Jeremy Dyson is co-creator of the [W...]
Stories, and a founding membe[...]
winning BBC series *The Le[...]*
written for and script edited many [...]
is the writer of a novel and three [...]
the Edge Hill award winner *Th[...]*

Andy Nyman is co-creator of the West End hit play and film *Ghost Stories,* and an actor, writer and magician. He co-created much of Derren Brown's award-winning TV specials including *Russian Roulette* and *The Lottery Prediction* and co-wrote and directed his stage shows, including Olivier award winning *Something Wicked This Way Comes.* As an actor he is best known for *Peaky Blinders* and the Oscar winning film *Judy.* His *The Golden Rules of Acting* books are both bestsellers. In 2018 he was awarded the Magic Circle's Maskelyne Award for services to British Magic.

Praise for *The Warlock Effect*

'Sheer delight ... This enthralling, playful thriller can be enjoyed for its virtuosic recreation of the period and for its cheeky depiction of Cold War spooks as closer to Derren Brown than George Smiley. Perhaps its chief pleasure, though, is simply the magic it contains, from the beginner's card tricks ... to grand illusion' *The Sunday Times*

'The affection of Jeremy Dyson and Andy Nyman ... for the period and its magicians, among them Tommy Cooper, shines through in this delightful thriller.' *The Times*

'Two great masters join forces to explosive effect.' Richard Osman

'A gripping book that evokes the reality of working magicians ... A pure delight.' Neil Gaiman

'[A] serpentine thriller ... The theme of magic [is elevated] into something more universal - a matter of survival itself; it also becomes deeply moving.' *Spectator*

'Bond's manipulative trickery ... is echoed in *The Warlock Effect.*' *Observer*

'This book is huge fun - gripping, informative and very clever. I didn't want it to end!' Peter James

'All the hallmarks of a modern classic, with more twists and turns than the intestinal tract.' Adam Kay

'A delightful historical espionage thriller, packed with arcane secrets of stage magicians and illusionists, peopled with real denizens of the period.' *Irish Independent*

'Absolutely joyous, with twists and reveals I never saw coming. This book is in itself a beautiful magic trick. Wonderful.' Derren Brown

'It could have been grown in a vat especially for me ... I absolutely loved every twist, every turn, every blockbusting cliffhanger.' Steven Moffat

'A rattling good yarn with humour, action, and the chance to learn a few magicians' secrets.' *Peterborough Telegraph*

'A delicious confection from a pair of devilishly clever minds.' Steve Pemberton

'This book is exactly like some of the magic it describes, the odd sleight of hand or false deception wrapped around a terrific mystery. The period atmosphere and the Cold War detail feel like a Le Carré but it's the characters that you really care about. I hope we see a lot more of Louis Warlock.' Ian Moore

'Edge-of-your-seat stuff ... Heartbreaking and uplifting in equal measure, *The Warlock Effect* is a fiendish mix of history, horror and humour.' SJ Bennett

'A thrilling and ingenious work of wonder. Twisting, evocative and hugely entertaining, *The Warlock Effect* delivers on every level.' Chris Whitaker

'I just adored this compulsive, fun, unpredictable and surprisingly tender book.' Jenny Colgan

'*The Warlock Effect* is spellbinding. Jeremy Dyson and Andy Nyman skilfully depict a shadowy world of magic and espionage in this gripping tale that is entertaining, heartfelt and as twisty as any artful stage magician's signature trick. Highly recommended.' Adam Hamdy

'A superb story of espionage and human endurance which casts its own vivid spell. In the stage magician Louis Warlock, Nyman and Dyson have created one of fiction's most complex and beguiling heroes.' Jay Rayner

'Simply billing *The Warlock Effect* as an espionage thriller would be doing it a disservice: there's far more to take from it than that, as the action takes us across Europe and back, introducing a series of fascinating and complex characters along the way. The plot seems straightforward at first, but then turns on its head, and some clever writing guarantees you'll never see it coming.' *Buzz*

THE
WARLOCK
EFFECT

A NOVEL BY

Jeremy Dyson and Andy Nyman

**HODDER &
STOUGHTON**

First published in Great Britain in 2023 by Hodder & Stoughton
An Hachette UK company

This paperback edition published in 2024

1

A CIP catalogue record for this title is available from the British Library

Paperback ISBN 978 1 529 36481 1
ebook ISBN 978 1 529 36479 8

Typeset in Adobe Caslon by Hewer Text UK Ltd, Edinburgh
Printed and bound in Great Britain by Clays Ltd, Elcograf S.p.A.

Hodder & Stoughton policy is to use papers that are natural, renew-
able and recyclable products and made from wood grown in sustain-
able forests. The logging and manufacturing processes are expected to
conform to the environmental regulations of the country of origin.

Hodder & Stoughton Ltd
Carmelite House
50 Victoria Embankment
London EC4Y 0DZ

www.hodder.co.uk

For Nicky, Eve and Poppy –
the three miracles in my life.
JD

For Sophie, Macy & Preston –
you are my whole life. I adore you.
AN

The ideal subject of totalitarian rule is not the convinced Nazi or the convinced Communist, but people for whom the distinction between true or false no longer exists.

Hannah Arendt, *The Origins of Totalitarianism* (1951)

THE READER'S SECRECY COVENANT

I,...
as an admirer and appreciator of magic,
understand that within this book I will
learn many of the secrets behind the
numerous effects with which the author has
built his reputation. <u>In signing this</u>
<u>covenant I give my word to never share the</u>
<u>revelations described herein. I do so out</u>
<u>of respect for the noble art of magic</u> and
in acknowledgement that these are the
wishes of the late Louis Warlock.

Signed....................................

Date................/.............../............

---

*NB After the initial print run has sold,
the printing plates of this book will be
destroyed.*

THE WARLOCK EFFECT

by
LOUIS WARLOCK

Line Drawings
by
DINAH GROULE

FOREWORD

Hello my friend.

Forgive me for thinking of you as my friend, but first and foremost I think that's what you are to me. A kindred spirit. Some kind of magic has happened if you're reading this. The mere act of me imagining that you might one day read this book has brought it about in actuality. That is a miracle.

It's an act of faith, composing these words. What's made it happen? What's helped bring this miracle into being? It's the fact that we share something, you and I, dear friend, dear reader, something profound.

I'm not used to thinking in this way, but I'm allowing myself to do so now. As I close my eyes and bring you to mind and odd though it may sound, I've already spent many hours doing that, this is what I know about you. You're endlessly inquisitive. You have a genuine sense of fun, which is an underrated quality. I think it may be the secret to a happy life. Most importantly, in fact essentially, you still feel connected to the person you were as a child. And that is why magic appeals to you. It's a direct line to the wonder we

all see at the start of our journey.
Magic's biggest trick is that it keeps us
excited and ready to make humdrum moments
sparkle, for ourselves and for others.

As I begin thinking about committing
these secrets to the page — revealing the
real modus operandi that lies behind the
headline-grabbing stunts and effects with
which I've made my name — time and again I
find myself reaching the same conclusion.
It's all about simplicity. Everything
begins with blankness, with empty space.
Empty spaces can be terrifying. The
temptation is to fill them with all kinds
of nonsense.

But if you open yourself to empty
spaces, you can fill them with truth. And
the truth is never wrong.

Here's the truth.

I love you, fellow magician.

What I have to offer to you, these
secrets, take them as a gift. I want them
to fill you with joy every day.

You are my friend.

I love magic . . .

And I love you . . .

PROLOGUE

It was dark in the dormitory, darker than Ludvik had thought it would be. The silver-painted pipes gurgled above and behind him, presumably some kind of heating system that brought no warmth that he could feel. It had been warmer on the transport boat from Holland, and that was the coldest he'd ever been. How could they let the place be so cold? Maybe England was a particularly chilly country. The other boys clearly weren't bothered. Their snores burbled and rattled around him. He tried to find comfort in them. He yearned for the relief of sleep, but it wouldn't come. He was hungry, which didn't help. He hadn't been able to eat much of his pudding. When he'd put the first spoon of glutinous custard in his mouth at supper, he'd run his tongue around a hard furry object, which upon inspection had turned out to be a dead wasp. Formerly he would have thought the food disgusting, but the experience of going for three days without eating after he was smuggled out of Germany had changed him. The fear that there might come another time when the food stopped seemed to have stuck, so now he was grateful for anything he was given.

It was easier for him to understand English than to speak it, so the conversations he'd had, such as they were, were halting and brief. He'd hoped the other boys might be friendlier, or at least some of them. They'd decided he was called Fritz, despite him telling them his name was Ludvik. Fritz 129, because here you were known by the number they gave you rather than your surname. It was painted on the end of the iron bedstead. Mr Glückmann in Hull had said this was 'a progressive school, very modern, that's why the headmaster's agreed to take you'. Ludvik had thought there might be some other boys from the boat, but

3

there weren't. He'd tried to keep speaking to a minimum: 'who will set a guard over my mouth and a watch over my lips' – that was one of his father's favourite sayings.

That morning, they'd all gone to chapel, and Ludvik had had no choice but to keep his mouth shut. He had no idea of the words.

'Fritz doesn't know the Our Father,' said a big ruddy-faced boy who'd fixed him with a stare from the minute he'd arrived.

'He wouldn't, would he? Nazis only pray to Hitler.'

'I'm not a Nazi,' Ludvik had wanted to say, but the words wouldn't come out.

He lay there thinking of all the things he was going to have to learn about. He had to make the best of it. He had to make the best of it. He kept saying that to himself over and over again. He heard a muttering in the darkness to his side, where his hand was hanging out of the bed. He stiffened, aware of something, some-one moving close to him – the softest of sounds. Then he felt something on his fingers. A dampness, gently enfolding them. They were being dipped in water. Warm water.

'Don't wake him. It won't work if you wake him.'

'Shh,' someone hissed.

'How long do you have to leave it for?'

'Only a little bit. It works straight away.'

Ludvik lay as still as he could, pretending to sleep. That was preferable to engaging with them. He tried to work out what the best thing to do was. He wanted them to know he could be their friend, could be one of them. He understood why they were doing this to him. It was just what kids did. It would have been no different back home, not that he went to a boarding school there, but he had been to B'nai B'rith summer lodge – before the Nazis shut them down – and there were plenty of those kinds of antics there. He knew what they were trying to do. The theory was that if you immersed a sleeping boy's hand in warm water, it would make him wet the bed.

'Has anything happened yet?'

'You've got to wait for a bit.'

'Let's not. Leave him.' This was a younger voice, or a higher-pitched one at least.

4

'You're just scared in case they do it to you, too. Prick.'

Ludvik's belly iced at the tone of that voice. This was the instigator speaking. Neville, he was called. Neville 117. There was something insidious about him. He was a thinker. Clever. He planned. Like a chess game. Ludvik recognised that way of operating. He knew how dangerous those kinds of boys could be. But if he paid no attention to the fear – though the fear was real – there was something he might be able to do. It wasn't as simple as trying to get Neville to like him. There was no way you could get someone of his sort to like you. But you could buy him off. As long as you let him think – genuinely think – you were never going to rise above him, that you would always remain subordinate.

Moving his left hand, the one that was under the blanket, as slowly as he could, he reached up, over his shoulder and under the pillow. His fingers came upon what he was looking for, and immediately he felt something like relief. Or strength. What he was touching wasn't an imaginary talisman or amulet. It had real power. It was something he knew he could rely on, whatever the circumstances, wherever he was and whatever was going on around him. He took a breath, then jerked his other hand out, the one that was dangled in the bowl of warm water. He'd only meant to splash, but he ended up knocking the bowl over, so it tipped up on to whoever was holding it.

'Bloody Nora!'

'Shut up!' This was Neville, hissing. 'Matron will be in here. We'll all get done.'

Ludvik tried to sit up as if he'd just legitimately woken. Neville, however, wasn't fooled. 'You were awake. Prick! You've soaked me,' he said.

'What?' Ludvik had to remind himself to speak in English.

'You little Nazi prick. Nazi spy prick.'

'I'm not a Nazi. I was . . . I escaped from them.'

'Fritz.'

'Boche bastard.' This from a smaller boy, Edmund, who was clearly emboldened by being in Neville's presence, a loyal foot soldier.

'I've escaped. I escaped from the Nazis. They were trying to get us.'

'That's his cover story.'

'Why were they trying to get you?' The boy who spoke was clearly not entirely under Neville's sway, or if he was, his curiosity was at least firing independently of that. That was something Ludvik could make use of, surely – the frightening details of his adventure – if he was to turn these boys towards him. But before he could try, Neville had gripped one of his fingers, which was still wet from the bowl of water, and bent it backwards sharply, making Ludvik yell involuntarily.

'Shut up, Fritz. If Matron comes in here because of you, you'll get it. I don't believe anything you've got to say anyway.'

'Why were you running from the Nazis?' the other boy asked again.

Perhaps aware that he had one final moment before he lost the crowd, Neville jerked Ludvik's finger back harder.

'I'm a Jew. I'm a Jew, OK?'

Silence amongst the gathered boys. They seemed to move back slowly. There was a look of cold disgust on Neville's face, caught in a slice of thin moonlight from a transom window high above.

'I was put on a train. And then a boat. And now I'm here,' said Ludvik, catching his breath.

'Prove it.'

'What?'

'Prove it.'

How could he prove it? Show them his cock? But before he'd even turned his mind to trying to solve that problem, another urge took over, and he heard himself praying: '*Shema Yisrael, adonai eloheinu, adonai echoed, baruch she'm covid machoto, le'olam va ed . . .*'

The other boys stared at him as if he was some exotic animal in a zoo. As he came to a halt, he realised he was still clutching the item under the pillow. He pulled it out – a battered pack of Piatnik playing cards – and used the confused and slightly resentful silence to change the agenda.

'Would you like to see something?' His English was suddenly more fluent. He had already rehearsed this script in his head. He'd used it as an exercise on the boat to practise his language skills, running over the lines again and again until they came fluently, as fluently as the moves he was about to execute. With a deft flowing gesture, he unsheathed the pack of cards from their box and went straight into a single-handed fan, which he offered to Neville. It was a risky strategy, but he was confident it would work. 'Take one,' he said lightly, nodding at the cards.

It was a reflex response he knew he could rely on: what does anyone do when they are offered a spread pack of cards? After only a moment, with suspicion still in his eyes, Neville reached out and resentfully took a card. Immediately he clutched it to his chest. He wasn't going to make anything easy for Ludvik – whatever was about to transpire.

'Show the others. Go on. I won't look.'

As Neville did so, having committed the card, whatever it was, to memory, Ludvik felt his hands prepare the pack for the next stage of the trick, which he had found in the pages of the American magic magazine *The Phoenix*. No thought was required. He had done it so many times that every stage was habitual.

'Now put it back, anywhere.' He closed his eyes, turned his head away and offered the spread pack to Neville again. As the card was reinserted, his fingers conducted the necessary movements to bring the chosen card under control. He went straight into a relaxed-looking overhand shuffle to disguise the move, and thought unexpectedly of his father, the smell of his Calabash pipe: 'I know, I know, you think your hands aren't big enough to hold the deck. That's got nothing to do with it. You learn by doing, and practising. Each time you master another sleight, it's the same. You think: I'm never going to be able to do this. But you keep going. You hammer away at it, and then one day – something clicks. You've got it!' He'd leaned forward, his eyes glowing. 'And then it's yours for the rest of your life.'

Neville's card was now at the top of the pack, where Ludvik needed it to be. All he had to do was make it look like it wasn't. He riffled the edge of the pack in preparation for bringing that about.

'I'd like to try a little experiment. An experiment in probability . . .' He noticed that the boys who had moved away at the revelation of his outsider status as a Jew had now moved back towards him; if anything, they were closer to him than they'd been before, drawn by the promise of diversion, and perhaps wonder, that he was offering them. Closest of all was Neville 117. 'You placed your card back where you chose to; I didn't influence that. Agreed?'

Neville looked at him. If there was a moment when he was going to quibble about who was now running things, the momentum of the trick itself and the promise of magic had erased it. He just nodded.

'I've shuffled the pack freely and fairly. If I cut it one, two, three, four times . . .' for each number he made a one-handed cut, delivering the words and the divisions of the pack at such a pace that it would surely be impossible to keep track of any single card, 'it would be impossible, wouldn't it, for the top card of the deck to be the one you chose?'

'Yeah, it would.' Neville obviously liked the challenge of this – the thought that Ludvik might be caught out by his own cleverness and end up failing.

Confidently Ludvik turned the top card over – or at least that was what his impromptu audience saw. 'The six of hearts,' he said triumphantly.

'No. It wasn't. Prick.' Neville had got his wish. But Ludvik, with expert timing, adopted a carefully calibrated expression of discomfort that contained just a whiff of artifice about it, enough to let the onlookers know that the story wasn't over quite yet.

'Forgive me. As I said, this was more of an experiment than a piece of magic. Can I give you the six of hearts? One down, fifty-one to go.' This was delivered more as an afterthought, a matter of little consequence.

Rather than hand the card to Neville, he gave it to the curious boy who didn't seem to be one of Neville's acolytes. Then he turned the deck so that the faces were towards himself and ran through the cards, pausing at one and pulling it above the others with its back to his audience. 'Stupid! It was the nine of diamonds, wasn't it?'

'Yeah,' said Neville, frowning, 'but—'

'Maybe you'll allow me to correct my earlier mistake?' Ludvik made the lightest of gestures and then turned the card around. It was the six of hearts – the card he'd just given to the other boy. The audience turned as one to face their peer, who looked at the card *he* was holding for the first time. It was the nine of diamonds.

'What!?' he exclaimed.

'What is it?' asked Neville, his surliness absent for a moment, as if the captivating trick had made him drop the mask he normally wore, just for a second or two. The other boy turned the card to show him.

'How . . .?'

The illusion that the two cards had changed places was perfect.

'Sometimes it corrects itself,' said Ludvik, in a matter-of-fact way. He'd always been able to act, and whenever he presented this trick, he drew on that ability, playing the part of someone who absolutely believed he'd stumbled across some weird, quirky natural phenomenon yet to be categorised, like a primitive man faced with a magnetised needle swivelling north.

All the boys, including Neville, looked at him with smiles of disbelief on their faces. It was always interesting to Ludvik that mystification generated pleasure – rather than anger, or frustration, say. Everyone smiled whenever he performed this trick.

A low wail began somewhere in the distance, rising simultaneously in volume and pitch. The air-raid siren. The response was conditioned. The boys around Ludvik pelted back to their beds, reaching for their gas masks. A clamorous clattering sound filled the dormitory. It was Matron in a hastily pulled-on housecoat, rattling a steel ruler inside a saucepan. 'Downstairs. Downstairs. Come on. Come on.' The rush and hubbub of the other boys waking, going into the automatic routines they were trained for. This was still new for Ludvik. He reached for his own gas mask.

As they raced down the wide stairwell to the ground floor, Neville appeared at his side. 'Show me how it's done.'

Was this a command or a request? Ludvik wasn't yet proficient enough in English to pick up the nuance. He guessed it was probably a bit of both.

'I can't just show you,' he said, knowing this would provoke Neville. But before the other boy could speak, Ludvik added: 'I'd have to teach you. You'd have to want to learn. Then it would be all right. But you'd have to keep it secret.'

'I will.'

Ludvik just nodded. They would become co-conspirators, as all magicians were.

The siren was louder outside; there was a chorus of them, one in the school, more in the town, two miles away. But the approaching drone of twin-engine planes and the accompanying screeches of descent were louder. Ludvik knew what caused the latter – so called 'Jericho trumpets' fitted to the bombers with the sole intention of making that awful sound. Everyone was looking up, listening as they ran, trying to gauge whether the planes were coming in their direction. Ludvik stood there gazing at the sky.

'Come on,' said Neville. But Ludvik stayed where he was, watching. He'd found the flames of one of the engines. It was a clear night. Neville shook his head and ran on.

Ludvik wasn't afraid of the plane. The only thing he was really afraid of was that he wouldn't be able to remember his mother. Even now, he couldn't bring her face to mind.

The place was silent. Not completely silent, of course; there was the subliminal sound that Louis was so familiar with – a tangible, breath-held hush that the microphones were somehow able to pick up and broadcast to the nation. And there were the noises on stage, too. The creak of the water tank behind him, the water sloshing against its reinforced glass. Even with no music cue playing, one could feel the tense presence of the band waiting to strike up.

Dinah had been lowered head-first into the tank – an upright affair about half the size of a police box. She didn't need to be in there upside down, but it added considerably to the drama. Louis had worked out early on in his broadcasting career that what the audience in the Camden Palace radio theatre experienced some-how communicated itself to the audience at home. It must have been in all those tiny indicators: the low murmurs, the nervous laughter, the anxious shuffling. While it was obvious that crowd noise would add to the experience of listening to a comedy, it was less so when it came to the performance of magic. But it painted a picture, and Louis had grasped instinctively that radio was all about the pictures.

He was hardly the first broadcaster to have realised this, but he may have been the first magician (Orson Welles aside). Everything happened in the listeners' heads. It was his job to give the audience the raw materials out of which they could compose the images themselves. Danny Mahal had put it best. 'You're not painting a picture. You are spinning a world.' Typically for Danny, the idea was communicated in the form of a lecture on Hindu philosophy: 'You are Maya, my friend. When you are on stage, you are Maya. The great spinner of illusion. The all-powerful Creatrix, the goddess who generates the daydream of that which we call reality. Reality is not reality. It is no such thing. It appears solid to us, but it is fashioned by Maya. You have the same job. You only have to give them the dots, give them the lines. Their minds will fill in the rest. They are their own illusionists. You are merely the provocateur!'

So that was what this was. This whole elaborate set-up behind Louis, on stage at the Camden Palace, was there to give the listening audience the raw material necessary to make a miracle happen in their heads. And actually, it wasn't just the audience, because this was the third series of *Warlock's Wonders*, and now, on occasions, there were photo-journalists, from *Picture Post* or the daily papers, and even newsreel cameras if word had got out that Louis was going to be attempting something particularly spec-tacular. Louis' inner Maya (with the help of his loyal 'Brains Trust', led by Danny Mahal) had helped make his series 1952's second-most-listened-to radio show after *The Goons*.

So, Dinah upside down in the tank was another example of illusion-spinning. When he had told the audience that the blood pooling in her head would boost her telepathic abilities, it was more Maya. ('Bullshit might be another word,' said Ivan Wolf, another, less poetic member of the Warlock Brains Trust. His aversion to the lyrical was ironic given that he was a professional writer, not a magician.) Dinah being immersed in water was also Maya – it created an element of risk that stimulated the listener's imagination. Louis had announced that in three minutes she would be in danger of passing out, which created more drama, on top of the picture it painted. ('How long can she actually hang there?' he had asked when the idea first came to him. 'Thirty minutes, forty minutes – not a problem.' This from Phyllis Griffith, Ivan Wolf's writing partner and fellow Brains Trust adviser. Phyllis had collected information like this over the years. She was an expert on death, murder and mutilation. It was her hobby. You'd never guess it, though. She looked like a village schoolteacher.)

Louis knew, better than any other magician currently working in Great Britain, that all these details, the story they told, the

Maya they wove, were how the trick was really done. In comparison, the actual mechanics of it were almost irrelevant.

He stepped towards the microphone, facing the audience in front of him . But rather than addressing them, his mind conjured the people sitting at home in their kitchens and living rooms; the stockbroker driving his wife to the theatre, listening on the Motorola in the car; the workers in the factories on the late shift; the commercial travellers in their hotel lounges; the lonely schoolboy with his crystal set, straining to hear through a whispering earpiece.

'Ladies and gentlemen, girls and boys, let's remind ourselves what has taken place so far. One of my volunteers for the evening, His Honour Judge Reynolds, QC, has passed amongst the audience present here at the Camden Palace radio theatre in north London and collected a number of personal items – they'll all be returned to you unharmed, have no fear.' Mild laughter at this, but Louis was pleased to detect tension in it, a sense of anticipation at what was to come, alongside an apprehension that every passing second was costing Dinah – beautiful Dinah in her fetching Jantzen swimsuit – moments of precious consciousness. To that end, he allowed himself to be a touch more loquacious than he otherwise might have been.

'Those items have been gathered and laid out on stage. And please note, I was blindfolded throughout their collection, so I can have no sense of which item was taken from which audience member. Judge Reynolds, is that correct?'

The judge, who was sitting in front of a microphone to the right of the stage, observing everything, leaned forward slightly to answer, with no less gravitas than if he were presiding over a capital trial.

'Yes. That is correct.'

'Thank you.'

'And am I still blindfolded now?'

'Yes, you are.'

'Have I tampered with that blindfold in any way? Touched it?'

'No. You have not.'

'And these items that are before you now?' For the benefit of the audience in the theatre, Louis gestured behind him. He knew

13

there was a stainless-steel trolley in front of Judge Reynolds. He'd approved its choice himself. He wanted to be sure it was big enough to be seen by everyone in the auditorium, even though it was irrelevant to the listeners at home. 'These are the same items you collected from the audience?'

'Indeed, yes.'

'Very good. Thank you once again for your assistance. I call now on our second adjudicator for this show, Lieutenant Commander Hinchcliffe. Sir, you're currently on leave from the Royal Navy, where you're a serving officer?'

'Yes, I am.'

'But you've been kind enough to join us this evening. You helped seal Miss Groule into the tank. She has no connection to the outside world, does she? There are no wires or cables present – nothing other than the Aqua-Lung on her back?'

'Absolutely not.' Hinchcliffe's slightly dour Scottish brogue somehow lent weight to his presence. And as he often did, Louis marvelled at how instinctively these bona fide volunteers played along with the circumstances, how good human beings were at divining what was expected of them. They would freely offer up exactly what was needed – as demonstrated here by the seriousness with which Hinchcliffe spoke. It couldn't have been any better if it had been scripted and rehearsed. It was being in control of all these subtle elements that made Louis feel strong and confident in the moment.

'Lieutenant Commander, I'd now like you to choose an item, any item from those gathered in front of you. Let your eyes range across what is there.'

He counted six seconds in his head.

'Do you have one?'

'I do.'

'Do you want to change your mind, or do you want to stick with this item?'

'I'm happy with this one.'

'Very good. I would like you to pick it up and carry it over to Miss Groule. You will need to squat down, then hold it up to the glass, close to her, in front of her head. Will you tell me when you're there?'

Hinchcliffe didn't have far to go. The tank was directly behind him. It was on a raised dais so the audience in the theatre (and any attendant photographers) would be able to see exactly what was occurring.

'I'm in position, sir.'

Louis liked that 'sir'. It meant things were going as they should, that he himself was the commanding officer, which was necessary. He had to have complete control: of the audience, the volunteers, the listeners, all the staff here, the technicians, the managers, his own posse.

'Very good. You have your item, which has been freely selected from a range collected at random from members of the audience present tonight—'

'Ladies and gentlemen! Please, if you would . . .'

Somebody was shouting. Somebody in the audience.

'Ladies and gentlemen,' came the voice again.

Was there a fire? An air raid? Had war been declared? Were the Soviets attacking?

'Ladies and gentlemen, I am the editor of *Illustrated* magazine and I lay down this challenge . . .'

Louis' immediate thought was that he had to regain his authority, no matter what. There was an audience at home. They wouldn't hear this man, who wasn't microphoned; only silence.

'Please, sir, if you could sit down,' he said.

'Louis Warlock is a fraud and a cheat.' The man's voice was louder now. The listeners at home might just have caught that. He had some kind of amplifying device – a portable megaphone.

'Please, sir, I need you to sit down,' said Louis, working to remain calm. He was trying to assess what his options were. Dinah was in no real danger, but the audience thought she was. Control had been wrested away from him, which made him seem weak. That was the worst thing. And the man was insulting him and his reputation; it was audible in the audience, and now at home too. What were they doing in the control room?

'A fraud and a cheat.' The man was speaking faster now, aware that he was going to be interrupted.

Trakhtn, royk, trakhtn. A Yiddish expression his father had drilled into him: 'think, calm, think'. It was a mantra that Louis

15

had run in his head from his earliest days of professional performance. If something went wrong, if the spectator said the card wasn't theirs, if a prop broke or a mechanism froze, 'think, calm, think'. Let him speak. Make a conscious choice to let him speak. The listening audience might just think this was all planned. Whatever this man had to say – and Louis recognised the voice now – it could be turned. It could be played. It could be out-thought. Easily.

To help regain command of the situation, he removed his blindfold. He was at the front of the stage, facing out, still unable to see what was behind him, so it would not imperil the routine when he returned to it.

'If Mr Warlock is unable to prove he is *not* a fraud and a cheat – by locating something hidden somewhere within central London, under test conditions, observed by scientists of our own choosing, on the fifth day of next month – then the great people of this nation may take it as confirmation that the man is nothing but a self-publicising fraud unable to do in actuality a single thing he claims.'

Ushers had arrived at the man's side. Someone had shown the foresight to throw a spotlight on him, revealing a tall, thin individual in a loose-fitting raincoat. His high forehead was topped by a pile of grey hair, like day-old whipped cream on a cafeteria pie. The burly commissionaire from the foyer had arrived too, and he was now manhandling the disrupter along the row. The megaphone had been pulled from his hand.

'Ladies and gentlemen,' Louis began. He could see the stage manager gesturing desperately for him to continue according to the script. He didn't need to be told. 'I know we tell you to expect the unexpected on this show. I can assure you, even we didn't foresee this. But before we continue – and for Miss Groule's sake, we need to – let me tell you all, I will accept this gentleman's challenge.'

He felt the audience relax. They were his again, bemused but excited. Was what just happened intentional, in some mysterious Warlock way? they were thinking. And Louis had immediately adjusted his performance in the subtlest of manners to imply that yes, it was. Everything could be played. Everything. You just had to give yourself permission.

'Thank you, Dinah, for your patience,' he said gesturing to the tank behind him. 'To return to the task at hand, the lieutenant commander is holding a tortoiseshell snuffbox. Is that correct, sir?'

'Yes! It is,' said a suitably baffled Hinchcliffe.

'And it belongs to a Mr Graham Cunliffe, who was born in Streatham. Is that correct?'

A cry from the auditorium – legitimate. 'Yes, sir!'

And the audience relaxed further into their applause.

'Did you know what was going to happen? Did you? Because if you even had an inkling ...'

Jack Naismith, the BBC producer, was unusually angry, his pockmarked face ruddy behind his heavy-rimmed spectacles. Louis knew the poor man was going to get it from his employers. Of course he was. The BBC was like school. Exactly the same. Grubs on the ground. Wardens in the lower corridors. Prefects in the common rooms. Housemasters in their studies. And everybody terrified of the cane. He'd recognised the hierarchy from his very first meeting at the corporation. It was a public school erected as a national institution.

'You know there'll be hell to pay. I'm telling you now,' said Jack, struggling to light his pipe.

'Oh come on!' Louis grinned at him as he gifted Jack a defence. 'I've just guaranteed us front-page coverage in every newspaper in the country. Local and national. Not to mention the chance of an extra show – broadcast live – when I accept the challenge.'

'You're really going to accept? But how will you pull it off?'

'Same way I always do.'

'Which is?'

'That would be telling.' And Louis smiled at him.

AN UNCOMMON MEMORY

I've used this item for many years. It
relies on a method that can be mastered in
moments yet seems truly impossible. Don't
let that seduce you, though; attention to
detail is key to making it appear that this
is the result of a lifetime's work.

Get a pack of cards, shuffle them and
then spread the deck, face up, on the table
so you can see every card.

Now . . . memorise the order of the
cards.

(Using my technique I can do it in
fifty-five seconds, that's a second for
every card including the two jokers,
leaving a second spare.)

Why are you still reading? START.

*

I promise I will teach you in a moment or
two, but let me tell you how I got to this
solution.

Some time ago, during a run at the
Stork Club, I had an unnerving experience.
While performing my blindfold divination
routine, I found myself aware of a new
sensation — it was as though I could hear
every beat of my heart, every throb of my
pulse. It seemed to add an urgency to my
performance. I remember leaving the stage

both a little disturbed but also excited at this new-found momentum.

My excitement was somewhat diminished when, at my annual medical a week or so later, I learned that I had borderline hypertension, or in layman's terms, high blood pressure. An unusual condition in a young man such as myself: a small genetic gift from my mother's side of the family.

I was told by my doctor that not only must I cut out the post-show salt-beef sandwiches, but a more relaxed approach to life should also be explored. I called on an older man of my acquaintance, a former refugee called Ernst Juda. He'd led a truly remarkable existence, despite enduring the horrors of being held in Auschwitz; he was also one of the most content and seemingly 'at peace' people I've ever met.

While I sipped a lemon tea and watched Ernst devour a slice of Maison Bertaux's finest strudel, he shared with me what he perceived to be his greatest tip for survival and the maintenance of good mental health. 'Stop. Take a moment. Remember that no matter how bad things may seem, you are alive. Remind yourself of that every morning when you open your eyes. Learn to see that every second is a gift. <u>Every</u> second. You take it all for granted because you think you are standing on concrete. But you're not. You're standing on the thinnest, most delicate sheet of ice.' Then he said, 'Remember that you are a human <u>being</u>, NOT a human <u>doing</u>.'

This was a thunderbolt moment for me. 'Human being'. Two separate words both with their own essential meaning. This was like

the first time I witnessed the duck/rabbit
illusion. Once you see the change, you are
forced to re-evaluate, you can never undo
it.

DUCK . . .

. . . OR RABBIT?

I realised that so much of my existence
lay in being busy, instead of simply being
in the moment of life, something that has
only been confirmed for me by recent

events. The endless 'doing' was, in Ernst's
words, running the sand out of my timer.
Ernst taught me a simple meditation
technique that allowed me to spend ten
minutes a day 'being', just me and my
breath. 'Stopping', he called it. 'You must
learn to stop your thoughts, Louis.'

It was during one of these 'breathers'
that this blissfully easy technique for
memorising a deck came to me. As is so
often the way, I realised I was fixating on
the problem rather than the solution. I was
seeing the duck, not the rabbit. As soon as
I understood this, it occurred to me that
what I actually needed to achieve was the
appearance of memorising the cards, not the
actual feat itself.

So, once the pack is shuffled, place
the cards face up on the table and spread
them out.

Now *pretend* to memorise them. It's so
silly that a key part of magic is simply
lying! Pretending, like a little child,
that you are using your magic powers to
achieve something impossible! Back to the
job in hand. I find a great 'wrinkle' is
when you see two cards of the same value
next to each other, make a show of
up-jogging them a little from the pack as
if fixing them in your mind.

This gives the spectator something to hang their hat on. I would recommend spending about fifty seconds on this apparent deck memorisation to keep it feeling plausible.

Gather the pack up and <u>simply remember the face card</u> - let's say it's the eight of clubs. That's all. Just one card.

Place the pack behind your back, so that the eight of clubs is facing away from you.

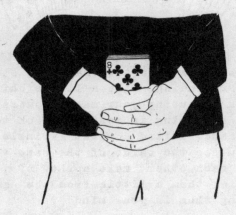

Explain that you will announce the cards one at a time in order; all you need the spectator to do is tell you if you are correct. As you explain this, you make the one simple move required: behind your back, you take the eight of clubs from the top of the deck and place it, face up, on the <u>other</u> side of the deck.

So, if you were to bring the deck out and look at it, you would see the eight of clubs on one side and another card - let's say the six of diamonds - on the reverse side. The eight of clubs is, in actual fact, face up on a face-down deck.

Next, say to the spectator: 'OK, the first card is the eight of clubs.' Bring the pack out from behind your back for real now, with the reversed eight of clubs facing them. As they look at that eight of clubs, you are seeing the <u>next</u> card, at the rear of the deck, the six of diamonds; it is literally staring you in the face! It's so delicious. Now remember that card as the

spectator confirms that the eight of clubs
is correct.

AUDIENCE VIEW →

MAGICIANS VIEW

   Place the pack behind your back once
more, saying, 'I'll slip the eight to the
bottom. And the next card is . . .' and do
the same move again: take the six of
diamonds and reverse it, placing it on top
of the eight of clubs.

While the pack is still behind your back,
complete the sentence you just began, naming
the next card, acting as if you are consulting
your memory: '... the ... six of diamonds.'
Then bring the pack out (reversed once again),
and as the spectator sees the six of diamonds,
you are staring at the next card – let's
imagine it's the three of spades.

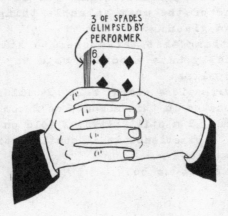

3 OF SPADES
GLIMPSED BY
PERFORMER

Once the spectator tells you that you are right, you do it all again. Behind your back, make the reverse move, then say casually, '. . . the next one is the three of clubs . . . no, hang on, spades.' The deliberate error is nicely convincing. Bring the pack out and then repeat the actions, picking up the pace slightly as you go from card to card. I have never actually needed to go further than about ten cards, as the demonstration is so utterly convincing for the spectator. What you will find astounding about this effect is that the audience won't for a moment suspect trickery; they will believe you are a memorisation master.

So there we are, my gift to you, a wonderfully plausible magic trick. But of course, dear magi, you already know a million of those. In truth, it's the other, more unexpected gift I would like you to take from me, the gift of 'stopping', the key to accessing the real miracle, the miracle of your creativity.

It's a gift that came to me through unwanted circumstances, and yet it's proved to be one of the most valuable things I've ever been given.

Something that threatened to kill me may actually have accorded me a way of saving my life.

Too dramatic a claim? Well, I will hold on to it, because in this moment, as I compose these words, I'm still alive. I hold on to that fact too. I experience it. I continue to be . . .

Let me be.

Please let me be.

2

If anywhere felt like home to Louis, it was Maison Bertaux. Yes, he had his rooms at York Place, but that was little more than temporary accommodation, no different in his mind from any number of less comfortable and less salubrious apartments he'd rented in the past. There was a chain of such places, crowded with creaking beds and mismatched dining chairs, all of them lonely, empty, impermanent. But Maison Bertaux was a Soho institution that had been there more than seventy years, a business founded on warmth and comfort and welcome and light: if Louis could have lived in there, he would have done.

To step off Greek Street and pass under that blue and white striped canvas was to walk into a refuge, a sanctuary of vanilla and cinnamon and roasting coffee and sweetened milk that transported him back to Europe, the cafés of his childhood. It felt like a warm bath on a cold day, or a cool room in midsummer. Even today, as he climbed the stairs and nodded at Monsieur Vignaud (who was expertly slicing a meringue cake and barely losing a crumb), it felt like the most perfect place in the world, despite the fact that the attic room he was headed towards currently held the possibility of complete professional ruin.

The Brains Trust had been meeting in the attic of Maison Bertaux for as long as they'd been convened. They gathered round an army surplus trestle table, surrounded by sacks of flour and golden caster sugar, and it only cost them £4 a month. If Louis had any true magical skill, it lay in the area of making friends. Not schmoozing people, not manipulating them, but forming genuine friendships that he maintained and fostered. He did his best to make friends wherever he went: at the barber's, at the theatre, at the dentist's, in railway carriages and grocers' shops. He'd discovered, as the war ground on through his school years, that he had an ability to connect with people in such a way that if any of them might have been able to help him in any fashion, they would have been insulted if he hadn't asked them. Monsieur Vignaud was no different.

'Of course you must use my attic room. Nobody goes up there. Nobody can hear you. You will be undisturbed, ignored, invisible. You must take it, Monsieur Louis. I insist.'

Louis had offered more than the sum Monsieur Vignaud suggested, but the proprietor wouldn't accept it.

'*Non!* Four pounds is what I asked for, and to charge you more would not be the act of a friend.'

'Here he is. The condemned man.'

This was said with glee by Ivan, who was holding up a half-eaten beignet. There was a dab of pastry cream on his neatly trimmed beard, and another on his Liberty-print bow tie.

'Be quiet,' said his other half, Phyllis, 'and wipe your face.' She wore owlish glasses and leaned across to swipe at his tie with her hankie. With her neatly parted hair and faded tweed jacket, she could have been his mother, but she was actually two years younger than him, and as a pair they were perhaps the most successful writers of radio comedy in the country.

Dinah, of course, was already there. She would have arrived first. She was responsible for bringing the cakes and the large flask of black coffee, from which she now poured a measure into a ceramic cup and handed it to Louis.

Danny Mahal was standing next to the back wall, which was covered from floor to ceiling with blackboard paint. He held a stick of chalk in one hand and a typed letter in the other. Unlike the others, he was in no mood to banter. The sober suit he wore, which hung off his skinny frame, had the unfortunate effect of making him look like he was attending a funeral. Despite being surrounded by flour dust and chalk powder, however, he remained immaculate. This was his most remarkable trick; no matter how filthy the surroundings, he was always impeccably presentable.

'Have you read this?' he said, holding up the letter; then, without pausing, he proceeded to read it aloud anyway: '"These are the circumstances of the challenge you have agreed to. Your assistant, Miss Groule, will be picked up from her home address and conveyed to the offices of the *Illustrated* magazine at number 364 Strand at 7 p.m. on the evening of 5 January 1953. You yourself will arrive there by 7:30 p.m. and you will be placed under close observation. At 8 p.m., Miss Groule will be taken to a location of our choosing, which will be within a three-mile radius of the magazine's offices. We agree to your stipulation that she will not be placed below ground. You will have three hours in which to find her. To complete the challenge, you must physically be able to place your hands upon her – i.e., have found her specific location within the general location we have chosen."'

'I hope they're not running this in the magazine. It sounds like it's been written by a chimp,' said Ivan, who was now on his second beignet.

'Oh, do shut up,' said Phyllis, pretending not to be amused.

Danny continued reading, ignoring the chatter. He always adopted the demeanour of the most sensible person in the room, although he was no more that than any of them. '"If you fail on any one of these points, you fail on all." Why this pompous tone? Like the God of the Old Testament?' Danny tossed the letter on to the table and pushed his hand through his thick black hair as if to wipe it. 'What's the matter with the man?'

'Ah,' said Dinah, who finally came to the table. She was wearing black ski pants and a dancer's wrap cardigan, which she loosened as she sat down. 'There's a little history there that pre-dates your presence among us, Dan.'

'Yes, it was while you were having all that fun entertaining the troops in West Berlin,' said Louis as he too took his place at the table.

'Some of us chose to build our careers rather than conjure them out of hot air and chutzpah.' The Yiddish pronunciation sounded surprisingly authentic in Danny's Bombay accent.

'You see, this particular editor . . .' continued Dinah.

'Mr Aldous,' said Ivan.

'Mr Aldous,' she agreed, 'had a run-in with Louis some time ago.'

'Unfinished business,' said Phyllis, who was getting a ball of wool out of her tote bag.

'Aldous used to edit the *Daily Herald*,' said Dinah, 'and when he was there, he felt that Louis embarrassed him deliberately in front of his own staff.'

'He did embarrass him deliberately in front of his own staff,' said Ivan.

'It wasn't meant to be embarrassing. It was playful,' said Louis, reaching for the letter, which Danny had cast on to the table.

'Playful,' said Ivan. 'Like a cat is playful with a half-dead bird.'

'Aldous was running a piece about hypnotism,' said Louis. 'A sceptical piece. And I was doing a mesmerism act at the time. I claimed I could prove it worked. So I put him in a trance and got him to sign a document saying that the English rugby union team were the greatest in the world, together with a memorandum asking his sports editor to run a full-page photograph of the declaration.'

'Very patriotic,' said Danny.

'Not for a Welshman,' said Dinah.

'A proud Welshman,' added Ivan.

'The edition very nearly went to press. Cost them a bit of money,' said Louis.

'And now he wants his revenge. Nicely chilled.' Dinah threw a look at Louis that expressed what everyone else in the room was thinking: Warlock is his own worst enemy.

'But for us, this is nothing more than an opportunity,' said Louis, apparently unruffled.

'You've got six days to come up with a method,' said Danny.

'That's right.' Louis smiled. 'And I think you mean *we've* got six days.'

'Don't you ever worry about slipping up?' asked Dinah, who already knew that the answer was 'no'.

Phyllis had retrieved her crochet hook and was knotting loops of woolly yarn into a small brown square. To Louis, this was a good sign. It was Phyllis's equivalent of a thinking cap.

'Yes, well – that's the first secret. The only secret. Release your fear of failing,' said Louis, putting the letter back on the table. 'And if you should fail, it's just another chance to exercise your creativity.' Despite the nobility of the sentiment, it was mere bravado on his part. Failure was a luxury he didn't allow himself. It hurt too much.

'Here comes the lecture,' said Ivan, reaching for a choux à la crème. Phyllis flicked the back of his hand with her crochet needle, and he dropped the cake involuntarily.

'Forget the lecture,' said Danny. 'Let's turn our attention to method.' He held his chalk aloft, ready to write. At the end of the session, it would be Dinah's job to compile the notes. She was an accurate and speedy typist and actually could have got it all down as fast as everybody spoke. But Louis liked the two-stage process, watching the board fill up with ideas, tracing the lines of thinking with his eyes as they unfolded; then later seeing Dinah's crystallised organisation of their thoughts.

He suspected that Danny took the role of minute-keeper because it absolved him of doing any of the heavy lifting. And yet Danny would often be the one to offer up some brilliant last-minute wrinkle, a twist on a twist. He was always frightened of getting it wrong, but he was better than he knew. He stuck to his dove act and his productions and his vanishes and big box illusions, and yet he could be so much more than that if he wanted. But he preferred to be comfortable. Did Louis conspire to keep Danny's brilliance from him so he could benefit from it himself? Yes, he did. Did he feel guilty about that? If he did, he would answer that guilt with his belief that we lay our own tables in life. Louis himself just observed carefully and chose from what was there. It wasn't his job to bring Danny to his fullest fruition.

'OK,' said Dinah. Her palms were pressed together, her index fingers against the little button of her nose. 'First thought. Let's narrow down the possible locations they could hide me in.'

'How?' said Ivan, sitting up. This was his favourite role: the aggressive prosecuting counsel. Like Danny, he was prone to avoiding the actual work of coming up with a way to do the trick. But his questions were the best. And the right questions ultimately led to the right solution. 'How do you narrow down all the houses, shops and miscellaneous buildings within a three-mile radius when they number in the tens of thousands?'

'Always with the mockers. Drink your *café au lait* and let the grown-ups talk,' said Phyllis. Ivan did as he was told. His writing partner, whose crochet needle was moving at great speed, turned her bespectacled gaze back to Louis. 'Why prioritise knowing the location in advance? Wouldn't it be better to concentrate on how we get the information on the day and then communicate it to you?'

'I'll take the second question first and the first second, if I may?' Louis smiled as he spoke. To him, the Brains Trust sessions were beautiful to listen to. Like Oxford philosophy. 'The problem is twofold: getting the information, and then passing it to me without them spotting it. And they will be watching me very, very closely.'

'So?' said Danny, who had already written 'location' on the board. 'We find out the information and get it to you *before* they start watching you.'

'Normally I would agree with you,' said Dinah. She'd grown up in Brussels, the daughter of a Belgian naval architect who'd lost his leg at the Battle of the Somme. Devoted to her father, she had spent her childhood playing chess with him. Consequently, she always thought at least three moves ahead. 'But this man Aldous, I don't trust him. He's not just wanting to set Louis a difficult challenge. He also wants to humiliate him. He wants revenge. So he's likely to do something slippery, like change the location on the day, or tell his team they're going to one place and end up going to another. It's not as simple as us bribing someone at the *Illustrated* to find out where they're taking me.'

'She's right,' said Louis, holding his chin. Dinah thought like he did, which was one of the reasons he loved her.

'But Aldous, despite being a bitter old sod, is not cunning,' she continued. 'He doesn't have the imagination. Which takes us to the next question. I can guarantee you they will choose a recognisable location.' She sat back, very sure of her assertion.

'Why?' said Ivan, with a touch of chippiness. He didn't like it when Dinah started riding one of her waves of thought, and he certainly didn't like someone else being further ahead than he was.

'Because Aldous, being unimaginative, is not one of life's rebels. He wants to be seen to be good at his job – which is, let's not forget, producing a national magazine with a circulation of over a million. For the story to have any impact with his readers, they'll have to recognise what they see in the pictures. Remember, it's the *Illustrated* magazine. So, readers in Birmingham, readers in Inverness, readers in Belfast – they'll all have to know what they're looking at. Readers who at best might have had one day trip to London before the war. They'll only have heard of a handful of places here. I'm pretty sure it has to be one of those places. And a three-mile radius of the Strand rules out quite a few of them – Greenwich Observatory, Kew Gardens, Hampton Court, for a start.'

'OK, I like it,' said Ivan, standing up now, reaching for the churchwarden pipe he kept in a specially elongated inside pocket in his blazer. 'And I'll go one further. Ken Aldous is a notorious *schnorrer*. I'll bet you anything he picks somewhere with an entrance fee so he can call in the favour of free VIP tickets for his family in return for the free publicity.'

'How do you know he's a *schnorrer*?' More perfect Yiddish pronunciation from Danny.

'Have you seen his shoes?' said Phyllis, not looking up from the fast-growing brown square of crochet.

'It seems a slender thread to hang a method from,' said Danny.

'Stop being so negative, Danny, or we're not going to get anywhere,' said Louis. Part of his job was to steer the conversation between pragmatism and creativity. He'd worked out a long time ago that it was good to favour the latter when in the early stages of the process. And he had to drive things, because ultimately it was his reputation that was at stake.

'If you're faced with a difficult truth, you'd always rather avoid it,' said Danny.

Louis ignored this, having caught on to Dinah's line of thinking. 'Say we get it down to ten possible locations – and they're watching me like the proverbial hawk. We could arrange the list of places alphabetically and number them one to ten. Then, rather than having to slip me a place name and address without them knowing, you'd only have to give me a number. Plus I could memorise the routes.'

'Why,' said Danny, who was already chalking numbers on the black wall, 'would you need to memorise the routes? You'll be sitting in the back of some car; you'll only have to say "Drive me to the Albert Hall", or wherever.'

'Yes – if I was doing it by their book.' Louis was already smiling. 'But I'm not going to do it by their book. I'm going to do it by mine. I'm going to do it blindfold. And I'm going to direct the car while blindfolded.'

'But they haven't asked you to do that,' said Danny.

'Exactly,' said Louis, and he pushed a whole chocolate eclair into his mouth.

3

At six o'clock in the evening of 5 January 1953, a black and silver Daimler Consort arrived at the flat Dinah shared with her sister on Richmond Way in Hammersmith. It was actually scheduled to collect her at seven, but it arrived deliberately early, presumably in an attempt to disrupt any plans Louis had made for following the vehicle.

'You know, he may not be cunning, but he is a *momzah* and he's going to want you to fail,' Danny had said.

'I know,' Louis replied, 'but that's why you'll have built in enough slack for me to be able to think on my feet if they try anything slippery, or if anything should . . . not go to plan.'

The first stage had been to employ a driver of their own, Frank Lorrimer – the best tail in London. Like most of the other specialist talent Louis made use of, the recommendation came from Beulah Hamilton, his fixer-in-chief. To say Beulah knew everybody was to understate the matter fivefold. She ran the Regal Review Bar on Poland Street, and most of the insalubrious characters in London owed her several favours, as did many of the more honourable ones. Frank Lorrimer was a disgraced captain from the Royal Army Service Corps, who'd served four years for being a driver on a payroll robbery when he'd fallen into debt after the war. He could follow any vehicle with a cushion of three cars in front of him and guarantee that the target would remain completely oblivious. This was a matter of great pride to him. He attributed his skill to his almost sociopathic ability to never get flustered. For a man who had let himself, and others, down with great frequency throughout his life, this was one thing he knew he excelled at.

Once Frank had seen Dinah escorted into the Daimler and watched it drive off, he waited until it rounded the corner and turned into Minford Gardens, giving it a few minutes before setting off himself. He was grateful it was evening. Other car headlights were just white blobs in the rear-view mirror, and so it would be harder for whoever was driving the Daimler to discern that they were being followed, particularly if Frank varied his distance as they went. The reg plate was 692 BUC. The BUC was easier to spot than some other letters might have been.

At Shepherd's Bush Green, it was a relatively simple job to keep an eye on the Daimler and hang back, further down Holland Road. From there it drove into Kensington High Street, and there was an unpleasant moment with the lights at Cromwell Road. Fortunately the traffic was slow, and by doing some gentle weaving and dodging, Frank had found his quarry again by the time he'd reached Brompton Oratory. His ability was uncanny. From there the only other moment of note was when the Daimler pulled into an underground petrol station at Hyde Park Corner. Frank debated whether to follow it in or wait outside. He hung back for a couple of minutes, then rolled his anonymous-looking Wolseley 1500 down the slope to the petrol pumps just as the Daimler was moving off. Leaving it as long as he dared, he gestured to the pump attendant that he'd changed his mind, and drove off.

A lesser man might have experienced another heart-stopping moment when the Daimler seemed to vanish altogether. But with his singular ability, Frank saw it just as it was turning into Grosvenor Place. It was a simple matter to keep his distance as it turned right down Wilton Street, round Eaton Square Gardens and into Sloane Square, where it pulled up. This was odd, but Frank had been told to expect some odd moments. He'd been given a numbered list of likely locations, and Sloane Square wasn't one of them. Before making the necessary phone call, he thought he'd wait until he saw Dinah get out. No need to jump the gun. Maybe they were just killing time, given that they'd set off twenty-five minutes ahead of schedule.

After a short while, the driver's door opened, but rather than coming around to the rear door to let Dinah out, the driver walked over to the green-painted cabman's café at the side of the road. He was obviously in no rush. Frank breathed a tiny sigh of recognition: because they were early, the driver and Dinah must be getting a sneaky cuppa. Fair enough. It gave him a chance to find change for the telephone.

It was 6.35 p.m., and Louis Warlock was standing apparently carefree and confident in the editor's office at *Illustrated* magazine. Since it wasn't a strictly news-based publication, even under normal circumstances there would only be a minimal evening staff present. But tonight, the place was empty, apart from Aldous and his team. The editor was so determined to maintain maximum security, to be certain that Louis and his associates could have no opportunity to bribe anyone for information, even the cleaners had been told not to come in.

Louis used the unnatural quiet to put himself into a composed and collected mode. He was only too aware that his greatest enemy at this point was not Ken Aldous or his organisation but Louis himself. It would be easy to give in to panic at any time. Once that began, it had its own momentum. And once it reached a certain pitch, it tended to take over. Keeping anxiety at bay, no matter what, that was the trick. They forgot the chosen card? Make the pack disappear. You got the prediction wrong? Bluff it out; make them think that somehow that was part of the plan all along and go on to wow them with something else. The one thing that was certain was that you couldn't get to that better place if you let terror take over, but if you managed to keep it cornered, it was possible to be creative in any given moment. Louis had learned in his youth the necessity of keeping fear controlled.

'Could I have a glass of hot water with six slices of lemon in it? Would that be OK?'

'Feeling sick, Warlock?' said Aldous, watching him with a cold apprehension that bordered on viciousness. He was clearly impatient for a fall.

'Not at all. The boiled water combined with the lemon's juices provides a concentrated dose of citric acid, which, science has proven, supports a focused mind.' Louis smiled politely at Ken's office girl, who headed off to the kettle.

Staring down at Louis, Ken pushed back his heavy Byron typewriter so it scraped noisily across the steel-topped desk. He picked up a folding map of London and shook it out to its full extent, laying it across the surface. Then he took a blue ball-topped pin from a packet and stuck it in place on the Strand.

'Gentlemen, we are here . . .' He looked up at the three photographers and assorted journalists (it seemed other publications were covering the story, too) who were gathered in the room. 'Miss Groule is somewhere in *here*.' With a heavy black pencil, he drew a crude, thick circle around a large area. 'If Mr Warlock's "clairvoyant connection"' – the latter word clicked out with disdain – 'is legitimate, then presumably her mental transmissions will allow him to locate her within the allotted three hours.'

Louis gave the lightest, most reasonable of nods.

'Further to that,' Aldous continued, like a QC summing up, 'we have included an additional challenge.' He turned to Louis. 'Miss Groule has been given a phrase that we've asked her to transmit to you along with her location. I'm sure it will be a simple matter for you to receive that too. When you are ready, we'll direct you to your driver and you can guide him towards Miss Groule's location yourself.'

'Of course,' said Louis. 'But I'd like to make a couple of stipulations, if I may.' *Here we go, here comes the funny business*, said the look on Aldous's face. But he was not prepared for what came next. 'Firstly, I would ask that we reduce the time allocated from three hours to two; secondly, I'd like to be blindfolded if I may, so that it's absolutely impossible for me to see where I'm going. If I'm deprived of my primary sense, it's much easier for me to pick up Miss Groule's mental signals.' He looked across to the other journalists in an affable manner. 'It's rather like extending the aerial on a radio receiver.'

Aldous was clearly torn: he couldn't help but admire Louis' ability to make the challenge even more extraordinary, but he loathed the way he also managed to not only hog the spotlight for himself but also brighten its beam as it picked him out.

'Obviously you may inspect the materials I've brought along.' Louis pulled from his pocket a bag made from black cotton twill, double-lined with grey silk. He also pulled out two rolls of medical tape, some sealed cotton bandage and two plain cotton wool pads. 'Mr Aldous, would you be good enough to apply these to my closed eyes, so that you're satisfied they're doing their job.'

'If you can't see,' said Aldous, already frowning, 'how will you direct the car where to go?'

'I will be navigating using Miss Groule's brainwaves alone, following them to their location. For that, I don't need to see. In fact, sight – as I've already explained – becomes a distraction.' Louis smiled gently. It was obvious, wasn't it? And he felt the tightrope quiver as he stepped on to it.

One step at a time. One step at a time. Louis spoke the words in his head as Ken Aldous led him down the granite steps of 364 Strand to the waiting car below. If it was possible to support someone deprived of sight in a resentful and unhelpful way, that was what Aldous was doing now. But the words Louis was repeating to himself were as much about the larger task ahead as they were about getting safely to street level. He had all the stages of the method memorised, and it wasn't complicated. The challenge was remaining focused and not allowing himself to become over-whelmed. He simply had to be clear about where he was and what he had to do next.

Two pairs of hands eased him into the nearside front seat of the car, which smelled of polish and cigarettes. The driver, whoever he was, obviously came from the higher end of his trade; Louis could detect Penhaligon's Blenheim Bouquet cologne (with a faint tang of body odour beneath). They must be using a hired chauffeur. This was a very large car, probably a Bentley, so they could fit Aldous and a couple of journos in it. Therefore it wouldn't be able to roar off at speed or make any sudden dashes ahead. That was reassuring, given what was to follow.

'Just to let you know,' came Aldous's Welsh burr softly in Louis' ear, 'I'm sitting directly behind you. To my right is Patrick Lowell, who is a professor from the University of London's physics and astronomy department. And to *his* right is Gerry Glover, the journalist assigned to write up the story for the magazine. We are all going to be watching you very carefully for the whole of the journey, like hawks.'

'I understand,' said Louis, keeping his voice free of emotion. 'Thank you.' He adjusted the bag over his head, which Aldous had examined with ludicrous thoroughness – presumably searching for hidden earpieces, wires, receivers and whatever else his paranoid imagination could conjure. But in the world of magic, it was a reliable truism: if you handed something out for examination, there was nothing to find.

Louis made a show of settling into the passenger seat. He reached across and casually wound down the window, leaning slightly against the door, then positioned his head, angling it towards the pavement, where he knew the photographers would be. After a moment – and without warning – he spoke up in a strong, clear voice:

'Could you please move off and drive straight ahead.'

The sound of chatter from outside was audible. A low buzz of excitement, augmented by flashbulb pops. Louis concentrated; he needed to stay focused in his mind. He called forth the image of the map of the Strand on the blackboard wall in the attic of Maison Bertaux, Danny pointing to each of the neat crosses he'd made in turn.

One step at a time. One cross at a time. There were four of them.

To know when the first one came, he had to count to 150. Which he now did.

'Would you pull over, please, on the left, at the first opportunity.' Louis felt the car slow almost immediately, before it came to a halt. 'I'm just going to step out on to the pavement for a moment.'

'Why?' came Aldous's suspicious response.

'Because I would like to attempt to better pick up Miss Groule's thought waves. Once I'm locked on to them properly, they'll be easier to follow and it won't be as stop-start. Please bear with me.'

Aldous said nothing, so Louis felt for the handle and opened the door. Using the edge of it to guide him, he stood up and moved out on to the pavement. He rolled his head around slowly, as if he was turning an indoor radio aerial, adjusting a signal. He did this for a couple of minutes. No need to count here; he judged it by instinct, knowing that longer than necessary would make it feel real. Then he got back in the car, saying no more than: 'Would you continue straight ahead, please, until my next instruction.'

There was a clear purpose to what he had just done, but it had nothing to do with Dinah's 'thought waves'. It was, in fact, something he had named 'faux-cess' (to rhyme with 'process'): a false logic that underpinned the story you wanted your audience to believe. It was important to define that story and its attendant logic upfront, to give the audience enough of it directly or indirectly as early as you could in the trick and then adhere to it with additional moments at regular intervals throughout the performance that followed. In this case, the logic and the story were simple: Dinah was sending out a mental signal from her secret location; Louis was receiving it and using it as a means to navigate by, just as an aeroplane will use radar to steer through a thick fog. If the acting-out of this faux-cess was going to work (and part of its job was to misdirect from the actual method), then the underlying story had to be strong and clear enough to engage the audience's imagination. Like all good stories, everything was about the details. The hot lemon water, for instance, a nonsense that Louis knew would keep Ken's mind focused in the wrong place. Hopefully it was the case here, too.

Now it was time for cross number two. This was why he had casually wound the window down as soon as he got in the car, something he was counting on no one really noticing. He was listening for the call of the newspaper seller outside Charing Cross station, who had been paid five pounds to extend his pitch until 7.45 p.m. and keep shouting loudly until the end of his shift.

'Final . . . Final!'

There he was. Louis counted another thirty seconds and said: 'We'll soon be coming to a large junction. I'd like you to travel round, keep left and go off at the fourth exit.' He felt the car take the corner and heard the tick-tick of the traffic indicator. Once he sensed them straightening up, he came to the third cross on his list. 'Would you pull over again, please. As soon as you can.' He spoke with some urgency, as if he was struggling, about to lose his signal. As soon as the car rolled to a rest, he jumped out and stood on the pavement again, his head tilted back. He didn't overdo it. He kept the move subtle, as if there was some real process behind it. He heard the back door open. Smelled Aldous's blend of stale sweat and pipe tobacco.

'Warlock. What are you doing?'

'I'd lost my connection. It's quite delicate.'

'Can you see through that thing?'

He couldn't, and Aldous knew it, so he felt no need to answer. He sensed the air move in front of him and assumed that Aldous was throwing a pulled punch to prove he had vision in some way. He gently lowered his head, relaxed.

'We can get back in now. Thank you,' he said, calmly.

Once the car pulled off, he listened for the next newspaper vendor who'd been similarly bribed.

'*Evening News. Evening News! Evening News!*' The man was really belting it out. Ivan must have slipped him a tenner. Louis was grateful for that, because it meant he was now very clear that the turning coming up on the right was Waterloo Place.

'If you could take the next right, please.' After the car had turned, he added, 'And keep going straight. But stay left if you could.'

In his mental map, he could see where Waterloo Place became Lower Regent Street. It would take them about three or four minutes to get there, and the car would slow as it approached the top end. About ten yards from the junction with Piccadilly Circus, there was a stall selling caramelised peanuts. The smell was designed to carry; that was part of the pitch – if you took one sniff, you had to buy a bag. As soon as Louis caught a whiff of the buttery, sugary goo, he would ask the car to pull over. Cross number four. These four crosses, as well as being faux-cess, were designed to allow some time to pass, enough for Frank to have tailed Dinah to her destination, then rung Danny, who was waiting in the stock room at Maison Bertaux. Danny would then go to Piccadilly Circus to arrange getting the necessary information to Louis.

And there it was. The rich caramel sweetness of the melting sugar.

'Please bring the car to a stop here,' said Louis, 'as soon as you can.'

The transfer of information was going to happen within three or four minutes of pulling over. He only had to get out of the car, as he had done before, to trigger it. 'I'd like to get out one more time. I'm nearly tuned in.'

'I think you've got out of the car quite enough,' said a truculent Aldous. 'Just stick your head out of the bloody window.'

Ignoring him, Louis reached down to pull at the door handle, but he was surprised to feel a hand reach over his shoulder, restraining him.

'I mean it,' Aldous said, irritation evident in his voice, menace even. Forcing himself to remain calm despite the provocation, Louis decided to stay in his seat. Angling his head towards the open window, he leaned out slightly, enough to make him visible and for the car to be identifiable.

'If we can just pause here then, while I re-establish my connection?'

'Well I guess we'll just have to, won't we?' said Aldous, his voice dripping with scepticism.

Louis moved his head around subtly, imagining what it would be like if he was actually trying to pick up some mental signal. He started counting to calm himself. Within two minutes, three at the most, he would know where Dinah was. He reached 120 on his count. Then 180. And then he was past 200, which he really hadn't expected. At 400, he stopped counting. He was surprised to feel the first tendrils of panic, an icy little chill in the base of his stomach. He was into his fourth minute at the side of Regent Street St James's, head bent out of the car's window, but the information had yet to come.

Louis wasn't the only one to be feeling cold fear in his belly. At that very moment, Frank was standing in a phone box in Sloane Square, wrestling with the awfulness of what had just taken place.

The driver of the Daimler with Dinah in it had emerged from the cabman's café with a single cardboard cup of tea, which he sipped from as he walked. Not very gentlemanly, Frank had thought. Maybe Dinah hadn't wanted one.

Being careful, but wanting to stay ahead of the game, he had casually got out of the Wolseley and wandered past the Daimler, which had its passenger window wound down. As he did so, he turned his head in a relaxed manner to get a glimpse of Dinah, hoping she would see him and be reassured. But the car was empty. There was no passenger inside.

His heart started racing. He must have made a mistake. He turned around, as if he'd forgotten something, and strode back along the pavement, pausing to bend down and tie his shoelace, taking a proper look inside the car. But there had been no question about it: there was no one on the rear seat. No one in the front. He had lost her.

And now he was standing in a phone box on the corner of the King's Road, his hands shaking as he fed coins into the slot.

'The bastards switched her out. It must have been at the petrol station. They must have had another car waiting. They knew I was following. They knew I'd wait before driving in. I'm sorry, Danny. I'm sorry. I should have known better. I'm sorry.'

It had never occurred to Louis that Frank Lorrimer, the best tail in London, could have lost Dinah. But that was why he had the Brains Trust. Because while Louis had considered that part of the plan to be flawless, Danny knew it was exactly where it would need reinforcing.

'You're a worrier, Danny,' Louis had said as he picked at the icing of a millefeuille.

'You don't have sharp steel blades fixed to gimmicked guillotines in your act, Louis. I do. If I don't triple-check everything, somebody might lose a hand.'

'It'll be fine.'

'Like I always say,' said Ivan, taking Danny's side, 'nobody needs fire insurance. Until they have a fire.'

So thanks to Danny, there was a plan B. But it was shaky. And it involved their nightclub-owning fixer Beulah calling in every favour she had with every press photographer on the circuit. With hindsight, perhaps this should have been part of the original plan, but hindsight is only useful for heading off future disasters. For now, all Danny could do was activate the strategy in an impromptu manner by sprinting to Beulah's club in Poland Street, where she was waiting for him.

She then sat on the telephone for twenty minutes, ringing round every photographer she knew – and she knew them all – to find out who had been booked out by *Illustrated* magazine that night.

The first fifteen of those twenty minutes had not been very productive. People either didn't answer the phone, or when they did, they were unhelpfully irksome (favour or no favour) or ignorant. Then, after chipping away at the unyielding rock for quarter of an hour, Beulah hit a promising nugget.

'Hello, is Dick there?'

'He's out, darling. Who's this?'

Beulah thought to modify her voice immediately; she didn't want to sound like the 'other woman', to this sharp-sounding Cockney wife.

'It's Beulah Hamilton, at the Regal.'

'Hello, darling. What's it all about?'

'We've got a late-night event needs covering – big star from out of town, very hush-hush. I know it's a long shot, but I need photos for the trade papers. Dick's the best. I was hoping I might be able to schmooze him with triple time.'

'Oh, he'll be peeved to miss that. He's working, darling.'

'Do you know where he is? Maybe he could squeeze both jobs in.'

'Funny you should ask, 'cos the one he's on is very hush-hush too. He wouldn't tell me.'

Beulah, who was sitting with Danny, squeezed his hand to let him know she'd finally got something, though it wasn't very promising.

'Do you know *anything* about where he is?'

'Sorry, Mrs H. I mean, I can ask him again. I'm just going to drop his sandwiches off to him. He'll never make it through the night without eating. He needs a round of corned beef and a flask of tea or he's finished.'

Beulah gave Danny's hand a double squeeze. 'Where are you meeting him?'

'Baker Street tube, twenty minutes – near where the job is. You were lucky to catch me. Just on my way out.'

Louis, meanwhile, ignorant of all of this, was fighting his own battle, a losing one, with rising panic. Because according to the plan, he should have had the information about Dinah's location more than fifteen minutes ago. And the tension in the car was palpable.

'I would have thought it might be more productive to drive around aimlessly and guess, rather than just sit here,' said Aldous, who clearly did not feel the need to disguise the contempt and delight in his voice. As far as he was concerned, Louis was staring at failure and simply putting off the inevitable: a braggart and a fantasist had been exposed, and now he was going to have to accept that exposure as it became national news. 'Seems to me her brain-waves aren't quite doing the job. You could have done with allowing yourself the full three hours I offered you. Oh well, you know best.'

Uncomfortably, Louis was feeling the same thing. And he was grateful for the blindfold so he didn't have to look at the faces of the other men in the car, who were chuckling lightly at his predicament. He had to find a way to break that cycle of thought.

Calmly he said, 'I would ask that you do what you can do to adjust this negative attitude. Hostility is what blocks the thought waves. Now . . . if you please, I need silence.' Hopefully this retort was enough to buy himself a few moments of quiet. He had to discover a creative solution to this problem. Creativity was unlimited. There were multitudinous possible responses, but fear would block all of them. *There's always a way. There's always a way.* He spoke the words internally, like a prayer.

The mantra was broken by a sharp rap on the windscreen.

'Excuse me, sir, can I ask, is there a problem?'

'Everything's fine, Officer.' It was clear from Aldous's response that he was being addressed by a policeman. 'I'm Kenneth Aldous, the editor of *Illustrated* magazine.' There was no disguising the self-aggrandisement in that introduction. 'We're here covering a story.'

'I don't care who you are, sir, you're parked in a no-stopping zone. I am going to have to ask you to move on immediately.' The policeman paused. He must have been taking in the extraordinary sight of Louis with the black bag over his head. 'Are you all right under there, sir?'

'Fine, Officer. I'm—'

'This is Louis Warlock, the entertainer. He's attempting an impossible task, without much success,' said Aldous, savouring his own words.

'I apologise for the inconvenience,' said Louis. 'Can I offer you two tickets for my next radio show? If you contact the Camden Palace, I can square it quite easily.'

47

The policeman sounded delighted. 'Goodness me. That's very generous. A pair in two weeks would be perfect. I'm on leave then.'

'Of course, Constable . . .?'

'Nuttall, sir. I'm still going to have to ask you to move on, I'm afraid.'

'Don't worry. We're going,' said Aldous. He must have tapped the driver on the shoulder, because the car began to pull off.

No one spoke as they drove. Louis' head remained cranked towards the open window. The only sound was the air flicking against the black cloth bag on his head. He could sense Aldous's delight at seeing him defeated.

With a sudden jerk, he straightened his head and seemed to sit bolt upright.

'Yes!' he said, suddenly reanimated. He turned towards the driver. 'When we get to the next junction, there's a large roundabout. Please take the third exit.'

'What?' said Aldous, jumping in, clearly surprised to hear Louis giving an instruction.

Louis ignored him. For the first time in an hour, he felt himself relax. From here on in, it was simple, because whatever the hold-up, whatever the reason for the twenty-minute delay, he was back on track, he was back in control. He let that knowledge warm him. He was back in control because he had received the information he needed. At least *that* part had worked smoothly.

The Brains Trust's plan had been based around a list of the most popular tourist attractions within a three-mile radius of the Strand. They'd settled on ten altogether: the British Museum; Buckingham Palace; Harrods; the Houses of Parliament (including Big Ben); the South Kensington museums; London Zoo; Madame Tussauds; the Tower of London; the Victoria and Albert Museum; Westminster Abbey. Once the selection was ratified and arranged alphabetically, each place on the list was assigned a letter, A through to J. That way, after Louis had memorised the line-up, which was a simple matter, the only outside information he needed on the day was a single letter.

The next question was how to pass the letter to him, unnoticed, while he was blindfolded in the car. Beulah was great friends with one of her local beat bobbies, Constable Alan

Nuttall. Piccadilly was his patch, and with enough notice, he could arrange his shifts so that he would be on duty on the evening of 5 January. Together the Brains Trust worked out a likely script for an encounter with a vehicle that had been parked for too long in a no-parking zone, say on Regent Street St James's. It would be a simple matter for Constable Nuttall to approach the vehicle and ask what was going on, and at some point in the conversation to ask Louis if he was all right. Louis would explain that he was, and offer tickets to his show. Constable Nuttall's reply would then begin with the requisite letter.

It had been made clear to Nuttall (who was himself an amateur conjuror) that the only thing he had to hit exactly was the first word of his response. The first possible location on the list was identified by the letter A, so the phrase paired with it was 'As long as I can bring my son and not my wife. He loves magic.' The second was labelled B, and its phrase ran: 'Blimey, that's very generous.' The third, C, was 'Could I trouble you for one in two weeks.' The fourth, D, 'Don't bother yourself, sir, though it's a very kind offer.' The fifth, E, 'Excellent. The missus'll be delighted.' And so on. PC Nuttall's response to Louis when he had approached the car at Piccadilly had been 'Goodness me!' Location G, number seven on the list, was Madame Tussauds.

At this point in time, Louis was ignorant of the fact that this information had been obtained thanks to Beulah's frantic detective work. Madame Tussauds was the only place on the list close to Baker Street tube, where the photographer's wife was dropping off his sandwiches. Committing to this location was of course a gamble, but experience and instinct told the team the odds were good.

So now there were only two challenges left for Louis. One was self-inflicted, and one had to be faced regardless. Directing the car to Madame Tussauds while blindfold was the first one; finding Dinah once there was the other. The Brains Trust team would help with the navigation by road, and Ken Aldous himself would be the means to accomplish the second.

To get from the Piccadilly Circus end of Shaftesbury Avenue, where the car currently was, to Madame Tussauds on Baker

Street, only three instructions were required. Two of these would be handled directly by Brains Trust members, namely Ivan and Phyllis, who were both keen cyclists. A taxi driver called Alan Chunz, who was also an amateur escapologist, would add his assistance.

Ivan went first. He was waiting at the corner of Shaftesbury Avenue in a spot where he could observe the business with Constable Nuttall and thus identify the car he had to follow (though to be honest, the man with the black bag on his head visible in the open passenger window was hardly inconspicuous). It was a simple matter then to keep up with it; there was a limit to how fast a vehicle could go along Shaftesbury Avenue, particularly as the evening's theatregoers were amassing. Once he was by the Cambridge Theatre, he pulled alongside Louis and tinged his bell four times. The bell had been re-engineered so its ring was a good six semitones higher than a standard affair, and thus immediately identifiable. Once Louis heard it, he would wait a few seconds so no causal link would be apparent and then say, 'Could you make a left turn at the next junction, please.'

Ivan did one other thing as the car rolled ahead of him: he reached down discreetly and placed a red ribbon with a magnet sewn into its end on the boot.

Phyllis, who was also on a bicycle, was waiting on Charing Cross Road, just below the Phoenix Theatre. She could see Ivan pulling round the corner and she could see the car he was behind. Once it had passed her, she could make out the red ribbon fluttering in the breeze as it drove along. It was a simple matter to cycle a few cars behind it and then put on a burst of speed half a mile later as they approached Warren Street station. Once she was close enough, she reached down and removed the red ribbon; then she pressed her bicycle horn three times. This had also been adjusted, so that it sounded two pitches at once. It was ugly, but immediately recognisable.

'And at the next junction, could you make another left turn, please.'

There was one pause, at the traffic lights after Great Portland Street, and then, not long after, the final instruction was given by the horn of Alan Chunz's taxi, which had been specially gaffed for the occasion to play a noticeably dissonant chord. This took place a good twenty yards in advance of the waxworks, so that Louis could count a further ten seconds in order to prevent any association between the unusual car horn and his command for the vehicle to stop.

They were there. Louis gathered himself, and then, with authority, launched himself into the next phase of his performance. He filled his mind with his manufactured story and faux-cess: where it had brought him, how it had got him there. He was also aware that (assuming the Brains Trust had done their job correctly) Ken Aldous would be experiencing mixed emotions – an unpleasant blend of cold fury and sheer bloody wonder. Gerry Glover, the journalist whose job it was to write up the story, would hopefully be more positive. But let's not get ahead of ourselves, Louis reminded himself. We've still got to find Dinah.

'Gentlemen,' he said. 'I have the strongest sense that Miss Groule is in a large building nearby. Could I ask one of you to guide me across the road. I could be wrong. Is it a candle factory? I sense generous amounts of . . . wax?'

He didn't know who it was that led him across the road, but he heard the sound of flashbulbs popping as they got to the other side. There was a thrum of activity as they moved inside, more flashbulbs, people calling out, 'Louis, Louis!' He was aware that the weird sight of the bag over his head would make for an excellent photo for the morning papers.

'Mr Aldous,' he said. 'Could I trouble you to take my arm? I'm going to ask you to do something for me if you would.' He felt Aldous's unwilling and suspicious arm slip under his own. 'I want you to do everything in your power to conceal from me any thought of where Miss Groule is in this building. Cast a veil upon those thoughts, imagine a heavy blanket thrown over them. If you feel my mind reaching inside yours: resist, resist, resist.'

This was, of course, a piece of unconscious instruction that would be impossible to ignore. However hard Ken thought he was trying to avoid it, he was actually taking Louis straight to Dinah. Every time Louis went in the right direction, there would be a subtle opposition from Ken. Louis merely had to pay attention.

51

As soon as he felt a staircase, he reached for the banister. He didn't need Ken to take him any further. He knew where he was, he could visualise it – and he had to acknowledge that Ken's sense for a dramatic photo opportunity was spot on. They were descending into the world-famous Chamber of Horrors.

And now another sense was about to take over. Louis coughed three times. That was the signal for Dinah to squeeze the gelatine capsule full of vanilla essence that she had in her back pocket and touch some of it to her neck. Perfume might have been too obvious; vanilla essence would not be identified in amongst all the other smells down there, the old tobacco smoke and carpet cleaner. Louis, however, was primed for it. He literally just had to follow his nose.

Once at the bottom of the stairs, he started to make his way along, still pulling on Aldous's arm intermittently. It would be foolish to indicate in any way that there'd been a change of method. But he did not have to pass far inside the chamber before he picked up the scent. It was like being back at Maison Bertaux. He cleared his mind and focused on the strength of the aroma. Deprived of sight, it was in fact easier to detect the intensity of it growing. It was definitely on his left. He could sense other people around, could hear the scurry of people behind him (presumably the photographers) attempting to be quiet – a further cue that he was approaching his destination. He felt another weight cast off, noticed that his heart was thumping (doubtless elevating his blood pressure), as it often did when he approached the final stages of an effect. It was a kind of excitement, a thrill at pulling off something difficult, combined with a vicarious enjoyment of what the audience was experiencing, so not an entirely selfish sensation. It was the same excitement one might feel in anticipation of a loved one unwrapping a carefully chosen gift.

And now it wasn't just the smell of the vanilla, it was the smell of Dinah, the memory of their first meeting, backstage at the Lewisham Hippodrome, a meal after the show – a lousy touring revue called *Knights of the Crazy Circle*. Dinah was in the chorus, Louis was doing his mesmerism act. There had been late-night pie and mash at G Kelly's, because Randolph Laks, the impresario, knew George Kelly and had persuaded him to stay open for the cast. Dinah had sat on the opposite side of the table, and her eyes had locked with Louis' for a shade longer than was polite. In the end, it was Louis who had to look away.

Standing there now, breathing her in, he dared to reach out for her hand, much as he had on the walk down Roman Road four years earlier. This time, he didn't know for sure where it was. But he didn't need to reach for long. It was her hand that found his.

And then something else. She was tapping his wrist. Morse code. Dash dash. Dot dot. M. I. Message incoming. The standard precursor to information coming his way. Morse as a secret means of communication was a method they had used so many times and in so many different situations that Louis was able to translate any message with barely any thought Dash dot dash dot. C. Dash dot dash dash. Y. Dash dash. M . . . He assembled the letters as they came. She was so good, it was close to actual mind-reading. CYMRU AM BYTH. It was Welsh. The petty-minded fool.

'Gentlemen,' he said. 'Would someone be good enough to remove my hood. You can leave the bandages on for now.' (He knew this would make for a better photo). 'Thank you. For the benefit of those now gathered, the gentlemen of the press,' he continued, 'let me recap the evening's events. I was charged with a challenge. An impossible challenge. Miss Groule, my fiancée and collaborator in the experimental science of mental communication, was taken to a location selected without my knowledge somewhere in London. This was done while I was held incommunicado in the offices of *Illustrated* magazine on the Strand. In order to help me focus my concentration on the mental messages she was sending out via brainwaves, I was blindfolded, to the satisfaction of these gentlemen here, Mr Aldous, the magazine's editor, and his journalists. Gentlemen, was it possible for me to see once this was done?'

'No!' said Gerry Glover, admiration clearly evident in his voice.

'In this manner, deprived of sight, unable to receive communication from another living soul, I directed the car from the Strand to the source of the mental signals I was picking up. Those signals led me here, to the Chamber of Horrors, beneath Baker Street, in the basement of Madame Tussauds waxworks – by the exhibit depicting the hanging of the infamous crippled murderer Charlie Peace, if I'm not very much mistaken.' Louis knew the Chamber of Horrors very well, and had groped around a bit, feeling the noose that was part of the display. 'This in spite of the stipulation I made that Miss Groule should not be placed underground. I am relieved to say that while this did disrupt the signal, as Mr Glover will confirm . . .' he imagined Glover staring at him now as if he were some kind of god, 'the connection between myself and Miss Groule is strong, which is how I know that she was passed an envelope with a message in when she arrived here, given to her by Mr Aldous. An envelope that she then sealed. Dinah, do you still have that envelope?'

'Yes, it's here.'

'Could you pass it to our friend Mr Glover here?'

Dinah passed the envelope as requested

'Sir, could you open the envelope once I've revealed what is written therein, and confirm whether I am right. The image in my mind is of words in a distinctive tongue: *Cymru am byth*, which I believe is Welsh and means "Wales for ever".' (Louis knew this, being a fan of international rugby.) 'Is there any way I could have received that information other than through the mental emanations of Miss Groule here?'

'No, sir.'

'Would you open the envelope.'

Glover did so, holding it up. The assembled photographers broke into spontaneous applause and cheers. Louis bowed his head humbly. Even though his eyes were still bandaged, he could picture very clearly the look of sickness on Ken Aldous's face – the expression of someone who'd seen his team lose a game he was absolutely certain they were going to win.

THE APPLICATION OF PATIENCE

I'm impatient. I wish I wasn't.

However, as I sit here composing these words, patience is a quality I'm being forced to acquire.

Like much else in life, if I'd been paying proper attention, I'd have realised it's something that magic has already taught me. Because patience can absolutely transform an effect.

Let's take as an example a situation that a hobbyist conjuror may find himself in. Imagine that in his pocket is the rather lovely 'card to matchbox' gimmick. For any readers unfamiliar with this item, the effect is exactly as you would imagine. A playing card, let's say the Jack of Spades, is held in one hand. The magician waves his other hand over the card, and it instantly transforms into a matchbox full of matches!

If you want to perform this trick, you can either buy it from your local magic dealer or make it yourself for a few pennies.

Take a bridge-sized playing card and glue its bottom half to the top of a suitably sized box of matches. Carefully fold the card over the box as shown in the

illustration and glue a cover from a
duplicate box on the back of the card so
that when the card is folded it looks like
an ordinary matchbox.

Show your audience the playing card.
The matchbox is hidden behind it. Bring
your free hand over the card, and under the
cover of a magical gesture, secretly fold
the top half down, over the box.

Remove your hand to reveal that the
playing card has been transformed into a
matchbox, and without missing a beat, push
the drawer of the box open, take out a
match and strike it.

Now here is the interesting thing. This
charming effect is much neglected. To my
thinking, however, the fault lies not with
the trick itself, but with how it's
performed. By changing your thinking and
simply being patient, the effect can be
transformed from a mere curio to a genuine
miracle.

Version 1

The magician is out with a friend. After a moment or two, the magi removes a playing card from his pocket. 'Look,' he says, 'the jack of spades. Now watch ...' He waves his hand over it, and the card transforms itself into a matchbox.

Version 1 - analysis

This version is the bare bones of the trick and consequently it's little more than a 'gag'. Here is what is running through the spectator's mind as he watches:

Oh, he's doing a trick now. Why's he holding the card in a slightly strange way? He's covered it with his hand and now it's changed into a matchbox. It must be a special matchbox that vanishes the card somehow. I wonder if I'm allowed to touch it. That was a clever trick.

When you see it laid out like this, you understand why the impact can only ever be mediocre. There's no real mystery, no actual magic.

Now look at what happens when just a few small but significant changes are made.

Version 2

The magician is with a friend. After a while, the friend takes out a cigarette and puts it in his mouth. 'I'll light that for you,' says the magician. He reaches into his pocket and removes a playing card and holds it to the friend's cigarette. The friend is rightly confused and asks, 'What are you doing?' The magi realises his error. 'Sorry ... it's been one of those days!' He then waves his hand over the playing card, which transforms itself into a matchbox. The friend is startled and amazed. The magi opens the box, strikes a match and lights his friend's cigarette.

Version 2 - analysis

Within this version there are subtle shifts in both the thinking and the magic on display, but you can see how different the effect feels. The first major shift is the application of patience. Rather than succumbing to the temptation that plagues so many of us - i.e., *I have something new that I am excited about and cannot wait to show you* - what one must do is wait. Wait for a moment that feels right. In this instance, that moment is entirely within the hands of the friend. If/when the friend takes out a cigarette to smoke, he provides the trigger.

And this is the second key weapon in the magi's arsenal: context. Giving the magic trick context changes everything. Suddenly the effect on display makes some kind of sense - a box of matches has appeared in order to light a cigarette. Now there is a logic to the effect that works to disguise the subterfuge. With context, instead of simply being an arbitrary trick, there is real skill on display. The magical ability to transform an object of no use (the playing card) into one that is needed at that moment (the matches). Trust me, the impact of that is huge.

Here is a version of what runs through the spectator's mind during this second version of the trick:

What the heck is he doing? He can't light my cigarette with a card!

This has made two things happen. Firstly, it has distracted the spectator from analysing the playing card or the way it is being held, and secondly, it has made them a participant in what is taking place and prompted a response, i.e., *You can't use that!*

Forcing an internal response from the spectator provides a moment of mental misdirection that allows you to wave your hand over the card and transform it into the matches. Suddenly this becomes a magical moment that they themselves are intimately involved with. It seems to happen because <u>they</u> requested it.

Of course, this strategy carries with it a risk. What if the moment to create the magic never arises. What if the friend decides not to smoke? Brace yourself. If that happens, you leave your 'card to matchbox' gimmick in your pocket and take it home unperformed! It's painful, of course, because you were excited to do it, but be patient, wait till the moment is right. It's worth the wait. Patience will lead to miracles.

Remember, you are a patient man.

You are a patient man.

Louis, remember you are a patient man . . .

The first real magic prop Louis ever owned was called the Cornucopia Cabinet. It cost one pound and ten shillings, and it was one of the premium items in the Harry Leat 1944 magic catalogue. Louis, who was in his final year in Westriver School, had a well-worn copy of the yellow-covered publication, which he would thumb through most evenings. No matter how miserable he was, how lonely or frightened, each of the tricks in the pages was a gateway to a promised land, a vehicle of hope. If I only had that, he would think to himself, I would be so happy.

Just browsing the items on a nightly basis was enough to generate an electric thrill in his stomach that served as a kind of narcotic, dulling the day's pain.

The magic tricks were depicted in neat, almost architectural line drawings, with no indication as to how any of them were done. Louis would gaze at them, imagining what it would be like to own one of them, to experiment with it, to discover the mechanism. Some of the items so caught his imagination that he vowed he had to possess them.

He'd been allowed to take on a job on Saturday afternoons at Seppings coke merchants in the village, sweeping out the front offices and the yard, and would return coated in black powder, hawking up tar-coloured phlegm, but clutching two half-crowns, which he'd put in an old gym shoe at the back of his locker.

He'd decided on the Cornucopia Cabinet because he simply had no idea how the trick could be done. The effect was this: the cabinet was the size of a can of cocoa, but square, made of lacquered plywood, with a small door on the front held shut with a brass catch. When you opened the door, the cabinet was completely filled with an apple. You removed the apple, closed the door, opened it again and it was now full of silk handkerchiefs (*use your own silks*, said the catalogue; Louis had already decided it would probably work with socks, because he didn't own any silks). You pulled out the silks – or socks – shut the door again, and when you opened it the next time, it was filled with a tin of baked beans.

Louis was already very conscious of the fact that a magic trick derived much of its power from its meaning. Tearing up and restoring a piece of plain paper was a much less interesting trick then tearing up and restoring a borrowed five-pound note – even though it was achieved in exactly the same way. Likewise, a little wooden cabinet that produced food at a time when food was rationed would grab the imagination of anybody watching, for the simple reason that everyone, including him, was hungry all of the time.

Once he had saved the money for the prop, together with the train fare to Charing Cross and the bus to Tooting, he travelled on the first Saturday he was able to gain permission for school leave. He could have ordered the trick by mail, but he needed to have the experience of actually going into the shop to view the glass-doored cabinets filled with the props he had only seen in the neat little drawings. He wanted to gaze on the burnished wood, the polished brass, the brightly coloured silk-screened cardboard. He wanted to know it wasn't just a dream that pulled him on from day to day. He wanted to know with certainty that there was a real place he could visit, stand in, untarnished by the threat of being bullied, or caned, or humiliated by bitter old teachers reminding him how worthless he was, or hateful wizened matrons, or vicious bigger boys.

The only thing that marred the hour-long train journey and forty-minute bus ride was the fear that something about the prop would let him down. That its mechanism, whatever it was, would make him shrug in disappointment because the method was poor, or obvious, or non-fooling. He needn't have worried. The gimmick was so clever that he sat playing with it for hours at a stretch for weeks afterwards, marvelling at its delicate intricacy.

To this day, Louis thought of the Cornucopia Cabinet every time he entered the Regal Revue Bar on Poland Street, because it seemed to have the same trick built into it. From its tiny door outside, the place looked like it could only contain fifteen tables at most, crammed into a single floor. But once you went down the narrow flight of stairs, accompanied by your own infinitely repeating orange-tinged reflection in the polished copper walls on both sides, you were staggered to see a space filled with more than fifty tables, walls lined with banquettes, and a balcony that ran round three sides with its own separate entrance via a spiral staircase. It was even more magical than Harry Leat's shop in Tooting.

And tonight, the setting could not have been more perfect. The Brains Trust were celebrating their triumph over *Illustrated* magazine. The next issue was five days away from publication, but the story had made every major daily newspaper, as well as two of the evening titles. (Dick, the photographer with the helpful wife, being a freelancer, had been able to sell his pictures several times over, encouraged in this enterprise by Beulah.) Louis may have been telling himself he never had any doubts about the outcome, but the truth was he still felt the burn of those eighteen minutes at the bottom of Piccadilly Circus and the fear of an impending humiliation. The pictures in the *Daily Mail* and the *Daily Express* had gone someway to ease the memory, but several glasses of Beulah's black-market champagne should finish the job nicely.

'Here he is. The man himself.' It was Ivan, waiting for him at the bottom of the stairs.

'Where's Beulah?'

'Sorting out a little spat. The house band didn't take kindly to the guest spot.' Ivan nodded behind him, and Louis immediately recognised the five-piece crammed on to the tiny stage: the Tony Kinsey Band. They usually played at Mack's restaurant on Oxford Street. Beulah knew they were Louis' favourite ensemble. She'd hired them for him.

'It should be me doing her a favour, shouldn't it?'

'You could say that,' said Ivan. 'Since she saved your useless backside.'

'Dinah here?' asked Louis, not wanting to think too hard about that.

'Come on, I'll take you up.'

They climbed the spiral stairs at the side of the stage that led to the circle, such as it was. There were a number of banquettes pressed into tiny alcoves, all angled slightly inwards, giving a view of the band. Dinah was sitting in one of the booths, wearing an electric-blue cocktail dress, her dark hair pulled tightly back, a tiny newly cut fringe tickling the top of her forehead. She was chatting to Phyllis, who in contrast looked like one of her mother's friends, in a floral-patterned cardigan buttoned up to her chin. There was a bottle of Beulah's hooky Moët in front of them, and it looked like they'd been going at it for a good half an hour.

Seeing Louis approach, Dinah jumped up in her seat and reached for him. Her blue silk scarf fell from her shoulders as she did, revealing her bare arms.

'Louis . . .'

'Started early?' he said, smiling.

'Or is it that you're late?'

'I couldn't find my cufflinks.'

'You mean you didn't look at the time until seven o'clock. I know you, Louis Warlock.' Her warm arms were around his neck, and she kissed his cheek. He could smell the bite of the alcohol beneath her Christian Dior perfume.

'Come on, you,' said Phyllis to Ivan, throwing him a stern look.

'Come on me where?' said Ivan, looking genuinely bemused.

'To the dance floor. Let's jitterbug.'

'Phyllis – no one's danced the jitterbug since VE Day.'

'Then we'll start a revival.'

'My legs are tired. I need to revive them with some booze,' said Ivan, who didn't want to dance.

'Come on.' It was clear there was to be no dissent. She dragged him away, leaving Louis and Dinah alone.

Dinah, her arms still snaked round Louis' neck, pulled him towards the banquette, sliding herself adeptly, particularly given her intoxicated state, into the narrow gap between the table and the cushioned seat.

'Beulah must have booked Tony Kinsey specially,' said Louis, who for some reason felt his limbs tensing up like the struts of an opening umbrella.

'You know what your trouble is, Mr Warlock. You're spoilt rotten.'

'I didn't ask her to.'

'You never ask anybody to do anything. But somehow they just do. You like everything your way, and you always end up getting it.'

'I can't say things went my way yesterday.'

'They did in the end.'

'Well, I've got you to thank for it. Giving me one barnstormer of a finale.'

'Is that all I've given you?'

'No, that's not all.' Louis felt his frustration rising, outside of his conscious control. It was in these moments – which came increasingly often, if he was being honest, usually when Dinah had been drinking – that he felt completely adrift, unable to fully understand what was in her head. It was as if the card had been selected, lost in the pack, and he'd gone ahead and found it only to see the spectator staring at him blankly.

'Would you like to dance?' he asked her. He didn't imagine that she did want to, but it was all he could think to say. He couldn't offer to get her a drink, because there were two more unopened bottles still on the table.

She pulled away from him to reach for her glass, refusing even to answer.

'Well, I might just ...' he struggled to think about what he might just do, 'go and see about some food.'

And he was up and away from the table. He was not even back down the staircase before he'd bumped into Ivan, who seemed to be similarly fleeing.

'If Phyllis asks, you haven't seen me,' said Ivan.

'What?' said Louis.

'Where are you going anyway? I thought you were supposed to be discussing your impending nuptials.'

That doused Louis in cold water. 'Am I? You know more than I do.'

'Not me, old chap. Phyllis.' Ivan tapped his nose in a conspiratorial gesture.

Louis hated that more than anything: the idea that he was a stooge in someone else's scheme. He carried on down the narrow stairs, letting Ivan squeeze past him. But Ivan turned as he did.

'Hey. Don't you dare go AWOL from your own party.'

'I'm just getting a drink.'

He headed towards the bar, to the right of the stairs. There was a cluster of bodies blocking the way, but he knew he could catch the eye of Spike, the barman, who would then immediately pour him a shot of Glenfiddich. But that comforting thought was interrupted by two large gentlemen in rather inappropriately sober suits stepping out in front of him.

'Mr Warlock?' said one of them, looking down at him. He was at least four inches taller than Louis.

'Yes?' said Louis, trying to work out who they were. The press? No. Their suits were far too good.

'Mr Warlock, would you come with us, please.'

Even in the dim light of the Regal, Louis could see that their haircuts had a military look. Both of them exuded authority, which momentarily put him into a defensive state. For a moment he was back at school again, cornered by two burly prefects.

'We've been instructed to collect you,' he was informed in clipped Sandhurst tones. 'Your presence is required.'

'Required by whom?'

'The highest level.'

'The highest level of what?'

'Her Majesty's Government.' This from the other man, who intoned the words testily, as if no such clarification should have been required.

'Is it about the Royal Variety Show?' said Louis. The joke was not well received.

No one from the club saw him being slid into the back of the black Austin A90 that was waiting outside, anonymous-looking but new and polished, as if it had just come from the showroom. It sped them towards Piccadilly, scene of yesterday's dramatic events, down St James's and Pall Mall towards Whitehall.

Neither of the men spoke, and despite Louis' nervousness, which was an odd mixture of excitement and agitation, he thought better of trying to engage them in conversation. Why he was being summoned on a government matter, he had no idea. But once again, as with the BBC, his school days were the ideal preparation. Authority was best deferred to in the short term, until you had a sense of what it wanted of you.

He did say one thing as the car propelled them through the night-time traffic:

'My friends will wonder where I've got to.'

'You'll be back within the hour,' came the curt reply.

The car arrived at an unmarked underground car park off Horse Guards Avenue. Despite the relative emptiness of the first level they came to, it continued driving downwards, navigating the narrow roadway at some speed, until it came to rest at the very bottom, four decks down. The men got out, opened the door for Louis and led him to what looked like a fire exit in the far corner of the parking area.

From here they strode down a concrete-walled corridor. From the look of it, the place might once have been an air raid shelter, but the new wood and the stencilled room numbers suggested it had been repurposed. And indeed, as they turned a corner, one of the men paused and knocked on a heavy oak-panelled door that would have been more at home in an above-the-ground civil service office than a corridor off a car park. The door opened and Louis was led inside.

Behind a commanding desk sat a grave-looking man in his sixties wearing the uniform of a senior officer. He looked up over the top of his gold-rimmed spectacles as Louis walked in.

'Mr Warlock?'

'Yes, sir,' Louis heard himself replying, without thinking.

'Thank you for coming at such short notice, and at such a late hour. I do appreciate it.' The man nodded at Louis' attendants, and they left the room as discreetly and silently as geishas.

Louis suppressed his instinct to make a quip, choosing instead to present himself neutrally and attentively, at least until he'd gained a greater sense of what the hell was going on. The man stood up and walked round from behind the desk. He was considerably taller than Louis, and he looked like he still had an athlete's build.

'Thorneycroft.' He reached out his hand, taking Louis' own in a light but firm grip. For the first time, Louis registered the large glass window to his right, which looked on to another room beyond. Its walls were painted hospital green and there was a surgical lamp with some large metal device on wheels beneath it. 'I run a special unit attached to the Ministry of Defence,' the man continued. 'Naturally I'm going to request that the following discussion stays completely within these walls. You understand?' There was no change in tone with this last question, but it was all too easy to detect the steel and the threat behind it.

Louis' eyes flicked back to the wheeled device, and he realised that it was an iron lung. Indeed, he could now see that there was a head poking out of one end of it, turned away from the window. A nurse entered to check on whoever was in there, and Louis looked away.

Thorneycroft stepped back to his desk to retrieve a cigarette box, offering it to Louis, who politely refused.

'Mr Warlock, have you heard of Oleg Hanikonikov?' he asked, toying with his lighter.

'Yes,' said Louis, completely thrown by the question, which in the circumstances was as surprising as hearing a Church of England vicar ask you if you'd seen any good stag reels lately.

'You know who he is?'

'Yes. He's a mentalist. What you'd call a mind-reader, or maybe stage hypnotist. Rather a good one, actually.'

Thorneycroft looked at him, wanting more, so Louis obliged. 'In fact, he's appearing at the Coliseum as we speak. A week or so left of his run.'

Thorneycroft nodded. For the first time, he himself turned to the window to his side.

'This man,' he gestured towards the figure in the iron lung, 'is an agent of ours. He was investigating Hanikonikov.' He paused, as if thinking about what he was going to say next. 'The poor bugger was caught trying to infiltrate his inner circle.'

'What's happened to him?'

Thorneycroft thought for a moment, as if trying to compose an answer to a difficult question. 'Hanikonikov ... hypnotised him, and somehow …' he swallowed, 'somehow he seems to have … rewired the man's autonomous nervous system.'

'What?' said Louis, trying to keep up.

'Our man, it seems, can now only breathe consciously as an act of will. If he forgets to do that, if he loses track, if he fails to consciously inhale or exhale, he suffocates.'

'Oh, come on. That's not possible. Surely.'

'No. It shouldn't be. But currently he has to sleep in an iron lung. Apparently there's nothing else we can do for him. The best hope is that somehow it will pass of its own accord, like any auto-suggestion, but we don't hold out much hope.'

Louis followed Thorneycroft's gaze to take in the man, his pale head emerging from the grotesque metal cylinder. It might as well have been all that was left of him. After a moment in which he let the sight speak for itself, Thorneycroft turned and walked back to his steel desk. He indicated that Louis should take a seat in front of him.

'The failure to predict the invasion of South Korea by the communist forces of the north two years ago has led to many terrible consequences, Mr Warlock. One of them is the ascendancy of what some have called brainwashing – the utilisation of techniques that turn the human mind against itself, allowing it to be used as a weapon or tool of torture. While we undoubtedly have the upper hand in matters atomic, for the time being at least, the Soviets seem to be on another plane when it comes to … things like this.'

Thorneycroft finally lit himself a cigarette, then settled back in his chair, taking a moment to consider what he was going to say next. 'Oleg Hanikonikov also goes by the name Major Oleg Kalugin. He's a Soviet agent. Before our operative was … compromised, he'd got as far as discovering that Kalugin had obtained a list of our own double agents, which he is planning to pass to his superiors via microfilm. All we know is that it's hidden in a magic prop of some kind. And it's going to be shipped back to the Soviet Union shortly. Until then, Kalugin seems to be keeping it close to his person at all times.'

'Do you know what this prop is?' said Louis, his mind already racing through the problem.

'Not exactly, no.' Thorneycroft tapped his cigarette on the edge of an onyx ashtray, staring at it as he continued. 'We need someone to find that out for us. And then ideally, switch it, without him knowing, for a duplicate.' At this, he looked up. 'It must be someone he won't suspect. Someone well known in the civilian world, with no military connections. Established in another area of life, highly practised in the art of deceit – but not in a way that would create suspicion.'

At once, everything snapped fully into focus for Louis, and he understood what he was doing there, fifty feet beneath the pavements of Whitehall. He looked again at the man in the iron lung on the other side of the glass.

'The Soviet Union is a tyranny,' said Thorneycroft. 'Not just another Nazi Germany – a totalitarian dictatorship engaged in power politics – but a unique and abnormal member of international society, inspired by a dynamic ideology that undermines every force, every element, that enabled you yourself to come to this country as a powerless refugee and entirely through your own wits and acumen turn yourself into the highly successful individual you are today. I think you understand that, don't you?'

But Louis didn't need the sermon. That fragile head on the other side of the glass, kept alive by the clanking machinery around it, was all he could think about.

'OK,' he said simply. 'I'll do what I can to help.'

There wasn't much of a reaction from Thorneycroft other than a small nod. However, the atmosphere in the room changed. Louis could sense approval and relief.

'Of course, it makes perfect sense for Kalugin to use a magic prop as a concealment device. They're hard to obtain in the Soviet Union and they'd hardly draw attention to themselves in a magician's luggage.'

'Can't you just seize everything of his before it leaves the country?' asked Louis, already fascinated by the tradecraft of espionage.

'We could. But we don't want the Soviets to know we know. And ...' Thorneycroft paused, perhaps unable to prevent his natural hesitancy at sharing such sensitive information, 'we would very much like it if they had another list of double agents.

A different one. A list containing names we ... approve of.' Was that a smile on his face, the first since Louis had entered the room?

'Because you'd rather have the Russians going after a load of their own agents who aren't actually betraying them, while the ones who are are able to continue with impunity?'

'The thing about the Soviets is they're on a hair trigger. The paranoia is so entrenched in their system that a simple accusation of working for the other side is often the only evidence that's required. In a nation where you are compelled to believe, it's very easy to think almost anyone can be a turncoat.'

'So,' said Louis, returning Thorneycroft's smile, 'you want someone to locate the prop and do a double switch? To take the prop, find out exactly where he's hidden the microfilm within it, then replace it with the counterfeit microfilm and switch the whole thing back again, without Hanikonikov ...'

'Kalugin.'

'... without Kalugin knowing.'

'That's about the size of it,' said Thorneycroft with an air of satisfaction. It was obvious he'd come to the right person. And Louis felt this powerful man's approval bathing him like sunshine on a cold day.

6

Louis was driven back to Poland Street in a different car, and with a different driver, who didn't engage in conversation. This was fine by Louis, who was trying to process the uneasy mixture of pride and trepidation around what he'd just signed up to. Checking his watch when he got to the Regal, he saw that he'd been away for a little under two hours.

Beulah was back at her post at the bottom of the stairs when he descended.

'Ah – the Prodigal Son returns. I wouldn't be expecting any fatted calf if I were you. Where'd you get to?'

'Business,' was all he said, reaching for a cigar from his inside pocket.

'Business! What business?' Beulah could smell a lie before the words were out of your mouth. She was the worst audience for any magic trick.

'The others still here?' Louis glanced over her shoulder and saw that the house band were now back on stage, playing their more conventional repertoire, currently a loose arrangement of 'You Belong to Me'.

He could only find Danny Mahal, who was dancing with Sabrina, his wife, who was also his stage assistant.

'Have you seen Dinah?'

'Come and dance, my friend. You're the king of kings.'

Sabrina whispered something in Danny's ear, and Danny laughed.

'What did she say?'

'She said you're king of the *schmerrels*.'

'So they've gone?'

'You need to find Dinah.'

As Louis walked out of the Regal, he told himself he would go to Dinah's flat in Hammersmith, but somehow he found himself walking back to his own rooms at York Place Mansions. As it was, when he got there, she was waiting for him.

'I came to find you,' he lied.

'Where did you go, Louis? *Why* did you go?' She was obviously hurt.

'I can't tell you.'

'What?!' She was affronted at this. Not drunk now, but not quite sober, she didn't hold back on her fury.

'I can't tell you. I don't mean I *won't* tell you, or I don't want to tell you. I genuinely can't tell you,' said Louis. 'I didn't choose to leave. I was taken.' Now he wasn't lying, so he invested the statement with as much passion and truth as he could muster.

'Taken? By who?'

'Let's go inside?'

'Don't think for a second that I'm staying the night.'

Louis thought about answering that with a quip, but stopped himself just in time.

Dinah sat in sullen silence while the coffee brewed. Louis had a little percolator that took about ten minutes to deliver a cup. It gave her a chance to calm down. Still, the question when it came was quite a shock.

'Why don't you want to marry me, Louis?'

'I do want to marry you.' He heard himself deliver this with all the spontaneity of an over-rehearsed line.

'Then why won't you set the date? We've been engaged for fifteen months.'

'You know as well as I do, it's hard to make a plan. We don't know where we're going to be with the radio show and the—'

'If Manny called you tomorrow and said, "Louis, I need you to clear ten days in your diary in August next year for a run at the Blackpool Winter Gardens", you'd say yes, and it would be in the diary five minutes later. Wouldn't it?'

Louis didn't even bother forming a reply. Dinah knew him well enough to know the answer, and now that she was more sober, her chess-playing side was restored to her. It had delivered him a typically astute checkmate.

That night, in bed, rolling from one side of the mattress to the other, Louis was flayed by the real reason he found himself unable to commit to a wedding date. It dated back to the first and last holiday he and Dinah had taken together. Ten days in Nice last year, after they had announced their engagement, staying at the Hotel Negresco, in a delightful room overlooking the Promenade des Anglais.

It was a big step for both of them. They had spent nights together in shared accommodation, but they had yet to go on holiday. Nice being Nice, there was more of an understanding about unmarried couples travelling together. It had all been very casual and very French, which would certainly not have been the case in an English hotel.

The first night had been relaxed, and Louis had looked forward to several days of blissful loafing in the company of his beautiful bride-to-be. Conversation with Dinah was always entertaining. She was sharp-witted, and if Louis was being honest, her encyclopedic knowledge of magical techniques was a constant diversion. It was, to say the least, very unusual to find a girl who even knew there was such a thing as a false shuffle, never mind that there were at least twenty-five different ones in common usage.

It was only on the afternoon of the second day that a cloud appeared in this otherwise perfect blue sky. Louis was reclining on a canvas sunlounger looking out to a calm Mediterranean sea, his hand trailing in the warm pebbles on the stony beach. Dinah had gone shopping, insisting that there was no need for him to accompany her. He would only be an impediment. Why not relax on the beach with his stack of *Hugard's Magic Monthly*s, and she'd be back by five o'clock, in time for an aperitif.

Louis had idly reached for his watch as he thought five o'clock was approaching. It was actually only quarter to. He had expected, hoped perhaps, that she would have been back by then, that she might have returned early. He put his watch down and tried to focus on the 'cut and restored' rope trick he'd been reading about in *Hugard's*. When he picked his watch up again, he was thinking it would be nearly five. It was in fact not quite ten to. The next ten minutes seemed to take thirty minutes to pass, with Louis checking the time every minute or two. For some reason, he was terrified that something had happened to Dinah. He knew this was completely irrational. As five approached, he started to anticipate the relief he would feel when she finally returned. But the hour came and she hadn't come back, and he found his heart was racing. He was hot, and his bowels were loose. Something had happened to her. Did he really think something had happened to her? He tried to engage himself in a debate, in the kind of self-talk he might make use of if a prop broke on stage or the spectator forgot which card he'd selected. *This is ridiculous, this is crazy* . . . but he didn't get much beyond that before the feeling that something terrible had happened to her began to reassert itself.

He had to go to the lavatory, his nerves were so great. The feeling was so intense, the fear so violent as he sat there, his heart pounding in his chest, that he had to speak aloud to himself. 'Calm down. She'll be back any minute.' But when he returned to the sunlounger, she still wasn't there. Had he missed her? Was she back at the hotel? He was paralysed, not knowing what to do.

In the end, Dinah found him wandering back and forth on the pavement on the Promenade. She was about fifteen minutes late. He was going to tear into her, he'd decided, but then he was so relieved to see her he immediately relaxed, and any thoughts of anger leaked away. He said nothing to her about his ordeal.

Horrifyingly, the same thing happened on two more occasions. The second time, he'd suggested he'd go shopping with her, but Dinah wouldn't have it, saying it would only spoil things for her. Louis felt like a child, needing to be constantly at her side. It was like some manic compulsion, and every shred of his prized competence and maturity evaporated in the face of it.

But here was the curious thing, he noticed: once they were back in the safety of their known world and back to their pre-holiday routine, crucially not living together but once again in their own individual realms, the episodes of anxiety did not return. Out of sight, it seemed, was out of mind. Once they were living apart, he did not find that he was obsessing about whether

Dinah had made it home to her sister's flat each night. He was not concerned about her fate to any neurotic degree when he knew she was out shopping in Shepherd's Bush or Holland Park. He had no idea why, but it seemed that the madness was only activated when they were together as if they were husband and wife.

He tried not to think too deeply about why this was. There was a dim awareness of some mental complex that a psychoanalyst would be delighted to make a three-course meal of if he got the chance, but Louis was not about to go down that route, not for one second. From the outside, in Dinah's mind and everyone else's, presumably, his reticence to complete their marriage ties was merely the everyday desire of a man to hang on to his bachelor rights. The reality – that he was unable to face the literal terror of being without her, should that event actually come about, and worse, that every unexplained absence provoked a flood of these unbearable feelings – was too shameful to even discuss. Instead, it could only be avoided. It was certainly nothing he could ever confess to Dinah. The demon that gripped him, whatever it was, was now in charge of things. And it was never going to give in to being married. But merely avoiding this was no solution, because Louis could not bear Dinah's anger, either. If only there was a way to square this circle. If only there was a way to appease her and maintain the status quo.

'I need to talk to you about something very important.' It was still early, not yet seven o'clock in the morning, and the first men in bowler hats were only just starting to appear on the pavement below Louis' window as he sat at the telephone, staring down.

'Louis, do you know what time it is? And you've woken Anna.' Dinah was angry, but she was still willing to speak to him. At least, she hadn't put the phone down on him yet.

'Can you meet me this morning?' he said.

'Yes.' She paused. 'What are you going to tell me? Something awful?'

'No. No. It's nothing like that ... I've got something I need you to do for me. But we can't tell anyone. I mean it. You can't say a word to anybody else.'

77

They arranged to meet not at Maison Bertaux, but in Holland Park, near the ruins of Holland House, because in Louis' mind, they were unlikely to be overheard there by any passing pedestrians. The place had been bombed in the Blitz and the work on its rebuilding seemed to be never-ending, so the noise of the reconstruction would mask any casual eavesdropping. Dinah was irritated by his mysterious approach, but she was also intrigued. Here was another thing they had in common: no mystery could be left unexplored.

She was wearing a bright blue woollen bobble hat and a smart duffle coat. Louis tried to discern what this said about her mood. As he approached her, her face turned out to be a more reliable barometer. Her expression combined a simmering anger with an air of anticipatory scepticism, ready to dismiss any hogwash that was about to come her way. Fortunately, the morning was bright and clear, too early for smog, fresh enough for the fragrance of the witch hazel and winter honeysuckle to be hanging in the air as they walked, and it lifted both their spirits.

'Shall we get a cup of tea?' said Louis, trying to be conciliatory without wanting to sound desperate or ingratiating.

'If you like,' said Dinah, a hint of her sulk still remaining.

There was a wheeled coffee stand near the old Ice House, and the smell of the beverage, stewed as it was, carried more cheer into the chill morning air.

Dinah suggested a bench nearby, but Louis asked if they could walk a little further, just so he could be more confident they were out of anyone's earshot.

After he'd told her about being taken to Thorneycroft and everything that followed, inevitably Dinah's first response was incredulity.

'How could this man be suffering in that way, unable to breathe? And why have they called on you of all people?'

'I was in the newspapers that morning. I was in their heads.'

'Come on. It seems crazy.'

'It *is* crazy.'

'Well, we've got to tell the others. We need everyone's brains on this.'

'No.' Louis was emphatic, remembering Thorneycroft's parting command. 'It has to be just the two of us. It's supposed to be just me.'

'Have they made you sign anything?'

He shook his head. 'It's all done on a gentlemen's agreement – with menaces.'

'What if they're watching you now?'

Louis couldn't help but look around. 'A man with his fiancée? Smoothing over a lovers' tiff? What's suspicious about that?' Of course, though he hadn't intended it, that was exactly what he was doing. Where was the best place to hide the gimmick? In plain sight, for everyone to see.

'As far as I can tell, it's a four-stage problem,' he said as they walked towards Holland Park Avenue. 'We need to establish what the prop is he's going to use to smuggle the microfilm, we need to get into his dressing room, obtain the prop and switch it, and find the microfilm.'

'A five-stage problem,' said Dinah her mind already working on it. 'You've got to get the prop back without him noticing, with the replacement microfilm in it. And how do you know the prop is in his dressing room?'

'My guess is that he'll keep it within glimpsing distance at all times. Wherever he is, the prop will be.'

'Why wouldn't he just have it locked away somewhere?'

'Because anywhere he might lock it away would be gettable by British intelligence. Think of the resources they've got at their disposal. The only way to be sure about it is for him to have his eyes on it at all times. At least that's how I'd do it.'

'Getting into his dressing room is probably the easiest bit.'

'True. Manny can arrange that, without any suspicion. Second easiest is finding out what the prop is.'

'How?' said Dinah. Her eyes were bright, alive, her pupils dilated. She was completely drawn in by the problem, as he'd hoped she would be. All irritation was forgotten, at least in this moment.

'Because I think he'll need duplicates of that prop. A prop not readily available in the Soviet Union. And it'll probably be a mentalism item, or a hypnotism item – something that would fit into his act, something he would plausibly perform.'

'But why duplicates?' she asked.

'I'm just thinking what I would do. If I had to gimmick something to secrete something in it – say, a false envelope – I'd start with three of the same thing. Three identical envelopes. Then I'd take the back of one, the flap of another, combine them all – make use of the fact that they were identical to start with to disguise the gaff.'

'OK.'

'So, I'll start with the dealers.'

'You boys,' said Dinah, not without affection. 'You do love your toys.'

7

There were around twelve magic dealers currently active in London, and Louis knew all of them intimately. He'd often thought that the relationship between a working magician and his dealer was probably closest to that of a whoremonger and his pimp. And the phrase 'turning tricks' could equally be applied to both trades. It wasn't quite that unsavoury, but there was definitely an element of compulsion and addiction in there. And of course, part of that was the obsession with novelty. What new item is there that might just inflame the desire of the jaded buyer who's seen it all? What new effect is there that is yet to be touched by another's hands?

He began a tour that took in Harry Leat's in Tooting. He tended to avoid the place now, as it was a little shabby after several years of austerity, which marred the joyful memory of his visit from school. Next it was on to Davenports on New Oxford Street (where George, the owner, was as snooty as ever), then the Hamleys magic department, which despite being in a children's toy shop was definitely worth a visit. It was currently run by Hugh Hunter, who was a working pro, and he kept a remarkably good stock. His ability to demonstrate an item was second to none, and when he recommended you a book, he would perform the best two items in it to prove you'd be getting value for money.

When none of these provided any obvious leads, Louis made a couple of excursions to the suburbs. Jack Hughes was out in Colindale, on the far end of the Northern Line. He dealt from his front room and normally admitted customers by prior appointment, but was willing to do Louis a favour. George Jenness had a similar set-up in his place on Inverness Avenue in Enfield. He mainly sold conjuring books, new and second-hand, but he had a sideline importing items from Tannen's in New York, so he was definitely worth including. But neither of these visits proved fruitful either, and Louis found himself back in the West End, on the doorstep of the Unique Magic Studio on Brewer Street.

Another appointment-only supplier, Harry Stanley was a genial individual with a moon face and an exuberant personality. He'd opened his studio shortly after the war, so it had been there as long as Louis had been living in London. It was, in fact, the obvious place to start, which was exactly why Louis hadn't started there. He'd assumed that Hanikonikov/Kalugin would be cautious about his preparations.

There was no shop front, just a plaque on the doorway by the entrance to the Lex garage, but up the steep, narrow stairs lay a luxurious space complete with a miniature stage (where Harry would demonstrate stage items), a well-stocked bar (where Harry demonstrated bar magic), a suede-topped restaurant table (where Harry demonstrated close-up magic and card tricks) and a floor area (reserved for cabaret items). Louis tended to favour the other outlets, because Harry Stanley was a lethally good salesman; though Louis was a mentalist, Harry was sharp enough to be able to persuade him that what he really needed was a rabbit-production box, a colour-changing fan and a substitution trunk delivered to his flat on receipt of the necessary cheque.

'Louis Warlock – you old devil! Look look look look. This just came in.' Harry was waiting for him on the landing. He was holding a silver ball about the size of a melon. 'You will not believe how light this thing is!'

'When am I ever going to do a floating ball?' Louis took off his hat. Harry had nodded at his assistant, a skinny young man with shaving rash, who reached over and took the hat and Louis' gabardine, hanging both on the metal coat stand behind the door. The walls were lined with light-coloured wood, and the floor was laid with an expensive wine-coloured carpet, giving the place the feel of a modern gentleman's tailor's. It was a long way from a toy shop (even though that was what it actually was).

'I know, I know, but you've got to feel this thing. It's a work of art.' And with that, Harry let go of the ball and it remained suspended in mid-air. It was undeniably impressive. The room was windowless, but it was well lit with small stage lamps as well as fluorescent strips, and there was no sign of any threads attached to the prop. As if following Louis' line of thought, Harry took a small bamboo hoop that had been hanging round his neck and lifted it over his head, passing it around the ball. It was the psychology of this that truly impressed Louis. Harry was relying on his insatiable curiosity, on the fact that he would happily pay the 14/6 for the item (after his ten per cent discount) just to find out how it was done.

This was the basic MO of any good magic salesman, but Harry's was the optimal version; he knew his customers' peccadillos all too well. It was good business to show Louis a cabaret item outside of his area of expertise, because he would be less likely to know the method. Thinking strategically himself, Louis allowed Harry to perform the rest of the floating ball, and several other (completely inappropriate) items, asking him to chalk them up to his account and arrange delivery. Harry even managed to sell him a book, a beautiful edition of Annemann's *Buried Treasures* that he'd just had privately printed. ('When are you going to write a book, Louis?' he asked, always on the lookout for commercial opportunity. 'I wish. I just don't have the time,' Louis replied.)

While he was making his purchases, Louis kept the chat as light and gossipy as he could, so that he could turn the conversation to Hanikonikov in as natural a manner as possible.

'Did you catch Hanikonikov at the Coliseum? I hear he's good,' he asked, allowing a note of suppressed envy to creep in, as if he wanted Harry to counter the good notices and thus provide him some comfort. Keen to keep his buyer sweet, Harry obliged.

'Oh, he's all right. People make a fuss because he talks with a foreign accent. It's nothing you weren't doing three years ago.'

'Really? I hear he's very charming in person,' said Louis, fishing without wishing it to sound that way.

'Well, that much is true. A good customer – for a communist. But then I guess there aren't that many dealers in Moscow.'

The challenge now for Louis was to sound as casual as he could. 'No! What did he buy?' A flicker of resistance on Harry's face. In theory, it was a dealer's place to maintain discretion. A working pro's act was sacrosanct. It was his livelihood, and no salesman wanted the reputation of undermining that in any way.

Balanced with that, Harry had a living to earn, and Louis was one of his best customers.

'Oh, what you'd expect. Slates. Cards. Blindfolds.'

Now, how to phrase this. 'What did you show him that ... impressed him the most?' Louis was trying to state it in such a way that it was only about him trying to find out what effect of Harry's he himself might have overlooked when it really should be part of his own repertoire.

'Well ... it's funny you should ask. Because there was one thing he loved.'

'How do you know?'

'Because he must have been planning on performing it a lot, back in the mother country. And I can understand that. It's a knockout.'

'What do you mean, planning on performing it a lot? Did he come back and tell you?'

'In a manner of speaking. He came back and bought two more of them. Maybe he's going to deal them on the black market. Exchange them for nylons for his assistant.'

Louis worked to conceal his excitement, concentrating on playing the part of the jealous performer. 'What is this miraculous item? And why aren't I performing it?'

'Who says you're not?'

'Am I?'

'Actually, no. Not your style.'

'But he's a mentalist.'

'Here he's a mentalist. I think he does all sorts over there.'

'Well go on, what is it? Rope? Silks? Coins?'

'Cards.'

'I do card tricks.' Louis didn't have to try very hard to sound put out.

'Rising cards.'

'A haunted deck?'

Suddenly Harry was tight-lipped.

'Come on, Harry. It's me you're talking to.'

'He paid over the odds for me to keep shtum.'

'I'll pay over *his* odds. And I'll still be here when he's back in Moscow.'

Harry looked over his shoulder to check his sore-faced young assistant wasn't about.

'From Scotland, of all places. Only came in three weeks ago. The guy who makes them produces a few a month. A semi-pro, would you believe, called Harry Devano. But it's wonderful. I've got three left.' He stepped over to the back wall of the store, where there was a line of wooden drawers, and pulled a key from his lapel pocket.

'A chosen card, freely chosen – and I mean freely chosen – rises out of the deck. By itself.' He opened a drawer and slid out a pack of cards, wrapped in yellow paper and elastic bands, then turned back to Louis. 'You won't believe the mechanism. No threads! Smooth as butter. One hundred per cent reliable, guaranteed for life. Like a Swiss watch.'

Louis' wallet was already in his hands. 'I'll pay cash for these. And I'll take all three.'

'Cash? This Russian's got right under your skin, hasn't he?'

He took out a sheaf of notes. 'Do us a favour, Harry. I know you just tipped me the wink about our Russian pal, but I'd appreciate it if you kept it quiet that I've bought these.' And Louis affected great sincerity at this point – just as he would if he was performing an effect and needed to manipulate the spectator in a particular direction. 'Let's keep it between you and me.' This spoken as if he was sharing a true confidence with a good friend.

'Louis! You don't need to ask. You'd *never* use a dealer item in your act. Nobody knows that better than me.' And Harry pocketed the money with a satisfied wink.

Communication with Thorneycroft's department was to be kept to an absolute minimum. If a face-to-face consultation were needed to discuss matters for any reason, it was to be requested and arranged in advance. Otherwise, straightforward progress reports were to be made every Monday, Wednesday and Friday for as long as the operation was proceeding, unless otherwise directed by either side. This was to be achieved via postcards to be left in the pages of a particular book in the London Library, a private institution for which Thorneycroft gave Louis a guest membership card in his name specifically for this purpose. 'You'll find no one will bother you, Mr Warlock. It's a very sedate establishment.'

The library was in the north-western corner of St James's Square, two doors down from the East India Club. Louis had made sure he dressed in suitably sober clothes so as to draw no attention to himself. He was well used to adopting whatever persona a routine demanded, and this was no different. It was a skill that dated back to his earliest days as a performer. Sure enough, no one challenged his entrance. He merely had to sign himself in, as any member would. The aged retainer on the front desk was not the type to take too much interest in who was coming and going. Louis had been instructed to make use of a book to be found in the reference section on the gallery level, one highly unlikely to be referred to by any other member: Volume 3 of *The Rural Cyclopedia, or a General Dictionary of Agriculture, and of the Arts, Sciences, Instruments and Practice, Necessary to the Farmer, Stockfarmer, Gardener, Forester, Landsteward, Farrier &C*, edited by one John M. Wilson.

The report was to be written on a normal-sized blank postcard and references were to be made to imaginary school friends, using the initials of the real people concerned (OH for Hanikonikov, LW for Louis and TT for The Target – aka the prop in which the microfilm was to be concealed). If there was anything else, Louis was encouraged to use his imagination. 'We're pretty sharp in this department,' Thorneycroft had said drily. 'We'll work it out.'

Louis took the book, together with a couple of other titles randomly pulled from the shelves nearby, to a desk in an out-of-the way corner of the library floor. The large reading room, flooded with light from huge Georgian windows, was a comforting place to be. He enjoyed the silence, the monastic feel. The peppery smell of dust and age could almost have been incense.

He withdrew a sheaf of newly bought blank postcards from his inside pocket together with his Parker 51. Pulling the cap off the pen, and making a show of referring to the pages of one of the now-open books in front of him, he wrote:

I got hold of Tom Tallis – or at least his double, that is. I'm going to persuade him to make the change next week. We're going out together Wednesday afternoon to talk about it.

He used another postcard as a blotter, then inserted the message into the open frontispiece page of the *Rural Cyclopedia*, ensuring it was tucked well into the gutter, and casually closed the book to secure it. He spent five further minutes pretending to read one of the other books he had pulled out, making some bogus notes on the postcards scattered in front of him. Then, once he was satisfied that even the most acute of casual observers would by now be bored beyond reason, he returned the *Rural Cyclopedia* to its resting place on the upper gallery shelves.

When Dinah came to his rooms for an update, she made a show of being resistant, still perhaps nursing a simmering resentment that the two of them were no closer to fixing a date for their wedding. But the reality was – and Louis saw it as soon as she arrived – she was as hooked on this new game as he was.

There was one thing that had occurred to him – a crazy idea that had come in the night – and it didn't relate to Hanikonikov or the mission. While things were more relaxed between them, since they had this other problem to work on, would it be possible for him to make a confession to Dinah about his unhinged neurotic fears concerning her being taken from him? Perhaps there was some way of talking the whole thing through with her. Confessing to the irrational thoughts and feelings he'd experienced in her absence. As he lay there – at 3.45 in the morning, the occasional taxi rumbling past outside – he began to believe such a thing might be possible if he approached it in a detached and descriptive manner. He could perhaps talk about it as if it was happening to someone else; a curious phenomenon that they were observing together, something they could both be wryly amused by.

With that thought he drifted back into a restless and fitful sleep, and woke with a vestige of the idea still lodged at the back of his mind. And it was still lodged there now, as Dinah sat in front of him pouring the tea through his old broken strainer, which she always complained about ('You're earning a hundred pounds a week, Louis – you can just go into Woolworths and buy yourself a new one').

He was shuffling one of the Devano deck of cards he'd bought from Harry, or at least the portion that could be shuffled. Idly he spread them out for Dinah to make a selection.

'Do we have to?'

'Just take one.' She did so, and he casually offered her the deck for her to replace it. Then, without comment, he stood the pack upright in the sugar bowl.

'Louis . . .'

He just nodded at the cards. Slowly, very slowly, one began to creep its way out of the pack, under its own motive power.

'What!' She immediately reached out, waving her hand up and down in between Louis and the cards.

'No threads.'

'What is it, then?' She reached to grab the pack.

'Gently . . .' He retrieved it.

'What's the mechanism?'

'Take a look. '

He handed Dinah the cards and she carefully fanned them out. At first glance everything looked normal, but a closer examination revealed a brilliantly intricate mechanism devilishly well hidden within.

'It's gorgeous,' she said.

'Hanikonikov bought three of them. This is what he's using to smuggle the microfilm.'

'Are you sure? How do you know?'

'Why else would he buy three? Each gimmick is guaranteed.'

They looked at each other, both aware that this was going to be the trigger for the intimidating and challenging task that lay ahead.

'I've already spoken to Manny,' said Louis. 'He's organising tickets for the matinee. Hanikonikov's more likely to be distracted if he's in between shows.'

'And what if the cards aren't in his dressing room?'

'We can only try,' he said, smiling. Dimly, another thought tugged at him, the idea that had come to him in the small hours about confessing his neurotic craziness to Dinah. But the possibility of doing that was already slipping away, like a piece of newspaper in water, dissolving into its constituent fibres, falling apart, beyond all chance of retrieval.

SHARED THOUGHTS

Imagine this: myself and my other half,
Dinah, are at a party socialising, and at
some point the conversation turns to the
extraordinary mental connection we share
with each other. We decide to
demonstrate.

I leave the room, and Dinah asks each
of the group to think of a capital city.
They call the names out and she writes each
one on a small piece of paper. When about a
dozen cities have been named, the papers
are crumpled and placed in a bowl.

Dinah asks a spectator to mix the
papers and to remove just one. Once done,
she takes all the other pieces and places
them in her pocket so they are no longer
'in play'.

The spectator now opens the selected
paper and shares with the group what the
randomly selected city is.

Dinah explains what will happen next.
She will stand facing the group, away from
the door. One of them will collect me and
stand me so I am back to back with her; she
will not look at me or say anything. The
spectator who chose the city will say
'ready', and Dinah will attempt to send the
name of the city to me.

Exactly as described, I am brought back in and stand back to back with Dinah. No words are spoken other than the spectator's 'ready'.

At this point, the group fall silent, and Dinah and I attempt to lock into each other thoughts. After a moment's concentration, I declare, 'I am seeing a building, tall . . . pointed, I think it's the Eiffel Tower. The target city must be Paris!'

The group explode into excited applause – a direct hit. Our reputation is secured by this demonstration . . . and soon yours will be too!

Dinah and I have used this effect not only socially, but many times on the radio and occasionally on stage too. It is so direct, and joyously simple. Think about it for a moment. The spectators can call out any cities and they can choose any target paper – it is out of your control. How on earth can this be possible?

As a follow-up, Dinah leaves the room and a spectator picks one of the other cities. Dinah re-enters and reads the spectator's mind, correctly naming their second chosen city!

What I am about to teach you is a simple method that creates a truly huge impact. It is a party trick I learned as a boy. The secret has been around for aeons and is disregarded by many in the magical fraternity as being too simple to fool, but it is precisely that childlike simplicity that I adore. The sheer joy of the method's chutzpah makes performing it wonderful.

You and your accomplice/partner decide
in advance on the target city — let's
imagine it's Paris. Once you're out of the
room, your other half grabs a notepad and
pen and asks the group to call out capital
cities. No matter what is shouted — London,
Paris, Washington, Tokyo, Rome, Berlin —
they simply write PARIS on every piece of
paper. That's it! Obviously if Buenos Aires
is called out, they must feign writing more
letters, but the secret is simplicity
itself. No matter which paper the spectator
picks, they will get PARIS. So that is
stage one.

Now to stage two, in which the
spectator sends the thought.

In the description above, you will
remember that once the first target paper is
chosen, the other papers are put away in
Dinah's pocket so as not to be a distraction.
Well . . . they go into Dinah's left pocket.
In Dinah's right pocket are a set of a dozen
or so papers with genuinely different cities
written on them. After Paris has been named
and the first effect has them amazed, Dinah
pulls out the papers from her right pocket,
with the different cities on them, and lays
them on the table. That way anyone who may
be suspicious can look through them. This
allows for the killer follow-up, should you
want to perform it. With the regular pile on
the table, Dinah leaves the room and then
when she's outside, I grab one of the cities
and ask the spectator to try and send the
thought to Dinah. The spectator reads it to
themself, then concentrates. After a short
moment Dinah re-enters and instantly names
the city . . . ROME!

This is another extremely cheeky method. In your pocket is a crumpled piece of paper with ROME written on it. You and your accomplice know this will be the second city. Once the first effect is over, I offer to repeat it, instructing Dinah to move to step out. As she does so, I casually reach into my pocket and remove the Rome paper. As soon as she's looking away, I move my hand to the pile of papers on the table and apparently select one at random. In fact I'm simply bringing the Rome paper out that was already in my hand. I then give it to a spectator and say, 'I'd like you to try, please. Read it to yourself and then send that city to Dinah.' Yet again, a great effect achieved by the simplest of techniques. There's no question, the more straightforward the method, if it's carefully used, the easier it is to be fooled.

And as I sit here reflecting on everything I've ever learned, or failed to learn, that devastating fact is more evident to me than it's ever been.

Multum in parvo – much in little.

8

The Coliseum was the largest theatre in the West End – and a notoriously unpopular house to play, at least if you were a magician. 'A great big stinking barn' was Danny Mahal's verdict on the place after he had appeared there in the Royal Variety Show two years earlier. The stalls were the size of a football field and there were three overly capacious tiers on top of that. Even the largest stage illusion was dwarfed by that huge proscenium. Since the end of the war it had mainly housed American musicals, and consequently Louis had never played there himself.

But a rare five-week lacuna had manifested itself in between *Call Me Madam* and *Guys and Dolls*, and so impresario Jackie Liveright (nephew of the infamous Horace Liveright) had stepped in with a thrown-together variety bill designed to milk the early summer tourists. A night of unchallenging fare under the title *Would You Believe It!* – an oddball blend of acrobats (Maurice French and Joy, the Balancing Wonders), novelty turns (Mickey Vine and Karen, balloon jugglers) and dodgy double acts (Joe Baker and Jack Douglas, the Crazy Kids). By far the most interesting item on the bill was Oleg Hanikonikov, the Modern Rasputin. The whole thing was what was known in the trade as a bank raid. Pay the cast peanuts and screw the theatre on their cut, because otherwise they'd be dark for five weeks, making nothing on their bars, kiosks and ice-cream trays.

The plan was for Dinah and Louis to attend the show together – a perfectly natural thing for them to do. No need for disguises or anything incognito, quite the reverse. Why wouldn't Britain's favourite mind-reader be appraising a rival from across the waters?

Then, once the show was over, Louis would 'go round' and visit Oleg in his dressing room. Dinah would wait in a rendezvous point backstage, and they would liaise there to do whatever was necessary.

'Louis, you need to be very careful,' said Dinah, fretting as they made their way into the auditorium.

'On the contrary, I think I need to be very relaxed.'

'Wouldn't it have been simpler to sneak into his dressing room while he was on stage?'

'It's never empty. His tour manager's in there at all times. A proper Rottweiler, apparently. This way is going to work fine. Trust me. He has no reason to suspect me of anything. We're brother magicians. I can slip straight in to talking shop.'

'Brother magicians don't generally resort to acts of unprecedented mental violence,' said Dinah, referring to the fate of the unfortunate agent who'd last crossed the Russian's path.

'I'm literally just going in there and doing a switch, like for like. Do you know how long I've been doing switches?'

'That's why I'm urging you not to let your guard down. He's going to be extremely vigilant. And he's not a magician. He's a major in the Soviet intelligence service.'

Louis accepted the latter point, though he felt the need to counter it. 'If I go in there thinking that, I'm finished. This is no different to handing a gaffed deck to a spectator and asking him to examine it. If you're terrified he might find something, you'll signal that to him and he'll spot it straight away. You've just got to believe what you're handing him is kosher. Lo and behold – he doesn't even look.'

He was more scared than he was admitting. But he managed to suppress his fears enough to keep them on the periphery of his inner vision; until, that is, he overheard two gentlemen behind him in the stalls, prior to curtain up, talking in a most ungentlemanly manner.

'This fellow – the Russian.'

'Hanikonikov,' said his friend, reading from the playbill.

'A colleague of mine saw an after-hours show he did.'

'After-hours?'

'Private show – some party up at Cliveden House. One of those debauched affairs. And the Russian . . .'

'Hanikonikov.'

'... he's an unscrupulous devil, I'm telling you. He gets this chap's friend's wife up on stage, such as it was. Young girl – they'd only been married a few weeks . . .'

'Go on.'

'He hypnotises her into believing she's taking a bath – on the sofa! Gets her to run it, imagining she's turning on the taps, tells her it's her honeymoon night and she's getting ready for her husband. Well . . . my friend said he'd never seen anything like it, not even in a stag reel. This girl strips off, stark naked in front of everyone, and gets on this sofa—'

'The dirty bastard! Then what?'

Fortunately, the band struck up that point, a muscular arrangement of 'A Little Bird Told Me'.

Hanikonikov closed the first half. It was an extraordinary act, featuring members of the audience, who seemed, as far as Louis was able to tell, completely bona fide. There was an impressive levitation with the assistant mesmerised into a state of rigidity, balanced on a number of upright broom handles, which were taken away one by one until she was resting on two alone. And as if that wasn't enough, Hanikonikov took a large surgical needle and inserted it into the top of her leg and she didn't even flinch.

And then a second audience member, a postman from Canning Town. Hanikonikov hypnotised him to believe he'd been born in Leningrad and had him speaking fluent Russian with a perfect accent. It was a baffling feat, and if the postman wasn't a stooge, Louis had no idea how it had been accomplished.

The attendant on the stage door recognised Louis through the glass, and the door was opened for him before his hand had reached the bell.

'Mr Warlock – very fine to see you. Having an afternoon off?' said the attendant.

'Working, Ernie. Sizing up the competition.' Louis shook the old man's hand. According to rumour, he'd been on that door since *Blackbirds of 1934*, the longest-serving concierge in the West End.

'Afternoon,' said Ernie, nodding politely at Dinah. 'You know where you going?' he asked, turning back to Louis.

'Dressing room number . . .?'

'Four, sir. Up two flights, turn right, first on the left. You can't miss it.'

As Louis and Dinah climbed the steps, they made their arrangements, keeping their voices low.

'Toilet and washroom on the top floor,' said Louis.

'And if I'm challenged?'

'Nobody uses it – it's not properly plumbed in. Bolt the door.'

'Usual code?'

'Dot dot. Dot dot dot. Dash dash. Dot. "Is me".' Dinah turned to kiss him and ran on, carpet bag slung over her shoulder.

Dodging show girls in flesh-coloured tights and a distinctly unjoyful-looking Joy (of Maurice French and Joy), Louis knocked confidently on the door of dressing room number 4. There were voices inside; it seemed he wasn't the only one to have gone round. Hanikonikov's was immediately discernible, but the other was English, high and slightly nasal, also familiar. In the few seconds before the door was pulled open, Louis tried to calculate whether it was a good thing or a bad thing that there was another person present. The answer was, of course, it depended on how he played it.

The door was opened by a severe-looking young woman with scraped-back hair and minimal make-up. This was, presumably, Hanikonikov's notorious tour manager. Louis knew immediately that she must have an intelligence role too, and he felt his stomach tighten. He hadn't expected there to be another pair of eyes watching him. He realised now that he'd been naïve, a victim of wishful thinking. The woman looked at him unsmilingly and he immediately turned on the charm.

'Good afternoon. Louis Warlock. I've just come to say hello.' He gave his broadest, most friendly smile, the one he employed whenever he was meeting anyone in a professional capacity

'Your agent said to expect you,' said the young woman coldly. 'Were there not going to be two of you?'

'My fiancée sends her apologies. She's meeting a friend.' It would perhaps have been better cover and provided more distraction if Dinah had come with him, but he needed her elsewhere. If only he could have had the full Brains Trust on hand, but of course, he couldn't.

The young woman moved out of the way, still unsmiling, exuding an air of irritation. She gestured to the far side of the dressing room, where Hanikonikov was deep in conversation with a short, skinny young man in thick-rimmed spectacles. Louis knew the other man, and thanked the gods of magic for his presence, because he could provide necessary cover while Louis did what he needed to do. It was William Wallace, though he was better known in the community by his stage name, Ali Bongo. He looked about fourteen, but in fact he was a bright young kid in his twenties. He worked part time for Harry Stanley, helping out in the studio and contributing tricks and drawings to Harry's monthly magic magazine, *The Gen*. His intense questioning and burning curiosity would be a good magnet for Hanikonikov's attention.

Louis reached out with his right hand as he walked towards the Russian.

'Mr Hanikonikov, a pleasure and an honour.'

A quizzical look, followed by a softer voice than the commanding baritone he'd used on stage. 'You are . . .?' Was this manipulative? Or genuine ignorance? Either way, it was most effectively met with more charm.

'Louis Warlock. Admirer and fellow professional.'

'Mr Warlock. Yes.' And that was all Louis was going to get.

'Ali. A pleasure to see you too.' Louis held out his hand to Wallace, having chosen to use his stage name, which he knew the young man preferred. 'Extraordinary routine, Mr Hanikonikov,' he said, turning back to the Russian, 'with the postman.'

'Routine?' Was he questioning the word or its use? If the latter, he could well be one of those performers who resented being bracketed with magic and magicians. If his skills were genuine (and, Louis reminded himself, somewhat uncomfortably, he was here precisely because he felt those skills *were* genuine), Hanikonikov would no doubt be insulted to have them reduced to mere conjuring tricks.

'The final item in your . . . in your performance,' said Louis. 'It was remarkable.' He smiled, letting his genuine marvel at what he'd seen show through.

'Thank you. The man was an excellent subject. That is not always the case.' So Hanikonikov was capable of humility, even if it was of the faux kind.

'Mr Hanikonikov, do you have strategies if a spectator – a member of the audience – gets on stage and is *not* a good subject?' asked Ali Bongo. This was a genuine question, of course. Ali had the callow fanaticism of a magic obsessive, driven to soak up any information he could whenever he had the chance, and wasn't shy about asking.

'In truth, young sir,' said Hanikonikov (and Louis thought it wise to remind himself once again that this man's name was actually Major Kalugin), 'by the time I have selected the subjects, I already know that they will be suitable for the experiment that is to follow . . .'

His answer didn't stop there, thankfully, which gave Louis the opportunity to sweep the room with his gaze. He was looking for the distinctive mustard yellow of the cardboard case that the Devano deck came in. This was a skill he had developed a long time ago: to be searching for something while concealing the fact that you were doing so; talking to a spectator while scanning the spread-out cards, looking for the marked one, or indeed just locating the positions of the four aces in a freely shuffled pack. He let his eye lightly graze all the surfaces of the dressing room he could see. He was confident that the deck would be placed in a position where it would be in Hanikonikov's gaze at all times. (Why not in his assistant's pocket? Would he really trust his assistant? Wasn't everyone capable of being turned?) He thought his best policy was to ask a question, in such a way that it would keep Ali Bongo in the conversation too; then, once Hanikonikov's attention was on Bongo, Louis would complete his reconnoitre.

'It's a funny thing,' he said, looking the Russian in the eye. 'My experience with hypnotism is very limited – I wouldn't presume to have an opinion about it in your presence, sir – but when it comes to the selection of spectators for a conjuring item, perhaps there is an overlap. One develops a . . . horse sense.'

'Horse's sense?' said Hanikonikov, frowning.

'An instinct – for who will be effective on stage and who will be difficult. It's a felt thing. Ali, what's your experience with spectators?' And with that question, Louis turned his head to Ali Bongo, hoping it would cue Hanikonikov to do the same.

'Well . . . I, um . . . I . . . my experience is that yes – yes, now you mention it . . .' The young man wanted to carry the weight that Louis' question had given him, even as he struggled to match it with his narrower experience of performance. Louis meanwhile took the opportunity to resume his survey. He felt the ludicrous frailty of his plan, the number of assumptions it rested on, not to mention all the impractical things that would then have to be achieved if he did manage to lay eyes on the Devano deck. But even as he was tormented by his own doubts, his heart flipped over in his chest – for his eyes had registered that precise shade of mustard yellow in a smear over by the make-up and face cream, beneath the illuminated mirror on the opposite side of the room.

He allowed his gaze to drift back slowly to confirm his apprehension. And it was correct. There were the cards in their case, the black edges around the yellow pattern so distinctive. Immediately this fact caused several things to lock into focus. Firstly, it dispersed the host of doubts that had accumulated: that his hunches were mere fantasy, that the job was impossible. Why else would the pack of cards be there, in Hanikonikov's eyeline, if it did not contain the prize? And why was there only one of them, and not the three Harry Stanley had said had been purchased, if it was not for them all having been cannibalised in some way, as Louis supposed.

He felt in his trouser pocket for the outline of the replacement pack. He was one action away from completing the first third of the mission, perhaps the most difficult part. And even as he had that thought, he felt a shadow fall between himself and its completion. Hanikonikov's assistant was holding him in her own steady gaze, watching him as his eyes had come to rest on the Devano cards. Thought number one. There must be a way to occupy her for the twenty-five seconds it would take to accomplish the switch.

'Excuse me,' he heard himself saying in his most polite voice, leaning towards her, 'would you have an ashtray? I couldn't see one.'

She gave the barest of nods, but he was relieved to note there was no additional suspicion on her face. Unfortunately, he'd only got as far as taking a step in the direction of the dressing room mirror, having turned his attention back to Hanikonikov, before she had plonked a rusty tin lid in his hand. When he glanced casually over in her direction, he could sense she was still staring at him. He did his best to pick up the thread of the conversation between Ali Bongo and the Russian.

'. . . I've heard it called the Eye Count, or the E.Y.E. Count.'

'The Eye Count?'

Knowing what they were discussing meant it was easy enough to jump back into the conversation.

'Teddy Victor's count, isn't it. It's a way of counting three playing cards, one at a time, while keeping one hidden,' said Louis, and he demonstrated by counting three imaginary playing cards into the air. Even as he was doing this, he found himself thinking, I'm completely screwed. Caught in a pincer movement. How am I going to get out of this? Almost exactly as he had the thought, there was a knock at the door.

In that moment, as everyone glanced over to the dressing room entrance, he seized the opportunity he'd been gifted. He casually placed the ashtray on the surface nearest the Devano cards and used the move to make the switch with the replacement deck, which was already palmed in his right hand. By the time the door was opened and the visitor received, he was back standing in his original position, with his attention fixed on looking to see who the visitor was, the same as everybody else. The exhilaration he felt as he pocketed Hanikonikov's Devano deck was as intense as anything he'd ever experienced.

'Hello, good afternoon, I hope you don't mind – I just called to see Mr Hanikonikov. Is he in?' said the caller.

Louis recognised the voice immediately. Polite, calm, Indian. What the hell was Danny Mahal doing there? What interest would he have in Hanikonikov, who for all his expertise had never been near a dove or a big box illusion in his career? And what gods had arranged for him to walk in at that precise moment, when he would be of maximal use to Louis' operation. But of course, it wasn't the gods who'd arranged it. It could only have been Dinah.

9

As Louis ran up the grey concrete steps to the top of the backstage area, he tried to process his conflicting feelings. On the one hand, he was furious that Dinah had broken his trust and involved Danny. But equally, he was immensely grateful for her initiative and her nous. In fact, if she hadn't betrayed their agreement, he would not now be striding towards the top-floor lavatory with the treasure in his pocket. She must have foreseen the challenges, thought it all through with her chess player's brain, and worked out how essential an extra distraction would be.

Nevertheless, as he rapped out his Morse code on the pink-painted toilet door, he struggled to contain his anger, which he'd been harbouring even as he excused himself from the dressing room. He was hoping his departure would be read as politeness as much as anything, since the room was now more crowded. He'd made sure he'd done one thing before he exited, and that was to leave his cigarette lighter, discreetly, near the ashtray and the switched cards.

'Well?' said Dinah as she opened the door.

'What the hell were you up to?'

'Have you got them?'

'Dinah—'

'Have you got them?' She raised her voice firmly.

Unable to resist her command, and the opportunity to demonstrate his prowess, he slipped his hand into his pocket, producing the Devano cards with a flourish.

'*That's* what I was up to,' she said, as if her case was now fully made.

'But Danny . . .'

'Danny doesn't know anything, OK?'

'Then what was he—'

'I just asked him to turn up there, and said he'd be doing you the most enormous favour.'

'What favour?'

'Do you want to know the mark of his loyalty? He didn't even ask,' she said sharply.

Louis couldn't let this argument spiral out of control. The matter at hand was too important. Dinah had already laid out her tool kit: a square yard of green felt, two scalpels, a bottle of Sanford's photo glue, a small metal rule and the two remaining packs of Devano cards. He tossed Hanikonikov's deck on to the felt next to them.

'Well, we've got the cards.'

'So, our worst-case scenario right now is that they don't get to smuggle the names of those double agents out of the country – right?'

'I suppose so.'

'Even if you don't go back into the room.'

'But I've got a duty to.'

'A duty?' Her question brought Thorneycroft to mind, the spirit of his authority, the desire for his approval.

'It's my duty to complete this. Who knows what chain reaction it'll set off if I don't.' There was more to it than that brief account he'd given her, but he wasn't about to share the complicated swirl of feelings he was having, the tug of guilt, his sense of honour.

Somewhere in the pack of Devano cards in front of them was a piece of microfilm about a quarter of the size of a postage stamp. He knew that was what they were looking for because he'd been passed a replacement to switch it with. They really had no more than fifteen minutes to achieve this. Because by then, Hanikonikov would be ready to usher any visitors from the dressing room, and the tour manager would be standing guard again. The window of opportunity would have gone.

'There's a finite number of places it could be,' said Louis, as he stared down at the deck in front of them. 'So let's just work through them logically, shall we?' He knew one thing with certainty at this point – the same lesson as always: 'do not give in to panic'. 'It could be in the gimmicked section of the cards. It could be in the mechanism itself. It could be in the ungimmicked cards. You start there – see if you can find anything. I'll do the gimmicked parts.'

They worked quickly, but neither approach yielded anything. Louis turned his attention to the mechanism. The thing was to be methodical. He disassembled it piece by piece. Whatever element contained the microfilm could be repaired with the replacement packs. But within a few minutes, it was clear that there was nothing concealed in there at all.

They stared down at the mix of cards and beautifully crafted mechanics. Louis was taut with frustration. Thankfully, however, Dinah's faculties were still functioning.

'What if you're going about this the wrong way?'

'Well, clearly I am,' said Louis.

'Stop feeling sorry for yourself and think.' The rebuke stung. Dinah continued. She had something in mind. 'You're expecting this thing to be hidden in the most obvious place.' She nodded to the bits and pieces laid out on the felt. 'In the mechanism of the gimmick and the parts that surround it. You've been admiring it since you bought it, haven't you?'

'Yes, I suppose,' said Louis grudgingly.

'Well, what if he's using the trick itself as misdirection.'

'What do you mean?'

'Any casual observer, magician or otherwise, is going to be immediately drawn to the gimmicked bits, because it's so fascinating to look at. Anyone searching for something hidden in the deck is going to start there.'

'OK,' Louis said, damping down his desire to contradict her.

'But what if he put the microfilm in the most boring part of the whole prop? No one is going to look there.'

He stared at her, still not really sure what she was talking about. She looked down and picked up the mustard-coloured card box that had been casually thrown to the side of the felt mat.

'What if it's in here?' She smiled at him. And Louis loved that smile.

All card cases were constructed in the same way – one piece of card folded and glued together at three points. Given how intimate Louis was with them, it only took three slices from the scalpel and the entire thing was laid flat out before them. He pressed his fingers along the surface like a blind man reading Braille. It didn't take long for his sensitive fingertips to find a small indentation on the side of one of the flaps. He glanced up at Dinah, who registered the hope and excitement in his eyes.

Working carefully, he prised apart the layers of cardboard. Nestling there in a little hollow where a neat square of one of the layers had been removed was a square of celluloid microfilm. Using the end of his scalpel, he carefully levered it out. He reached into his pocket for a stamp collector's cellophane envelope and slipped the item into it, immediately closing the flap and putting it back into his jacket. Then from his ticket pocket he pulled out a different-coloured cellophane envelope.

'Colour coding. Very important to avoid mix-ups.'

'Where did you get that?'

'Stanley Gibbons, on the Strand.'

'Not the envelope. What's in it,' she said, referring to the replacement microfilm.

'It was left for me.' He was not about to tell her of his arrangement with the London Library.

It was a relatively simple operation to slip in the replacement microfilm and seal the cardboard around it. Sanford's photo glue was always the gum of choice, because it dried so quickly with very little scent. Soon the box was reassembled and one of the pristine Devano decks inserted, after Louis had spread and shuffled the cards several times, to simulate a few weeks of ownership. He and Dinah looked at each other.

'Now all you've got to do is get it back into his room. Without anyone noticing.' She didn't say any more, but he knew what she was thinking, because he was thinking the same thing himself. Why not quit now, while they were ahead? The important thing was that the Soviets wouldn't get their list of double agents. But that wasn't what Louis had agreed to. And he really needed to show Thorneycroft that he had come to the right man. The risk was exposure. But the risk was always exposure, in one way or another.

'I'll see you in the Lamb and Flag in fifteen minutes. It's a straight in-and-out job,' he said calmly.

'All right.'

Unless Louis was imagining it, he detected some satisfaction in Dinah's response. And a touch of admiration.

As he descended the stairs, he went through in his head the necessary moves he was about to make. He'd left his lighter by the ashtray, near the mirror, next to the make-up items where he'd deposited the duplicate Devano cards. This was actually a piece of magical thinking, learned at the feet of the Professor himself, as he was known, the magisterial Canadian magician Dai Vernon: every move has to be motivated. If you need to ditch a secretly palmed coin in your pocket, you must construct a reason for the move. You could, for example, talk about how you have to wipe your hands with a handkerchief because they're sweaty and they must be dry for the next part of the trick to work. Now you've got a reason to reach into your pocket, where you can ditch the palmed coin. The forgotten lighter was the equivalent to the sweaty hands, and the return to the dressing room was the handkerchief in the pocket. It was all entirely and reasonably motivated.

He knocked on the dressing room door, and Hanikonikov's assistant greeted him coldly. When he saw Ivan and Phyllis squashed in there too, he was relieved, grateful and only slightly irritated at this further example of Dinah's disobedience/perspicacity.

Ivan nodded at him. 'Mr Warlock! Always a pleasure. Were you in this afternoon?'

'Oh yes.'

'Wonderful—'

'Sorry, not stopping. Just realised I left my lighter.' And there it was, still in position on the side by the mirror. As he leaned across to get it, he palmed the replacement Devano cards, gripping them between the heel of his thumb and the pad of his right little finger. This was a deck switch of his own devising that he'd made a thousand times, used for replacing a freely shuffled pack with a stacked one. But now all eyes were on him. And this wasn't a stage, it was a room no larger than a modest study. But he couldn't break the momentum either; if he stumbled, that would be fatal.

Suddenly a clatter came from his right. Phyllis had dropped her box of Maltesers, which were now rolling around the linoleum. With a commendable lack of grace, she was already on the floor picking them up, her backside in the air. It had only been four years since the end of confectionery rationing. Anyone with a sweet tooth would understand this. Louis took the gift she'd given him, moving forward in one graceful action, picking up his lighter and holding it triumphantly in the air to further distract from what his right hand was doing. As he pocketed the lighter in his trousers, his other hand sleeved the switched deck. A quick scratch of the face was enough to let gravity slide it into the crook of his elbow, where he could press it in place against his body until he was out of the room.

'Thanks again,' he said to Hanikonikov. 'And safe travels.' And with that, he was free.

10

Louis had always assumed that the final handover of the target (or Tom Tallis, as he had come to know it in his head, from the description he used in his postcards) would be at the London Library via *The Rural Cyclopedia*. Although he hadn't been asked, he'd gone as far as creating a gimmick for the job. He'd brought three duplicates of a tourist's picture postcard, split it into its constituent layers and fashioned an empty square in the top right-hand corner, where the stamp went. The microfilm would be hidden within it. But then, unusually, he'd received a direct telegram from his 'Uncle Len', who'd gifted him his library membership:

> Sorry for short notice. Your cousin Ben will be in town tonight. Wants to try one of these new coffee bars he's been reading about. Could you meet him at Moka at 7 p.m.?

Louis was taken by surprise that the transfer was to be made so directly. The Moka Bar was one of a small number of such establishments that had opened in and around Soho in the past year or so. It served Italian-style coffee from a polished chrome machine, dispensed in tiny cups at inflated prices. But kids starved of glamour and excitement had latched on to these places as a promise of a world to come. The women all had short hair and short-sleeved jackets, the men wore open-necked shirts and reeked of Brylcreem. And it was so loud with the thrum of delighted chatter and the constant hiss of the steamer that it was virtually impossible to have a conversation. It was certainly impossible to overhear one, which was why Louis imagined they were meeting there.

As the rendezvous approached, he felt a growing excitement and an attendant sense of nervousness – an intoxicating blend of anticipation, satisfaction and risk.

Almost as soon as he entered, he felt a hand on his arm. A short, nervous-looking man with bright, intelligent eyes behind round-rimmed spectacles.

'Cousin Louis! It's good to see you here. Right on time, seven p.m., just as Uncle asked.' He looked up at Louis expectantly, like a turn on stage waiting for a response to his cue.

'Cousin Ben. It's good to see you,' said Louis, improvising his response. This was the greatest game he'd ever played. He didn't think he could ever love anything as much as he loved magic. But this was like magic times ten. 'I have actually got something for you. It's been so long. I thought you might like—'

'Ben' cut him off immediately. 'Cigarette?' He held out a pack of Player's, from which one cigarette poked out ostentatiously. Louis was clearly supposed to take it, so he obliged.

'Would you like a cup of coffee?' he asked. But Ben was still fussing with the pack of Player's, pulling another cigarette half-way out with noticeable care.

'Take another one, for later. You can smoke it when you get home.' He lifted the pack up, closer to Louis' eye level. Louis looked down and could see the fag he was being offered had been doctored. It had no tobacco in it, but instead contained a rolled-up piece of paper.

'Thank you. I will. I'll smoke it with dinner.' He took the second cigarette and slipped it into the handkerchief pocket of his jacket.

'Actually, shall we head outside,' said Ben. 'It's rather stuffy in here. That demon throws out quite a lot of heat.' He nodded at the coffee machine, which was spitting and sputtering behind them.

'Good idea. At least we'll be able to hear ourselves think.'

Ben turned first, moving through the crowd, mostly kids, caught up in their own carefree worlds. Louis wondered what they should talk about once they were out there. But the moment Ben stepped on to Frith Street, any association with Louis fell away. He just kept walking, and within twenty seconds he was simply another evening commuter on his way home to Kensal Rise or Parsons Green. Within forty seconds, Louis had lost him in the crowd.

As soon as Louis got home, he fished in his handkerchief pocket with his forefinger and middle finger, pincering out the fake cigarette Ben had given him. Wanting to be as careful and diligent as possible, he fetched a scalpel from his drawing room table and sliced the side of the cigarette paper open, revealing the rolled-up tube within. He flattened it out on the table in front of him. A long, narrow strip of a kind of paper stock he wasn't familiar with (and he was familiar with most types; they'd all featured in magic gimmicks of one kind or another over the years). This was light, like cigarette paper but stronger. It was written on in a small, fine hand, in block capitals. Clear and legible, tiny, but just about readable with the naked eye:

Go to Richmond Park on 18 February at 10.30 a.m., to the new Isabella Plantation. If you take the footpath that leads from the west side of Thompson's Pond (see over) towards the rhododendrons, after 500 yards you will come to a litter bin on the right-hand side of the path. Walk ten paces from this into the bushes and you will come to a small clearing. There will be a white-painted stone in here. Pick it up and you will see that it has a slit in its bottom. Insert the item (in a stamp collector's celluloid envelope) in here. Return the way you came.

The 18th was the day after tomorrow. Presumably the extra day was included to give him a chance to clear any prearrangements. How considerate, he thought.

The morning came, and Louis found he woke early, again in a state of some excitement. It was a fine day in mid-February. There was a light breeze that made him grateful for his scarf as he walked to the Tube. The anticipation of the trip out to Richmond, via Hammersmith, was not unpleasant. The rush hour was dying down (he'd left at 9 a.m.), he could relax, read the morning paper and savour the thought of the ten-minute walk through the lush greenery at the other end. He knew Richmond Park well enough not to be anxious about finding his way. Then there would be the thrill of locating the stone. Again, the game of it.

As he rode out on the rattling train from Baker Street, he found himself thinking about Dinah. He was in a new world now. The operation had been a huge success, in the face of apparently insuperable odds. Surely he had proved himself to be an invaluable asset to the intelligence services. And surely they would be calling on him again, accepting him into their confidence and their esteem.

His heart was racing as he walked the path from Thompson's Pond past lines of pink-flowered camellias, the ground scattered with trampled petals. It was quiet, which was why Louis imagined this was the chosen location for the handover. Yes, there was a tension, but it wasn't unpleasant now. It was closer to the nerves you might feel during a game of cards. Not real stakes, more a safe simulation. Nobody was going to die. The worst thing would be that he wouldn't be able to find the stone. So be it. He'd just contact them via the London Library. Or they'd reach out to him. They must have their reasons for doing things this way. Maybe it was just their orthodoxy. Magicians too had their own fixed routines, which in truth could be achieved in other, simpler ways. Maybe if his career in espionage was to continue, he could offer some suggestions for improvements, as a fresh pair of eyes.

In the end, it was a simple matter to find the stone. The little clearing was so out of the way, it would not conceivably have been stumbled upon by a casual dog walker, or even an assiduous groundsman.

Louis looked around once more, checking he was truly alone, and truly unobserved. He picked the stone up. It was cast from resin, presumably in a mould taken from a random piece of real rock. The surface had been painted to look natural, and then painted again in smeared whitewash, so it stood out to him but not to any casual passing eyes. He admired this attention to detail and the psychology behind it. The underside had a narrow slit cut into it, about four inches long and no more than a sixteenth of an inch wide. It would be a simple matter to slip the stamp collector's envelope in without there being any danger of it falling out.

He took the envelope from his inside pocket and placed it inside, then returned the stone to the ground, as close as he could to the spot where he'd picked it up from, restoring it to its unobtrusive position in the earth. In a relaxed and confident manner, he pushed himself out from the bushes, checking that there was no one on the path before he rejoined it. There wasn't, so he strode on, following the track for a while, allowing it to take him on its course for ten minutes or so. Only then did he start paying attention to where he was and making his way out of the park.

There wasn't any sudden burst of elation at having successfully completed his mission; rather, it was a slow-dawning sense of his accomplishment. By the time he rolled into Earl's Court to change on to the train back to Baker Street, he was experiencing a sort of dizzying disbelief that he'd achieved what he'd been asked to do. It was only as he was walking past Druce's Depository towards York Mansions that it truly hit him. He'd done something extraordinary. Surely new and profitable paths were now opening up before him. But even as he had that thought, he knew it wasn't about gain of any kind. There was something deeper beneath it all. His value would now be known by the authorities. His loyalty. His effort. He'd spent the war years at Westriver School carrying the weight of being despised for his lack of Englishness, even as he'd worked to lose his accent. Now, surely, he'd proved beyond question that he was a British citizen.

As soon as he got home, he telephoned Wilton's restaurant on Jermyn Street and booked a table for two for eight o'clock that evening. Then he called Dinah and asked her if she would join him there. There was much to celebrate.

He ordered the cold salmon, and Dinah had the baby lobster, since Louis was paying.

'You *are* paying?' she said, only half joking.

'Of course. We're celebrating. And I'm also saying thank you. I wouldn't have done it without you.'

'Well, nothing new there, then.' She was being sharp, but she was smiling too. He topped up her wine from the carafe and felt his belly tighten. He had something to say, and he wanted to do it while the smile was still on her face.

'I want you to know, I've been thinking about . . . everything. And . . . well, I'm going to be . . . I'm going to make changes.'

'Changes?'

'I'm going to start doing things, taking things more seriously.'

'Oh yes.' He could feel her anticipation.

'Obviously I'm . . . I'll be hearing from Her Majesty's Government soon enough. And when I do, I'll know where I stand.'

'What do you mean, know where you stand?'

'I think this is going to be big, Dinah. Really big. I think they're going to want to use me again. But I think that's likely to involve some official shenanigans. I mean, hoops I'll have to jump through. For things to be put on a more official footing.'

'What are you trying to say, Louis?'

'I'm not . . . I'm just saying . . .'

'Yes?'

'I'm just saying, as soon as I know where I am with all of this . . .'

'Yes?'

'I'll be in a position to . . .' He found himself trailing off.

'Position to . . . ?'

'Position to know where I stand. And then . . .' he went on quickly. But he wasn't able to form his words any more precisely. What *was* he trying to say? 'And then we can . . . make our arrangements.'

'I see.'

'It's just a matter of waiting for the official feedback.'

'And when you say "our arrangements" – there are arrangements to make?'

'Of course.' He smiled. And then found he was looking down at his salmon, the mayonnaise in a little oval on the plate next to it. He picked up a large flake with his fork and dipped it in the sauce, carefully coating it all over.

'I don't see why we can't talk about it now,' said Dinah, with greater clarity than he could manage. 'We don't need the government's approval.' These latter words carried a catty bite.

'I just . . . We can. I just thought . . . It's about doing everything in the right order.' He was improvising, but not very well. 'I need to see where I am.'

There was a moment, balanced on a very fine point, where it certainly felt plausible that Dinah might stand up and walk out. But she didn't. Whatever inner battle she was having came down in favour of staying put. But there was not much joy in the rest of the meal. The conversation was muted, and there was little air of celebration.

As he lay in bed alone that night, listening to the lorries rumbling past, Louis searched for some thought that would compensate for the uncomfortable feeling that had settled in his chest, the tightness, and attendant agitation that wouldn't allow him the release of sleep. He didn't find one, but he did eventually slip into unconsciousness.

He was woken by a loud and insistent knocking on his front door. His first thought was that it was Dinah. As he scrambled into his dressing gown and the knock came again, he felt, if he was being honest, a rising hope. He didn't care if she'd come to have some final furious reckoning with him. He just wanted to see her again. He was sure he could win her round by communicating to her how much that was the case. He swung open the door, ready with a winning smile. But there was no Dinah. Instead, a severe-looking man in an Ulster coat flanked by two uniformed police constables.

'Louis Warlock?'

'Yes,' he said uncertainly, trying to work out why they were there. He didn't have any surviving next of kin to be notified about, unless something had happened to Dinah. But surely they'd go to her sister. There was relief in that thought.

'I'm arresting you on a charge of treason against Her Majesty's Government. You do not have to say anything, but anything you do say may be taken down and given in evidence in a court of law.' And the man nodded to the constable on his left, who reached for a pair of handcuffs. The other constable took hold of Louis, and not in a gentle manner, and swung him around while the handcuffs were fixed on his wrists.

'I'm sorry. I don't understand.'

'You'll come with us.' And that was the last word that was said to him as he was hauled without ceremony down the narrow staircase of York Mansions and out into a dimly lit dawn, the sky a dull grey lid overhead.

THE DEADLY ASSISTANT

If you ask people to talk about a
magician's act, they will very often refer
not only to the magician, but also to their
assistant. Friend, it is a much
misunderstood, much underrated role. The
truth is, assistants are needed to both
openly and covertly help make the magic
happen. Night after night I find myself
amazed at the effortless misdirection
provided by an assistant. In a nightclub
setting, they're often clad in a sequinned
leotard, fishnets and high heels, and it's
impossible for the audience's eye not be
drawn momentarily to them as they move
across the stage, fleetingly releasing the
magician from any scrutiny and thus freeing
him to invisibly 'flick the switch or make
the ditch'.

There is, however, one assistant I wish
was never on stage with me. 'The Deadly
Assistant', as I christened her. She often
appears unwanted, at the worst possible
moment. Unlike trained and rehearsed
assistants, this lady isn't working on your
behalf. She is there for one reason only:
to destroy you. Let's remove the veil and
call her by her actual name.

Doubt.

Doubt works not to misdirect the audience, but to misdirect you. And she is powerful. For example, having watched you perform a classic force of the necessary card - even though you've done it perfectly and discreetly - there she is whispering in your ear, 'Damn, which card did you just force? Are you sure it was the right one?' So convincing is she, so persuasive, that you stumble and, just like that, the moment has vanished and the magic has gone.

Even worse, when creating a new effect, there she is, wearing her most lethal disguise: common sense. 'I don't see how this can ever work. You should just stick to what's been done already.'

How to silence this troublesome assistant is an ongoing challenge, and with one style of effect in particular, it becomes a matter of life and death. I call those effects 'the Injurers'.

The Injurers are effects that are not only magical but carry with them a genuine physical risk. From the possible impalement of your hand during the petrifying Card Stab, through to the truly perilous risk of internal ruination while performing an Acid Test, these are not to be performed lightly. Now, of course there is a level of artifice and safeguarding intricately bound into the methods of all these effects, but even with those precautions in place, doubt can truly scupper you: 'What are you thinking? What about those fatalities! Don't create . . . don't take crazy risks - stay the same, stay safe.' It's up to us to hear the truth behind her siren call - the

lie she is really peddling: 'Be
mediocre . . . you'll live longer.'

Recently I have been dreaming of an
effect that I am yet to find the perfect
method for. It needs to be rock solid,
because the danger that accompanies this
barnstormer is totally real.

A gallows stands centre stage; six
nooses are on display for an audience
committee to examine. Five are legitimate
hangman's nooses, the sixth a breakaway
rope that can hold no weight even though it
looks identical to the others. The nooses
will be fairly mixed and then the audience
committee will freely select one of them,
which is then affixed to the gallows. Once
that noose is in place, I shall be led to
my potential death. My head will be placed
appropriately, and after a moment's pause,
I'll be dropped either to my extermination
or, preferably, on to a waiting crash mat
and resounding applause.

But I have come to realise that the
hideous simplicity of the dreadful thing's
mechanics renders it almost gimmick-proof!
I even managed to entice Mr Albert
Pierrepoint to Maison Bertaux for a lesson
in the physics of how a man's weight
affects the speed of his demise. It
transpires that if calibrated correctly,
the snap of the neck and death is
instantaneous. (As a side note, should you
ever have the pleasure of meeting our
Queen's most efficient executioner, he is
most partial to a cream horn.)

When it comes to this effect, I keep
reminding myself that the challenge is
actually a basic one, to simply 'force' one

item out of six - in this case the safe noose from the lethal. Unlike forcing a card, though, these objects are out of my hands, which means the method has to be psychological. With those type of forces, the margin for error is much greater, as they rely on utter confidence and audience control to ensure their compliance. It truly is a challenge that terrifies me, but I feel I must solve it, for my own peace of mind.

If, as I leap off those gallows, I find my neck is in the real noose, my last thought may well be of the Deadly Assistant whispering in my ear: 'Told you you should have stayed mediocre.'

11

The cell was spartan in the extreme. A concrete floor and walls. A single tiny window, too high to see out of. An iron bed frame without a mattress and a plain wooden chair.

Louis had asked to be allowed to go to the lavatory and was brought a zinc bucket with a block of carbolic in the bottom and a folding lid.

'I need to make a bowel movement,' he'd told the policeman on duty, as if the man were a doctor. The information didn't make any difference – the bucket was going to have to suffice. There was no toilet paper.

After he'd finished, he tried to think straight. At some point they would have to feed him. He would have to be given access to water, a shower. Eventually he heard the key clanking in the iron door. His heart started racing. He was trying to keep the tightest hold he could on his fear. He had been since his arrest. He must not give in to panic. Once again, school was a good preparation. He had never actually been locked up, but there were plenty of times when he'd had to wait in the housemaster's study, often accused of something he hadn't actually done. He had some experience when it came to appealing to authority, the mix of humility, deference and sincerity required.

The door was opened by a more senior policeman to reveal a short, balding, sweaty-looking man in his fifties. He wore a pair of spectacles with thick browline frames, which he adjusted upon seeing Louis. He wrinkled his nose, presumably at the smell emanating from the bucket. His double-breasted suit was shiny in places and a little ragged around the sleeves, and even from where he sat, Louis could see his tie was stained. He carried a pigskin briefcase, which he held in front of him as if it were a shield.

Louis stood up, trying to look compliant and cooperative. The most futile thing he could do, at least while he was in this cell, was to make a fuss, no matter much how he wanted to. Realising that the smell wasn't going to help matters, he turned to the policeman.

'Excuse me? Could you . . .' He nodded down at the bucket in the corner of the cell. The officer just looked at him as if he were mad, and then shut the door, locking it behind him.

Louis gestured to the battered chair, since the policeman had not brought an extra one for the man to sit on, a polite sign of respect. Without disguising his irritation and displeasure, the man sat down, putting his briefcase on his lap and unbuckling the straps.

'I'm Baldwin. And this appears to be the definition of an open-and-shut case.' This statement had the unfortunate effect of seeming to be a joke, because it coincided with him opening his briefcase. However, it couldn't have been more obvious, given his demeanour, that any appearance of good humour was completely unintentional. He removed a buff-coloured file folder and continued: 'The facts are clear, and ostensibly watertight.'

'Mr Baldwin,' Louis said, calmly and authoritatively, 'if you could just arrange for me to make a telephone call, I'll be able to contact my brief.'

Baldwin looked up at him, incredulous now as well as irritated. 'I *am* your brief,' he said with barely contained contempt, then looked back down at his notes.

'Surely I'm entitled to—' began Louis, but that was as far as he got.

'This is a military matter of the highest security. In these circumstances, you're only allowed to take the representation assigned to you. Do you understand?'

Of course, Louis' immediate instinct was to fight back, but his strategic side quickly regained control: *Hear him out. Don't make an enemy of him, no matter how unhelpful and contentious he seems to be.*

'Yes,' he said, quickly adding, 'I think so.' However strategic he was being, he didn't want to appear to be a pushover.

'I am your brief. I have been assigned to you. And I'm here to recommend that you plead guilty to this charge of high treason. You, Louis Warlock, aka Ludvik Weinschenk' – and Baldwin somehow managed to squeeze out every available drop of un-Englishness from those four short syllables – 'have been caught in flagrante, working directly with Soviet agents against the interest of your own country. The very same country, I might add, that harboured you when your life was threatened in childhood. There is, I'm afraid, clear and unambiguous documentary evidence of you stealing military secrets and passing them directly into Soviet hands.'

Louis sat down on the edge of the iron cot and clasped his hands together. He wanted to demonstrate, as subtly as he could, that he was calmly and sincerely gathering his thoughts before he spoke.

'Mr Baldwin. I understand what you're saying. But I need *you* to understand, as my representative, that this is a misunderstanding – a terrible misunderstanding. I don't know how it's happened. I'll admit my naïvety in these matters – it may be that there are competing departments within the British military – but all you need to do is contact one Major Thorneycroft of the intelligence services, and I promise you, he will be able to give a true account of what actually has taken place. The simple fact is that I was working *for* British intelligence, not against them.'

'Yes, Mr Warlock. This is what you said at your initial police interrogation, the military interrogation that followed, and the intelligence interrogation that followed that. It seems that you're determined to cleave to this story.'

'Yes. And it's a story that Major Thorneycroft will be able to confirm as fact.'

'So you've said. Unfortunately, there's no serving officer called Thorneycroft in the British army, navy or air force, or any of the intelligence services. There is simply no such person.'

'But he gave me orders, he—'

'Orders? What do you mean, orders? You're a civilian. And why would he order a civilian to steal secrets from one of our own agents? Mr Warlock, there's little I can do for you if you're not prepared to accept the reality of your predicament. They'll be transferring you to jail, where you'll be held on remand until the trial. I will come and see you again once you're there. Until then, I'd like you to reflect on the facts that are arraigned against you and consider again how you want to respond to them. You must know that you are facing a potential capital charge here.'

Louis let this bombast go without comment. He needed time to think. Well, he was to have plenty of that, it seemed.

Within ten minutes of Baldwin's departure, the idea came to him. And despite the stuffy temperature in the overheated, oven-like space of the cell, he went so cold his teeth began to chatter. What if it wasn't a matter of competing departments within the intelligence community, or poor communication between officers, or a misunderstanding somewhere within the corridors of power? What if it was Louis himself, 'Great Britain's most brilliant magical mind', as the radio announcer described him every week; what if he had been hoodwinked by a bit of cheap chicanery, so effectively that he'd sold his own soul to it? What if he'd been fooled and then done up like the proverbial kipper and played by the other side? What if Hanikonikov was working for the British? In fact, Baldwin had just told him this – *order a civilian to steal secrets from one of our own agents* – and bound up in his own denial, Louis had let it slip by uncommented upon.

Over the course of the next fifteen minutes, he reconstructed what he imagined had actually taken place: the microfilm that he had retrieved from Hanikonikov was actually supposed to be on its way to *British* intelligence, not the Soviets. Hanikonikov was an agent working for the British, not the Russians. The microfilm hidden in the Devano cards must have contained details of Soviet double agents working in the West. Why it hadn't been passed across earlier Louis didn't know, but he guessed it was something to do with preserving Hanikonikov's double-agent status. He was a genuine Russian citizen who'd been recruited by the British, but this status must have been compromised by the Soviets without British intelligence knowing it. So the Soviets were in a position to flip the whole situation to their advantage – using Louis as their unwitting operative, getting him to steal the secrets back for them before they could be passed to the British. At some point, relatively late in the proceedings, British intelligence must have got a sense of what was going on. Louis was guessing Hanikonikov's suspicions might have been the trigger. Which meant that all the while Louis was congratulating himself on a smooth operation backstage at the Coliseum, Hanikonikov must have realised that he had switched the cards and obtained the real microfilm. He must have got word to his (British) superiors, and surveillance must have begun immediately.

The next day, Louis asked to see Baldwin as a matter of urgency. It was late afternoon before he was taken from his cell to a badly lit interview room on another floor.

'Could I trouble you for a cigarette?' he asked.

'I'm a pipe smoker, I'm afraid,' said Baldwin, though there wasn't much of an apology beneath the words.

'I think I know what's happened,' said Louis. And he proceeded to unroll his theory. To be fair to the man, he was attentive, and he started to make notes almost immediately. He didn't comment, and he let Louis speak until he was finished. Then he looked at him, cool and hard.

'And is there anyone who can corroborate any of the details of this account?'

Of course there was. Dinah. Dinah could corroborate every aspect of it, at least in the sense of confirming exactly what Louis had said to her. But before he'd even begun to form the words to tell Baldwin about this, an inner voice called out, with violent conviction: *No!* Because if Louis even mentioned Dinah's name, she would immediately be arrested and be pulled into this night-mare. And heaven knows what other accusations they might try and pile on her. They would be perfectly willing to destroy her life too. Not to mention the lives of the rest of the Brains Trust, despite their marginal involvement. And that must not happen. If he could still achieve one thing, it would be to make sure that didn't happen.

'There was no one else involved. That was the point of it,' he said, firmly and calmly.

'What do you mean, the point of it?'

'They wanted me to believe – beyond question – that they were British intelligence, and that Thorneycroft was a high-ranking officer. It was impressed upon me, very effectively, that if I were to speak to anyone, anyone at all, about what was being shared with me, there would be serious consequences.'

'So you didn't discuss this with any of your associates? Involve them in any way?'

'How could I, under those circumstances?'

Baldwin looked at him, an inscrutable expression on his face, before finally speaking. 'Then we don't have very much in our favour when it comes to building a case. Do we?'

'I suppose not,' Louis said quietly.

'You see, Mr Warlock, the prosecution have a plethora of evidence. From their agent's sworn statements about your inter-actions with him. Photographic and material evidence of you passing state secrets of the highest sensitivity for collection by known Soviet agents, who unfortunately were able to elude capture themselves. All you have in your defence is this one, frankly unbelievable account. And are we seriously expected to accept that you took at face value the assertion that a man had been hypnotised into not being able to breathe?'

Louis felt himself swallow. Why *had* he believed it? Because of Thorneycroft's prestige? The man had given such a convincing performance. But Louis knew himself that one man speaking a lie with absolute conviction, if the requisite care had been taken to build up the supporting circumstances, could win over an entire audience. And it seemed he too was not immune to such deception. Of course he wasn't.

'It's all I've got,' he said. And it was all he was prepared to give.

He asked if he was allowed to write a letter. He'd had no contact with anyone since his arrest. Baldwin made it clear to him that he could do so, but that his correspondence would be read before it was sent on and anything that was deemed a matter of national security would be censored.

'Your case is currently embargoed, Mr Warlock. No one is allowed to write anything about you. You may recall the business with our two agents Burgess and Maclean, who went missing in rather startling circumstances a couple of years ago. "Government employees", it said in the *Express*. But everybody knew that meant they were spies.'

'They went to Moscow, didn't they?' said Louis, remembering the scandal.

'They did. And consequently our secret service people are somewhat – shall we say – paranoid. So now, I'm afraid, everybody's being a lot more cautious. The *Express* will not be writing about *you*. Nor indeed any of the papers. And anything you try to say to the outside world . . . well, it will be restricted.'

'Surely I can let those who care about me know that I'm alive and well. They're going to be worried. They'll have no idea what's happened to me.'

'You can say you've been arrested. And that your case is under investigation. Use whatever euphemisms you want. If you don't want the letter turned into Swiss cheese, choose your words carefully.'

Louis was desperate that Dinah should conceal any hint of her involvement. Whatever else happened, from here on in, he was determined that everything was going to be clean. It was just him. Nobody else. He stayed awake all night trying to think of a reliable way of getting that message out to her.

By the morning, he had a method. He carefully wrote her a letter with a borrowed Parker pen on plain writing paper.

Dearest Dinah,

I've been arrested for a crime I most certainly didn't commit. I'm not able to tell you any more at this stage. There will be a trial in due course, and I have every confidence that everything will be sorted out by then. I just wanted to write to you to let you know that I'm well, and safe. This is a military matter apparently, hence this absurd high security.

Please do not worry. You know I'll be all right and I'll be able to work out what to do.

With love
Louis

PS I owe Beulah £4.6.7 for the do the other night. The free bar was rather expensive! I've no idea how long I'm going to be in here. Please can you arrange to pay her the exact amount, <u>down to the last penny</u>. You know what she's like, I don't want her out of pocket. Please do this.

The postscript was a cipher, but there was nobody in British intelligence who would be able to decipher it. In fact, there was nobody beyond him and Dinah who would be able to decipher it. This was what it said:

Stay silent.

And this was how it said it:

The previous summer, Dinah and Louis had been alone in a train carriage on the Great Western Railway. They were on their way to the Bristol Hippodrome to perform in a musical variety show with Winifred Atwell and Reg Dixon topping the bill. Louis was reading the paper, and there was a story about a new piece of experimental music that had had its debut that week at a concert hall in New York. It was called *4'33"* and consisted of four minutes and thirty-three seconds of silence. Louis immediately looked at the date on the front page to check that it wasn't 1 April. The story was so ridiculous, it was like something from a Chaplin film.

'Listen to this composer.' He read aloud from the article. '"People are missing the point," Mr Cage said. "What they imagine to be silence isn't silence at all. It is something else entirely. But they just have to learn how to listen."'

Apparently the pianist took to the stage, laid out the music on the piano, and then closed the lid, to indicate that the piece had begun. He opened it again at the end of the first movement, closing it at the start of the second, and so on until the whole piece was finished, after precisely four minutes and thirty-three seconds, at which point he opened the lid again. Louis read all this out to Dinah, because he couldn't believe it. And as he read, they both got more and more hysterical.

After they had calmed down, it was Dinah (of course) who said:

'You know what?'

'What?'

'That's a great code word. For us.' They were on a permanent trawl for personal code words. Innocuous phrases that would have no discernible second meaning for anybody else hearing them but that would immediately land for Louis and Dinah. Whenever one presented itself, Louis would make a note of it on a small postcard and add it to an ever-growing pile that was arranged alphabetically by meaning. Then, when they were devising methods that relied upon information being passed between them, it was a simple matter to refer to the 'lexicon', as he had dubbed it, to see if there was anything useful.

'What's the code word?' he asked, not cottoning on.

'"Four minutes and thirty-three seconds". We're never going to forget that it means "silence". Or "absolute silence".'

'*Very* good!' Immediately he'd reached in his pocket for one of the postcards he always kept about his person and made a note. He'd learned long ago that whenever an idea arrived, from whatever source, it had to be written down straight away.

So now, only six months later, he had no doubt that Dinah would make the connection. He'd underlined 'down to the last penny', because £4.6.7 was equivalent to 433 pennies. She would know straight away that he didn't owe Beulah any money for the celebration do; it had been Beulah's gift to him. So she would be alerted to look out for something. And it would only take a moment for her to get to 433. Silence. Absolute silence. She was a smart girl. She would understand.

12

Louis was relieved when he discovered his case was going to be heard on Tuesday 17 March. Apparently there was a great imperative for matters to be resolved hastily. He found dealing with uncertainty draining and debilitating. Facing something concrete was always preferable.

The proceedings were going to take place in camera, which meant no press, no reporting and no jury. Baldwin insisted that this was in Louis' interest. If the hearing was to be fair, then all the available evidence needed to be laid before the presiding judge. Given that much of it referenced details of the highest level of national security, this could hardly be done in the presence of the press and the public.

He woke early on the morning of the trial. Five days previously, he'd been transferred from Wandsworth, where he was being held on remand, directly to another prison, the location of which was kept from him. The journey had taken about three hours. He was allowed into the refectory for his meals, but he had to sit apart from the other prisoners. From overhearing their conversation, he was able to determine that he was in a glass-house – that is, a military prison – called Cornhill, although someone else referred to it as Shepton Mallet. So, he was in Somerset, which was inconvenient for visitors, but then he wasn't allowed any visitors anyway.

At first he'd felt a numbness to his situation. He'd allowed a safety curtain of denial to descend, acquiescing to a vaguely magical belief that somehow things would sort themselves out. If he examined himself more closely, he knew that something in him had been crushed by the wrongness of what had taken place.

He was full of disgust at his own stupidity. He could feel the pull of self-pity, the temptation to give in to it. He knew he must wrestle with that, but the weight of it was so heavy. The worst thing was the feeling that he'd been robbed of his future. He saw clearly how right across his life he'd relied upon the idea of ever-improving circumstances to sustain him. That was gone now, and he knew it.

Eventually he hit upon the strategy to pull himself out of this abyss. It involved searching for some pleasure in the now, even if it was just a crumb or a morsel, in the hope that it might offer a first step back to a more positive mindset, which he desperately needed if he was going to get to a place he could build from. He had to find some of his old steel.

Meals were a source of enjoyment, simply because he was hungry most of the time. Hot showers too. Visits from Baldwin offered surprisingly affecting moments of human contact. Even trips to the lavatory yielded something. Gradually he found he was able to use all these events as stepping stones, or handholds to get him across the void of each day to somewhere a little better.

Normally he would have aimed for connections with other prisoners, but he was kept completely apart from them. They were little more than ghosts to him, unreachable apparitions in grey clothing drifting past in the distance.

He'd thought he'd be able to connect with his guards, to use some of his notorious charm on them. But of the two who'd been assigned to him, one wouldn't even look him in the eye and the other proved to be completely immune to it. He was tall and etiolated, with baggy skin and a harshly lined face that sat all too well with his cold and contemptuous manner. Louis had assumed when he'd arrived at the jail that his celebrity might carry weight, be a tool he could use in some charismatic way. It was a shock to find how ephemeral it was. Its power seemed to have evaporated almost overnight.

The trial, Baldwin informed him, was going to take place at Taunton Crown Court. Normally cases such as these would have been heard in London, but the secrecy surrounding the affair meant the authorities actively embraced being out in the West Country.

Inevitably, Louis spent much time running possible scenarios over and over in his mind. There were only really two. He was either to be acquitted or found guilty. If he was found guilty, he would immediately appeal. Baldwin had reassured him about this, along with the fact that it would be a protracted process. So, jail – more of this – was as bad as it would get. The question was, how much more jail?

If he could have had a pack of cards, he would have been all right. He had seen one down in the recreation area, but he was not permitted to spend time there. It was of course calling to him, his oldest friend. It was hardly a surprise that much about his experience was reminiscent of the worst aspects of school: the plain and flavourless food; the regimented day; the enforced times for sleeping and waking. He was back there, slipping all too easily into the miserable grooves and ruts worn deep within his psyche by that oppressive regime. Stop it, he told himself. Take control of your thinking. You can do better than this. If he couldn't get playing cards, he would try something else.

In front of him there were a number of cardboard tubes he'd collected, from the insides of toilet rolls – four of them in all. He took one of them and carefully disassembled it, unfurling it on the floor. Then he tore it into four equally sized pieces and dipped one in the water in his sink until it turned into a mulchy mush. This he squeezed in his hands until it became pliable and clay-like. Once this had been achieved, he rolled it into as neat a ball as he could fashion and laid it underneath the hot-water pipe that ran around the outer side of his cell.

He made another three balls, ensuring as far as he could that they were all of equal size and shape. When they were dry, they were pretty solid and easy to handle. Soon he was practising a magic routine with them, his own variation of a trick known as 'chink a chink', usually done with coins or, as its originator the great Max Malini did, sliced-up pieces of wine cork. (The trick's title derived from the noise the coins would make as they moved around; the cork eliminated that sometimes problematic element.) He spent two hours or more finessing the moves and exploring the possibilities that the props presented. He was still absorbed in working on it when he heard the sound of the key in the lock of his cell door.

The journey to Taunton took a little more than an hour. As soon as they'd set off, Louis' stomach had tightened, a tightness that quickly rose into his chest, increasing his heart rate as it did so. The police van was blacked out, so he didn't have the distraction of looking at the Somerset countryside as they drove. But for all his nervousness, there was a kind of comfort in the sense of impending resolution.

'The defendant, Ludvik Weinschenk, also known as Louis Warlock, will take the stand.'

There was no disguising the disdain with which Louis' birth name was uttered. But he couldn't deny that Ludvik was still there somewhere in his centre, like the solid little figure inside a nest of Russian dolls.

He had never been in a courtroom before. The only thing he had to draw on to orient himself were the handful of court scenes he could remember from the movies: *The Paradine Case*; Will Hay in *My Learned Friend*. Neither of these, it became apparent, would be much use as a guide here. There were far fewer people present than he had expected. The judge, of course – identified as Mr Justice Beddows – who seemed to be entirely constituted of the accoutrements of his position: the red robes, the elaborate white starched collars, the dusty-looking wig that draped over his shoulders and across the top of his chest. Then there was the prosecuting counsel, a tall, sardonic man called McGilchrist, who had the sharp avian features of a Ronald Searle cartoon. Baldwin, of course, and his assistant, who was meek and prematurely balding; and a small group of figures in military uniform who sat in the shadows on the small upper gallery. There were no press, no members of the public. Just Louis, held in the penetrating gaze of Mr Justice Beddows. Once again, it was school that came to mind, and Louis was in the position of something low and verminous whose mere existence was an affront to the good functioning of society, of life itself.

He found himself listening to the proceedings with an odd sense of detachment, despite his nerves, as if it was a description of somebody else's activities, so divorced did it feel from his own recollection of events. Baldwin had advised him to keep quiet and speak only when asked to. 'Don't make the mistake of thinking that your demeanour will have no impact on the judge. He's known as "the recording angel" on the circuit because of his ability to peer within a defendant's soul.'

The prosecution's opening volley had been particularly stinging:

'Your Honour, what I'm about to describe to you is a shameful account of the most callous and treasonous activity I've come across since the last war. At great personal cost to himself, and placing his family at risk, our agent, Mr Oleg Hanikonikov, had been able to secure a list of Soviet operatives who were embedded in positions of trust in Great Britain and were passing state secrets regarding matters of national security, military planning and intelligence operations. Careful arrangements had been made to transfer this information to British officers, and yet prior to this taking place, the defendant, Mr Weinschenk, intercepted this information, substituting it with a bogus version that would have caused great damage to innocent British and Allied operatives while he returned the precious original material to his Soviet masters.'

'How does your client plead?' said Mr Justice Beddows, turning to Baldwin. His voice was commanding but dispassionate.

'Not guilty, Your Honour.'

'And yet,' the prosecuting barrister fired straight back, 'we have clear documentary evidence of the transfer being made, using methods straight out of the Soviet playbook. Before our agents were able to intervene, the material had been removed.'

'It's a pity our agents weren't able to operate quicker,' the judge said, with more than a hint of disapproval. 'Perhaps if they'd been less concerned about photographing the defendant and more astute about what he was up to, we would still have that information.'

'It's a fair assessment, Your Honour. The intention was to do both – to document the defendant's collaboration and apprehend the other agents. Unfortunately, those agents were able to evade capture. However, that misfortune does not pertain to Mr Weinschenk's guilt or innocence.'

The judge harrumphed. Louis was pleased to observe the prosecution had scored a point at the expense of Mr Justice Beddows' goodwill.

When it came to Baldwin's turn to present the case for the defence, Louis experienced a rush of relief, the first he'd felt for some time. The man went for it like a whippet dropped into a race track, proving himself to be a highly capable defending barrister. His somewhat truculent and irritable manner turned him into the best kind of advocate, and he did an excellent job of presenting Louis' account. His manner and his aggression had the effect of lending anything he said an air of being the only truth possible, and for anyone to question it would be an act of indulgent idiocy. Louis himself certainly couldn't have done a better job of describing, from his point of view, exactly what had taken place.

'Your Honour, my learned friend, Mr Weinschenk is the true victim in this case. A victim of a diabolical confidence trick designed to use his own acumen against himself, in service of the malignant plans and designs of the Soviet Union. Most diabolical of all was the appeal made to his loyalty and love of country in order to deceive him into serving the very enemy he thought he was acting against. He was insidiously manipulated into carrying out the wishes of the Cheka, or the KGB, as I believe it is now known. Mr Weinschenk was shown what appeared to be the worst of the Soviets' actions in order to persuade him of the urgency of the matter at hand and the necessity of using his unique skills to fight their depravity. I reiterate the fact that he genuinely believed he was serving his own country – and in fairness to him, it's hard to see how he could have believed anything else in these circumstances.'

When his defence was completed, Baldwin sat back down with an air of a man who had presented an ironclad case on behalf of his client. Where the prosecution had been florid and overly dramatic in their account, he had been fair and factual. And holding this encouraging thought in mind, Louis stood for the cross-examination, turning to face the questions with as much confidence as he could muster.

'Mr Weinschenk, you gave in evidence here, and in your initial statements to the police, an admirably clear description of what happened to you on the night of your collection by these "agents" from the Regal Revue Bar.'

'I've tried to be as cooperative as possible at every stage.' It was school again, and he was presenting himself to the headmaster.

'You've certainly been clear. Well rehearsed, you might say.'

'Objection, Your Honour,' said Baldwin, standing commandingly.

'Sustained,' said the judge, again hovering with an air of disconnection from the noisy drama the prosecution was trying to conjure.

'I merely mean, Your Honour, that the defendant presented a remarkably coherent account of what had happened to him – full of an unusual amount of detail.'

'I have tried to answer every question I've been asked as clearly and honestly as I could,' said Louis, turning to the judge, not being afraid of letting through a flash of genuine emotion.

'Of course,' said the barrister, unfazed. 'One fortunate consequence of this is that it has been possible to reconstruct your journey on that night. It culminated on Horse Guards Avenue, did it not?'

'Yes, sir,' said Louis, not sure where this was going. He turned to Baldwin, but the man's face was impassive.

'Would you take a look at these photographs?' A clerk handed Louis a sheaf of black-and-white prints. 'Was this the underground car park you were taken into?'

Louis looked down at the images. When it came to the photograph of the entrance to the subterranean parking area, he recognised it straight away. There was no point in concealing this fact. He was tempted to look to Baldwin again, to see if there was any cautioning expression on his face, but he realised that would immediately undermine his position. He was going to trust in the truth.

'Yes,' he said. 'This is the building.'

'And if you'd take a look at this next set of photographs, of the lowest level of the car park. Was this the area the car drew up in?' Again, when the photographs were handed to him, he immediately recognised the layout of the concrete bays and the narrow doorway in the furthest corner of the basement area.

'Yes, sir – I believe it was.'

'Good. And that doorway, in the third photograph – was that the way you were led.'

'Yes. I think so.'

'You think so?'

'It looks like the one I can remember.'

The prosecution was satisfied with this. 'Very good. Your Honour, if you'd look at this further set of photographs. These were taken by the police after Mr Weinschenk had given his full sworn statement. You'll see they reveal the area beyond this door – which was in a state of considerable disrepair. It is in fact a decommissioned area built at the rear of the Cabinet War Rooms as an emergency overflow in the event that a bomb attack damaged other areas. It has never been used – as you will see. There was up to a quarter of an inch of dust along the central passageway in photograph B. The other photographs reveal similarly disused areas throughout. None of this matches a single detail in Mr Weinschenk's account of what he saw when he was supposedly the victim of a confidence trick at the hands of Soviet agents.' His delivery of the words 'confidence trick' contained a triumphant amount of disdain. 'Can you explain why this might be, Mr Weinschenk?'

'Well, obviously they've covered their tracks. They must have gained entrance there as part of their plan to fool me – and then as soon as they were done, they returned the place to its former state.'

'I see. Your Honour, if you'll look in particular at photograph C, you will see evidence of a considerable and well-established infestation of rats. In photographs D, E and beyond, you will see the individual rooms that were accessible. Others had been sealed with aerated concrete blocks. These photographs provide straightforward evidence of a period of several years of undisturbed dilapidation. How might you account for this discrepancy, Mr Weinschenk?'

'I can do so easily: they were very good,' said Louis. He realised immediately that this reply might risk sounding too flippant, so qualified it. 'In my professional world, the world of magic, the quality that marks out the very best practitioners is an obsessive attention to detail. If I want you to believe that one card is actually a different card you've already seen, I will neurotically match every last crease and fingerprint. And further, I'd add: if I was an agent working with these people, why would I bother to describe a set of circumstances in my carefully composed alibi when I know it will be immediately contradicted by a cursory examination? Why would I even waste my breath?'

'I don't know, Mr Weinschenk. I'm not the one who is on trial here. I suppose you had to say something. But I do know this. We have clear documentary evidence of you intercepting and stealing national security secrets of the highest possible value and passing them to other agents of Soviet origin via means known as a "dead drop", means that are a hallmark of the procedures of those agents. You did all of this while living as a British civilian, in the employ of the British Broadcasting Corporation, no less. These secrets, had you not intercepted them, would have been of the greatest possible value to ourselves and our allies in closing down a deadly circle of espionage that even now seriously threatens British lives and British interests.'

Baldwin, who seemed surprised by this unexpected and forceful parry from the prosecution, made the best defence he could, but it involved little more than restating the case that Louis had himself just made.

The judge brought proceedings to a close with a rather brief summing-up in which he asked Louis if there was anything else he wanted to say. Louis could have kept silent, but he felt he should take the opportunity to reassert his innocence and energetically stand up for himself, even though his heart was hammering in his chest.

'Your Honour, I can only say again, as clearly, directly and forcefully as I am able, that I'm not guilty of these charges that have been brought against me.'

He tried to find the judge's eyes beneath the absurd grey curls of his horsehair wig, which was the same colour as his bristly eyebrows – both of which seemed to have the consistency and fullness of a Brillo pad. Staring as directly as he could into the man's pupils, using every means he had to communicate the absolute truth he was appealing to, he continued:

'Everything I did, I did because I genuinely believed I was acting on behalf of the British government. What was communicated to me, the people who presented their case to me, the instructions they gave me – there was never a single moment when my faith in their account wavered.' He had thought about admitting to naïvety, or stupidity, but now hesitated – it was better, he thought, just to state the bare facts, rather than passing any judgement on his own character. 'It's both a nightmare and a tragedy for me to discover that those actions, which I considered to be an act of service, were the very opposite. I thought I was using my skills and abilities for the good of this nation, the country that has harboured me since giving me refuge as a child. To discover that my well-intentioned instincts were hijacked by operators of a hostile power, and put to an opposite purpose, is a source of shame and dismay. There's nothing else I can say.'

'Thank you, Mr Weinschenk,' was all the judge said in reply. And with that, Louis was returned to his cell.

13

Louis did not have to wait long. By the time he was collected from the tiny cell, less than a couple of hours had passed. It felt longer, of course, much longer, but the clock on the wall visible as they entered the chambers said otherwise.

Everyone was already assembled, all the characters who'd been present at the trial. In fact, there seemed to be a few more – two or three shadowy figures Louis glimpsed in the gallery high above. There was an air of silence, and expectancy, as if all who were present had as much at stake in the outcome as he did. He tried to catch Baldwin's attention, hoping for a moment of 'it's OK', or anything, any indication of which way the judge might be leaning. But Baldwin studiously avoided his eye, instead staring at a set of notes on a legal pad in front of him, pulling the cap on and off of his pen, twitching like a malfunctioning automaton.

'The court will rise,' said the ancient-looking clerk, and the judge swept in, seemingly bent under the weight of his robes. Louis stood, and was immediately aware that his leg was trembling. He felt weak and shaky. He tried to find a handle on his thoughts, something he could grab on to. Some way of maintaining calm, being himself, finding that solid little ledge he'd managed to discover all those years ago in the dormitory at school – that essence of who he was, buried inside the thing that was called Ludvik, and later called Louis.

'Ludvik Weinschenk. I have listened carefully to the competing accounts presented to me today. Your testimony as to what happened to you is both compelling and fascinating. If what you say is true, you have been the victim of a diabolically ingenious attempt to fool an innocent man in order to gain his acumen, his abilities and unique talents and set them to nefarious purpose without his knowledge. Worse still is the use of that man's patriotic instincts as a weapon against the country he in fact loves, via a covert manipulation and inversion of those noble impulses. Rarely have I encountered such an egregious deceit. In fact, I would have to say, it could only have come from a mind of quite uncommon cunning.

'The difficulty I have is the fact that this account has emanated from a mind already proven to itself be in possession of a quite uncommon cunning. Indeed, your reputation, which you claim has been so unfairly besmirched, has been built on this same devilish deviousness. And since there is not a single piece of material evidence you can offer in support of your version of events, no matter how compelling this story is, it's impossible for me to avoid the fact that you are a man who trades in such falsehoods on a daily basis. Therefore, it's also impossible for me to come to any other conclusion than the fact that you are actually the source of this account rather than its victim. Given that fact, the prosecution's points are well made.

'You, Ludvik Weinschenk, have by your actions potentially sacrificed the lives of many brave British operatives in the field by the interception of material that would have undoubtedly protected those lives. You have also irreparably harmed the interests of our allies in a grave struggle with enemies who seek to undermine and destroy everything that we hold dear. The fact that the information was stolen from a man who risked everything to obtain it is merely an obscene flourish on an already terrible enterprise. All of this means I have no choice but to find you guilty of the crime of high treason.'

Louis' heart was quivering, running at such a rate that he felt he might collapse there and then. He realised in that moment that he'd never thought, when it came down to it, that the judgement would go against him. But the shift in his thinking that accompanied that realisation still failed to prepare him for what came next. The judge reached down to his side for something and placed it slowly and deliberately on his head. It was a square of black cloth. In a grave and stern voice, he began to speak, as

Louis watched. It felt curiously as if he was now sitting in a theatre, watching a scene in an ongoing drama. It certainly couldn't be real. It was dreadful, but it could only be a temporary state of affairs. Surely?

'Prisoner at the bar, you have been convicted of high treason, therefore the sentence of the court that follows is mandatory. You shall be taken from this place to a lawful prison, and from there to a place of execution, where you shall be hanged by the neck until you are dead. And may the Lord have mercy upon your soul. Remove the prisoner.'

What followed was increasingly feverish and dreamlike. At first a hazy sense of disbelief descended, as if he'd just woken from a nightmare but was still in the grip of its after-effects. The dread would dissolve if he could just claw his way back to waking reality. But by the time he'd reached the tiny cell, three flights down in the court basement, the nightmare was still ongoing. What seemed to have happened had indeed happened. So he tried to rationalise himself out of the terror that was settling over him. Surely this was more political posturing, more theatre, nothing other than that.

After a brief period staring at the cream-coloured paint covering the bricks, with these thoughts racing round his mind, Baldwin's arrival was heralded by the clattering of the key in the old iron lock.

'This was not the result we were aiming for,' he said, without any indication that this was a joke. 'But you must rest assured, Mr Weinschenk, that I've already begun the process of appeal. What you have to understand is the element of display that's present in this judgement. The Yanks are watching this one very closely. There was a real sense of humiliation that we'd let Burgess and Maclean get away in the face of the Americans' warnings. You've got to remember they lent us nearly four billion dollars just so our country could stay afloat after the war. They really do get to call the shots in quite a frightening way. So High Command have been looking for any opportunity they can to demonstrate their assurance and their competence. Unfortunately, I'm afraid to say, you seem to fit the bill.'

Louis looked up at him. He hadn't bothered to stand when the man came in. 'I didn't do it,' he said, sounding like a child.

For the first time since they had encountered each other, Baldwin placed a hand on his shoulder, squeezed it.

'We shall fight on,' he said. 'I will come and see you as soon as I have news.' He turned his back and nodded at the constable outside the cell.

Louis found he was calling after him as he left. 'What will I tell people?'

'I'm sorry?'

'What will I say to people?'

There was a moment's silence. And then:

'That you are appealing.'

Write it down. Make it real. *I am appealing. There will be an appeal.*

Louis didn't know how much of his letter would get through uncensored. An appeal was a real and tangible thing, and it was possible that he had a part to play in the process even as he was sitting in his cell. He remained an active participant in his own fate. While there was still breath in his body, he could choose to act. And he would. He would. He would apply himself as he'd never applied himself before.

The authorities were still going to be reading his letters, he knew that, so here was a place to start. He could pour all his truth, all his sincerity into missives to Dinah, to Ivan and Phyllis, to Danny, to Beulah, in as intelligent a manner as possible. There would be little point in writing something they would cut half the words from. Rather, he could compose his letters carefully so as to hold back on any detail that pertained to the military and intelligence aspect of his predicament and focus on what he felt about what had happened. And then trust that the truth would out. One letter in and of itself might not directly affect his fate, but the sentiment expressed therein, if communicated with force, could work its way up the chain of command and catch with somebody enough to give them pause.

Dear Dinah,

My darling. What can I say? I am caught in circumstances that are beyond my comprehension. I have no idea what the newspapers are reporting, if anything, or what you know, again if anything. I have been sentenced to death for high treason. Like Lord Haw-Haw, except my charge is working for the Soviets. None of this is true. I was fooled into it. I was stupid. I didn't ask enough questions. I allowed myself to be swept up in someone else's dreadful plan, like a spectator ushered on to a stage to play his part in a performance. I have to accept that I did the thing I'm accused of, there's no way around that, but I genuinely believed, didn't question for a second, that I was working for our side, for British intelligence. I've no idea what you've read, what you know, as they've kept the papers from me and I'm in solitary confinement. My lawyer claims he has done his best and has begun the appeal process.

Dinah – I don't know where to start. I can't give way to despair. I have to believe I'll see you again. I

And here Louis' plan broke down. Because he couldn't complete the sentence. He wanted to tell Dinah what he felt about her, what he truly felt. But he couldn't get to those feelings. He'd thought he would be able to. He'd thought he would just write them down. But they took on the quality of a mirage. Something you could perceive off in the distance only to find that it disappeared, dissipated as you approached. Unless there'd been nothing there at all.

In the end, he found himself copying out the letter again and discarding the last two sentences. He thought it was better to send something. He was trying to keep strong. He'd forged himself – he liked to think he'd forged himself – on one simple idea: that there was no failure, there was only giving up. That one strove to meet what was in front of oneself minute by minute, hour by hour, day after day, week after week, month after month, year after year, decade after decade if necessary, facing it calmly, attacking the obstacles whatever they might be, forging a path through the rubble. What good was that course, that way, if he gave up on it when he needed it most?

He did receive a letter, but it was formal, in a brown envelope with a typed address. It was from Baldwin, stating simply that a date had been set for his execution. Three weeks hence. The absolute shock of reading this. It couldn't be so. And in fact, Baldwin went on immediately to give sweet relief. Louis must not be too concerned at this, it was merely a formality, and things were proceeding well with the appeal. He expected there to be more news soon. He had every confidence in the process.

Things are proceeding well with the appeal. Louis held on to this sentence like a shield, but every so often that shield would crack and a bit of the terrible harsh glare it was keeping out broke through. In those moments, his mind slipped its reins and began to conjure the moment of his own execution, his own death. What was beyond it. Or wasn't. Each time, he exerted maximal will to keep those thoughts at bay.

He wrote back to Baldwin, asking him why no other letters had come through. Surely his friends would want to reply to him. Baldwin replied to say it was possible the letters were being withheld for security reasons. He would look into it.

Tuesday 7 April. A day redolent of springtime. Of early sunshine. Of the sweet smell of freshly cut grass. Of a weekend by the sea with his parents. His parents. The thing he rarely thought of, never spoke of. He remembered walking along the *Seebrücke* at Sellin, the promise of a long day of joy ahead. He pushed back against the thought. He felt that if he let it take him, he would disappear into it, he would give up, like a drowning man, giving in to the enveloping embrace of death.

He returned to his chink-a-chink routine, the little cardboard balls. Anything to engage his mind. He vowed that once he was out of this (and he would get out of this), he would work it into his act somehow, he would tell the story of how he made himself a magic set out of toilet rolls, and kept his spirits up and maintained his sanity by rehearsing with it.

After his sentencing, he had been transferred back to Wandsworth. He was housed on E wing, in the condemned cell, which had unexpected advantages. The space was the largest he'd been placed in yet. It had its own bathroom facilities and lavatory, and even its own kitchen. Everything was about keeping Louis from being seen by the other prisoners.

He found himself wondering if he could use this isolation to his favour in some way. For the first time he seriously put his mind to the idea of escaping. He had some of the requisite skills after all. Could he get out of there? Disappear? Flee the country? He ended up talking himself out of it. Somewhere within him there was a residual faith in something absolute that would keep him from his demise. That order would be restored in some way, because at the bottom, it didn't make any sense that it wouldn't.

There were two prison guards who alternated their watch, and he was under observation twenty-four hours a day. Despite his attempts at belief, there were intermittent bouts of extreme fear that became increasingly physical in their manifestation, closer to disease than an emotional state. Hotness, sweatiness, shaking, a feeling of illness, a permanently clenched stomach. Watery bowels. A complete loss of appetite. The sense of being trapped began to grow, the horror of not being able to escape even if he tried. A state of absolute despair without any hope or light, broken only by flashes of sadness. Deep, deep sadness at the thought of not seeing Ivan again, or Phyllis or Danny or Beulah. Or Dinah. He searched for a scrap of comfort in the memories of the happiness he'd experienced in their company, but it was no consolation.

He had to keep faith. People didn't understand the true meaning of that phrase, which was about holding on in the face of seeming impossibility. So even as the evening of the 22nd approached, and he was told he was to be given a choice of his final evening meal, he repeated to himself over and over again that the reprieve was coming.

He didn't think he would sleep, but somehow he did. It was fitful, and he kept waking to the view of the grimy window and a smear of moonlight behind it. Each time, the thought of what was imminent descended on him like heavy boxes filled with stones, falling on him from some unseen shelf high above. But he answered the dread thing with the knowledge that the message was coming, it was on its way. Baldwin would arrive, panting perhaps, like something from a cheap B picture, and Louis would be taken from the condemned cell, transferred to another prison and his life beyond.

But now it was getting lighter, and he felt sicker and colder. If it reminded him of anything, it was of one of his bouts of internal wrestling when he was in Nice with Dinah (Nice – imagine it, being in Nice), worrying that something had happened to her, that she had died. The sane and rational part of him told himself to calm down, to get a grip, that it was absurd and ridiculous to allow such thoughts to take hold. And suddenly he realised that it was the hope that was insane and the terror that was reasonable. He'd been keeping that unbearable thought at bay for as long as he could, but now that it had broken through, the glare of it was all he—

BANG!

Like a shot from a gun, a door in the wall opposite burst open. He'd never even registered it was there. It was an arbitrary detail. An ordinary locked door that he'd assumed led to another cell – like an adjoining room in a hotel. It was the kind of door you passed every day of your life. It had been there for all the time he'd been confined, looking at him, presenting itself to him, and he'd thought nothing of it. And now three prison officers he didn't recognise were marching through it, like soldiers in a play.

'Stand up. On your feet. This way.' Two of them were at his side, looping their arms under his, lifting him to their height so his feet were almost off the floor. He wanted to resist going through that door, seeing whatever was on the other side of it. But it was too late. He was through it and into a room twice the height of his cell, with white-painted walls. The floor was made of dark wooden planks, polished and lacquered. It was like a dance hall. Like the Hammersmith Palais. If Louis stopped moving his legs, the two officers could slide him along it with ease, like Fred Astaire being pulled by Ginger. There was a handle poking out of the floor, unnaturally large and erect. It looked like something from a railway signal box. Stop. Go. On your way. Directly behind it was a large white rectangle embedded in the floor, with more polished wooden boards within its frame. And across it, from front to back, two large planks had been laid, parallel to each other, about four feet apart. Louis was marched right in between them, in the middle of the platform.

'Drink this.' The other prison officer, the oldest one, with the fierceness of a furious drill sergeant, handed Louis a shot glass, pushed it into his mouth. What was it? Brandy. It burned as it went down. Another man stepped forward, sober, round-faced, in his forties. He wasn't wearing a uniform, but was dressed in a dark funereal suit. There was a heavy rope in his hands, half of it covered in leather, like a giant dog lead, looped back on itself through a metal fastening.

It couldn't be . . . This wasn't happening. Louis was struggling now, struggling hard, even as the officers held him fast. He tried to move his head out of the way, dodging the noose (for that was what it was) as the older officer passed it over his head. But it was there, and the officer was behind him, pulling it tight. A movement at his side. The white-painted walls. Light from the window. Now? Here? No. No. Someone was growling. It was him. He was the one snivelling, moaning like an animal.

A vast clatter, echoing off the ceiling as the handle at his side was hauled back. The world fell away beneath him. It was there, then it was gone, and he fell and he fell and he fell into a cold blackness that closed around him like clay, as Louis Warlock died.

MY EXTRAORDINARY PAL ARCHIBALD FIBBS

A dear friend of mine was a gentleman
called Archibald Fibbs. A ludicrous name,
but one that suited him perfectly. He was a
greengrocer, but more appropriately a
compulsive liar. Consequently, I always
referred to him as 'Fibbing Archie'. On one
of our many days together, Fibbing Archie
told me he had developed an extraordinary
memory and used numbers as his aide-
memoire. He produced fifty index cards —
they were numbered 1 to 50 on one side and
on the reverse each one of them had a
ten-digit number written on it.

5279651673

14

He handed me the cards, asked me to check that they all had different numbers and told me to pick any one of them. If I then told him which number card I had chosen, he would tell me the memorised ten-digit number on it. Filled with doubt, I did as instructed. I chose card 14, and to my amazement, he reeled off the number written on it: 5279651673. I thought maybe I had been duped, so quickly picked another card. Surely Fibbing Archie hadn't actually transformed into an honest human being who could be taken at his word? I took card 46. Quick as a flash he proclaimed:

'I love that card, 7527965167,' and sure enough, he was right. I immediately wanted to develop this same ability, and luckily Fibbing Archie was more than happy to teach me . . . for a small fee, of course.

* * *

Guess what, it's a stunt! Completely fake. When he told me, I found myself shouting at him, 'Fibbing Archie! Fibbing Archie! Fibbing Archie!'

I am about to teach you this stunt, safe in the knowledge that not only will it help you amaze people, but more importantly, it will also blur the edges between what is real and what isn't. In fact, while we're talking about blurring the edges, I should come clean and tell you that the entire Fibbing Archie story is made up. But the secret that allows this deeply plausible stunt to work is one I can still attribute to him . . . as you will see.

Before I teach you this brilliantly simple method, a word about mental stunts and mentalism in general. If you have dipped your toe into performing any mental effects, you will learn very quickly that the impact on an audience is unique. Unlike with a vanishing coin or a lady sawn in half, spectators believe mental effects to be real. An audience member older than seven or eight innately understands that what is happening in magic is a delicious artifice, a performance, a piece of theatre. But with magic of the mind, a different reality steps in: 'Look what people are capable of!' 'There's so much about the brain we don't understand.'

The staggering thing is that this phenomenon, this desire to truly believe in the power of the mind, kicks in when an audience sees even the most basic of mental effects. So be aware, you have real power and real responsibility.

This stunt is based on the following equation. The numbers are generated by setting $F0 = 0$, $F1 = 1$, and then using the recursive formula $Fn = Fn-1 + Fn-2$.

So there you go! Easy, isn't it?

Forgive me, I couldn't resist. But that truly is the mathematical formula upon which this stunt is based – the Fibonacci sequence.

Sound familiar? Fibonacci? Fibbing Archie! You see, as always, method to my madness.

So here is the trick.

Let's start with the number 1.
No matter what number is chosen (in this case 1), we will always add 11 to it.
So, add 11 to it. 1 + 11 = 12

Reverse that number = 21
These become the first two numbers written
  on the back of card number 1: 21

Now add those two numbers together to get
  to the third figure: So, 2 + 1 = 3

The resulting number is 213.

Now add these last two numbers together
  again. 1 + 3 = 4.
Our number becomes 2134.

Do it again . . . 3 + 4 = 7.

21347.

    Now, when you add 4 + 7, you get 11, a
double-digit number. In such cases ignore
the first digit and use only the second one
— here that would be a single 1, but if it
was, say 9 and 7 you were adding together,
that would make 16. In that example you
would just use the 6.
    So following this, the ten-digit number
written on card number 1, the number you
would call out, would be:

2134718976.

    Let's try card number 2.

That would be 2 + 11, giving us 13, which we
  reverse to give us the first two digits:

31.
Then, 3 + 1 makes 4.
314.

1 + 4 makes 5.

3145.

4 + 5 makes 9.

31459.

Then 9 + 5 makes 14, and we just take the
    4, which gives us 314594 . . .

Now keep going yourself. What's your
    ten-digit number (don't look below until
    you've got it)?

It should be:

3145943707.

    Did you get it right?
    Now all you need to do is get fifty
index cards and write out each sequence. On
the face of each card write the card number
- 1 through to 50 - then on the back write
the number the Fibbing Archie sequence
gives you, starting with the one generated
by the number on the front of the card.
    You now carry with you a deeply simple
yet incredibly plausible memory stunt. The
hardest part of this effect isn't the stunt
itself, it's the lying afterwards. The
spectator will want to talk about your
incredible memory and how on earth they can
learn to do the same thing.
    Here's the remarkable thing about this
effect. In the guise of improving your own
memory, you are creating new powerful memories
for your audience. It changes how you will be
thought of and remembered, long after you're
gone . . . and who doesn't want that?
    To quote my fictional friend: 'Guard
this secret well, it carries with it a
great responsibility.'

On 17 February 1953, the following story had appeared in the *Daily Sketch* before being picked up and circulated by other papers, both national and local.

> A popular radio entertainer who was arrested by officers in Marylebone for being drunk and disorderly was found actually to be suffering with a serious mental illness.
>
> Louis Warlock (who was born Ludvik Weinschenk), aged 26, was determined upon examination by a police surgeon to have fallen victim to a psychotic illness. It is thought to have been triggered by nervous exhaustion.
>
> The arrest came after a concerned member of the public alerted police following an incident on Marylebone High Street in the small hours of the morning late last week. Mr Warlock has been transferred to a secure institution for his own safety and will be treated there for his condition.

Prior to this story going public, the members of the Brains Trust had already been alerted to the fact that something odd was taking place when they were individually arrested by the police and brought into custody for questioning in connection with their visit to the dressing room of Russian magician Oleg Hanikonikov earlier that month.

There was much that was peculiar about this, not least the fact that no one outside their immediate circle knew who the Brains Trust were or that they had any connection to each other, apart from a vague show-business acquaintance. Their collaborative existence as a group was Louis' best-kept secret.

When the four of them compared notes afterwards, they discovered that they'd all been asked variations of the same questions. What were they doing in Hanikonikov's dressing room? Why had they chosen to go there that day? Had anyone asked them to be present? In actual fact, each of them was there because Dinah had asked them to attend at a specific time. She hadn't told them why, other than that it was very important to Louis that they do so. Her requests for absolute secrecy were hardly necessary, and certainly none of the others was going to make reference to the fact that she had instructed them to be there, even under caution.

Danny had a straightforward alibi. He was in the business, and in the business it was common courtesy for magicians to 'go round' when conjurors with an international reputation were in town. Phyllis and Ivan, meanwhile, who had no apparent connection to the world of magic, had already had the foresight to concoct a cover, in case Hanikonikov himself had asked them what they were doing there: they were researching an episode of *Educating Archie* that they'd been commissioned to write (they were depping for Sid Colin and Eric Sykes because Eric had been moved across to write for *Frankie Howerd Goes East*). Phyllis had come up with the idea that Peter Brough could have taken Archie to see an exotic stage hypnotist: 'We thought it would be funny if Archie was hypnotised but doesn't go under, but Peter Brough does.' All of this could be confirmed by the BBC if anyone cared to ask.

They were each released after an hour or so's careful questioning, which they came together to discuss over coffee at Maison Bertaux. Danny had already worked out why they'd all been arrested.

'It was the strangest thing. When I was being taken in to Charing Cross police station, you know who was being taken out? Ali Bongo. He looked completely *shvach*. Grey. Sick. Like he'd been in there for hours. And he wouldn't even look at me. They must have been questioning everyone who was in that dressing room that afternoon, whoever they were.'

Dinah, who could have told them more at that point, refrained from doing so. But when the story about Louis ran in the *Daily Sketch* six days later, following on from the already alarming fact that he'd been AWOL and incommunicado for the previous four, she called another official meeting of the Brains Trust and they all gathered once more at Maison Bertaux.

She'd organised coffee, but no cakes. It didn't seem appropriate somehow. In truth, she herself couldn't have eaten anything. She was tense, and sick with worry. It wasn't unheard of for Louis to disappear, but never for more than a couple of days, and never without leaving a message (particularly now that they had their arrangement with the Turk for that very purpose). And never, never when there was a show to rehearse. In fact, within moments of her seeing the newspaper story, there had been a call from Jack Naismith at the BBC to say that *Warlock's Wonders* had been curtailed and replaced with a new series called *In All Directions*, starring Peter Jones and Peter Ustinov – a show that was apparently improvised and performed entirely by the pair themselves, so it needed very little preparation.

Phyllis and Ivan were the first there.

'Dinah – what the hell's going on? What's the matter with him? There's never been anything like this before,' said Ivan.

'Louis having a nervous breakdown? I don't believe it,' added Phyllis.

Until then, Dinah had kept everything in, which was her habitual response to anything connected with illness or hospitals. Her father had suffered much ill health, and she'd effectively been trained to be like that from an early age. But now, held by Phyllis, breathing in the mumsy mix of Johnsons' talc and lavender engrained in her sweater, all her self-control left her.

By the time Phyllis had let go of her, Danny had arrived, exhibiting the same incredulity the others had.

It was strange for them to be sitting around that trestle table without Louis. But the combination of the show's cancellation and the newspaper story was unequivocal confirmation of the facts. He was gone.

'You must have heard something. Why hasn't he called you?' said Ivan to Dinah, and Phyllis immediately thew him a withering glance.

'She's not next of kin,' she said, 'not in law. Their engagement's informal.'

'Who *is* next of kin?' said Danny.

'I don't think Louis has any living family. He never talks as if he does.'

'They died,' said Ivan darkly.

'What?' said Dinah.

'In the camps.'

'Do you *know* that?' she asked, hating the fact that she felt angry because Louis had never said anything to her.

'He muttered something about it once. I filled in the rest. We didn't really talk about it,' Ivan added quietly.

'We need to speak to his doctor,' said Danny.

'The paper didn't even say which institution,' said Dinah.

'We'll go to Marylebone police station and ask. There'll have to be a record,' said Ivan, his rising anger all too apparent.

They went in a group, not caring that they were revealing their connection to each other. The circumstances were such that everything was overridden. Including the unwritten rules of magic. Without even discussing it, they knew that their combined will stood a better chance of shifting the dead weight of bureaucracy.

'We can't pass that information across, I'm afraid,' repeated the desk sergeant. 'It's confidential.'

'She's next of kin,' said Ivan.

'I'm sorry, miss. Not legally.'

'Who's your superior?' Phyllis barked the question with a military authority.

'Inspector Collins.'

'Tell Inspector Collins that Miss Dinah Groule, who is well known to nearly three million listeners of the BBC Home Service, will be speaking to the *Evening Standard* very shortly about him and his uncooperative desk sergeant, who are keeping her from attending to her fiancé in his hour of need, and doubtless the paper will be calling on him for a comment.' The desk sergeant took account of the fierce resolve in her voice.

They were there for another fifteen minutes, a shorter wait than they might have expected. The sergeant returned with a slip of paper, which he handed to Dinah. It said simply *Broadmoor Institute*.

'You're to keep that to yourself, miss,' he said firmly.

'Broadmoor's for the criminally insane,' said Ivan. 'Why on earth would he be sent there?'

'Not exclusively for the insane,' said Phyllis. They were all growing increasingly grave.

'We'll go to mine,' said Dinah. 'It's nearest. We can call from there.'

The phone call didn't last long. They were told they had to put their request for a visit in writing to the institution's head physician, Dr Howson. Dinah sat down and wrote the letter. It was posted within the hour.

She received a response three days later. It was polite but clinical. The patient, Mr Warlock, was being kept under observation on a secure ward for the time being and for his own safety. Visiting was not possible. If Miss Groule would like to write to him, her letters would of course be passed on. She would be notified when there was a change in his condition. She must rest assured that he was receiving the greatest level of care.

Dinah was infuriated, frustrated, increasingly sceptical. She knew that none of this made any sense. And so she reconvened the Brains Trust once more, this time after hours, and at her Hammersmith flat, rather than at Maison Bertaux. She wanted absolute privacy.

'There's something I've been avoiding telling you,' she began.

Phyllis was sitting perched on the curved red sofa, reaching down and playing with the tasselled fringe that hung between the base and the floor as Dinah spoke.

'What do you mean?' said Ivan, who was leaning forward, frowning, expecting even worse news than they'd had already.

'Had Louis been ill?' said Danny, who was voicing what Dinah imagined the others were thinking too: that she knew something about the state of his mind and had been keeping it from them.

'No,' she said emphatically. 'He hadn't been. And that's not what I've gathered you here for. Not directly.' She was stalling, putting off the inevitable. But there was no getting round it, so as calmly as she could, she finally told them everything that Louis had told her about his mission. His recruitment by the

157

intelligence services, and why she had asked them all to be present in Hanikonikov's dressing room back at the start of February.

'I couldn't tell you any of it earlier. It was too—'

'You could have told us after we were interrogated,' said Ivan, interrupting her.

'Even less then,' she said, defending herself against this unfairness. 'For your own protection. But it's different now. This business. This incarceration. A mental institution. I don't believe it. Not for a second.'

'Just a minute, just a minute,' said Ivan, 'I want to know more about this secret mission. Hanikonikov a Soviet agent?! Louis working for the government. Really? *Really?!*'

'I'm telling you what he told me. Word for word.'

'None of that is relevant to our main concern,' said Danny, aware how easily they could go off course. 'Our priority is this *mishigas* around Louis. We need to find out what's going on.'

'Exactly,' said Phyllis

'But how on earth can we help him if he's up to his neck in all that?' said Ivan.

'We can let him know we're here, thinking about him. Give him a chance to communicate with us. But to do that, we need to find out where he is and what's really happened to him,' said Dinah. 'We have to try.'

'We must,' said Phyllis, looking exclusively at Dinah. 'We will.'

There was a pause. Ivan was the first to speak.

'Clearly he's not in Broadmoor.'

'Why clearly?' said Phyllis, who now had her crochet in hand, her needle conjuring a cradle hat for her cousin's newborn.

'Because what he's been involved with is the stuff of the highest security. Espionage, state secrets. And his "arrest" and "mental breakdown" happened within days of him completing his mission.'

'He's never had a single episode with his nerves in all the time I've known him,' said Dinah. 'And think what we've been through.'

'Agreed,' said Danny.

'And you've heard nothing from him since his disappearance?' asked Ivan. It was a touch too accusatory for Dinah's liking.

'Nothing.'

'You're sure.'

'Yes!' she said, making her irritation known.

'Because you've lied to us once.'

'She didn't lie,' said Phyllis, snapping. 'She did what Louis asked her to do.'

'We don't have secrets,' said Ivan.

'Well in this case we did,' said Phyllis.

'Yeah – and look where it's got us!'

Danny spoke up, gesturing aggressively with his open palms. 'We cannot fight each other like this. We must focus our minds.' And in that moment, Dinah saw exactly what Louis did when he was there. He was their leader. And he led them exceptionally well. Somehow she was going to have to step up and be the one to take his place. So be it.

'This is what we're going to do,' she said, in a voice much louder than she was accustomed to speaking in. 'Someone, somewhere knows where he is. We'll find that person.'

It was Beulah who came up with the connection. And it was Dinah's decision to go to her: 'Who do we know who knows everybody? Royalty, politicians, soldiers . . .' And so it was Dinah who sat down with Beulah at the back of the Regal Revue Bar while a cleaner roared around the stage with a furiously buzzing floor polisher, providing the perfect cover for their clandestine conversation. No one nearer than a foot away could have overheard anything.

Beulah was noticeably less resistant to the apparent absurdity of Louis' recruitment than Ivan had been.

'Honey – it's not even the strangest thing I've heard this year,' she said, sipping a Bloody Mary.

'How can we find him?'

'Why do you want to find him?' Dinah looked at her, shocked at the harshness of the question. 'I'm serious. What do you think you can do for him? He's got into this of his own free will. What can you do for him now?'

'I want to let him know I care. We care. After that . . . It depends where he is. What's happened to him.'

Beulah went quiet for a moment, mulling over Dinah's answer, mingling the request with her own complex feelings about Louis. After a minute or so filled with the cycling roar of the floor polisher, she spoke again.

'There is someone I can think of who might know something. But you'll have to leave it with me.'

'I need him to know we—'

'Leave it with me,' said Beulah firmly. 'I know how you're feeling, darling. But you're going to have to leave it with me.'

Sir Guy Hollingworth Cox was one of the most senior judges in the country. As Admiralty Registrar, he was responsible for overseeing the Admiralty Court, handling all cases relating to shipping and maritime disputes. He'd been admitted to the bar in 1924 and begun a distinguished career that led him to become a King's Counsel in 1939. He'd volunteered on the outbreak of war, but was deemed too old for active service, and his legal talents were such that he was instructed that the best way he could serve his country was to remain in his occupation. By 1944, he had been appointed Recorder of Richmond upon Thames, and in less than three years he was asked to become a judge at the High Court of Justice. His position as Admiralty Registrar had come at the turn of the decade.

It was perhaps a surprise that such a senior figure in British society was a regular customer of Beulah's, and also a regular visitor to the Regal's premises. Beulah had many customers she served privately. And she kept rooms on the top floor of the Regal building for that very purpose. Unlike most of her peers, she didn't pimp, and had strong feelings on that subject, but she did offer other services that weren't available elsewhere, particularly to gentlemen of standing who were cautious of their reputations. Sir Guy, or Walter as she knew him (it was his second name), was one of her best customers.

Once a week he had a regular appointment, usually on a Friday afternoon. He would arrive in a low-key way, not brought there by his usual chauffeur, but rather as an anonymous-looking pedestrian, wearing a cheap and worn two-piece suit and a slightly too large bowler hat pulled down over his brow. Beulah herself would always open the door to him and show him upstairs. He was so reliable that over the years he had become one of the few fixed points in her sometimes-turbulent life.

This afternoon was no different, at least not on the surface, but by the time they'd mounted the narrow flight of stairs and reached the third floor, Walter, being a sensitive man, could discern that something was up.

'Is all in order?' he asked as she opened the door to the well-appointed room with its dark embossed wallpaper and narrow garret window.

'Sit down, Walter,' said Beulah in a quiet voice. Ignoring her for the moment, he started looking around. Part of their arrangement involved the handing-over of a cardboard laundry box wrapped in brown paper and tied with twine. 'Walter ... please sit down.'

Because the box wasn't on the table, Walter knew something was up. Panic began to stiffen him: the fear that he'd put to the back of his mind and had ceased naming years ago, because he trusted this tough, reliable woman opposite him, believing, perhaps stupidly for someone so well versed in the law, that there was honour among thieves, figuratively speaking. Their narrowly defined but always dependable ritual, unchanged for many years, was being disrupted, and it could only mean trouble.

Beulah, defiant in the face of the battle she knew was coming, gestured to an overstuffed Edwardian armchair by the boarded-up fireplace.

'Walter, how long have you been coming here?' It was a rhetorical question. Merely an opening gambit. She didn't expect him to answer. 'In all that time, I've never asked for anything from you, have I?' He looked up at her with dark, intelligent eyes. His years as a prosecuting barrister had ingrained in him a prognosticator's ability to see ahead. He knew immediately what was coming.

'There's something I need to know,' said Beulah, 'and I'm not able to pass over your goods until I have that knowledge. I'm aware you might go elsewhere, but it won't be easy for you now. Not in your current position. Plus, you trust my supply. And rightly so. It's medicinally pure. And I can guarantee it.'

There was fear in Walter's expression at the thought of being denied what he needed, terror even. Everything Beulah had just said was true.

'I know our relationship is based on trust,' she continued. 'And I'm breaking that trust. I've thought long and hard about it, but friends of mine are in need, and this is the only way I can help. The one thing I'll say is, I'll never ask another favour of you after today. This is it. Grant me what I need, and everything goes back to normal – I promise you that.'

'What *do* you need?' he said. There was darkness in his response. Anger, and shame too, shame that he was even in this position.

Beulah told him what she needed.

'I can't,' was his simple response.

'Then I can't either,' she said. 'I'll have to withdraw the supply.'

Involuntarily Walter let out a moan, low and animal. He might have been saying no – or he might just have been expressing what he felt through the inarticulate sound.

But he gathered himself, then repeated simply, 'I can't, Beulah.'

'This is important. Very important. Do you think I would be asking if it wasn't?' The statement hung there as the traffic rolled by and the market men called from three floors below in the ordinary, workaday world outside.

He looked into her eyes, an expression of such need and desperation that she couldn't bear to hold his gaze. But she did. She wouldn't be the first to look away. In the end, it was Walter who hung his head, dropping his face towards the floor.

Three days later, on Monday evening, he came back. He'd called her on her private number to say he would be doing so.

When he arrived, his eyes went straight to the Victorian bureau underneath the window. It was open, the desk down, and laid out on the green hide writing surface was a clean syringe and a cardboard box, its lid off, the eight exposed glass vials reflecting the flickering light from outside. He handed Beulah a slip of paper, folded in half.

As he removed the jacket of the threadbare suit that constituted his disguise, Beulah headed for the door. There was a little sound as she opened it, somewhere between a cough and a cry.

Involuntarily she turned round. Walter was holding the syringe. He didn't look at her, but he knew she was looking at him.

'I want you to know,' he said in a quiet voice she could barely hear.

'Know what?'

There was a pause, as if what he was about to say had involved some decision, one that wasn't quite yet made. But then he spoke.

'I was sent to France in 1918, in the spring. I was only seventeen, but I'd volunteered, you see ... We were supposed to be stopping a German advance. They were getting closer to Paris. We were under shell fire for three months, non-stop. But we held our section of the line . . .' The notably long silence that followed somehow spoke something of that experience. 'After we got back, it was my commanding officer who suggested I try using the stuff. It was easier to get then. It worked for him and he thought it might help. It did.' Another brief pause, and he added, 'It does.'

Beulah nodded and turned back towards the door. When she got outside, on to the landing, she unfolded the slip of paper. It had seven words typed on it:

Transferred to Wandsworth prison. Three weeks ago.

And so the Brains Trust found themselves reassembled, back at Maison Bertaux. Beulah's information, however it was obtained, had lifted Dinah to the point where she felt less helpless and more positively motivated. So much had been confirmed by those two brief sentences. Louis was obviously caught up in something that involved the authorities lying about him at the highest level, spreading falsehoods to who knows what end. It also proved that he hadn't gone mad, that he wasn't sick. But why was he in Wandsworth? Whatever it was he'd been arrested for, it wasn't something that could be stated publicly.

'Well, it's obviously something to do with this spying business,' said Ivan, always wanting to sound like everything was clear and self-evident to him, even it wasn't to anybody else.

'Yeah, all right Mr Pilot ACE computer. If it's so bloody obvious, what exactly is it? Why's he been arrested?' said Phyllis, always irritated by this know-it-all stance.

It was Danny who spoke up here. 'I think Section One of the Official Secrets Act can help us,' and he proceeded to read from a pocket notebook he pulled from his jacket: '"If someone obtains, collects, records, publishes, or communicates to any other person any secret official code word, or pass word, or any sketch, plan, model, article, or note, or other document or information which is calculated to be or might be or is intended to be directly or indirectly useful to an enemy; he shall be guilty of felony."'

They all looked at him, surprised by this expert knowledge. 'I did what Louis would do. Stopped by Westminster Reference Library.'

'Very good,' said Dinah, pleased to see they were stepping up their activities. Now it was her turn to try and think like Louis and ask some probing questions. 'They think he's been passing secrets to someone when his mission was to rescue secrets from being smuggled out by a Soviet agent – right?' They looked at her, not quite following. 'Right?' she said again.

'Possibly,' said Danny wanting to keep the conversation moving.

'So how can we help?' she asked.

'You could tell the authorities what you know,' said Danny.

'No,' said Ivan firmly, 'That's not the way. Certainly not without more guidance from Louis himself.'

'He's right. For once,' said Phyllis, catching on. 'If we blunder in without enough information, we risk getting arrested ourselves, or making things worse. The quicksand principle. Struggling when you're caught in it only means you get pulled under. We need to think.'

'We need more information. And we need to set up a line of communication. Nobody's better at coded exchanges than me and Louis,' said Dinah. 'If we can just get that line going, we can speak freely and no one will know what we're saying to each other.'

'Yes, but the authorities are keeping him incommunicado,' said Danny. 'I know,' he added straight away, heading off Dinah's objection, 'I don't mean to *kvetch*, I'm just restating the parameters.'

'I know, but even if they are, the four of us know there are ways round that. We've built Louis' career on that fact. Does anyone know anyone in Wandsworth? A prisoner? Staff? Any connection at all?'

'I don't think we can ask Beulah again,' said Danny, with some awareness of what that last favour had cost her.

'We don't need to,' said Ivan excitedly.

'Why?' said Dinah.

'Alan Chunz.'

'Taxi driver Alan?'

'Yeah.'

'What about him?'

'His brother-in-law's a screw.'

'How do you know?'

'I've been out with him.'

'When?' asked Phyllis, sceptical of Ivan's tendency to overstate and embellish.

'A stag night, if you must know.'

'Stag night! You!'

'Never mind the details. Is he a screw in Wandsworth?' said Dinah, feeling the urgency.

Ivan's brow creased. 'Dunno.'

'It doesn't matter,' said Dinah, hope growing. 'It's somewhere to start.'

They met Alan at the Coach and Horses that night, having got a message out to him via the taxi company's radio dispatch. It turned out his brother-in-law worked at Brixton, but he was a keen member of the Prison Officers' Association, so he might know someone at Wandsworth. Dinah had insisted on caution in all of this. 'We don't tell Alan the specifics. We just say it's a matter of great importance to Louis. And if he asks how Louis is, we tell him things are OK and we're just helping him. But we can't say any more.'

As it turned out, Alan was fine with it. Everyone wanted to help Louis. That was all they cared about.

Two nights later, they were in the Chop House on Farringdon Road, with Stanley Powell – Alan's sister's husband, the Brixton screw – happily chewing on mouthfuls of lamb and mint jelly as he spoke.

'McGarvey, he's the head PO at Wandsworth. And he's a right old b—' Stanley checked himself, mindful of Dinah and Phyllis sitting opposite. 'Not the kind of man to do you a favour.'

'How *might* we turn him? If we had to,' said Ivan, trying to find something of the working man in himself to appeal to Stanley with, which was in truth a vain enterprise.

'You can't. He's an effing bruiser, 'scuse my French, ladies. He could kill you with his bare hands. He ain't scared of nothing, apart from his missus, who's even scarier by all accounts.'

And there it was. For Dinah, that was all they needed to know. There was no point in being subtle. That wasn't going to work. So she went to visit her hairdresser, Monsieur Alexis, who had a salon on Southampton Row.

'You want to go blonde!' The last word spoken with two syllables to express his shock. *Blon-duh.*

'More than just blonde, monsieur.' And she unclasped her handbag and produced a folded cover torn from *Picturegoer* magazine. It was Diana Dors, hair in fixed cascading waves, frozen like a meringue down the side of her head.

'But Miss Dinah, this is not you! *Non non non non non!*'

'It's for a show. A part. A part I very much want, monsieur.'

'Why not just wear a wig?'

Dinah shook her head. 'That won't cut it. Demanding producers. I really need to convince them. They have to think I *am* this woman. Afterwards, I can get a pixie cut.' She'd thought it all through.

Monsieur Alexis looked doubtful, but if that was what madame wanted . . .

The County Arms had stood on the edge of Wandsworth Common for a hundred years. As much of a local landmark as the prison, it was built around the same time to serve the officers and staff. It was busy from the early evening onwards, and the saloon bar in particular could be boisterous, attracting working men and commercial travellers who would happily walk there from Clapham Junction a mile and a half away.

It was bold for an unaccompanied woman to sit alone in the saloon bar, but Dinah's plan depended on it. The others would only countenance it if she agreed to their unobtrusive presence in the room with her. At first she resisted. If she was going to do this and succeed, she needed the freedom to be unobserved. Any hint of self-consciousness on her part would throw her off. Ultimately, they reached a compromise. Ivan and Danny would sit in the snug with Alan Chunz, peering through the door every so often to check she was all right.

'It's a busy pub. It's early evening. What do you think's going to happen to me? When it's time to go, I'll walk through the snug and we can all leave together. It'll be done by then anyway.'

There was no guarantee McGarvey would be in that night, but it was a Friday, and his shift ended at six o'clock (that much Stanley had been able to find out). Dinah knew what he looked like from the photo Stanley had found in the Prisoner Officers' Association summer magazine. She'd taken a seat at the bar at 6.15, not wanting to leave too much time in which she'd undoubtedly be bothered by other men, given the unsubtlety of her outfit and the fact that she was alone. She looked exactly like what she hoped McGarvey would think she was. The fact that the publican was only a short distance away on the other side of the bar gave some measure of comfort.

A clean-shaven man with ruddy cheeks who reeked of peppermints offered to buy her a drink within three minutes of her taking up her position on the stool. It was easy enough to decline, and inform him she was waiting for her fiancé, who was coming over from Wellington Barracks.

A few minutes later, a younger man with pomaded hair and a tweed blazer tried to charm her by complimenting her on her smile, which was odd, because she hadn't been smiling. She told him the same thing as she had his predecessor, though in a crisper voice. This one had a whiff of halitosis. She'd preferred the peppermints.

McGarvey entered not long after that, loudly, with a group of his colleagues, all of them with uniforms visible beneath their overcoats. Dinah felt herself tense up. It was one thing to have gone through this plan in her imagination and rehearsed it with Danny, Ivan and then Alan. It was quite another to be faced with the brutal reality of a heavyset thuggish stranger probably twice her age, knowing she was going to have to appeal to the worst in him in order to get what she needed. He had a squat, egg-shaped body with a loose pouch of a neck, red-tinged hair combed severely back from his forehead, and a wide, narrow mouth with surprisingly girlish lips.

It was enough to start with a few glances. She tried to imagine she was the kind of girl who liked the physically strong, masculine type. If she was playing that part, who would she be? There was a moment when he saw she was looking at him, and she immediately returned her attention to the mirror behind the bar. Within a couple of minutes he was there at the counter, ordering three pints of best stout. She kept her gaze assiduously in front of her, nowhere near him. Alternating between interest and disinterest was the policy she'd decided on as the most likely to gain results.

She could hear his loud voice. Its rough tinge was alarming in itself. Keep that from your mind, she told herself. Cleave to your character and focus on what has to be done. First contact was the cue for her to prepare the next stage. She unclasped her handbag, pulled out the tube of Angel Skin hand cream that Danny had doctored so it would do the job it had to do. Part of that modification involved the addition of a strong but not unpleasant scent. It was Phyllis's idea – it would provide an immediate talking point, and also a motivation for what needed to follow.

Once he'd returned to his mates, it only took two more glances. She couldn't hear their conversation, but it was clear McGarvey was being encouraged.

He walked over to the bar, directly towards her. Dinah mentally accessed her prepared script as she smiled at him.

'Sorry,' she said. 'I thought you were my cousin. You look just like him. I haven't seen him for years. Sorry for staring. He lives in Wolverhampton, so I thought it couldn't be.'

'On your own?' he said, as if he hadn't taken in anything she'd said. 'Can I buy you a drink?'

'That's very kind' – as if she'd never been asked this before in her life. 'I'll have a port and lemon. And some potato crisps if they've got any.'

While he caught the barman's attention, she rubbed another smear of cream into her hands.

'I thought perhaps you might be waiting for someone,' he said, attempting politeness. His clumsy attempt at good manners was almost endearing. She tried to use that thought to spur herself on.

'Oh no. Waiting for my train – killing time – then back to Basingstoke. I prefer it here to sitting at the station. You get bothered less. I have to catch the seven fifteen; it's the only one that stops at Hook.' She was trying to sound chatty and a bit airy – like Joyce Carey in *Brief Encounter*. And as she was talking, Phyllis's idea proved to be a good one.

'That's a nice smell. What is it?'

'Do you like it? It's this new hand cream. Pond's Angel Skin. Supposed to be really good for you. Relaxing, you know. They tell us we've got to be more relaxed, don't they? Do you want to try a bit?' This as if it was a spontaneous afterthought as she flashed him with the full force of her smile. It was possible he'd be suspicious at this point, but men were men, so it was more than likely he wouldn't, or at least he wouldn't care. Dinah was not a 'fast' girl herself and never had been, but life in the theatre was enough to cure anyone of their naïvety pretty quickly. Dressing room chat was not for the faint-hearted, and chorus girls were certainly not choristers.

'You've got proper working man's hands, I can see that. Aren't they big?' She squeezed a bit of the cream on to her own, considerably smoother hands and then reached for his, taking them in a matter-of-fact way, as if she were a nurse, or a mother with her child. The airy characterisation helped here. She was just being impulsive. Daft. Enjoying the flirt. She moved slowly and thoroughly, smoothing the silky cream over his coarse skin. Having his hands rubbed in this way soon began to have an impact.

'Like it?'

'Mmm . . .'

'Nice, isn't it. It's funny. It gives me a little lift. You know – if I'm halfway through the afternoon at work. Little things like that keep me going.' She smiled at him in an open-hearted way as she smeared the cream into his hands, as if it was the most innocent, normal thing she could be doing. Confusion was apparent on his features. This was obviously far beyond his regular daily experience. But there was something narcotic in it for him too. And he wanted it to continue, even as he seemed a little scared of it. Her hands applied pressure, allowing his thick fingers to slide in and out of the lubricated sheath she'd created around them. It was quite possibly the most sensual experience the man had ever had. And though there was intense pleasure in it, it was overloading something in him.

'I'm going to have to go back to my pals. They'll wonder where I've got to.'

'Oh, that's all right. It's been nice to meet you. And thanks for the drink. What's your name, darling?'

He swallowed. Was he contemplating lying to her? Dinah thought about those traditions in witchcraft that advocated caution about telling someone your true name. It gave them real power over you.

'Mick,' he said simply.

'Thank you, Mick.' And she picked up her glass of port and lemon and raised it to him. 'Maybe you could walk me across the common later, to my train. Only if you were going that way. Nicer to have company. If I'm going on my own, I'd walk the long way round, but I can leave a little later if I go with you.' This hook was a necessary part of her script, they'd decided, if she was to ensure he'd come back for the second half.

As she watched him return to his little gang, the other members of whom were laughing in a ribald way as he joined them, Dinah experienced a temporary relaxation. She'd accomplished the first part of the plan, the technically difficult part. It couldn't have gone more smoothly. The rehearsals had paid off. But this relief could only be fleeting, because emotionally speaking, the really difficult part of the operation was still to come. How long to leave it? Five minutes, they'd decided together. Rhythmically this was about right, and about as long as she dared risk without there being a danger of him leaving the pub. She took her timing from the old wooden clock on the far side of the bar fixed to the chimney breast.

As the minute hand reached its cue point, she swivelled slightly on her stool and angled herself noticeably so she was facing in McGarvey's direction. She was holding her drink, and she took a sip, slightly lowering her gaze, waiting for him to look at her. In the event, it was one of his friends, a shorter, squatter man with a severe short back and sides, who nudged him. More laughter from the others. When McGarvey looked at her, she jerked her head to one side with a little 'come here' flick, the slightest of smiles playing around her eyes. There were audibly course cackles from his group, which didn't deter him from approaching her. No doubt what happened in the saloon bar with his mates was kept from Mrs McGarvey by a strict code of honour.

When he was close, close enough for her to whisper, she leaned towards him and said, 'I'm glad you've came back. I've got a secret for you.'

'What?' he asked, not sure he'd heard her correctly.

'I said I've got a secret for you.'

'What secret?'

'I've got something of yours.' And she reached across and lifted the man's left hand into the air

He was frowning, so she had to nod at him to encourage him. She realised that every muscle in her body was tense now. As if she was preparing herself to receive a physical blow. She looked at his heavy, booze-loosened features, struggling to understand this strange chain of events. She was going to have to help him further. She removed her hand from his, leaving it suspended in mid-air.

'Third finger.' And she waggled her own.

He looked down again. Now he got it. His face dropped.

'Don't worry. I've put it somewhere safe. You want it back, I'll need a little favour.'

A moment's silence. She could see every emotion playing out on his uncomplicated face. Shock. Confusion. Deep disappointment. And then anger. It started around his lips, which moved themselves into a sneer of fury, and then spread to his eyes, which opened wide, losing their pigginess as indignant rage took hold.

'You give me that fucking ring now, you filthy fucking tart.' The words were spat in a low voice that despite its lack of volume revealed the violence of the man. Now Dinah had to access her own steel.

'You'll get it back, but this is what you have to—'

'I said give it to me.' And he grabbed hold of her wrist, squeezing so hard he could have broken it there and then. But she spoke over him, with just enough volume to risk drawing attention.

'This is what you have to do. And I suggest you listen. Because a friend of mine has a photograph of you holding my hand that's going straight to your missus – with a very believable story that doesn't cast you in a good light. Now, none of that has to happen, but you have to listen to me.'

His mind was rolling over the possible outcomes. What could he tell his wife about the wedding ring? And the photos, if that was true? What would she believe? The dawning horror of having to face her seemed to deflate him, sucking something out of him from within. It was not an unpleasant thing, to watch a bully being so easily diminished.

'Louis Warlock is in Wandsworth prison,' said Dinah simply. 'I know he was transferred there nineteen days ago. I just want to get a message to him. A signed reply from him gets you your ring back. And that's the end of the matter. That's it.'

His nostrils flared as his eyes remained wide.

'I can't,' he said, definitively. And he was unexpectedly pleased with this answer, which threw her.

'You'll have to.'

'I can't.'

'You will.'

'I. Can't.' This almost growled through clenched teeth.

'Really. And why can't you?'

'Because they fucking hanged that fucking traitor two weeks ago. I saw them take his corpse away. Good riddance to him. And I ain't lying.'

She could see by his triumphant eyes that he wasn't.

16

His fingers hovered, and gently – very gently – he moved his hand closer. The lightest of touches. A provisional caress. Roughness. Thin crêpe bandages. There was no surprise in that. He'd been repeatedly told not to touch, for his own good. That he had to heal. That he had to trust. At first his arms had been restrained, tied loosely to the bed where he lay for much of the time. But when they were finally released, he'd obeyed the instruction, partly out of fear at what he was going to find.

But today, he'd been assured, he would get to see who he was. Today he could touch.

And he sat there remembering, reviewing, thinking.

The fear had faded. As had the absurd bursts of hope. Now his mind was trying to work through everything in a more analytical way. Trying to get ahead of them. Trying to out-think them, in order to buy himself some advantage, however small.

The very first thing he remembered . . . Light. There had been light. But he hadn't been able to see anything other than that. Only whiteness. A soft, cloudy brightness. There was a tightness around him, and something softer beneath.

Am I dead?

A natural thought to entertain, given the last thing he could remember leading up to this.

'You're probably thinking, "Am I dead?"' The voice had been nearby. Faintly amused, English. Very refined.

Oh God! Please don't let heaven be yet another version of school.

'Sorry,' the voice had said. 'Didn't mean to startle you. I saw you move. Anyway, in answer to that question, yes, you are dead. Technically speaking.'

A hint of something else in that voice, beneath the refined accent. Was this an American?

'Louis Warlock, aka Ludvik Weinschenk, is no more. He's gone. May he rest in peace. Sorry to be so blunt, but that's the truth of it, so there we are.'

Not American. That odd twang. What was it? African. Yes. Like that touring Highlife band from Ghana. Just a hint of it. Odd against the plummy public-school tone.

'So,' the voice had continued, 'how to account for the fact that in spite of the death of Louis Warlock, aka Ludvik Weinschenk, you are still here. Well . . . thereby hangs a tale.'

An abrupt swishing sound, and everything had got brighter.

'My name is Strath. And I represent – how to put it – a certain department of the Secret Intelligence Service of the British government. Don't worry. You haven't heard of us. Nobody has. Nevertheless, we exist.'

'Where am I?' Ow. It hurt his throat to speak. Like someone was attacking it from the inside with a rasp.

'In Aldershot. In a military hospital.'

Not heaven, then.

'Aldershot?'

'Yes.'

'So I'm alive.'

'Oh yes.'

His legs were tingling. Pins and needles. He was alive. A momentary burst of joy. Relief. So sweet. With life came hope, surely . . .

'You said . . .' He'd coughed, trying to clear his throat.

'Go easy, old chap. Throat'll be a bit sore for a while. Have some iced water.' The clink of ice in a glass jug, the sound of pouring.

'Why can't I see?'

'You can see. It's just your eyes are bandaged.'

He'd leaned forward from the pillows behind him, sipped at the water gratefully.

'You said I was dead. And I remember—'

'I shall keep saying it. Because Louis Warlock *is* dead.'

'But I'm here.'

176

'*You're* here, yes. And we shall have to give you a new name, but we can choose that together, down the line. For now, let's call you Patient Paul.'

'They hanged me. I . . .' He didn't want to remember that. The terror. The shame of his fear.

'Paul. From the Latin for "humble". Pointing to the most sacred of rebirths.' He was deliberately obfuscating. That high-class voice with its odd tinge. 'I want you to see the light, too. But I want you to rest first, and I'll be back later, when you're a little more in the land of the living.' This last sentence had been spoken with a flourish, as if the man were an MC in a music hall.

The flashes of joy and relief kept coming for a while, but more overpowering were the questions. Where was he? Why was he there? What was to come? What had they done to him?

Think. Think . . .

His nose hurt, inside and out. The back of his ears ached. His lower back was bruised, as were his ribs on both sides. One of them might have been cracked. Louis knew how to stage a fake hanging, and the injuries he was afflicted with were all consistent with that. When he was being led to the gallows, at some point in the proceedings they must have fastened a girdle around him and pulled it tight. There would have been a hook of some kind on the back, maybe two, and a wound steel cable bound into the rope with loops that would have been fastened to the hooks. The hooks and the girdle would have taken his weight, and if the drop was adjusted to be only a foot or two, rather than the customary five employed in a genuine execution, he would have experienced little more than an abrupt jar. His ribs would have taken the brunt of his weight, hence the bruising.

And the unconsciousness? Well, he was given that brandy. Most likely there was a strong, fast-acting sedative mixed in with it. Chloral hydrate, the so-called Mickey Finn? This was the hard edge of the intelligence services. SIS, the man had said, well versed in dirty tricks. Who knew what chemistry they had access to? There must have been thirty seconds between being given the drink and the drop, if not more.

Satisfied at least that he'd worked out the method, he moved on to the harder question. The more intractable question. Why?

That answer came slowly, partially, dribbled out in small, carefully distributed packets of information. He had to be softened up first, it seemed. Slowly marinated or hung up like a game bird and left for some time until, in this man Strath's judgement, he was ready for the oven. Well, let Strath think that. In reality, it was Louis who was biding his time.

First came a lecture about the state of the world in 1953. Then an explanation of the role Louis had to play in it.

'... You, through the consequences of your own adventures, have presented us with a rather unique opportunity. We have an absolute responsibility to take advantage of that opportunity.'

The grey shape he could discern against the brightness bobbed down, as Strath presumably sat himself in a chair.

'From a legal point of view, the case against you was pretty solid.'

By now, Louis had recovered a little more of himself. Affecting acquiescence was part of his game. They'd stripped him of everything, committed an act of unforgivable violence against his psyche. And he was going to have his revenge on them. If he was sure of one thing, it was that. But he was going to get it right. And that meant patience, playing a part, misleading them as to his true state of mind. All of that was fine. He had time.

'The case against me might have been solid, but if I'd been allowed my own brief, I assure you, I could have knocked a fair number of holes in it,' he said, in answer to Strath's point. If he was too acquiescent, he felt they might suspect he wasn't playing straight.

'You could never have been allowed your own brief,' Strath said, sharply, more of his concealed accent revealing itself in this flare of authentic feeling. 'You're an intelligent man. More than intelligent. You don't really need me to explain why that was the case, given the issues of national security involved.'

He calmed himself, regained control before continuing. 'Please listen carefully. We currently face an enemy the like of which we've never faced. In many ways they're worse than the Nazis. Ultimately, the Nazis could never have triumphed, because the flag they marched under was rotten. The flag the Soviets march under isn't tainted by the same rot. There is nobility in their cause, which most people understand. But the actual outcome of their ideology when it's applied is not noble at all.

Under the late but unlamented Mr Stalin, the corpses have piled high, and the pile is getting higher. Hundreds of thousands. Millions possibly. It seems to be the inevitable fruit of the Soviet way. We, here in this country, us, our allies, we're not perfect. If we were, God knows, you wouldn't be here now, under these circumstances. You'd be on stage somewhere making people happy. And frankly, that would be a better use of your abilities. But listen to me, listen to me . . .'

At this point, Strath did something unexpected, momentarily throwing Louis from his avowed path of retribution: he took both of Louis' hands in his, squeezing them tightly. The action was so spontaneous and apparently authentic that Louis felt tears gathering in the corners of his bandaged eyes.

'This is not a perfect world. But I believe that this country, however far from perfect we are, however much we've failed across the centuries, it's still just about the best we've managed thus far, as human beings. We have a responsibility to try and preserve what we've managed to achieve, so we can improve upon it. You yourself survived the terrible circumstances of your child-hood, as was pointed out at your trial, because of high ideals enacted by imperfect men.'

Strath stood up, started to pace about again. This wasn't a rehearsed speech. He genuinely seemed to be formulating his thoughts as he spoke.

'So here's the problem we face. The doctrine that drives the Soviets is gaining momentum, it's finding traction in our own country and in other parts of the West, among young people who are quite understandably attracted by the lustre of fairness it presents. But they're unable to see the malignancy it opens the door to, because their idealism doesn't admit to the worst aspects of human nature, which are, sadly, dormant in all of us. All of us.'

Louis would be lying if he didn't admit to being wrong-footed by this lecture. He hadn't expected to encounter such thoughtful-ness or articulacy. His concealed rage at his confinement, the torture of being forced to face his own demise had led him to believe that only shoddy motives lay behind it. Punishment, humiliation, retri-bution. But this man was a thinker. And whenever he spoke, a ghost of sympathy for Louis seemed to enter the room.

'Despite what you may be thinking, you can't leave, I'm afraid,' said Strath. 'You're under military confinement. And though you weren't actually executed for your crimes – and why that is the case is a matter we will come to in due course – the verdict against you still stands. You were found guilty in a court of law. So you will have to remain here, or somewhere similar, most likely until the end of your days. For what it's worth, I don't personally believe the case they made against you. I never thought you were guilty of treason, and I did try to intervene on your behalf, I really did. But there were louder voices than mine, I'm afraid. And they had a greater reach. I was able to save your life, however, by proposing . . .' and he paused, trying to get the words right, 'a certain scheme.'

A certain scheme. So he's behind all this. It is his doing.

'What exactly have you done to me?' Louis asked bitterly. As he spoke, he made to press his hands against his bandaged face. Strath stopped him.

'Don't. Not yet. You'll injure yourself. Really. Leave it be.'

'What have you done to me?' Louis heard himself saying again, in a lower voice full of desperation and fearful despair.

Strath stood up and clapped his hand on Louis' shoulder. 'In time . . . in time.' He clicked his fingers; the shade of a nurse entered, another grey shape against the whiteness, and Louis arms were restrained once again.

All through this stewing period, Louis was not permitted any contact with the outside world or with other prisoners, if there were any. There was no radio, no newspapers. Every so often a gramophone was wheeled in, and a selection of light classics were played. He could hear the unseen nurse solemnly slipping discs from their sleeves, and the ghost of a Strauss waltz or a Chopin prelude would float from the speaker.

The next phase of Operation Schmooze, as he had dubbed it, involved a change of circumstances. They started taking him for walks outside, supported by a nurse, or by Strath, who seemed to be working to some predetermined timetable. Louis found he was immediately grateful for the breeze, be it warm or cool, the scents of springtime: cut grass, blossom. Even the sound of aircraft low overhead spoke of a world comfortably continuing in his absence. On one of these expeditions, Strath surprised him by talking unguardedly about Louis' predicament.

'I did argue that if you'd had things put to you directly, you more than likely would have cooperated. You really do have a unique set of talents. A unique mind. You know that, I think. And now that you're . . . officially dead, you may well be the most powerful secret weapon we have at our disposal.'

'Cooperated with what? What are you talking about? What do you mean, secret weapon?' Louis wasn't going to hide his indignation.

'Has it ever occurred to you that you were carefully selected for the role you ended up playing?'

'By you?'

'Not by me. Before all of that. By the Soviets. I'm going back to the beginning of this.'

'Well . . . I suppose they needed a certain set of skills to get their hands on the microfilm. So yes.'

'I'm not talking about that. What you say is true. But you were also a target in and of yourself. Someone wanted you brought down.'

'Who wanted me brought down?'

'How are you on international magicians?'

Magicians. Magic. The words still did something to Louis, even in this unhappy place: a little pull in the stomach, a lift to the spirits. It was ridiculous.

'Have you heard of a magician called Potash?'

'No.'

'Not a surprise, to be honest. He's secretive. But by all accounts, he's some kind of magical genius. Of the type that doesn't seek the limelight. Full name, Chananel Potash. A Pole. Moved to Moscow after the annexation. He was, shall we say, an enthusiastic party member. He saw early on that his talents for deception might be used to serve the cause. A man of great vision, perhaps.'

'Very interesting.' Louis was keen to return to the original topic. 'Why did he target me?'

'We'll come on to that. What you need to know first is that Potash was successful at capturing the attention of the higher echelons of the party. The MGB were very interested.'

'Who are the MGB?'

'The Ministry for State Security. Very powerful. Very ruthless. More so than our equivalent – my lords and masters.'

'I'd say you were pretty ruthless.'

'And I'd say if you criticised the state like that in dear Mother Russia, it would be enough to see you cremated alive, so these things are relative. Potash went to them with his idea for a department of espionage that drew on his own particular skills.'

'How do you know all this?' Louis said, still sputtering his questions in a resentful tone.

'A high-level defector. Moscow occasionally offers up its own versions of Burgess and Maclean, I'm relieved to say.'

'OK. Who is this defector? Take me to him. I want to speak to him.'

'Yes – that would be useful, wouldn't it. I suspect there's a lot you could ask him that we would never think to. Sadly, that opportunity has passed.'

'Why?'

'The Soviets managed to poison him, even though he was over here. Some kind of batrachotoxin. You only need two grains of the stuff. They're very good at that side of things. Lot of history with it.' Strath let that sink in before continuing. 'Potash's outfit are known simply as the K, short for the Otdeleniye Kolduny.' His Russian pronunciation was notably impressive. 'The Department of Sorcerers. An elite faction within the Russian secret service. They've weaponised their powers of deception to a powerful degree.'

'Why aren't we doing that?' said Louis, the magician within him already bristling that his own team had overlooked his abilities.

'That's why you were targeted. You see, Potash had had that thought too. And being a thorough sort, he'd already informed himself about the competition. Surveyed the field. Identified you as a potential rival.'

'Why me specifically? Why not . . .'

'Yes?'

Louis didn't continue.

'Not a long list, is it? And you were at the top of it.'

'I've had enough of this buggering about. I want to know the truth. I want these bandages off. I want to know what you've done to me. I want to know why. I want to get to the bottom of it. The bottom of everything.'

'Tomorrow. Tomorrow everything will be unveiled.' And Strath clapped him on the shoulder.

The next morning, Louis found himself asking:

Who am I?

The question kept echoing. Not casual, not philosophical, but urgent, pragmatic, full of fear.

What have they done with me?

He stiffened as he heard footsteps. Not Strath. One of the nurses. He recognised the smell of Palmolive and TCP.

'We're just going to uncover your eyes.'

The light dimmed as the curtains in the room were drawn. Even in that dimness the light was overpowering as the bandages were gently pulled away. Reflexively he kept his eyes squeezed shut.

'It's OK. You can open them.'

Slowly, very slowly, he dared to do so. Things weren't clear at first. Those tiny muscles around his pupils that brought things in and out of focus hadn't had to do any work in days, weeks. Gradually they began to wake up. Easier with the nearer things. The nurse's face. Clean, scrubbed, without make-up. Pure, like a nun's.

'Lieutenant Colonel Strath will be here shortly,' was all she said before leaving, departing with an even step.

He sat there letting the sparsely furnished room form itself around him. It occurred to him that this whole thing, his recuperation, his bandaging, the restriction of his vision, might have had no medical purpose at all. Perhaps it was just more mind games, more stewing, more marinading, more faux-cess designed to prepare him for whatever was coming next.

After some time – hard to say how long given that there was no clock on the wall and no watch on his wrist – he heard the approach of Strath's familiar tread. Which didn't prepare him for the shock of seeing the man himself. Despite the ghost of the accent he'd heard, Louis had envisaged a clean-cut, fair-haired captain-of-the-cricket-team sort, given his sharp breeziness, his air of confidence. The man who walked in was dark-skinned, with thick black hair barely disciplined by its military buzz cut. He had a proud, questioning face, slightly plump, that seemed to read Louis' reaction to his appearance.

'Not who you expected?' Louis gave no answer, so Strath continued. 'My father was an engineer, a former army officer stationed in Sierra Leone. My mother was a nurse. I fought my way to this position. Too bright for them not to make use of me.' This was clearly a speech he had made on a number of occasions, a pre-emptive answer to the unvoiced questions racing around the minds of anyone in the service who met him. 'How are we feeling?' he asked, swiftly swerving the subject away from himself.

Terrified. Furious. Abused.

Louis didn't say any of that. Instead, he pointed to the wrapped package that Strath was holding.

'What's that?'

Strath held up the package and attacked it with unexpected vigour, tearing off a layer of brown paper to reveal a mirror with a simple narrow wooden frame.

'It's ironic, isn't it, that there are people who would pay everything they owned to be gifted this opportunity. The chance to begin again. Unencumbered by their mistakes, by their regrets, by their shame.'

Louis felt himself flinch as Strath held up the mirror. He wanted to close his eyes again.

By what authority has this been done? By what authority?

What followed was the strangest sensation he could ever recall. It was like experiencing the wonder of a brilliant magic trick in which the sight that met your eyes didn't just fool you, it defied every expectation you were carrying in your head. The person staring back at him from the mirror was not him. His slightly hooked nose with its convex bridge and downward-turned tip was no longer there. Without thinking, as if he was simply at the barber's, he found he had turned into a three-quarters profile to better comprehend what he was looking at. That nose – his nose – had been replaced with a neat, pert, more modest button. Turning back full face on, his hands went to his jawline. Where it was formerly, overly broad, noticeably so, it had been narrowed, made more discreet. His ears, with their long lobes, had been shortened and brought closer to the sides of his head, and his heavy brows had been lightened. Staring at his eyes, he realised they were a different shape too. Those he was accustomed to seeing – slightly hooded, Mediterranean – were now wider and rounder. Added together, all these changes made him look like somebody he'd never met before, somebody distinctly northern European. Somebody from an old family with no outsiders in the bloodline. Celtic, maybe, or Nordic. Not a trace of Jewishness. If it wasn't for the dark hair, he believed he could have passed as a German officer.

He moved his head from side to side as if to confirm he was actually the person he was looking at in the mirror. He placed his hands on his face, pressing it in different places. When he spoke, finally, it was with a question.

'Who did this to me?'

'We have a team, led by a man called Ravilious. He's been specialising with burns victims since the war. Airmen in particular, giving them back their faces, as far as he could. Yours . . .' Strath paused, considering how to put it. 'It's a new face. Designed to blend in.'

'Not a Jew, you mean,' Louis said softly, to himself as much as Strath.

'Maybe you'll like blending in. See how the other half lives . . .' said Strath. Was there a touch of bitter irony in that quip? A moment of shared understanding? If so, it was short-lived. 'Well?' he asked, impatiently. 'What do you think?'

It was beyond Louis in that moment to articulate that. But he knew what he was feeling. The liquid ore of fury that had been smelting in his guts was forming itself into an ingot of determination. And he resolved in that moment that whatever their plans for him were, he was going to tear himself away from them. He was going to flee. He was going to escape. That would be his revenge. He would burn up all their careful manipulation of his life in that act. He would get back to the Brains Trust. He would get himself to Dinah. And together they would plot their way out of this catastrophe. He looked at the stranger in the mirror and thought only one thing.

Who am I? Louis Warlock. No one – no one – is going to take that away from me.

THE REAL MAGIC WORD

My dear friend. Are you still there? Are
you reading this?

If you are (and you are, aren't you? I
know you are. I know you are), I want you
to think of a magic word. Got one?

Well, I'm guessing you either thought
of 'hocus-pocus' or 'abracadabra'. Yes,
there are a few other obscure ones out
there, like 'gazumba' and 'sim sala bim',
but ultimately it boils down to a choice of
two. Think about those two choices while I
remind you what a magic word really is. It
is a spell, an assembly of letters that
possesses an ancient other-worldly power,
accessing and bringing forth a force that
ordinary people cannot command. Now close
your eyes and whisper them both, but don't
just speak the words; as you say them,
imagine that you command and affect that
real power. The power to bring something
into being, make something appear, to bring
it forward into our realm, however
unlikely, however impossible it seems.

Which one of the words felt to you like
it had the most power? Somehow 'hocus-
pocus' feels silly, doesn't it, like it's
made for children. Maybe that's because
it's an invented word, it has no real

grounding, no absolute power. It was first created to describe the frivolous tricks that sixteenth-century jugglers performed.

But 'abracadabra' is a different beast. Whisper it again. As the word trips off your tongue, you can sense that there is something beneath it, something deep and ancient. It is there in its rhythm, its sound, its music. Without you even knowing it, that word, a word that has survived since the second century AD, evokes a response that you can't put your finger on. You can feel the dark, ancient power of it. 'Abracadabra' is a corruption of the Hebrew ארבדכ ארבא, *ebrah k'dabri*, meaning 'I will create as I speak'. In other words, the very act of speech will create new realities. Words have power once they are formed.

This I know to be true.

But there is a buried secret that I want to share with you. 'Abracadabra' isn't the most powerful magic word; there is another.

I have no idea what year you will read this, but as I conceive this book of conjuring thoughts and routines and the thinking behind them, the planet is but a few years into grieving and healing from a period of unfathomable loss. Our sense of what humanity is has been truly shaken. The world finds us looking to repair ourselves; hope is tugging at us, trying to blossom. So how can we help? I feel weak. I feel lost. I feel helpless. All those things appear to be irrefutably true. What can we do? What can I do? Magic, my dear fellow magi, my brothers in arms, is so much more than tricks. It can ride this hope, show anyone who comes into contact with it, with you as a practitioner, that yes – the impossible is possible.

Do I believe that? Can I hold on to that thought? That's the question. That's the question.

I'm going to tell you something. The most powerful magic word on this glorious planet is . . . your own name. Not said as an incantation, not said to bring forward imaginary powers, not said to harness other-worldly forces, but given as a covenant, a sign of goodness, a sign of hope.

When you started reading this book of routines, you signed a secrecy contract. (Even if you didn't sign it physically, you read it, considered it, imagined it.) Let's be honest, in real terms, it's meaningless. What's going to happen if you break that clause? Will I somehow find out, hunt you down and spend inordinate amounts of money in legal costs suing you for breach of contract? No. Of course not. So why bother? Because, my friend, there was a time when giving your word meant something deep. The idea that being a fellow who could be trusted to stand firm and be decent was something to aspire to. The power of your name.

Well, here we are, in a world that feels like it's been ruined. Your magic has the power to mend that. Heal it. Bit by bit. Act by act. Day by day. Reputation by reputation. Because here's what happens if you break the clause: you betray your name, maybe not in anybody else's eyes, but in

your own. But if you cleave to the covenant
you've made, if you abide by your vow,
you've built something solid inside,
however small. Something true. And you can
carry on building from there. Really
building. That's when the magic begins. If
you can do that when it feels impossible –
in the darkest of hours – and keep going,
good things will happen. I promise you.
That's your covenant.

I've vowed to compose these words.
Commit them to posterity. In my mind first,
then on the page. That's my covenant. And
I'm going to keep going. I put my name to
that.

Something will happen.
I will create as I speak.
Abracadabra.

17

From the moment of the unveiling, Louis had decided that the most effective thing he could do was play the part of being plausibly cooperative. That meant being less than one hundred per cent obliging and obedient, and at first not even fifty per cent obliging and obedient, which was easy. He only needed to channel his authentic feelings.

Without it being explained, it was clear what Strath's immediate plan was: a period of settling, allowing Louis to get used to his new appearance, before any further briefing.

After the unveiling, he had said: 'I shall be away for a few days. I have to go to town for a short while. I want you to concentrate on getting well. When I return, we'll discuss what comes next.'

'What if I don't want anything to come next?'

'We'll discuss that too,' Strath said.

Louis didn't think for a moment Strath was going anywhere. He was confident that the man would be staying exactly where he was, keeping Louis under close observation, seeing how well or otherwise he was mentally coping with his change of appearance and the ongoing situation they were putting him through. Strath had spoken of Louis being a powerful secret weapon. If he was telling the truth, and this wasn't hyperbole, Louis didn't think for a second that there wasn't a highly detailed plan that had begun with his fake execution, continuing with many stages beyond, all carefully leading to his ultimate deployment in the field.

His first session in the gymnasium had boosted his sense of optimism about the possibility of escape. Ironically, it was the high security they'd adopted around this that had given him that hope.

Strath had apologised that they were having to keep him handcuffed when they transferred him to the gymnasium, given that it was on the other side of the airbase compound. It was just a temporary measure while he continued going through this period of acclimatisation. (Louis had let the look on his face do the protesting. There was no need for speech.) But as one of the cuffs was fixed around his wrist and the other around the uniformed soldier who was accompanying him, he observed that they were using a standard-issue set of Hiatt A1167 police hand-cuffs from the early 1940s. Well, he knew how to get out of those in about thirty seconds flat. He wasn't going to do so now, but it demonstrated as clearly as it could that this institution was being complacent about its security arrangements. All he had to do was pay attention and audit all the similar gaps.

Sure enough, adopting that frame of mind began to yield results. He noticed, for example, that they were still locking the door to his room but they were no longer bolting it. It was secured with a Gibbons rim deadlock of a kind he was familiar with. He knew it was possible to pick such a lock with a steady hand and a couple of thick wires with right-angle hooks bent into their ends. He started searching the sparsely furnished room for anything that might do that job. He thought the bedsprings could be the way to go, but he lacked the tools to separate them from their fittings. In the end, he found that the curtains were strung on their rail by open rings of brass that were thin and malleable enough to be unfurled and worked beneath the leg of one of the beds until a suitable hook had been fashioned.

There were guards posted outside, sitting opposite the door on the other side of the corridor. Three of them, one at a time, on eight-hour shifts. There was a porthole window with wire-mesh fire glass. If Louis turned the lights off and stood on the chair at the back of the room, he could see through the window to the guard beyond. The one who had the afternoon posting was an older officer who clearly had trouble with his waterworks. He could be relied on to disappear for a sneaky two-minute bath-room break at least twice in his shift. He seemed to provide the perfect opportunity.

Louis had allowed himself a day to rehearse. He waited with his unfurled curtain ring poised. Once he began the lock-picking, he would start counting in his head. If it took more than thirty seconds, he would wait for his next chance. It was crucial that he was out and gone within a minute, so that he could be round the dog-leg of the corridor with his door shut before the guard returned. Then there would be nothing to immediately alert any suspicion. As far as he could tell, the man was not in the habit of checking anything upon his return.

As for the next part of his plan, it was the handcuffed walk back from the gymnasium that had delivered it to him. He had no other clothes but a dressing gown and a pair of pyjamas. He certainly wouldn't get far in those. But on his return from his unhappy exercise period, being led down a corridor about forty yards from his room, a familiar smell had hit his nostrils, wafting up from a basement area.

Chlorine.

A swimming pool.

Whether it was for training purposes or leisure, a swimming pool would have changing facilities. And as if to confirm the thought, he heard the sound of splashing, the echo of a blast of a whistle. He would just have to get down there in his pyjamas and dressing gown and hope there was no one around, or if there was, that he could hide until they'd gone.

But first he had to get out of the room.

Poised for his cue, he cheered inwardly and immediately felt pangs of stage fright when the older guard slowly shuffled off to the lavatory. Jumping off the bed, he squatted down next to the lock, inserting his improvised tool. Then silently, carefully, he turned the knob and pulled the door open, shutting it behind him as softly as he could. If he could have done, he would locked it too, but it was more important that he used the time to disappear. He would just have to gamble on the guard's lack of care upon his return.

Next problem: what if he encountered someone on the corridor as he headed towards the pool? Well, he just needed to walk with confidence and purpose. The odds were that whoever he met wouldn't recognise him, unless it was Strath.

Fate was on his side, at least thus far. He could hear the sounds of distant splashing up ahead. There would be at least one set of clothes to be found. He had to keep his pace up, even as he maintained his ongoing caution.

He rounded the corner and headed down the short flight of stairs. It led directly to a small changing room. In its centre was a set of benches with an upright section in the middle. Hanging from pegs were two sets of clothes on one side and one on the other. The ones nearest him were civilian in appearance; those on the far side carried the blue shade of an airman's uniform. He went for the uniform. This was an airbase after all – you were less likely to be challenged if you were a serving officer.

As he dressed, he stayed as alert as possible. The jacket and shirt were a reasonable enough fit, but the trousers were too long. If he gave them turn-ups, it would look odd. He opted for folding up the excess length inside the trouser legs. The boots were loose too, so he pulled the laces as tight as he possibly could. He felt within the pockets of the jacket as he started walking. There was loose change. He would need it. He was going to find a telephone once he was out. He was going to call the Turk.

As he left the changing room, he passed a mirror. They'd put one up in his hospital quarters, but he had avoided looking at it. The shock of catching the occasional glimpse and not seeing himself reflected back had only served to drive his desire to escape even more. But now he wanted to see, even though every second was vital. Partly it was the instinctive urge to adjust his outfit, check it for acceptability. But partly also it was the dark fascination of confronting what they'd done to him, somehow more tolerable now that he'd taken back control of his own destiny. He held the airman's cap in his hands, pulled his head upright, lifting his chin. He looked into those wider, rounder eyes, trying to find himself in them. He had never been one for studying his own reflection.

What are you looking for? came the thought. *How would you even know if you'd found it?*

His me-ness? His Louis-ness?

It was all too ethereal. He didn't have time. He stepped away from the mirror and ran up the stairs in search of his exit.

Walk with purpose. A disguise wasn't just about what you were wearing. It was also to do with how you carried yourself, your gait, your general demeanour. 'Always walk with confidence,' his first agent had told him, 'especially when you don't know where you're going.'

There were other people around now. That was fine. He didn't stand out. He couldn't have looked more at home in his RAF uniform (as long as he ignored the flap-flapping of his feet against the parquet flooring). He kept his gaze ahead, adopting a slightly preoccupied look, as if his mind was elsewhere, pre-emptively keeping any eye contact at bay. Every so often there were signs, as in a hospital or public building. He assumed that sooner or later one would say 'exit', or 'reception'. Occasional windows showed him where the airfield was, so it wasn't going to be in that direction. Security would not be as tight leaving as entering. This wasn't a prison. All attention would be on preventing people without authority from getting in. He did what he could to convince himself this would be the case.

There was a manned guardhouse just outside the main building. The entrance was attended by a uniformed security officer who was currently accepting a delivery from a postal van. Visitors had to pass through his guardhouse on the left side of the road-way. Those leaving simply passed through a turnstile exit on the other side. It wasn't attended. There was an exit barrier in between the two preventing entrance by road. And that was it. Louis only had to keep walking.

A small group of people had gathered ahead of him. Some were in uniform, but there were two women in civilian clothes. He just needed to stay calm, ignore his racing heart. Not draw attention to himself. He would be through in a matter of seconds. Just start counting. One to ten. Ten to twenty. As each number passed, a thought in his head intervened: surely he was pushing his luck; surely they must have raised the alarm . . .

But now he was at the turnstile, like gaining entrance to a racetrack. It clicked and rattled around him as he walked through.

He was out on the pavement, which curved slowly around, following the two women in front in their knee-length raincoats, one camel, one tweed.

Keep looking straight ahead. Keep walking with purpose. Don't speed up, whatever you do. Maintain your pace.

Within a minute, he'd reached the main road beyond the airbase. There was fencing on the left-hand side next to the pavement, which the pedestrians in front of him continued to walk along. On the other side was a verge running parallel to a line of scrubby woodland. Would it draw more attention if he crossed the road, walked into the woods, took shelter there? There was no question that each passing minute drew him closer to the discovery of his absence.

Get off the road.

The pull of it was too great. With a couple of glances over his shoulder, he walked briskly to the other side. Aware that he was momentarily free of anyone's passing gaze, he darted into the woods, but kept walking, seeing if he could find some kind of path ahead of him. It didn't really matter where it took him.

There was a sort of route amongst the brambles and the undergrowth, but it ran in the same direction as the road, so it didn't really offer much in the way of concealment. He didn't care where he was going – he just needed to steal a coat and find a telephone. Telephone first. He could see through the trees that there was a traffic roundabout at end of the road he'd just left, and beyond it a parade of shops. Immediately that became his destination.

It did occur to him that he could wait in the woods until nightfall. But the thought was batted away. They might have dogs. They'd sniff him out. *Keep moving. See how far you can get. Just call the Turk first.*

It would have been good if there'd been a pub, but there was only a café: the kind that catered to workers rather than housewives taking tea. Briskly he crossed the road and went straight inside. There was a phone on the wall next to the window. Make the call, buy a cup of tea, while looking for a coat that would cover the uniform. (Given his guard's lack of conscientiousness, it was likely the uniform would be missed before Louis was.)

He pulled a couple of pennies from his pocket and put one into the slot on the top of the phone. He dialled o for the operator, pressing the A button as soon as she answered.

'London Gerard 5358, please.' While he waited for the Turk to answer (please let it answer, please don't let Danny have dismantled it yet), he scanned the room for a coat rack. There was one over by the lavatories. Things were going his way! Five rings the machine was set for. He'd just opened his mouth to speak when—

THWAMMMM.

His head went bright with pain.

And then blackness.

The Turk was perhaps the highest embodiment of Louis' vanity and Danny's indulgence of it. Dinah often complained about Louis' spendthrift ways – scrimping on practical necessities like cutlery and bed linen while blowing large amounts of money on whims and fancies, particularly if they could be justified as a business expense. While magic props were a legitimate purchase even as they were an indulgence, camera equipment, Wurlitzer jukeboxes, deluxe slide projectors and two-way radios remained good examples of caprices that were less easy to justify to the accountant.

The Turk – perhaps the greatest of these extravagances – had begun life when Louis had read an article in *The Gen* about Harry Jansen, aka Dante, the famous Danish/American magician having just taken delivery of something called an 'electronic secretary' – a machine that answered the telephone even when no one was there to take the call. It combined a record player and wire recorder. The record player contained a specially recorded message asking the caller to leave one of their own. It then switched over to the wire recorder to receive it.

'You know what would be great?' said Louis to Danny the next day. 'To have something like Dante's set-up, so that if I get an idea when I'm out and about – on tour, at a venue, wherever – all I'd have to do would be to find the nearest telephone, dial the machine and speak my idea down the line. You could instantly pick it up, wherever I was, and get going on it.'

'What's wrong with a stack of postcards and a bookie's pencil,' Ivan had said, scowling.

'Time,' said Louis, as if it was obvious. 'With this thing, you'd gain days. Instant communication. I might want a prop built or a repair. I can call straight away and the message is collected. It's brilliant.'

Everyone knew it was an indulgence, but perhaps there was something in it that might just give them an edge somewhere down the line. Plus, Danny loved nothing more than a technical challenge. Their version could be simpler than the commercially available alternative. There was no need for an outgoing message, just the wire recorder. A simple circuit could be triggered by the incoming phone call, and Louis just had to put the phone down to shut it off. Once it was built, they paid to have an extra telephone line installed at Maison Bertaux. To complete the system, Danny had set up a bulb that flashed in the cafeteria's main office if a message had been left. Monsieur Vignaud had kindly agreed to call Danny when it did.

At first Louis had made use of the device on a number of occasions, but the novelty soon wore off, and after the first few weeks it enjoyed only intermittent employment. It was nick-named the Turk after the fabled automatic chess player from the eighteenth century – although where that had been a mere illusion, Danny's version did actually work by itself.

Standing in the Aldershot café, Louis' intention had been to leave a message on the Turk to give the Brains Trust advance warning that he was alive and free. Then, once he was in a safer locale with some semblance of a disguise, he would try ringing them individually until he got hold of one of them. But the first word of his initial message hadn't even made its way out of his mouth before the cosh came down on the back of his head. Something had been recorded, though. And that something was enough to provoke debate.

It was Danny who took the call from Monsieur Vignaud. Within forty minutes they were all in Maison Bertaux, in the corner of the third-floor room where the Turk was installed. The large wooden port box that kept the dust off had been lifted, exposing the squat wire recorder inside. They all sat on their haunches, staring it at like caveman round a sacred fire, as if the object might offer up a super-natural message from the great beyond.

'Have you listened yet?' asked Phyllis, the first to break the silence.

'Yes.'

'Well?' said Dinah, unable to disguise her frustration that Danny hadn't already given any kind of account of what he'd heard.

'I'm just going to play it,' said Danny. 'You all need to hear it.'

'Well go on then,' said Phyllis, also irritated.

Danny reached for the switch on the top, pushed it to the left. The mechanism started up. Sound began to crackle from the internal speaker. There was a brief noise, a burst of something behind it, a swell of hiss, a clatter. And the recording ceased. It couldn't have lasted for more than five seconds.

'Well?' said Ivan, irritated.

'That's it.'

'That bit of noise? That's the message?'

'Yes.'

'Is that all that's on there?' asked Dinah.

'I replaced the wire about three months ago. This is the first message that's been left since then.'

'That isn't a message,' said Ivan.

'Play it again,' said Dinah.

'There's nothing there,' said Ivan.

'Play it again.'

Danny reached for the switch again, pushed it to the right. The brief message reversed with a high-pitched sucking sound. He clicked the switch back in the other direction and played the recording again, stopping it once it had finished.

'You can slow it down, can't you?' Dinah asked.

'Slow what down?' said Ivan sceptically. 'There's nothing there.'

'Just do it,' said Dinah. 'Please.'

Danny obliged, fiddling with a dial on the square front of the machine. When he set the recording playing again, they all listened intently.

If one paid attention, there were three distinct stages to the sound. An initial hint of something vocal, like a single syllable softly spoken. Then a crumpled percussive sound, much louder, that smeared away, quickly falling in volume to become part of the ambient hiss. And then the rising of what must have been background noise – a low clatter of some kind. Cutlery on crockery? Whatever it was, it was abruptly cut off.

'That first sound,' said Dinah, her eyes wide, her tone urgent.

'What do you mean?' said Danny. 'It's *gornisht.*'

'It's Louis.'

'What's Louis?' This time it was Phyllis asking, confused.

'That sound. It's the sound he makes when he's about to speak. It's a bad habit. And it always used to drive me mad. It's unique to him.'

'What are you talking about?' said Ivan. But Phyllis thumped him on the top of his leg.

'I'm serious. Come on, you know what I mean. When he's trying to form words, and he hasn't quite decided how he's going to say something, he makes that little clicking noise. Like he's pulling his tongue of the roof off his mouth.'

Nobody said anything. There was just embarrassed silence.

'Play it again. Normal speed,' Dinah said. 'Please.'

Danny did as she asked.

'There,' she said. And she mimicked the sound herself.

'I can't hear it,' Danny said, apologetically. Dinah looked to Phyllis, who after a moment shook her head, her lips pressed together tightly.

'I think,' said Ivan, in a softer voice this time, 'it's a wrong number.'

'How can it be a wrong number?' said Dinah, trying to disguise the desperation that flickered in her own voice. 'Have we ever had a wrong number on the Turk?'

Danny didn't answer.

'Danny? Have we?'

'I don't think so,' he said.

'That doesn't mean we couldn't have one now,' said Ivan. 'Does it?'

No answer again.

'Danny? Does it?' said Ivan.

'Technically speaking, it doesn't. If it was a local call from this exchange. Someone could have misdialled.'

They all stared at the machine. It was clear to Dinah that they'd made their minds up.

'He's not dead,' she said eventually, breaking the painful silence. No one said anything at first. Then Phyllis spoke up, gently.

'Dinah . . .'

'He's not dead. I know it.' And she stood and walked towards the stairs.

The others remained where they were, as if they were conspirators, convinced in their belief that Dinah was merely running from the bitter truth they all knew to be the case. They listened to her diminishing footsteps hurtling towards the ground floor, and when they had covered enough distance, Danny picked up the port box and lifted it over the Turk, as if he was rolling a stone in front of a tomb.

'You don't think . . .' Phyllis started.

He turned to look at her.

'Do *you?*' he said. She didn't answer him, but that was an answer in itself.

18

One day, Louis was taken outside and sat on a bench beneath a rather pleasant chestnut tree. It was warm, a picture-perfect May afternoon, the kind that would have formerly gladdened his heart. Now it was merely something he looked at, seen through glass, or in a photograph. It had nothing to do with him.

After a few moments, Strath appeared, walking across the recreation ground that spread out beyond the tree. He was holding a leather folio and wearing a light linen suit that served to emphasis the darkness of his skin

He had, of course, had Louis followed on his attempted breakout. He'd thought (he explained after the event) that such an escape bid was inevitable, or at least highly likely, and had regarded it as an opportunity to see Louis using his natural field abilities, his initiative, his wiles. But the moment Louis attempted any interaction with a civilian, his shadows were under strict instructions that he was to be immediately interrupted and apprehended.

Strath sat down next to him now and smiled. It was a complicated smile. It contained sympathy, and something paternal, and a kind of weariness at the task immediately ahead, whatever that was. Before he could speak, however, Louis got in first with his own pitch.

'I want to speak to my fiancée,' he said. His voice was small, quiet. His throat was not sore now, but his spirit was diminished. Maybe 'Louis' really was leaving him.

Strath's mouth moved oddly, as if he were swilling the remains of a cup of cold tea. Then he said:

'Your fiancée wasn't pregnant, by any chance?'

'No!' The question was like a glass of cold water in Louis' face. The sudden, unexpected intimacy it suggested.

'That relationship is over. You have to start again.'

Louis stood up. 'Do you know what you can do with all of this. Stick it up your arse. And if you try and send me over there, do you know what I'm going to do, the minute I arrive? Defect. Willingly. And tell the Soviets everything I know. Everything.'

Louis thought it would take a day or two, but Strath was actually back in his room that afternoon.

'I'd very much like your opinion on a couple of things. If you'd like to come with me.' It was as if Louis' outburst had never happened.

He was taken in a large elevator down to a basement level where there were no windows and everything was illuminated with the harsh glare of fluorescent strips.

The corridors branched, turned back on themselves, twisting like a fairground maze. Eventually they came to an anonymous room with dark walls painted a military green, lit by bulkhead lights. An old trestle table had been set up in the middle of the floor, with two swivel chairs behind it. On it there was a lidded cardboard box.

'Come and have a look at this,' said Strath. He lifted the lid and shook the box slightly. Inside was a parcel wrapped in white tissue paper, as if it contained some relic bound for a museum. 'Go ahead,' he said.

Louis was still angry, full of resentment. But he was also bored. And there was immediate intrigue here. Without thinking about it too much, he carefully unwrapped the parcel, revealing an item made from polished brass, about five inches square, like a large powder compact. It was hinged at one end. He lifted the lid part to find that the underside of its top was mirrored, a layer of polished silver. The inside of the case (where the tablet of powder would have been if it had contained make-up) was most curious. It was made of five concentric discs nested within one another. Each was patterned in a similar way, with narrow spiralling arms of highly contrasting black and white enamel. However, on alternate discs the arms of the spiral sloped in opposite directions: on one they leaned from left to right, while its neighbour's leaned from right to left. Just staring at this arrangement for a moment made Louis' eyes flicker, as with the onset of a migraine.

'Beautiful, isn't it?' said Strath, avoiding looking at it.

'Yes . . .' Something was stirring in Louis. He thought he knew what the item was. 'They come from Moravia,' he said, gazing at the thing in wonder.

'You know what it is?'

'Read about them. Made by a man named Boileau. Pierre Boileau. Does it work?'

'Work?' said Strath, surprised.

'The mechanism?'

'You already know more than I do. Our technical department thought it was a clock. Or an astrolabe. It's awaiting more specialist examination.'

'It's getting that now,' said Louis scathingly.

'Who was Pierre Boileau?'

'Prop-maker, nineteenth century. Worked with Jean-Eugène Robert-Houdin. You've heard of Robert-Houdin?' More scorn in this.

'Magician?'

'He had a number of startling routines that all relied on automata.'

'Clockwork, you mean?'

'Well, you could call it that, but it's a bit like calling the Sistine Chapel frescoes "decorations".'

'Was this' – Strath nodded at the item – 'a magic prop?'

'No,' said Louis, still gazing at it. 'Where did you find it?'

'Amongst the possessions of one of our agents. He'd been working under cover. In Czechoslovakia.'

'Makes sense.'

'Why?' said Strath, intensely focused on each of Louis' answers.

'Like I said, it was made in Moravia. In Czechoslovakia, as it is now. Boileau lived there. These were his obsession. He made them for himself. *Boîtes à rêves*. Dream boxes.'

'Dream boxes?'

'Uh huh,' said Louis. He was pressing and prodding as gently as he could, attempting to find some switch or mechanism.

Suddenly the thing clicked into life with a soft tick. The circles on its surface began to turn, but in opposing directions and at slightly different speeds. It was impossible for the eye not to be drawn into them. If one focused on the inner circle, one's eye was pulled towards its centre. If one switched to the neighbouring circle, one's eye got pushed outwards. Moving from one to the other was dizzying, confusing, instantly vertiginous. Louis held the device up, looked at it. As he did, he felt his mouth start to open. His face slackened. His head began to nod forward.

'Hey,' Strath called to him, with unexpected sharpness. He patted him on the shoulder.

Louis turned the dream box over in his hands so that the turning circles faced away from him. He experimented again with the different combinations of pushes and presses. The mechanism came to a halt.

'Why "dream boxes"?' said Strath. There was a gravity to the question, an urgency. It wasn't just a casual or curious enquiry.

'Why do you think?' said Louis, flashing the dizzying spirals and their anti-spirals at the other man, who involuntarily turned his head away, as if he were scared of it. 'Boileau was fascinated by mesmerism, hypnotism. How to induce hypnotic states. So he turned his craft to constructing devices that would bring about such shifts in consciousness. Clearly you're looking at one. Or not looking at it.'

'And are they . . . rare? These devices. How many of them did he build?'

'They're certainly rare. As I say, I've never even seen a photograph – only an engraving. The monograph I read said they were only ever in Boileau's private collection. There's another school of thought that says they were just pipe dreams. Fantasies. That they were never built. I think this' – he waved it gently in the air – 'dispenses with that theory.'

Strath led Louis back into the twisting narrow corridors of the subterranean labyrinth, pausing as they arrived at a pair of double swing doors.

'This business with Potash,' he said, 'you need to know it was never just about you.'

The doors were of the kind that opened on to a hospital ward.

There was a smell in the air of bleach and carbolic, but it couldn't quite mask the more unpleasant smell beneath: vomit? Effluvia? Death? Louis couldn't quite define it. He only knew that it smelled of despair.

The room beyond was tiled, like a communal shower, or a rugby players' bath. But there was no plumbing, just rows of white tiles, gleaming in the strip lights. At the far end was a single door. It was padded, and secure, with three separate keyholes, one at the top, one in the middle and one at the bottom. There was a glass porthole in its upper portion. Strath went over to it and rapped his knuckles briskly on the glass, three times.

'*Vesel'ye Zhiloy-Dom* in Russian. The best translation might be "the Funhouse",' he said.

'What?' said Louis. He found that his resentment and bitterness were still receding, intrigue and curiosity taking over. 'What's any of this got to do with a Funhouse?'

'It was a phrase that started coming up on intelligence reports, about eleven months ago. Other Allied countries had lost their agents to the Funhouse. That kind of thing.'

'What does "lost their agents" mean?'

'What is says. They went into this Funhouse – whatever it was – and they didn't come out. At least not . . . intact. Five of them to date.'

'What is it?'

'Yes, well, we wanted to know that too, as a matter of some urgency. The only thing we were able to find out initially was that it had some connection to Potash. So we sent one of our men in to try and find out.'

'And did he?'

There was a brief pause before Strath answered.

'I think the best thing, perhaps, is if you meet him.' He reached out and laid a hand on Louis' forearm. 'I should warn you, you might find it a bit . . . unnerving.'

This was all starting to feel very familiar to Louis, which was unnerving in itself.

'Just so you know, I've been stung like this before,' he said, assuming Strath would pick up on the reference to the fake iron lung, where all of this had begun for him.

'Yes,' was all Strath said, but again there was that gravity in his tone that seemed to carry its own authority, dispelling any sense of deception. He looked through the porthole in the secure door, then stepped back.

The sound of three keys turning one after the other, and then the door opened, inward. A white-coated orderly backed out pulling a wheelchair, in which sat a dressing-gowned figure, slumped to one side.

'Patient Paul, meet Lieutenant Colonel Richmond.'

Louis might have bristled at Strath's persistence in using that asinine alias, but when the wheelchair was swivelled around, it pushed those thoughts from his head. He went cold. The man wasn't disfigured in any way, and yet the visceral sensation Louis experienced was as if he'd just seen somebody who'd been shot in the face and survived. That very particular mix of pity, disgust, and self-reproach for feeling disgust at all. Except the man's face was unmarred. He was in his late thirties, maybe forty. He had thinning rust-coloured hair that was neatly brushed and flattened in a severe side parting, together with a full bushy moustache. On the surface he was an ordinary-looking chap, the kind you wouldn't glance at twice if he were sitting opposite you in a railway carriage or a waiting room. And yet in his eyes, in the haunted and vacant expression on his face, in the frozen clutch of his pale hands, in the smell of illness and old age around him, there was something terrible, something dreadful – the sense of a young, healthy man who'd had his vitality and his sanity taken from him.

'Colonel Richmond was operating undercover behind enemy lines in Czechoslovakia when he disappeared. We assumed he'd been captured. But under normal circumstances, if that had been the case, we'd have been made aware of the fact pretty quickly.'

Louis was listening to Strath, but every so often, rather like looking into one of Boileau's dream boxes, his eyes were pulled back to the man in the wheelchair, who just sat there looking straight ahead. Louis noticed that his fingers moved individually in some random sequence, as if he were pressing the keys of an invisible typewriter.

'We heard nothing. No snide attempt to humiliate us with his arrest and exposure. No request for a prisoner swap. None of what you'd expect in those circumstances.'

'And his mission had been to find out about this Funhouse?' Louis had lowered his voice, as if out of consideration for the unfortunate agent.

'Yes, he'd been charged with finding out what it was. Where it was. What happened in there. General information-gathering. Anything he could discover. Anything at all.'

'And you think they put him in there?'

'Yes.'

'And . . . this is the result?'

'It rather seems that way. Sadly, he's not able to tell us about it.'

'Does he . . . talk at all?'

'Sometimes. Why don't you ask him something?'

Louis' stomach tightened. He'd rather avoid engagement with this human shell if he could. It reminded him of something from his childhood – his early childhood, before the war, when he'd been at his school in Freiberg. They'd been taken to sing Christmas carols to the men in the old soldiers' hospital. He hadn't thought much about it until two days before, when one of his schoolmates, Werner Fuchs, had told them about the horrors they were going to see in there: 'There's men with no legs from the stomach down. There's a man with his face missing and he's still alive. He can only drink. He lives on warm milk and beef soup.' Louis had dismissed this as Werner showing off, teasing, wanting to scare them. But when they'd been ushered into the small assembly hall in the hospital and the audience had been brought in, some of them on crutches, most of them in wheelchairs, he realised that Werner had been telling the truth. It was like being sprayed with freezing water. In that moment he'd have given anything to get out of there, rather than having to sing to them, to take in their ruin. He'd focused on every single word of 'Alle Jahre Wieder' just so he didn't disgrace himself by revealing anything of what he felt.

And now he had the same feeling, even though there was no physical sign of injury before him.

'Colonel Richmond?' He spoke softly, as gently as he could.

The man surprised him by turning his head sharply. It was almost a jerk, a bird-like motion. He fixed his empty eyes on Louis'. Two holes in their centres where a person should be.

'Colonel Richmond. Can I ask you something?'

No answer.

'Can I ask you if you . . . know anything about the Funhouse?'

He waited. It was a stupid question, of course, because he'd clearly been asked it already, many times. And the initial moment of silence made him think there wasn't going to be any answer at all. But then he realised it wasn't silence. There was a low moan, like a distant wind, that built very quickly. It was a rumble, a purr in the man's chest, and as it rose in volume, it formed into a groan. It was like language, but a language without words. The groan transformed itself into violent bursts of sound, low-pitched screams, one after the other, the cry of a desperate animal caught in a trap, trying to tear its own leg off. And all the time Colonel Richmond's empty eyes held Louis', like a lover.

After a few seconds of this, Strath nodded at the orderly and the creature was wheeled, still raving, back through the door.

'Yes. I'm afraid that's the most we can get from him,' said Strath, as the slamming of the door echoed tightly around the tiled chamber.

'What happens in there?' asked Louis, glancing over Strath's shoulder to the glass porthole.

'We look after him as best we can.' Strath smiled, in a melancholy way.

Louis had a sudden memory of the man in the iron lung. Was he like a gullible spectator to a magic trick, being forced the same card twice? He could have made the point out loud. He'd already alluded to it. But he decided to keep the question to himself. He had others.

'Did they do anything to him physically? Brain surgery? Lobotomy?'

'We gave him an extremely thorough physical examination, under sedation. No signs of scarring on the scalp, on the head, inside his nose or on the roof of his mouth. Teeth intact. X-rays revealed nothing. The same could be said for the rest of his body.

All clear and clean, in good physical condition. There was some muscle wastage around the middle of the body. The only aberration was one small scar, about an inch and a half, to the right of his abdomen. Again, X-rays revealed nothing. In truth, until he dies and is given a post-mortem, we can't know for sure what that was about.

'And he was found with the dream box on him?'

'No, no. That was in his things, in the apartment he was renting, well concealed beneath a loose floorboard – a safe location only his liaison knew about.'

'Where was he found – after his disappearance?'

'He was left at his place of work. The place where he was supposed to be working as part of his cover, that is. He was as he is now, as you've just encountered him. Doubly incontinent. Even more distressed. We got him back as quickly as we could.'

Louis took in the information, reviewing it and storing it away.

'I'd like to go back to my room now,' he said to Strath, simply.

One thing was clear beyond doubt: Louis had to determine to his own satisfaction that this man Richmond's condition was real; that he wasn't being played once again by someone else's carefully constructed deception. He'd had enough of that. There was an old Chinese proverb: 'A person must fall in a hole many times before they learn to walk around it.' He was determined to speed up that process as far as he could. He flung open the door of his room and started yelling, undeterred by the fact that it was 3.45 in the morning.

'Hello! Hello. Staff. Hello.' He was bellowing so loudly that a middle-aged nurse in starched pale blue uniform appeared within a moment, as if he'd summoned a genie.

'What's all this shouting? What's the matter?' Her irritation was unsurprising. Inevitably, perhaps, the orderly running of her ward came before the comfort of her patients.

'I need to speak to Strath. Now.'

'What are you talking about?'

'I need to speak to him now. Within twenty minutes.'

'You need to—'|

'Listen to me! Listen. Your lords and masters want me to do something for them. But I will not do it unless Strath is here within twenty minutes. And you will be responsible for that. You alone. It will have been your choice And I will make that very clear to your superiors.'

The nurse glowered at him, but she could see the intent in his eyes.

When Strath arrived, he was muted, but not dishevelled. He was a senior military man after all. He would have had a war full of being woken at ungodly hours, and his rise through the ranks would have been driven in part by his ability to show up, alert and useful, at a moment's notice, regardless of the time.

'Explain,' was all he said.

'I want to know,' Louis said calmly, straightforwardly, 'that his condition is exactly as you described it to me. Seeing him at the shortest possible notice will give me confirmation of that. No costume, no preparation, no actor playing a part.'

'I see.'

'I also need to see every piece of documentation that you have to hand concerning Colonel Richmond. Don't bother with any excuses about official secrets or national security.'

'Very well,' said Strath, who clearly grasped why Louis was asking for what he was asking for.

The documentation arrived before Colonel Richmond did. There was an identity card, a file with a haphazard selection of his military papers: letters of promotion, certificates of rank, medical reports. There was a pile of personal effects: letters from family members, membership cards to the Army & Navy Club and the RAC, a library card. Everything seemed authentic. There were no signs of faux ageing or post-hoc paper-crumbling, methods Louis was all too familiar with. In fact, the best testament to the authenticity of what was to hand was both its volume and its arbitrary nature. What he knew of Operation Mincemeat, where a fake personality had been created around a dead body in order to fool the Nazi High Command, was the surprisingly small amount of information that the fraud rested on. There must have been about five times as much material piled up here on his bed now. These were genuine items, and they proved beyond reasonable doubt that Colonel Richmond was a genuine individual.

At least four of the documents had his photograph attached, including a group picture from his passing-out ceremony at the Army Training Regiment in Winchester. Louis was holding this one when the door of his room opened. There was a loud bark, a sound of distress and aversion of the kind a frightened animal might make. Louis looked up and saw Colonel Richmond, in pyjamas and tartan dressing gown but with bare feet. His toenails were neatly clipped and filed, as if by a pedicurist, an odd detail, but one that signalled the level of care the man was receiving.

'I'm sorry to disturb you, Colonel Richmond, at such an early hour.' Louis' statement hung there, sounding absurd in his own ears. And yet the man turned to look at him, the same alarming emptiness, or brokenness, in the centre of his eyes. Louis held his gaze for a moment, searching for something he recognised. And that was the thing ultimately that convinced him of the reality of Richmond's state: the very alienness of what he found there. Whatever state the man was in, it was something Louis didn't recognise, couldn't understand, had never encountered before. If this wasn't true, then nothing was.

'Thank you,' he said, nodding to both the lieutenant colonel and Strath.

Strath turned to the orderly and indicated that he could wheel Richmond back. As they set off, the man made a noise somewhere between a low growl and a whimper. Louis may well have been imagining things by now, but it seemed like it was intended for his ears. Was it too fanciful to think it was a warning?

19

From Louis' point of view, things moved rather quickly from there on in. It seemed many elements of the exercise had already been in the planning stages. Colonel Richmond had been deployed in Czechoslovakia, so that was where Louis was to be sent. Fortunately, he already spoke the language, since it was used around the house when he was young (his grandfather had referred to it as 'Bohemian'). The familiarity, the connection it gave him to a past that he'd worked so hard to bury over the past decade or more made the sessions he spent with his trainer unexpectedly emotional. In the turbulence of having his post-war life torn away from him, he appreciated the fact that it gave him something else to hold on to, however tenuous. Did that mean there was to be an element of going home in what was to come? It was a thought he had never allowed himself. He kept it close to his heart. It certainly wasn't something he was going to admit to Strath.

Strath's department had compiled a modest list of new identities based on deceased Czechoslovakians who in their own country would be categorised as 'missing, presumed dead'. One individual stood out to Louis – a man who'd been in his early twenties when he died, without any known spouse. He was called Radoslav Kaznelson. After the Germans rolled into France in June 1940, Kaznelson had fled to Great Britain and joined the Czechoslovak depot at RAF Cosford. He ended up flying in 313 Squadron and lost his life in 1942, in the Dieppe Raid.

'A brave young man, who despised the Nazis by all accounts,' Strath said. 'I don't think he'd mind his name being used in this way. Hard to see him approving of Potash's tactics, don't you think?'

Louis didn't answer. He just looked at the tiny, faded photograph on the dead man's enlistment papers. He wasn't yet completely sure about this idea of doing as he was told. But he was keeping those doubts to himself.

'One other thing that will be useful to us,' said Strath. 'Kaznelson was an orphan, according to his papers. Makes him more of a *tabula rasa* from the point of view of officialdom, much harder to cross-check retrospectively.'

Louis nodded. The reasoning was sound.

'Now,' said Strath, 'if he was a magician – which we want him to be, of course, if he is to catch Potash's eye as a potential recruit – what stage name might he take?'

'Something punchy and alliterative, perhaps,' said Louis, searching his own mental catalogue of performers' alter egos, 'with a tie to his actual name. Like . . . Karel Kay?'

'Excellent,' said Strath, 'and very convincing. Patient Paul, from here on in, I dub you Radoslav Kaznelson, aka Karel Kay. Karel Kay the Extraordinary.'

'Karel Kay Mimořádný,' said Louis, correcting him.

Now that the job of building his new identity was under way, Louis had been moved to an airbase a few miles away at Odiham. He was barracked there in a private room, with everything that was needed for his training at hand. He was aware that he was still under close observation, but as a mark of growing trust, he'd noticed that doors were no longer routinely locked. As the tempo of preparations picked up, Strath called him to a formal briefing in a small room overlooking an expansive airfield. Every so often planes hummed in and out, underlining the fact that all too soon Louis would be on one of them.

'Objective one,' said Strath, 'is to find out as much information as you can about the Funhouse: where it is, how it works, what techniques are used. Objective two is to infiltrate Potash's outfit, the Kolduny, and gain any intelligence you can about their operations. Of these objectives, it's the former that is of paramount urgency, but it's the latter that is of the greater importance. If you can convincingly embed yourself in the Kolduny, win Potash's trust, that will be of incalculable value. If you fear you're under suspicion at any point, there may be an argument for cutting and running with any information about the Funhouse you've managed to gain.'

'Can I just say at this point that we are missing a trick,' said Louis, 'by not drawing on some civilian expertise in our preparations.'

Strath looked at him, his expression shifting from donnish to something more martial.

'The perfect man, or rather man and woman, for a job like this. Ivan and Phyllis, who used—'

Abruptly Strath swivelled, grabbing a lengthy wooden ruler from the gutter of the blackboard and swiping it down with tremendous force on the desk a few inches from Louis' fingers. If he had been less accurate in his aim, those fingers would undoubtedly have been broken.

'No! Never. Do you understand me. Warlock is dead and his associates are dead to you. They have no existence for you, for me. No relevance. They are dead. All of them.' These words were shouted not just with force, Louis was surprised to discern, but with anger. 'Do you understand, Kaznelson? Do you understand me?'

'Yes.'

'Yes, what?'

'Yes, sir.'

'Yes, sir. You are Radoslav Kaznelson, formerly of 313 Squadron, returning Czechoslovakian citizen, and if you doubt that, we may as well return you to Wandsworth and put the noose around your neck for real, because that will be an infinitely preferable outcome to what is likely to follow.' Strath stared Louis straight in the eye. This wasn't theatre on his part. It was fact.

His fury was chastening. But it served to make Louis' own barely contained anger resurface. He'd been corralled into this position by events, by other people's decisions, by fate, by everything other than his own will. He'd been torn from his life, his friends, his career, his reputation, his loves, his future, his hopes, for the second time in his life. And if he ignored Strath and somehow managed to contact the Brains Trust (even though he had failed before), the consequences that would follow were unpalatable, unthinkable. Not so much his own death – which would probably come sooner rather than later in one way or another – but the outcome for Danny, Phyllis, Ivan and even Beulah, which would be imprisonment for aiding and abetting treason. And for Dinah. Dinah locked up, deprived of her youth, her life . . .

There was another decision Louis could make. Take the anger and use it. Focus it. Like a follow spot on stage, direct it at Potash. Let it burn him when it found him. Potash was the source of all this, Potash was the cause. Let him suffer the consequences of his actions. He must be the target of this rage.

In the end, Kaznelson's story came easily to Louis. He wrote it up in a single morning, as if it was a school composition exercise: 'Pen portraits. You have a double period to explain what happened to Radoslav Kaznelson after he was shot down over France during the Dieppe Raid in August 1942.' Having been washed up on the beach, Louis decided, he made his way inland and hid in a barn on a small farm. Something terrible happened there, which Kaznelson will not speak of to this day (the implication being that he murdered an old farmer in order to have somewhere to hide out until the end of the war, living on the produce without having to venture into town). Carrying the guilt and shame of this, he made his way across Europe scratching a living as an itinerant worker: pot-washing, fruit-picking, labouring. After the war, he settled for a time in Liège, gaining work at a small *pension*, where he tried to maintain a stable life and forget the traumas of the previous five years. In this he was no different to half the population. He rekindled his childhood love of magic and started performing small shows in the bar. With this new-found skill, he was able to move on, playing at children's parties and working as a street performer (Louis thought it wise to keep the engagements semi-professional, making double-checking with existing venues impossible and unnecessary).

Having tired of this itinerant existence, and as a communist sympathiser driven by hatred of the Nazis, Kaznelson set his heart upon returning to his home country after the Soviet invasion in 1948. Given his orphan status, and his desire to put the horrors of the war behind him, adopting a low profile and choosing to start again in Prague made more sense than returning to the Košice of his youth.

Strath read the account over quickly, a smile growing across his face.

'Pretty good trick. Perhaps your best.'

'What do you mean?'

'Being able to conjure a whole life from nothing. From nowhere.' He looked down at the paper, as if the subject was trapped within it, captive in a cage. 'I feel for you, Kaznelson, I really do,' he said. 'You've had a rough old time. I hope you find some solace on the stage.'

'There's nothing like the glare of the limelight for blotting out the horrors of the world beyond,' said Louis, meaning every word.

Vienna had been exciting when he'd first arrived. In the dark, as the black Lancia Aurelia had rolled them through the streets from the airfield into the city centre, only a small amount of it was lit, so it was easy for Louis to project the memory of his one visit in childhood on to the fragments presented to him through the black glass: lights in high windows; slivers of narrow cobbled streets like the skin on some huge reptile's back; elegant stonework, slices of baroque architecture caught in the spill of street light – it was all as he remembered it. And most unexpectedly, a sudden wave of joy washed over him. It was the recollection of the Wurstelprater – the amusement park dominated by the huge wheel of the Riesenrad. But it wasn't just the idea of the wheel that enchanted; it was everything that went with it: the smell of cotton candy mingled with cigarette smoke in the cold evening air; the thrum and rattle of the engines that turned the carousels; the swoosh of the swing boats; the shrieks and cries and calls of excitement, adults and children alike, the thrill of danger harnessed for entertainment. It had been everything that he loved, distilled into half a mile of concrete and wood and iron and coloured light bulbs – the promise of magic in the darkness.

That magic didn't last. Even as the lights of the city brought ripples of his past to him, thoughts of what actually lay ahead returned all too quickly, like an overflowing tide.

'We can get you into Vienna. That's straightforward enough,' Strath had told him in his final briefing. 'What comes after will be trickier.'

'Why?' Louis had asked.

'Don't be dumb, Kay.' Strath had already taken to referring to Louis this way. If it began sounding like an affectation, it very quickly transformed into a new norm, for Strath at least. 'How do you think we're going to get you to Prague, hmm? Fly you in on a Bristol Britannia? There are three walls of barbed wire, eight feet high, between Austria and Czechoslovakia. And on the other side, a huge clearing strewn with landmines. And where there aren't landmines, the fence has six thousand volts running through it. It's nicely decorated in places. The bodies hang off it like baubles on a Christmas tree.'

'I'm looking forward to it more by the hour,' said Louis.

When he awoke on his first morning in Vienna, what he saw soon extinguished the little spark of joy any nostalgia had kindled. There was more rubble than architecture, at least in the district he could see from his hotel window. Many of the baroque buildings appeared to be still standing, but they were mostly facades, like ghostly sets on a broken stage. Even the Prater, he would soon discover, was smashed and weed-bound, with most of its attractions gone, though the Riesenrad still turned slowly and mournfully, like some animated monument to the agony of war.

Still, that first night had not been without comforts. He was barracked at the Hotel Sacher, just round the corner from the Café Mozart. Apparently it had become the sole preserve of British officers involved in the occupation. In Louis' childhood (and long before that), the Sacher had been Vienna's equivalent to the Savoy. Its velvet-curtained Red Bar had catered to the highest of Viennese society. Now it seemed to be a kind of souped-up officers' mess, serving sausages and beans and NAAFI-style tea to the senior soldiers who lounged about on noticeably threadbare settees and dining chairs.

It was here, in one of the dark-walled cubbyholes, that Louis encountered his Viennese contact from British Field Security. He had been informed he would be met by someone in civilian dress called Devon, who worked as a fixer on the division's behalf. He didn't have any more information than that.

He had been told to wait in the Red Bar, where Devon would find him. After half an hour and a second cup of lukewarm tea, made almost undrinkable by the condensed milk it was served with, he was about to leave, assuming that either Devon wasn't coming or he himself was in the wrong place. It was only as he stood up to go and leave a message at the understaffed reception desk that he noticed a tall, fair-haired woman staring at him. She strode towards him with surprising purpose.

'Kay?'

'Yes?' said Louis, keeping his still-awkward reaction to the use of his new name veiled.

'Devon.' She moved her zippered folio into her left hand and held her right hand out. 'Journey all right?' She must have been in her late thirties. She exuded a severe, unshakeable authority.

'Very good, actually. It's a long time since I've been anywhere, so it was rather a treat.' Louis smiled broadly, trying to keep up. No one had told him his liaison was to be a woman. Devon herself didn't acknowledge anything out of the ordinary, continuing in a brisk and sober manner.

'Good. I don't know how much you know, but the most important thing you need to understand is that Austria is still sliced up into its four zones – American, French, British and Soviet. Vienna itself is entirely surrounded by the Soviet zone. So this is not a safe place.'

'I have to say, coming from London, it doesn't feel that way.' Again Louis smiled, grinned even, wanting to infect this woman with some warmth so they could communicate properly. But still there was nothing back from Devon, no reaction at all. She clearly didn't waste words. Perhaps he wouldn't even have noticed this if she'd been a man. But because she wasn't, he instinctively found himself reaching out, trying to establish some kind of emotional connection.

'The city too is divided into four sectors, apart from the First District, the Innere Stadt, which is policed collectively. That's the key to the little intelligence we've gained about what's going on in Czechoslovakia. It also affords us opportunities to probe and provoke. And as far as your mission is concerned, it gives us a place to recruit you a second, which is what we're going to need to get you to Prague alive.'

'Do I get a say in who that person might be?' said Louis, who had switched into a businesslike mode himself. If breezy charm wasn't going to get him anywhere, emulation might.

'That's not how I've planned it.'

'Well, it's how *I'd* like to plan it.'

'With respect, Kay, I'm in charge of running this side of the operation. I'll select the personnel.'

'With equal respect, Miss Devon, it's my life that hangs in the balance when it comes to that choice, so I'd like to participate.'

'I don't know what assumptions you might be making, Kay, but let's get them out of the way now, shall we. My authority is no different from any other officer you might serve under. I was an active member of the resistance behind enemy lines throughout the war, and I've faced tougher decisions than any you're likely to have made at any point in your career. This isn't an ENSA casting call. Understand? At any one time we have a very modest pool to draw on.'

'Sounds *exactly* like an ENSA casting call.' Louis' hope was that a joke might leaven things, rebalance this testy beginning. Was that the flicker of a smile from Devon? Was there a human being under there after all? 'I understand,' he continued, thinking it might be wise to show he was capitulating. 'I'm not looking to question your command. I just want a little input. That's all.'

It was agreed that they would reconvene the next day at Schönbrunn Barracks, on the edge of the city. This was where military intelligence ran their operations from and where Devon had her office. As Louis rolled his way across the city in his transport jeep, he observed that many of the buildings they passed had the same three Russian words stencilled on their corners: очищен от врага. He asked the taciturn driver if he knew what it meant.

'"Cleared of enemy",' he said. 'The Russians drove the Nazis out house by house round here.'

The war had ended over eight years ago, but only as a date on the calendar. In people's lives, in their minds, it was clearly still rumbling on. Not just in the stubborn Soviet graffiti, but in their emotions, their shattered sense of who they were, what their life was, their civilisation. There was to be no relief.

Devon was waiting for him with a cup of cocoa. It was watery, and not particularly sweet, but Louis was grateful for it. Somehow it was another little human touch from this woman who otherwise maintained her impenetrably formal edifice.

'As I was explaining yesterday, you need a second to get you safely to Prague. We can get you across here . . .' Devon gestured to an area on a map pinned to the wall. 'Plenty of forest. And the terrain limits the border patrols. Once you're a couple of miles north-west of here, you should be fine. But there's only so much you can learn about the territory from a map. You'll need a native to chaperone you once you're there. Someone who knows the place well.'

'And what kind of person might that be?'

'Well, it's luck of the draw, generally speaking. Who's been picked up by field operatives. Who we're able to cajole, coerce, threaten into giving us their assistance.'

'Threaten?'

'Kay, this is what you need to understand. We don't have a vast profusion of trained double agents to hand. In fact, the actual number answering to that description is currently around zero. There is a resistance movement on the other side, but it's chaotic and spasmodic in its effectiveness. So instead, if we have something we need to do over there, someone to spy on troop movements, say, or to get a radio set to the resistance, or some forged papers, we generally have to make use of an individual who's just defected. That means persuading someone who's risked life and limb getting over the border, tunnelling, or swimming, or just running, to go back over there, right back to the hell from whence they came.'

'You don't have trained couriers to do that?' Louis was a little shocked.

'We did. But the border's been tightened recently on their side. A whole network of operatives has recently been rolled up.

And now we're back to square one. So instead, we have to find someone we can motivate. Someone who wants a new life in Britain or Australia.'

Louis wasn't prepared for the first candidate. Again he'd assumed it would be a man. So when a young girl who looked like she was still a teenager came in, he was a little startled.

'Kay, this is Miss Stivin. She's been with us for over a month now.'

'Miss Stivin.' Louis stood up and nodded as politely as possible. The girl seemed terrified. 'Would you mind if I asked you a few questions?'

She looked to Devon, as if she was frightened of getting it wrong. Devon nodded her assent. Miss Stivin was a slight figure, emaciated even, with dark circles under her eyes. A prominent nose and high cheekbones gave her face a bird-like mien.

'Do you speak English?'

'Bit.' She looked down, shy and uncomfortable.

'That's all right,' Louis said in Czech. 'We can just talk normally.' This was a good opportunity for him to do so, given that in a few days he was going to have to do this routinely. She was immediately relieved.

'How did you make it over here?'

'I walked.'

'How did you get past the border guards? That's not easy, surely.'

'I went at night. I walked. Then I swam.'

'She was picked up on our side of the Morava river,' said Devon, whose Czech was obviously serviceable enough to follow what was being discussed.

'Why did you come?'

'They were going to court-martial me. Send me away.'

'Why?'

'I was in the Zemědělská Divize.'

'What we'd call a Land Girl,' said Devon.

'I was posted in Malacky. My grandmother was ill. I wanted to go and see her. They said no. I had to work. I went anyway.'

'Did they catch you?'

'No. I came back. But then they arrested me. For being away without leave.'

'You're a brave girl.'

'They've been good to me here. But they ask lots of questions I don't know the answers to. Will they send me back?' There was fear on her pale face. And a great need. Because Louis could speak her language, she immediately assumed a kinship. She did not want to go back.

'It's all right, Miss Stivin. Nobody wants to send you back. Thank you.' Louis nodded to Devon. There was no point in questioning her any more.

The obvious truth occurred to him as she shuffled out of the room: the place she was so desperate to flee from was the very place he was trying to get into. Hopefully the next candidate for Sancho Panza to his Don Quixote would have more potential.

'OK,' he said. 'Shall we see number two?'

'I'm afraid that's it,' said Devon, without looking up from her notes.

'What?'

'There was another. An older man. A black marketeer. But he was shot by the Soviets trying to steal copper wiring in their sector.'

'So that's it.'

'It's not ideal. But she has good local knowledge. And she looks younger than she is. Paired with you, she'll deflect suspicion.'

'She doesn't want to go.'

'No one would, Kay. But we're offering her the chance of a better life. a speedy and guaranteed passage straight into a new identity in the free world. No long years in a squalid refugee camp on half-rations. No grinding uncertainty or fear of deportation. Instead, instant freedom – upon accomplishment of the mission.'

'You could give her that anyway.'

Devon looked up, straight at him, considering her reply. There was something unfathomable in that moment's silence. Something that spoke of her own youth, scarred as Louis' had been.

'If only we could, Kay. If only we could.' And she returned her attention to her clipboard, ticking off an item before returning her pen to her pocket.

FRAGILE ANIMATION

I want to share with you one of the last
times I was well and truly fooled. The
biggest lesson I learned was that the thing
that fooled me wasn't the method. You'll
see.

Whenever I could, in my old life, my
blessed life, I used to spend my Sunday
mornings walking through Petticoat Lane
market. For those who have never
experienced the joy, it is a truly giddy
mix of the latest fashions, fruit and veg,
and London's finest grafters pitching their
swindles. Many of the lessons I have
learned in terms of structuring an act have
come from these mavens. The clarity needed
in building your tip, setting up stall,
shpeiling them in and then passing the
bottle is fundamentally the same as any
great magic routine.

If you follow their example, your act
will have a great foundation.

Building your tip
- Why exactly are you there? What mystery
  is about to unfold?

Setting up stall
- What are you selling? What premise is so

incredible that the crowd dare not leave
for fear of missing something amazing?

Shpeiling them in
- How do you keep them watching you?

Passing the bottle
- Bring it to a punchy close and make the
sale. What's your killer finish that
means they simply have to applaud? And
then buy what's on offer?

One particular morning as I strolled
down the lane, I heard the strains of Kay
Starr's 'Comes A-Long A-Love' drifting from
a nearby café's jukebox. Standing outside
was a man clapping his hands in time to the
music as he *shpeilled* to the crowd: 'He
doesn't need feeding, my love . . . all he
needs to keep him happy is a good tune.
Shame the same can't be said for your old
fella.' The lady, her rather rotund husband
and the crowd roared with laughter.
I pushed myself to the front and
couldn't quite believe what I was seeing. A
small cardboard sign read 'Dancing Charlie
Chaplin', and there on the floor by the
man's feet was a paper cut-out of the
Little Tramp himself. The likeness was fine
enough; the pencil-drawn black suit, bowler
hat, walking stick and moustache made it
unmistakably Chaplin. Incredibly, the four-
inch-high paper doll was standing upright,
bobbing and dancing to the beat of the
music from the café.
'He bounces and moves, and not just to
swing tunes, my darling; tickle his tummy
and whisper the dance you want him to do

and he'll do it for ya.' As he said that, the man bent down, lifted the paper doll up from the pavement and handed him to the lady. 'Go on, my darling . . . whisper what you want him to do.'

The laughing woman did as she was asked, and as she whispered, the grafter bellowed, 'I can read lips, you naughty girl. He ain't gonna do that for two bob, it's Charlie Chaplin, not your milkman!'

The crowd exploded with laughter as he took the doll back from the lady and held it up by its head. 'This little marvel hides a secret invented by the Yanks that baffled the great Winston Churchill himself.' With that, he put the doll back on the pavement, and unbelievably, it started dancing immediately. 'He'll dance on your table, dance on your floor, dance in your kitchen and dance by your door. This is my last few, and when they're gone . . . they're gone for good.'

With that, the grafter grabbed half a dozen envelopes from his pocket. 'In this envelope you get Charlie, you get the secret technology and I've even gone to the trouble of writing out a list of the songs he most enjoys! Today only, two bob. Who wants one?'

The crowd couldn't buy them fast enough, and once the half-dozen in his hand had gone, he opened his suitcase showing at least another hundred ready for sale.

I walked away, my new 'Dancing Charlie Chaplin' envelope in hand, excited that I now possessed the secret. As soon as I opened the envelope, I had the dawning moment of realisation that despite my vast knowledge, I was no better than the rest of the *schmucks* who'd just thrown their hard-earned two bob down. Even more humiliating, it was a method I knew so well. The envelope contained a tatty piece of paper with Charlie Chaplin drawn on it, another piece of paper with a list of ten songs written on it, and finally the hidden 'technology' . . . a line of fine cotton thread. The instructions on the reverse of the song list simply stated:

1 Tie one end of the cotton to the leg of a chair
2 Tie the other end to your ankle
3 Hang the paper doll from the small flap at the back of his bowler hat
4 Tap your foot and watch him dance

That was it! As you read this, do not disregard the brilliant simplicity of this method. Try it at home and you'll be amazed how wonderful it looks.

Once my frustration subsided, I was reminded of young magician Ron Macmillan's adage: 'If it fools you, it's threads or magnets.' And yet I felt utter joy too. Why? Had the grafter just stood there silent while the puppet danced, I would have looked at it and in a heartbeat worked it out. But no, the *shpeil* and the laughter had created a concealing fog around it. I was fully fooled and I didn't even mind; it felt fantastic. Once again, the lethal misdirection lay within the performance and the story. When I heard there was a secret American technology involved, I was sent off in a spin of what that might be. It was perfect.

A fragile bit of cotton and a
delicious, charming lie had me drawn in and
gleefully parting with money I could barely
afford. When performing your tricks,
remember that dancing Charlie Chaplin and
bring them to life. In the words of
legendary magician Max Malini, 'We are all
lambs to the slaughter at the hands of the
right butcher.'*

-----
* I pass on another tip to you. Always be on the
lookout for opportunities. I went back to Petticoat
Lane the following week and fooled the grafter with
a couple of tricks of my own. I taught him them in
exchange for him letting me work the stand with him.
He was happy for the break as his knees were shot.
Six months later I bought the site from him and
boosted my income grafting for the next year. Sell a
man a Charlie Chaplin and make him dance, and he'll
feed himself for life!

20

Dinah stood in the small queue at the Empire, shaking out her umbrella. It was raining outside; not hard, but there was a constant drizzle. You only had to walk ten yards and you were soaked, as if by a proper downpour. She didn't mind the wait. The foyer of the Empire was palatial. She'd always liked looking up at the twin chandeliers and the wood panelling, as if she were in some stately home rather than the middle of the West End. This was the second time she'd seen the film. *Genevieve*. A silly comedy with John Gregson and Kenneth More about a race to get to Brighton in old cars. She didn't really care for it. She just liked being transported somewhere else for an hour and a half, away from the thought that devoured her. Louis Warlock, his absence and the hole it had made inside her.

She stayed there for most of the movie, but by the time Genevieve was crossing Westminster Bridge, she'd had enough. She'd determined where she was going to go next. It was only 5.15.

It was a short walk, barely five minutes, round the back of the cinema and up Gerrard Place. Monsieur Vignaud stayed open until six o'clock. He remained quietly welcoming, pleased to see her, gently sympathetic without a hint of patronising pity. He didn't question why she was there; he just let her go up the stairs to the third floor as if she were a paying tenant.

Dinah lifted the port box, stood there staring for a moment at the squat silver wire recorder, the black cabling that Danny had rigged up emerging from its back like a tail, worming its way into the wall. It might ring again. Why couldn't it? If she stayed here long enough, she might be here when it did.

She sat down with her back against the wall, staring at the machine as if it were an oracle, as if it might give her information about what lay heaviest in her heart.

It wasn't the fact that Louis was alive somewhere, unable to get in touch with them. It was the fact that she somehow knew he was in danger, in terrible danger. Three and a half years of simulating a psychic connection had allowed her to internalise the idea that it might actually be real. Louis would be the first to dismiss it as a fantasy. But wherever he was, Dinah could feel it, the thing that was coming for him, like a black shape hiding in the thickest fog. And there was nothing she could do to stop it.

'It's not fair to the girl. She's risked everything coming over here already. For us to send her back . . . She's little more than a child.'

Louis had been troubled in the night. The thought of forcing that young girl back into the peril she'd just managed to escape for the sake of his mission seemed unconscionable. 'What exactly are we offering her if she does this?' he asked.

'A fast track to a new life in Australia, all her papers, full citizenship.' Devon barely looked up from her clipboard.

'And what if she doesn't help us – what's the likely outcome for her?'

'The way things are at the moment? Minimum of six months in the refugee camp, maybe a year. No guaranteed outcome. It's quite possible they'll hear her case and hand her over to the Soviets.'

'Are you saying she might actually end up being worse off than if she got picked up in Czechoslovakia?'

'It's a serious possibility.'

'If I take her, I'm giving you notice now that I'm going to do everything I can to see she gets back.'

Devon contemplated this for a moment, before speaking. When she did, it was calm and unequivocal.

'It's your neck at the end of the day. If that's your preference, so be it.'

'Noted,' said Louis calmly.

'Is that all?' asked Devon, who was clearly keen to get on with the rest of her day.

'There is one other thing,' said Louis.

'Yes?'

'I'll need a vent doll.'

'A what?'

'A ventriloquist's dummy.'

'Why?'

'Because I've been thinking. They'll be on the lookout for any new magician who suddenly arrives in town from nowhere. And that's a conundrum, because the fact is, I want to gain the attention of the Kolduny's "talent scouts". But there are other ways of getting on variety bills.'

Devon sat silently for another few moments before speaking.

'Kay, my knowledge of your mission and its objectives is limited. My main responsibility is to get you across the border safely and without detection. But ventriloquism, conjuring, juggling and any other kind of fairground chicanery are simply beyond my expertise and judgement.'

'I don't need your help. I just need to go shopping. Find a ventriloquist's dummy.'

'You'll have to be chaperoned.' She sighed. 'I suppose I can spare somebody. Does it have to be now?'

'Yes.'

'Very well.'

The private's name was Millican. A refreshingly chatty young man from the north of England who turned out to be surprisingly good company. There was a large indoor flea market in the remains of an old tram depot in the city's Neubau district. They'd gone in on the off chance, on their way to a costume shop near the Theater an der Wien. The place was expansive and busy, a mixture of legitimate traders with stands and painted signs and more desperate-looking individuals with impromptu collections of their worldly possessions, hoping to make enough money to feed themselves and their families for another week.

'Do you know what a vent doll looks like?' Louis had said to Millican, who clearly saw his current posting as a day's paid holiday.

'Sure! Like Archie Andrews. Or Charlie Brown.'

'Spot on. OK, let's split up.' Louis saw Millican stiffen. The soldier had obviously been given orders not to let Louis out of his sight. 'Private, you can trust me. I'm not going to make a run for it.'

'Orders are orders, sir.'

And Louis knew that was true. 'All right, but we can walk the aisles together, yes? I'll look on one side and you look on the other.'

It was as they were doing this that Louis began to feel uneasy. He had the prickly sense that he was being followed. Was this just paranoia, after his conversation with Devon? Or was it legitimate instinct? There was a feeling that somebody behind was pausing whenever he did, and picking up speed at the same time too. While he was trying to work out whether this was actually the case, Millican pulled at his sleeve, like a little boy.

'I think I've spotted something.'

As casually as possible, Louis turned around and let Millican lead him to a stall about twenty yards back. Behind a collection of old toys, wooden cars, train sets, doll's houses and xylophones was something bulky and green with a grotesque brightly coloured head sporting locks of rough grey-brown hair with a protruding tuft at the top. The hinged jaw, separate from the rest of the carved face, immediately spoke of puppetry. This was not a conventional ventriloquist's dummy, neatly made and professionally costumed. It looked more like something thrown together by an amateur, or a parent on behalf of a child. The costume, such as it was, seemed to be a First World War Russian army jacket with papier-mâché hands sewn into the sleeves, and child's trousers with a pair of little boy's boots attached. Nevertheless, with a touch of paint and a bit of imagination, it could provide Louis with exactly what he needed.

'OK, here's what I want you to do,' he said softly. 'Go to the stall and without drawing attention to yourself buy that dummy.'

'The big ugly thing?'

'Exactly. But I want you to buy three or four other things too. Doesn't matter what, but make them memorable, so that the dummy becomes just another item of bric-a-brac. See if they'll bag the whole lot up for you too.'

He handed Millican a clutch of schilling notes from the wad Devon had issued him with.

'Now, I'm going to go over to a stall on the other side – don't worry, I'll be within your view at all times.' Before Millican could protest, Louis added firmly, 'Thing is, Private, I'm pretty sure I'm being followed. And it's very important, operationally speaking, that I lead whoever it is up the garden path. Understand?'

Sensing the seriousness in his voice, and recognising the tone of a superior officer (even if that status was theoretical rather than official), Millican curtailed his objection.

'So, with that in mind, I'd like you to stay where you are for a few moments, while I walk off as showily as I can and start snaking around some stalls on the other side. Then, very quietly, you head over to that stand and do your business. We'll meet casually by the entrance in about ten minutes – with your items bagged or rolled up so that an observer can't see what they are. OK?'

Again Louis' authority had taken over, and Millican was now fully in a subordinate role.

'Sir,' he said simply, and off he went.

Whether he was being followed or whether he wasn't, Louis behaved as if he was. His reasoning behind adopting the persona of a ventriloquist was this: just say for a moment that his paranoia was justified, and somehow, despite the fact that Louis Warlock was dead, the Kolduny were alert to the possibility of the British sending over a magician to penetrate their operation. If that was the case, then anyone new who turned up doing magic tricks would be an immediate target for suspicion. But someone who turned up doing something else that still might gain him entry into the variety theatre circles of Czechoslovakia – say via a very serviceable ventriloquism act – might be able to slip in under the radar. And then, after a while, he could allow his ability as a conjuror to creep out. Though it had been a while since Louis had practised the ventriloquial art, he used to perform a rather nimble act of that kind when he first stepped on to the circuit that involved borrowing personal possessions – clasp bags, wallets, purses, anything in which a puppeted mouth could be improvised – and getting them to reveal secrets about their owners.

Having purchased some random items to throw any observing party off his scent (while keeping attention away from Millican), Louis headed for the exit. Seeing that Millican was already there, he nodded at him as casually as possible to head outside. The private had done his job. His purchases were well concealed in a large grain sack. Once back on the street and heading in the direction of the Theater an der Wien, Louis gradually walked closer to the lad until they were side by side.

'Mission accomplished?'

'Yes, sir. But it's an ugly-looking thing.'

'Well, that ugly-looking thing may well be my ticket into Prague society.'

The doll was indeed ugly, but it was full of character, and its amateurish nature was easily professionalised with some paints from the barracks carpentry store and a needle and thread. As he sat there with the absurd bundle of cloth, wood and papier-mâché on his lap, doing his best to remember how to execute a back stitch, Louis found himself thinking of Dinah with a sudden pang, so acute that he wanted to cry. It was a lurching ache of loss, right in his centre. His hands went limp and fell on to the dummy, and he let out a great gulping wail. Almost immediately, he tried to gain control of himself. After a second burst of muted howling, he managed to do so.

These feelings were not an option for him. It wasn't possible for him to indulge them. He could not allow it. He had made his choice – which wasn't even really a choice; he had been delivered where the fates determined – and the only thing to be done was to acknowledge that there was no way back from it. Instead, he had to contain these sentiments, govern them and focus on the task at hand. That was the guard rail he had to cling to – his mission, his quest, his revenge on Potash for setting in motion the whole accursed chain of events. That was his path, and he must cleave to it with renewed determination.

Miss Stivin, Louis' new chaperone-to-be, didn't reveal much when she was presented with a summary of what lay ahead. Devon had decided that Louis should be the one to explain things to her, which he did. He found his Czech was getting more fluent. It would at least be beneficial for him to spend time conversing with her.

'Miss Stivin – can I ask you, what is your Christian name?'

'Elena.'

'Elena. I have something to put to you . . .'

Slowly and fairly, he took her through what lay ahead. He explained all that would be expected of her – how she would have to guide him from the border, once they had crossed safely, towards Prague. The safest thing seemed to make the journey by rail. She only had to get him to the nearest small town with a railway station, help him make his arrangements. He was confident that once he reached Prague, he could take care of himself.

'If I travel to Australia, will I be able to bring my grandmother?' she asked. 'Could you get her out too?'

Louis already knew the answer to this.

'No. That won't be possible. But you will be able to write to her as soon as your passage is under way. And she will have the satisfaction of knowing that you will be well looked after by the British government and established in a new life in a free country.'

'What if they hold it against her if they know I am working with the British?' Despite the bleakness of the question, this was encouraging to Louis when it came to their mission; it showed the girl was in possession of a questioning intelligence.

'You don't have to tell her that you're working for the British. You just say you've found a good job over there. They will find you a job, by the way.'

'I don't want to live there any more – in Czechoslovakia.'

Louis risked a further question. 'Are you sure about helping me, Elena? They can't guarantee you'll get back.'

'God will guide me,' she had said. And that seemed to be enough for her. How Louis wished he could share her faith.

Everything from there on in was focused on the crossing. Numerous methods were discussed, but Devon's preference was clear from the start.

'I want to do it this way because we've managed it before. It has a relatively high record of success.'

'A hundred per cent?' said Louis.

'Nothing's a hundred per cent.'

'What then? I'm someone who likes to know the odds.'

'Let's just say it's over fifty.'

They left it at that, for the present.

Louis and Elena were taken to meet the quartermaster, Captain McCunn, a brisk Scotsman in his forties with a crest of bright red hair and a neat moustache to match.

'I'll need to weigh you both before we can issue the equipment.'

'We haven't been told what the equipment is yet,' said Louis, who was hovering somewhere between excitement and terror. As far as he could, he was trying to consciously favour the excitement, a technique he'd adopted with any of his stage performances that felt particularly daunting.

'One thing at a time, eh?' said McCunn, leading them to a large set of luggage scales of the kind used by shipping agents. 'If you'd both stand on here ... You'll have to huddle up.'

He recorded their height as well as their weight, and while they were standing together measured them around their waists and hips.

Once this was done, Elena was released, to be taken back to her room in the barracks, while Louis was given the full briefing.

'No point in making the girl sit through it. She won't understand it and it'll only scare her. Once you're up to speed, you can tell her what she needs to know.'

Louis sat down in the small meeting room dominated by an expansive blackboard, which filled most of one wall. Inevitably he found himself thinking of Maison Bertaux. I would give my soul for a choux bun and a cup of black coffee, he thought. He let the image go and tried to focus on McCunn, reminding himself that it wasn't just his own life that depended on what he was about to be told.

'We've done this a few times and we don't think they've cottoned on yet. We try to keep them guessing, so we don't always attempt it, but we know it works.'

Louis was impatient to know what 'it' was. He watched as McCunn began to draw on the blackboard with confident strikes of the chalk.

'You're going to fly yourselves in by balloon. It might sound crazy, but there's nothing much to worry about. You don't have to be Phineas Fogg.' A diagram of the balloon with measurements began to take shape on the board. 'The thing's made of black silk. You're going up at night. I swear to God, you might as well be invisible. You need never go higher than a thousand feet.'

'Won't the air burner be visible?' asked Louis, his mind already teeming with questions.

'It would be – if we were using one. This uses helium.'

'And how will Miss Stivin make her return journey?' Louis felt himself stiffen. If there was any sense that they were treating the girl as dispensable, he would call it off himself.

'That's all taken into consideration. You've got sixty-five thousand cubic feet in here,' McCunn said, pointing to the drawing of the balloon. 'That'll lift three people. She's about two thirds your weight, and you're not exactly heavy, so I'd say we've got a good two hundred pounds excess. So, we can send a canister that holds enough gas for the return journey.'

'How will we hide a balloon and its basket?'

'Here's the clever thing.' McCunn was starting to come alive in a way that was completely recognisable to Louis. His enthusiasm was energising. 'The basket is large enough to take the two of you and your kit, but it's made of chainwork. Once you're on the ground, it collapses and folds flat. Then you cover it with the black silk, and anything you find locally goes on top of that. Bracken, leaves, foliage. Where we're aiming for, it should be easy enough to find a good hiding place.'

'Yes – and that's my next question. How exactly do we aim it?'

'The wind'll do that for you. Like I said, we've done this before.'

McCunn wiped off his hastily drawn balloon with a board rubber and replaced it with another exuberant diagram.

'You'll take off from the top of a high hill – here. You're actually at the lower end of the Carpathians, not far from Bratislava. At night, as the air cools, there's an automatic breeze that blows down from the summit to ground level. You'll control the speed of your descent with the gas valve and the release mechanism. And rest assured, that downward breeze blows on either side of the hill, so the return journey for the girl is the same; she just has to launch herself from the other side of the summit.'

They spent the next week on an airfield about twenty miles north of Vienna. The Brumowski base was under American jurisdiction, but there was a section that had been commandeered by the British. 'You'll be a long way from any prying eyes,' Devon had assured them, 'and there's plenty of other blimp activity, so a balloon going up and down won't draw too much attention.'

They were to be tutored in all aspects of ballooning, or at least those aspects that were necessary for taking off and landing, deflating, disassembling, reassembling and reinflating.

'What about navigation?' Louis asked . This was greeted with a curt laugh from McCunn.

'You go where the wind blows you – unless you call going up and down navigation. Which I suppose it is, after a fashion.'

Having located a clear patch of ground, away from trees and buildings ('and you needn't worry about the buildings – apart from a cow shed or two, there's not much around'), the skill was going to be in making the call as to when to descend, and at what speed. There was some rigidity in the basket once it was assembled and clamped in place, but they couldn't afford to go too fast.

Within a day, they'd got the basics of going up and down, keeping away from the trees (or at least the fence and the pylons, in this environment). And there was a thrill that Louis relished in rising into the air and feeling the earth fall away beneath them.

The balloon they were using initially was large and white ('It'll blend in better with what else is around us here'). But on the fourth day, they were told to meet after sunset and introduced to their actual vehicle. Now they would have to accustom themselves to flying at night.

Throughout all of this, the girl was calm, attentive and straightforwardly practical. She let Louis take the lead initially, but once the first few trips up and down were out of the way, she seemed keen to try the controls herself. Louis was pleased to see that she didn't panic and didn't emote. Something about that reminded him of Dinah. Just having the thought physically relaxed him, but brought a rush of melancholy too.

There was only one incident, when the balloon made a sudden drop after he'd miscalculated how long to keep the gas relief valve open on an otherwise uncomplicated descent. She'd grabbed hold of him instinctively and squeezed him tightly. In truth he'd had the same instinct, so it hardly counted against her.

By the time they got to the night of the journey itself, they both felt so well versed in the art of ballooning that they might as well have been training for a month rather than a mere week. Louis was grateful for that. When they weren't on the airfield, they were being drilled in the details that were going to come into play on the other side. Czechoslovakia was approaching – coming towards Louis like the ground came towards the basket as the helium ran out of the black balloon above.

They'd been taken to a mountainous region about an hour's drive from the airbase. It was a cloudy but calm night; the air wasn't completely still, but the wind speed was low – or so they'd been assured. Conditions were perfect. The balloon would be practically invisible against the night sky, as would their dark clothes. They put blacking on their faces, which they would have to wipe off by the time they were seen in public ('Get Leichner number 12,' Louis had told them, 'it'll come off easier'), but they had each other to help with that task.

Their trainer took them out to the mountain. He was going to supervise the launch. Much of what followed went so fast that Louis was barely able to take it in. But as soon as the balloon was inflated and they were rising into the air, everything seemed to calm again, despite the anxiety about what was ahead.

Together he and Elena watched the ground fall away and felt the world open out around them. Soon, when the downdraught caught them and began pulling them to the ground on the other side, they would have to make a decision about how fast to descend. But for a few minutes at least they could float in the blackness and let it carry them where it would.

The strange thing was that her understandable nervousness had seemed to subside once they had taken off. He felt her next to him, leaning slightly against him, her skinny arm pushing against the sleeve of his overcoat. Maybe it wasn't a conscious move towards him, but naturally he felt something protective within him reaching out to her. And then a quick flash of himself on the boat to England when he was a child came to mind. Alone, desperate to find someone to trust. He pushed the memory away. They had to focus. They had a concrete task to achieve. What was coming was beyond their control, it was simply a matter of being taken.

21

The doll was called Franz. His hair was shorter now and his colouring was different. Louis had tried to make him look younger. He'd reddened his cheeks and widened his eyes, as far as he could. The costume helped, given that an adult-sized jacket had been used to fashion the figure's upper body; however inadvertently, it looked like a child dressed in its father's clothes. He had just nudged it more in that direction.

Of course, it was common for a ventriloquist to cast his dummy in the mode of impudent child. Answering back, cheeking off provided instant comedy and instant conflict. And the difference in the pitch of each voice – from adult tenor to youthful soprano – enhanced the feel of puppeteer and doll being separate characters.

Ventriloquising in another language proved no more difficult than in one's natural tongue. And however carefully Louis had cultivated it over the years, English wasn't actually his natural tongue. The Czech he was now speaking was in fact far closer to it.

The one preparation he'd made was to write himself a script. Allowing himself to improvise would have been too risky – there was always a danger he might slip back accidentally into English. So he wrote a number of routines, relatively quickly, and made it his job to memorise them until he was fluent.

As he was working on this act, he slipped so easily into enjoying it – being back in the role of an entertainer – that he had to remind himself what the real job was. This was only a means to an end, something to get him noticed by the Kolduny without raising suspicion that he'd been planted by foreign agents. The actual task in hand was a graver one: to get himself recruited and embedded in the Kolduny and then find out what the Funhouse was, and how exactly it was turning able-bodied officers into ruined shells. One step at a time, he told himself as he studied his script, one step at a time. And don't hurry.

The pitch he had found was a good one: on the front concourse of the old Franz Josef station. It had meant bribing the platform manager, but he managed to earn back that bribe within two days. Tips were sparse at first, but as he felt his way into the role, he got better at knowing how to elicit cash from the audience. And once he'd run in the mind-reading routine, he was pulling in double his initial daily rate. As expected, he noticed that his money tended to go up if the jokes had a satirical tinge. While targeting the current government or the Soviets was completely taboo, the Americans were, of course, fair game, and he could be clever about how he played it:

'You know, the Yankees really get on my nerves,' said Franz.

'Why?' Louis asked, deadpanning, looking from the dummy to the crowd.

'They're always boasting. I heard this Yankee going on to a Czechoslovakian about how the United States was a truly free country because there he could stand in front of the White House and shout "To hell with the Marshall Plan." "So what?" says the Czechoslovakian. "I can stand in front of the Straka here and say exactly the same thing!"'

A huge laugh from the gathered crowd. It seemed they enjoyed the dig at the Americans, but even more the chance to laugh at their own regime, however benign the joke seemed. This bit of local political knowledge – that the offer of participation in the Marshall Plan had been rejected when the country went fully communist in 1948 – had actually come to him via Elena on their journey in. As he performed the routine, he wondered how she was doing now. Was she safe? Was she already on a ship to Australia? It had been more three weeks since she'd left him.

Their landing via balloon had been a terrifying scramble, both physically and emotionally. The double fence at the border had been just about visible on the other side of the trees through the murky night air. Their view had been clear when they'd risen above the pines on the Austrian side, their trainer clearly visible, diminishing beneath them. But very quickly a mist had seemed to gather, coagulating around them as they began their descent. It was good for concealment, but very bad in terms of their chance of making a safe landing. And if it had got much thicker, they'd have struggled to see where the forest ended.

Ultimately it was patchy enough for them to be able to navigate, but they'd misjudged when to begin heading down and had ended up being much closer to the fence than Louis had intended. They'd made it, but with a sharp thump that knocked the breath out of them both. Louis felt it like a whack to his stomach. But there was no time to recover. They needed to get as far away from the fence area as they could, and fast. Up till now, the intelligence had been correct. There was no sign of a watch, or any approaching patrol, but they knew that the longer they lingered, the more they were trying their luck. Their days of drilling and repetition paid off. They didn't have to think, and Louis was grateful for it. They were both running like automata: unscrew the basket bolts on all sides; pull out the helium tank; collapse and fold; deflate; roll up the silk; cover the basket.

Then a search for branches and foliage. Once again, the intelligence had been fruitful. There were patches of thick bracken just about visible in the blue-black gloom around them. And down a small sandy slope there was a large boulder that would serve as a landmark for Elena's return. They lifted the package of silk and chain-linked metal and rolled it up lengthways behind the boulder, then covered it with several layers of bracken fronds and deadfall. They were done in twenty minutes. Before they left the area, Louis found a small knob of sandstone on the ground and chalked a snaking line on the base of the rock – inconspicuous to the casual eye, but immediately apparent for the searcher in the know.

'Remember it,' he said to Elena, 'Remember where it is. So you know what to look for.'

'I will.'

'You sure you'll recognise it again?'

'You're worrying too much. I've got it.'

He *was* worrying. But he'd rather she didn't notice. He'd been trying to mask his concern, knowing she would pick up on his anxiety and that would only make things worse for her.

It had taken about half an hour, maybe forty minutes, to make it down the scree. He'd hoped they could manage it before sunrise, otherwise they would be dangerously prominent – a moving point in the landscape. When they emerged from the mix of scrubland and trees into open meadow, dawn was still an hour away. There was a line of low wooden fencing about thirty yards to the right, with a ditch in front of it. Louis headed towards it, and once there, he sat down, indicating that Elena should do the same.

'We won't be visible here,' he said, looking around. 'We can rest for a while.'

She had joined him gratefully, squatting on the ground, leaning on the cracked fence behind her.

'I want you to take a good look at this,' said Louis, gesturing at the view. 'This is the way you must come back. You're going to have to retrace your steps as accurately as you can.'

Elena nodded. She was a smart girl. Not fast, maybe, but attentive. She absorbed things and processed them in her own time.

Wanting to help her, he said: 'If you look over there, what's the most recognisable thing?'

'The poplar trees.'

The isolated trees were stark like pylons against the sky.

'Let's make a cross here on the fence.' He picked up a stone from the ditch, turned round and scratched a thick cross in the old wood, gouging as deeply as he could. 'If you stand here,' he said, turning back round, 'and hold your thumb up to your eye, how many thumbs is it from the poplars to the bottom of the hill where we came down?'

Carefully Elena did as she was instructed.

'Three and a bit,' she said.

'Make a picture in your mind so you won't forget – a poplar tree curled into the shape of a number three, with a little bit extra shaped like a giant thumb flopping off the end.'

He waggled his thumb around and was pleased to hear her laugh. It lightened her.

'When you come back here,' he said, 'you'll see the poplars and you'll see that strange bendy number three-and-a-bit in your imagination, and you won't forget it. Three and a half thumbs from the poplars.'

She looked at him with a smile of wonder on her face, as if he'd just shown her how to turn lead into gold.

It was a short trudge across the field to a muddy potholed road, more like a farm track. They wiped their faces clean as they went, using two old brown handkerchiefs that would disguise the presence of the make-up on the cloth. When they'd finished, they stuffed the handkerchiefs in their pockets. As they passed a turnip field, Louis rummaged in his rucksack, digging beneath the bundle of dirty clothes that Franz was wrapped in (the smell would hopefully put anyone off investigating too closely – not that the dummy was an immediately incriminating item). Eventually he found what he was looking for – a worn hessian shopping bag.

Looking around to check there was still no one in sight, he scrabbled in the earth and pulled up three of the turnips, breaking off the foliage so they resembled something on a market stall. Then he put them in the bag and handed it to Elena.

'Makes us look that bit less suspicious, don't you think, if you're carrying a shopping bag. Just a couple of people on their way somewhere with a bit of food.' Though a tiny detail, it was the thinking of someone who understood how to manipulate his audience.

The muddy track came to a junction after about half a mile, where it joined a better-defined road. There was enough of a verge along the side of it for them to be able to walk safely, not that there was any traffic.

'This is the road,' Elena said.

'Are you sure?'

She nodded. 'I know it.'

Louis took a tiny compass from his pocket and checked the direction. Bratislava was to the south, probably six or seven miles from where they'd landed. It should take them less than two hours even going at a gentle pace.

For all that he wanted to project a calm and assured demeanour, he found he was affected by the landscape around them. Day was beginning to break, revealing a moody, heavy sky with hunks of grey cloud that seemed to merge with the mountains looming over the valley. He felt like he wanted to dart back under the scrubby trees, to stay concealed. But they had to hit the road at some point.

Wanting to hide his anxiety from Elena, he chatted about anything that came to mind – mainly his memories of Prague from when he was a boy. He attempted to take comfort from the fact that they were safer walking in this direction. Border guards were far more concerned about people heading out of the country than those travelling inwards.

'I've got a game we could play,' he said, trying to sound as relaxed as possible.

'What game?'

'Why don't we make up a story about who we are and where we're going?'

'I know who I am,' said Elena. 'Justyna Horackova. That's the name on the false papers they gave me.'

'Not just the name – where do you live, Justyna, and what are you doing with me?'

Elena thought for a minute before saying in an impressively fluent manner: 'I live in Bratislava. I moved there three months ago from the country, where I'd been in the Zemědělská Divize. You're my cousin Karel who's lodging in Zohor, which is where we're going now.'

'Of course I am. I wonder what I'm doing in Zohor.'

'I don't know,' she said, suddenly seeming agitated, 'but I do know that I need the bathroom.'

Louis relaxed. He'd thought from her tone that there was a bigger problem than that.

'It's fine. There are some trees over there,' he said, pointing to his left. 'I'll wait here. Leave the bag.'

He stood at the edge of the silent road, deliberately turned away from the small copse he could hear Elena trudging towards. As he waited, the huge desolate hills rising over him on one side, he suddenly felt completely alone and vulnerable. Some protecting veil had been torn away from him and he was now fully exposed to the brutal elements. With no real distractions, and a sudden psychological break from his mission, he felt his demons calling him and his anxiety rising. His instinct was to dive to the ground, to crawl under something and hide, but there was nowhere to do so.

Almost exactly as this feeling overcame him, there was a rattling rumble on the narrow road ahead: an approaching truck of some kind. As it came into view, Louis saw from the dirty green of its livery that it was a military vehicle. He willed himself to relax, to become as loose and insignificant as possible, of no more moment than a clod of mud, a foraging crow, a ragged bush bristling in the wind. But there was no way to disguise how odd he looked, standing immobile at the side of the road. He didn't want to start walking for fear that the truck would move past him, only to stop at Elena when she rejoined the road.

As it approached, the note of its grumbling engine began to lower in pitch. By the time it was upon him, it had come to a stop. The driver's cab had three soldiers in it, and there were two more sitting on the open flatbed behind. One of the men, a pink-faced, loutish-looking type of around Louis' age, with close-cropped straw-coloured hair, shouted to him:

'What you doing there?'

Louis should have answered straight away, held his gaze disinterestedly, or even just shrugged. Anything. Any kind of response. But he found he'd frozen. His heart was thudding away, and a state of cold terror had evicted any coherent thought from his head.

'You. What are you doing? Don't just stand there. Answer me.'

There was another soldier visible next to him, grinning – but there was no comfort in that grin. It was the smile of a bully, looking forward to the scene that was about to unfold.

'Come on. Speak up.'

But Louis couldn't. It was as if his throat had seized up. Inexplicably, he'd become thirteen years old again, his mind filled with the memory of racing to get on the transport boat from Holland, terrified of every soldier they passed on the way.

'He's OK. Don't worry about him.' It was Elena. She was behind Louis, speaking casually, a beautifully judged weariness in her voice, as if she was taking the soldier's side. 'He's slow.' She shook her head disparagingly, to show that Louis was her constant burden. 'That's why he carries the turnips.'

'Where you going?'

'Bratislava. See our cousins.' She'd somehow adopted a familial air, as if this soldier she was speaking to might also be her cousin. They were clearly of the same stock. Countrymen. Elena was self-evidently as much a part of this land as the mountains behind her. Regaining some of his faculties, Louis slowly lifted his bag. The shape of the turnips was clearly visible within.

The soldier nodded at Elena. There was no more fun to be had here. And the sense of honest suffering she exuded must have elicited some spark of sympathy.

'Don't let him walk in the road. He might get run down next time.'

'I know,' she sighed, and jerked her arm, indicating that Louis should follow her. She bowed her head slightly to the soldier and then set off without looking back, Louis trudging slowly a few paces behind her.

Once the rumble of the engine had diminished to half its volume, Louis risked a glance up. He was grateful to see the vehicle disappearing into a distant haze of dust and exhaust, showing no sign of stopping.

'You did very well there,' he said.

Elena just nodded. Louis let himself relax inwardly, and without a word passing between them, he felt Elena doing the same.

In Bratislava, it had been relatively easy to find the train station. Louis hadn't known quite what to expect, in terms of how the city would feel under Soviet jurisdiction. If anything, it seemed more prosperous and stable than Vienna, at least superficially. People were going about their mid-morning business contentedly enough. It took until they got to the station for him to perceive any authoritarian hand. There were armed uniformed soldiers visible on the concourse, checking the papers and tickets of people travelling. Why this was the case he didn't know. Was it routine? Or had there been some kind of tip-off?

'Is this normal?' he said to Elena, nodding at the soldiers.

'Depends,' she said. 'We're close to the border here.'

In as natural a way as possible, he eased her over to a refreshment stand by one of the big arches at the entrance of the station. He purchased two lemon teas while they waited to see if the soldiers would move on.

'You know, if you want to avoid them, you don't have to get the train,' said Elena, looking up at him, sympathy in her eyes.

'What are you thinking?'

'What if you got the bus to somewhere away from the border? Somewhere like Trnava. No one goes there.'

'But can I get a bus to Prague from there?'

'Yes. I think so. Soldiers don't patrol the buses. They're too lazy.'

In that moment, Louis was once again grateful to Devon and her wisdom in having him chaperoned.

'You can get a rover ticket from the tobacconist's. Or the news-stand. You can go on any bus you want then.'

As they stood at the newspaper booth on the far side of the road from the station, Louis reached a decision. It was his to make. Now that there was a crowd, a population around him, and he knew what he had to do, he didn't need her any more.

'You should go now,' he said.

'But we've only just got here.'

'You've done exactly what was required of you. You've delivered me to where I need to be. That's all you were supposed to do.'

She shook her head. 'But I should take you to Prague.'

He laughed at this. 'You don't need to take me to Prague. Once I'm on a bus, I just get on the next bus. And then I'm there. You need to get to . . . where you're going.'

'But when you're in Prague—'

'I know Prague. I've been there before. I can speak the language. Find myself a hotel room. Really. You can't stay with me the whole time. I want you to go now.' He handed her the bag of turnips. 'For the journey back. The perfect disguise. Put a few more things in there while you're here.'

'Are you sure? Will I have done enough for them to send me where they promised?'

'More than enough. Go.'

She stood there for a moment, uncertain. Then she turned slightly, making to set off.

'You can remember how to get it up? And how to control it?' he said.

'I practised enough times. You watched me.'

'I did.' He smiled at the memory. He took a step closer to her, lowering his voice, though there was no one around them showing the slightest interest in their conversation. 'And you know how to get in touch with Devon's people on the other side?'

'The letter's with the balloon.'

She only had to hand that missive to any Allied military operative in Austria, and they would take care of the rest.

'Remember what they told us. Wait till you feel the first pull of the downdraught from the other side, then yank the release valve.' Spontaneously, without thinking, he reached out and held her. 'Thank you,' he said simply. 'I wouldn't have made it here without your help . . .'

She just nodded. He could feel her frailty against him. It seemed to belie the strength and courage he'd seen her display. After a moment, he let her go. With little fuss, she turned and set off, back towards the road they'd arrived on. After a few moments, she was one of the crowd.

Once he'd lost sight of her, Louis suddenly realised how tired and hungry and cold he was. He looked forward to getting on the bus, sitting down. He had no idea what lay ahead, but he was here, and his mission had begun. The thought he had to push from his mind was that with Elena gone, he was fully alone. How the hell was he going to do this? Spontaneously, a voice spoke up in his head.

You're not alone. You've got me . . .

That was Franz. The voice he'd been rehearsing for the puppet before they left Vienna. There was little comfort there, but it was just enough to enable him to set off towards the bus stand and begin his journey to Prague.

22

Three uncomfortable nights in a cheap hotel had led Louis to find more permanent rooms in Smíchov, one of the less salubrious parts of Prague. This was enough to help him implement the next part of the coping strategy he'd decided upon: impose some order, some regularity, some routine, lay down rails to allow yourself to navigate the continuing uncertainty. So every day at 10 a.m., he strode across the Jirásek Bridge and walked to the station concourse to set up his pitch.

Within two weeks of starting his double act with Franz there, he had managed to collect something like a regular audience. He even began to recognise the faces of those who returned day after day.

One of the more popular routines revolved around Franz's critique of Louis' fondness for American cigarettes. This monologue was delivered by Franz with unsubtle irony as Louis smoked, letting the fag dangle from his mouth while the dummy talked, saving the moments of exhalation for vocalisations that required no articulation. It was a trick he'd been taught by an old Irish vent called Harry Hewson. If one blew, rather than sucked air in, the cigarette's end would glow in an identical manner. It was possible to form words while exhaling in a way one couldn't while inhaling, and yet the visible subtlety really helped the illusion. All the while Franz chattered away about the useless Americans who'd sell their smokes but not their wheat.

'If only we could eat Lucky Strikes, hey, then we'd be fine. Except I wouldn't, because this dummy' – gesturing to Louis – 'is so mean he wouldn't share them. I'm a bag of bones as it is.' Louis gave the doll a shake, as if Franz were shaking himself, and his wooden hands swung like little bells, which always got a laugh.

It was true that this dialogue wouldn't have troubled Ivan and Phyllis, but it played very well here. This knowledge of local antipathy to Yankee smokes was something else Louis had Elena to thank for. He vowed, if he got back home, to find out what had happened to her. If he got back home. Increasingly he'd been thinking of the prospect as hypothetical. That was a bad habit.

With his audience growing every day, it was perhaps only a matter of time before he received a professional enquiry. To maximise the chance of such an approach, he'd let the station clerk he'd bribed know the details of his lodgings, saying quite openly that if anyone should come asking about him, he could be contacted there.

And as it happened, that was how the approach came.

Louis was in his tiny room, having just lit the sputtering little gas ring to warm up some soup, when his crotchety landlord rapped on his door.

'For you,' the old man said, somehow managing to load those two syllables with three sentences' worth of resentment.

'I'm sorry,' said Louis, without being sorry at all.

'Downstairs.' These two further syllables were delivered with even more acrimony. How dare this shabby new tenant have the impertinence to have someone call on him?

When Louis came into the hallway, he saw a tired-looking man with a balding pate and a ruddy, acne-scarred face.

'You Kay?' asked the man, squinting at him suspiciously. Louis guessed that the shabby cardigan he was wearing over his stained collarless shirt didn't make the best impression. He also guessed that this man was a civilian. If he were there on state business, he'd be with an armed guard, and they'd probably have burst straight into his room without knocking.

'That's right,' he said, maintaining some coolness until he had enough information to calibrate the proper response.

'My name's Novy. I'm from the Karlín.'

'Uh huh.' Louis didn't immediately know what the Karlín was, but from the way the man spoke, it was obvious he was supposed to.

'The Karlín, more recently known as the Theatre of Folk Art. Except – would you believe – we're allowed to call it the Karlín

Musical Theatre again, since the city has managed to claw it back from the licensed bandits, otherwise known as the state, who tried to take it from us and make it theirs.' There were layers and levels of bitterness in this statement that hinted at a whole opera's worth of trials for poor Mr Novy. Louis gave a slow nod with just a hint of a smile, as if he was conversant with all of this and just as jaded about these matters of bureaucratic insanity as Novy was himself.

'How can I help?' he asked.

'You've been making quite a name for yourself, young man. For more than a week people have been saying I should drop by and see the clown at the station. Telling me he should be on my bill.'

Louis bristled at the word 'clown', but then checked himself. The further east you went, the more respect that word contained. A clown possessed more dignity than a magician over here.

'Your bill? What bill?' he asked. He didn't want to just jump because Novy had clicked his fingers. It was important to maintain the persona of a canny street performer.

'I've been charged, Mr Kay, with putting together "a cavalcade of Czechoslovakian talent". A *vaudeville* show.' And the disdain with which this foreign word was spoken made it clear exactly what Novy thought of the task he had been given. 'Apparently it will help lift the spirits of our citizenry and inspire them in their daily mission to serve the noble state.'

'Mr Novy—' Louis began.

'Please, there is no need for false modesty. All you need to say is that you will be prepared to join our company. I have numerous light opera singers, I have dancers, I have more acrobats than any audience could possibly want to see on one bill, but I have no clowns.'

'I am not exactly a clown, Mr Novy, you know – I'm a ventriloquist.' Louis very much wanted to say 'a vent', but there was no equivalent Czech contraction, as far as he knew.

'You make people laugh, don't you?'

'Yes,' he said, nodding.

'Then you are a clown.'

*　　*　　*

255

Louis was instructed to turn up for a rehearsal the following morning at ten o'clock at the Karlín theatre, and of course to bring Franz with him, together with any band sheets he might require and any props he might use. It wasn't quite a shoo-in – the proprieties of an audition process would have to be observed, of course – but Novy had already made his need clear.

The Karlín, it turned out, was not the second-rate music hall Louis had anticipated. It was, in fact, a majestic (if now slightly shabby) house on a par with a larger London theatre like the Palace or the Adelphi. The dilapidation was no doubt a consequence of the war and its aftermath, but the place hadn't lost its grandeur altogether.

The show Novy was putting on was called somewhat pompously *Ceskoslovenská Kavalkáda: the Fruit of the Third Republic*. This, Louis concluded after only an hour or so, was a rather hyperbolic title to lay on the shoulders of the motley assemblage of turns that the crumpled impresario had been able to corral in whatever impossibly short time span he had been given to throw it all together. It was also apparent that, for whatever reason, this was not a happy company. More than a few performers clearly didn't want to be there, and there was a general air of low-level resentment and grievance aimed at the management, without any obvious reason for it.

Louis always made it his business to avoid the grumblers and stick with the happy, so he applied the same strategy here. As he was discussing his play-on music with the band leader, he caught the eye of one of the violinists. She was shaking her head at the ill temper of the squat maestro, who, with his plump nose and heavy black glasses, looked like the East's answer to Billy Cotton. He was officious and determinedly unhelpful, and was pretending that he'd never heard of 'We're a Couple of Swells'.

'Irving Berlin?' said Louis, trying not to let himself become exasperated. 'You're aware of him?'

Before the man could reply, the friendly violinist helpfully offered up the melody from the song in question. It was enough to spur the rest of the band to follow suit. Given that Louis only needed four bars to get him and Franz on stage and another four for their exit, it seemed they were in business, regardless of the leader's antipathy. He gave a little nod of thanks to the red-headed violinist and she smiled wryly, a smile Louis returned. It was a moment of conspiracy between two kindred spirits who recognised each other's will to make the best of things despite the prevailing winds.

The ill temper of the various artistes was one thing, but gradually Louis became aware of something else: a sense of nervousness, even disquiet, that was markedly different from any of the usual anxieties inherent in putting on a show. This feeling was disconnected from concerns about the audience's displeasure, indifference or scorn. If he'd had to put a name to it, he would have called it 'dread'. On that first day, he wouldn't have been able to pin down what the cause of that dread was. By the end of the week, he would know.

The violinist, a girl of only twenty or twenty-one, turned out to be quite an ally. She was highly gifted, easily the best of the musicians in the pit, and bright too. They fell into easy conversation in break periods between rehearsals, after Louis thanked her for filling in the gaps in her leader's musical repertoire. She was pretty, with long, straight hair that hung down her back, and a playful smile.

'Happens all the time, so don't take it personally,' she said while they were eating lunch. Louis had an apple that he'd brought from his rooms, which he cut carefully into slices as they talked. Having levered the pips out with the end of his pocket knife, he offered her one of the segments speared on its point. She took it gratefully.

'He doesn't like being given instructions, particularly not by the turns,' she said, biting into the fruit. 'But you only have to act like you know your place. You don't actually have to *be* in that place.'

'Girl after my own heart,' said Louis with a gentle smile.

'You're Karel Kay?'

'That's right.'

'They're all saying you're a tramp who just got lucky.'

'That's about right.'

'Well – I'm pleased for you.'

'You're a marvellous violinist,' said Louis. 'How long have you been playing?'

It was obvious how much she loved her art. Her enthusiasm bubbled over in her response.

'Since I was five. My mother said I could barely lift the bow back then. I just loved it. The instrument, I mean. It looked so special. It was the most special thing in our house. It belonged to my grandfather. I'm Eva, by the way. Eva Palovic.' She wiped the juice from her long, delicate hand and held it out to shake.

As the days passed, the dread that the others were suffering soon began to creep its way into Louis' bones too. It was most obviously to be found in the sly glances from some of the acts, noticeably Gabriela the trapeze artist, who was often to be seen leaning against a wall or a door jamb in her tatty leotard, smoking a ragged self-made cigarette, spitting bits of tobacco on to the floor, one narrow eye peering round whatever part of the theatre she was in, as if collecting information she could use as a weapon against anybody unfortunate enough to have fallen under her gaze. She was a little too old and a little too out of condition to be performing acrobatics, and she avoided rehearsing whenever she could. Most of her ire seemed to be turned against the young women in the company, Eva in particular, although in practice it didn't seem to extend beyond a hard hate-filled stare. And now, given that Louis was associating more and more with Eva, that baleful gaze was increasingly turned in his direction too.

'She's a fully paid-up party member,' said Eva, when they both noticed her watching them sharing fruit. This had become a bit of a daily ritual – anything that could be sliced up they would lay out in front of them on a paper bag and pick at the pieces as if on a picnic. 'Enthusiastic, you might say.'

'She doesn't look like she'd enthuse about anything.'

'Oh, she enjoys not liking people, enjoys it very much.'

There were others, too, who seemed to be paying unhealthy attention to everything Louis said, whether they were conversing with him or merely within earshot, and so he got into the habit of taking notable care about what he allowed to pass his lips. The consequence of this was a slow and constant erosion of any kind of peace of mind. It seemed that, despite momentary experiences, one could never truly relax. The only time he felt any kind of safety was when talking to Eva. And even then a lurking thought struck him: what if his only friend wasn't a real friend after all?

He decided to use this low-level anxiety as a motivator for his mission. He wasn't here to get comfortable. He was here to get noticed. Any comfort he stumbled into along the way, well, that was a different matter, but his main purpose was to draw attention to himself with his magical skills. 'Have you heard – there's a vent at the Karlín who's rather nifty when it comes to magic' was the word he wanted to get out into the world. The fact that the walls had ears, and not just the walls, but the floors, the ceilings and all the fixtures and fittings too, was surely something that he could get working on his behalf. It was definitely time to introduce a little astonishment into the proceedings.

After two weeks, the shows were increasingly popular. It turned out that in spite of Louis' initial scepticism, Novy had actually done a good job at putting together an entertaining bill. Louis found his act was really making an impact. And Franz the dummy had gained his own billing on the hand-painted poster in the frame under the portico at the Karlín's entrance: *Karel Kay with FRANZ!* Given that he was now clearly identified as a ventriloquist, to the extent that it was the dummy who was gaining notoriety, it certainly seemed like the right time to move the act into more overtly magical territory.

Louis had already devised a psychometry routine that Franz could perform, based on one he used to do with Dinah. (Was he invoking Dinah more and more, to deter his burgeoning connection with Eva? No. Eva was just a friend. That was all.) The trick involved passing out a series of cloth bags amongst the audience and asking people to place small items inside. They would be gathered up and handed to Louis, and Franz would then divine what the item was, and more importantly, who its owner was, including several pertinent facts about them. It was by any standards a killer routine. A headlining mentalist would happily close his act with it. Given that it was in the hands of a ventriloquist's dummy, it moved up a whole other level, because no one would be expecting impossible magic to emerge from a stupid puppet and his supposedly passive operator. The effect gained an extra layer of deception and amazement.

It was only the second night of performing the routine when the following happened:

Louis had just got as far as handing the bags out to the front row, asking for them to be passed around the auditorium, when there was a commotion from the back of the stalls and four uniformed soldiers strode in at some speed, led by a non-uniformed figure in an open greatcoat, wearing a dark suit beneath. He headed straight for the stage, locating the treads at one side. Ignoring the fact that Louis was in the middle of speaking, he pushed past him and turned to the audience.

'Comrades,' he said, 'I'm here on a solemn but necessary mission, so you will have to forgive this interruption.' He had the blithe confidence of someone who knew he was the most powerful person in the room. There was no one here who could challenge him or cause him difficulty of any kind.

In the seconds before he continued, time slowed and Louis' heart rate began to rise. Everything sharpened. What were his options here? Running through the auditorium was out of the question. Was there a closer exit he could dash for? Could he make it to the wings? The men were clearly armed. He knew they would have no compunction about shooting him.

'We are here in the service of justice. I know you will understand why we must execute our duty.' He nodded at two of the uniformed men, who were now at the front of the auditorium, and they moved forward at speed, both leaping over the edge of the thin wooden wall into the pit. Alarmed and confused, Louis leaned forward, standing on tiptoes in order to see what was happening. There was a cry of protest, and he knew straight away it had come from Eva. She was being hauled to her feet, even as she tried to resist the brutality of the arrest.

'No . . . Get . . . No—' But a gloved hand was over her mouth, and they dragged her from her chair. Her skirts became caught on a music stand, which fell over at an angle, exposing her bare legs up to her thighs, but the soldiers just pulled anyway, even as she kicked at them like a furious child.

Louis' first thought was to dive in and help, to intervene in some way. But like everyone else in there – the musicians sitting around her, the audience, the stage management – he found that he was paralysed, watching the cold violence of the arrest play out. His right arm was covered with the stupid puppet, which was now hanging limp and forgotten like an absurd sleeve, only serving to draw attention to his own weakness and shame.

'This young woman is Eva Palovic,' said the official on stage, maintaining a grotesque calm. 'Her uncle is Jozef Koecher, who you should know has committed an unthinkable act of treason.'

By now, Eva was being held between the two soldiers, still struggling.

'Koecher defected from our country for reasons unknown and is now living somewhere in the United States of America. An act of treachery and sedition that brings with it unavoidable consequences. I am told that the niece' – and here the official gestured vaguely towards Eva without deigning to look at her – 'had a great future ahead of her in service of the nation, playing with the state orchestra, where she was fully expected to achieve a lifetime's tenure. Now the state has no choice but to prohibit her from any public performance or position in which she might earn her living from her musical abilities. But the state is merciful too, and as of tomorrow, she will report to the laundry at the University Hospital in the Nové Město, where she will still have the opportunity to serve her fellow citizens. Thank you, comrades.' The official nodded briskly and left the stage, walking past Louis as if he wasn't there.

There was a moment's silence in which a low moan was audible from Eva. Perhaps she had just realised what had been said. And then Novy's head appeared in the wings, nodding urgently at the band leader to strike up a chord. The man obliged, and Louis felt a spotlight turn on him, indicating that he should resume his act. It momentarily blinded him, thus sparing him the sight of Eva being dragged from the theatre, ending her professional career and any musical greatness that might have lain ahead of her.

She was the closest thing to a friend he had found in many months. He knew he would never see her again.

BEFORE I FORGET

Here's a strange shopping list. Read
through the list slowly and remember it,
please.

A balloon
A mountain
Some poplar trees
Three turnips
A truck
Some lemon tea
A bus ticket
A hotel key
A puppet
A penknife
An apple
A violin

Now cover the list with your hand and see
how many you can remember – in order.

How did you do? Most people can
remember the first two, strain for the
third item and then get lost after the
fourth. It's only twelve objects, yet to
many of us it feels like an impossible
task.

Here's what I've found. Within magic,
there are techniques and strategies that
are created to merely impress spectators

through artifice, but that actually develop capacities in the performer that can alter your life for the better. Unlike the illusory version of memorising a deck of cards I taught you previously, here the method employed for trickery achieves the very thing it is apparently faking. By simply shifting how we think, we can expand our mind's capabilities. You might be surprised what salvation this skill can offer you.

What I am about to teach you is a truly simple, extremely easy mind game that has remarkable potential. If you put a little time into this, I promise you will never have to write down another shopping list! This method doesn't rely on any mnemonic systems, or even the ability to 'remember' anything at all. The genius of this practice is that it relies on something that is programmed into all of us: the ability to tell a story. This technique can enable you to memorise anything. Anything.

Are you sitting comfortably? Then let's begin.

Once upon a time . . . an extraordinary thing happened.

A very unlucky man was flying in the air holding a **BALLOON**; it burst and the man landed on a **MOUNTAIN** - whose tip went into the seat of his pants! So shocked was he that he rolled down the mountain and smacked into **SOME POPLAR TREES** - ow ow ow! The last tree flipped him and he landed head first in a turnip field; his poor head had **THREE TURNIPS** stuck to it. He couldn't see and ran into the road, and a **TRUCK** crashed into him. Wheeeeeee, he went flying in the air and landed in a café, where the waiter was so shocked, he spilled **LEMON TEA** all over the man. The man went to dry himself with a towel, but it was actually a giant **BUS TICKET** and went all soggy! The man started crying and dried his eyes with his **HOTEL KEY**! Aha! I'll go to bed, he thought, so he went to his room and snuggled up with his **PUPPET** . . . which was hard to do as it had a **KNIFE** in its hand. He didn't have a pillow, so he rested his head on a giant **APPLE** instead. He drifted off to sleep listening to the sound of a lovely loud **VIOLIN**. THE END.

You've read that story once. Now run through it in your mind, counting the objects off as you do. I'll start you off . . . What did the man fall from?

I'll wager you remember most of them, straight away! If there's a couple you forgot, read it again. Now try all twelve. Amazing, isn't it?

But how can something that a moment ago felt impossible suddenly be simple, almost effortless?

This is a memory trick known as 'the linking technique', or as I like to call it, 'story time'. There are two key things happening here. Firstly you have to use your imagination to create each piece of the story. The odder and sillier the ideas, the easier it is to remember them. Each time you make a new list, you will invent a new story.

Here's the biggest thing that I have learned from this memory technique: so often life's challenges feel insurmountable when in fact they are not. Often, all it

takes is some simple, calm sideways
thinking and you can amaze yourself.

I believe that using genuine mental
techniques like this one, in amongst the
falsehoods, keeps me inspired and able to
show people what they are capable of. And
it shows me what I might be capable of too,
even as I doubt that I'm capable of
anything

Now before I forget . . . Remind me what
those twelve objects are?

You can do it.

You can do it.

23

Eva's miserable fate weighed heavily on Louis, but it served him in one way. Any notion of slipping into a pleasant routine or comfortable day-to-day existence while waiting for the Kolduny to notice him was definitively dispelled. He'd stood by and done nothing while they'd dragged the terrified violinist away, so now he would atone. He would devote himself with every aspect of his being to pursuing his mission, and in doing so hopefully quieten his shame too. He was there to infiltrate the Kolduny and find out what the Funhouse was. If he could, he would bring down Potash with it. If only he had access to the Brains Trust, he knew he'd be able to achieve it. But sensing Dinah's face beginning to form itself in his mind's eye, he dropped the thought like it was a burning coal. It was senseless to even indulge it for a second.

In the first instance, he just had to focus on making his act as brilliant as he could. That was straightforward, in its own way. But there was another side to his mission, and it involved the dream boxes. He needed as much information as possible. It wasn't a matter of that being a possible route to Potash; he needed Potash to find *him*, he needed to be talent-spotted. That was the only way if he was going to successfully infiltrate the Kolduny. But this side quest with the dream box was specifically about the second part of his mission: the Funhouse. Since meeting Colonel Richmond, facing the horror of a man who'd had his mind so casually destroyed, the determination to prevent that happening to anyone else had only solidified. And this meant gathering as much information as possible. But he had to proceed cautiously. Fine. He could be patient. He was used to it. It took patience to memorise a stacked deck of cards. It took patience to master any difficult sleight of hand. He knew how to be patient.

Go gently, go steadily, go determinedly. Forge alliances and relationships in an unforced manner. Don't give up. Persist and let events take him where he needed to go.

The most important thing was to begin casually. That meant doing a circuit of all the antique shops, junk shops, flea markets and pawnbrokers he could find. Colonel Richmond must have got his dream box somewhere in the vicinity. That was a very tangible lead to follow. If Louis made small purchases in each of the likely premises, he could begin to develop his contacts. Perhaps he should start by expressing an interest in something like 'novelty clockwork'. There was no point in mentioning dream boxes specifically. That would be too exposing, too clumsy. But if he became known as someone with a passion in that area, someone who was willing to spend money, it might just be that a dealer or proprietor would lead him there. Start small, perhaps with toys: jack-in-the-boxes, wind-up cars and trains; anything with a mechanism. From here he could move on to souvenir watches, cuckoo clocks, weather houses and musical boxes. Ultimately he hoped to find out what other dream boxes might have been sold, the size of the pieces – in truth, anything at all. His plan didn't stretch much beyond that at the moment, but he trusted that things would become clearer as he went.

The hope he had of engaging in friendly connections soon evaporated. Business wasn't good, particularly at the higher end of the market. Many of Prague's dealers had simply given up after the communist takeover in '48. Still, a careful and thorough exploration of the city, particularly when he ventured out of the centre, slowly began to yield results. There were two shops on the west side of the river, in the Malá Strana, that had boxes full of tin toys, including wind-up items. This was at least somewhere to start, and both had them priced reasonably enough that he could afford to make multiple purchases, which enabled him to engage in some good-natured bartering.

It was while he was doing this that he realised he was being watched. He felt it before he saw it, and so he turned as the items were being wrapped, as casually and unconcernedly as he could manage. Immediately he relaxed a little. His observer was an old man in a threadbare woollen suit, and shoes with at least one broken sole. He was watching Louis in a kind of fascinated way, rather than with malice. Maybe he was a little senile, Louis thought, nodding politely at him.

As he left the shop, the old man addressed him in a quiet voice:

'*Ata yehudi?*'

As the words registered, Louis worked to consciously relax his face and empty his eyes of any comprehension. Because he understood the question. The man was speaking Hebrew. He was asking 'Are you Jewish?' in the Biblical language. As quickly as he could, he adopted an expression of non-comprehending indulgence, as if to say, 'I know you're a bit mad, but I'll just smile politely so I can walk on past you.' But this was not enough to shake off the old man, who shuffled behind him out of the shop.

Once outside, he was a little bolder.

'*Bistu Eydish?*' he called out. There was a mournful tone in his voice. The sound of someone lonely, like the voice of a man on a desert island calling after the first ship he'd sighted in years, only for that ship to go sailing past without having seen him.

'*Bistu Eydish?*' was the same question asked in Yiddish. Louis thought it would be more suspicious to ignore this, so he turned casually and responded in Czechoslovakian.

'I'm sorry?' he asked, smiling kindly.

'*Bistu Eydish?*' the old man asked again, with a hint of desperation. He was holding out one of his hands as if ready to clasp a brother. Louis could see cracked and dirty nails and the nicotine stains on the inside of his fingers. The man seemed a little mad, and he decided to just smile again and leave, maintaining the fiction that he didn't understand.

There was something else troubling in the man's behaviour that only struck him as he walked away. He realised that he'd been unconsciously luxuriating in the sense that he'd been gifted a Gentile identity by the plastic surgery he'd undergone. It was one thing he didn't have to concern himself with, being seen as a Jew, even if he'd swapped that for many other burdens. But this old man hadn't seen him that way. There was too much else buzzing through Louis' brain for it to concern him now. But it had caught somewhere within, to nag at him later.

Back at the Karlín, where Louis was more than halfway through his run, things had quickly settled down after Eva's arrest. In terms of the general conversation, it was as if the miserable event had never happened. There was a development, however, that seemed to be related to Louis' psychometry act. As he was passing out the cloth bags among the audience during his next performance, he noticed a woman with short blonde hair in a grey suit sitting in the second row, watching him intently. Her gaze was unsmiling, analytical. It was possible that the bait of Karel Kay and Franz had finally been taken.

With that in mind, Louis thought it was time to up the magical content of his act even further. What he wanted was a killer item that would leave the audience speechless. There was one trick he could think of that he knew he could manufacture himself, provided he could get hold of some playing cards, some furniture polish or clear wax and some fine-grade sandpaper. It was a routine that magician Eddie Field had made popular some years earlier, called 'the Invisible Deck', in which a spectator imagined holding an invisible pack of cards, and reversed any one of them in their mind's eye. The magician then produced a real pack and revealed that a single card had indeed been inverted, and that it was the spectator's freely chosen card. But better even than that, the great magician Dai Vernon had come up with his own wrinkle that improved upon this apparent miracle. In Vernon's version, the card was not only reversed but had a different-coloured back to all the others. It was truly inexplicable.

It would take Louis a couple of days to manufacture the special pack, and he needed to give himself some time to practise.

The only real challenge, he realised, was how to have Franz perform the trick. His was still a vent act, after all, and it was vital that he maintained that fiction in order to maximise his chances of convincing the Kolduny that he was a clean and bona fide turn. But the climax required the pack of cards to be spread between two hands, and one of Louis' would be inside Franz.

He spent longer trying to solve this problem than he did rehearsing the trick itself. Eventually he had to go out for a walk in order to do so, even though rain was tumbling from the sky as if from in buckets. He was standing drenched on the Charles Bridge when the answer came to him, and he was so excited he started laughing. If he could have done so, he would have telephoned Dinah right there and then. But then he was so shocked that he was having that upsetting thought that he had to run back to his rooms until he was out of breath, hoping that the physical exertion would drive it from his mind.

The night of the new trick's first performance came, and at first Louis thought it might just be a dry run, because there was no sign of the steely-faced woman in the front rows. But as he asked for the house lights to be raised in order for Franz to get a look at the audience and choose a volunteer, he saw her. She was sitting about halfway back in the stalls, on the right-hand side, her gaze as intense and unsmiling as ever.

With the audience member selected, Louis went into the shtick he had come up with that would enable him to present the end of the routine and still keep Franz in control of it.

'Comrades,' said the dummy, 'we now come to the most difficult part of my presentation. I'm going to read this man's mind. As promised, I will do so blindfolded.' Laughter from the audience at this. 'And so as to rule out any chance of cheating, I'm going to ask my faithful assistant here ...' at this, Louis gave a long-suffering look to the audience, which provoked more laughter, 'to place me in the dark, in a sealed box, from where I will instruct him further.'

Franz was thus dispatched into a wicker crate that Louis had borrowed from the theatre's costume department, but despite being removed from sight, he continued to bark his instructions from within – or so it seemed. Here was another ventriloquial trick Louis had learned on the music hall circuit: to slightly deaden the pronunciation of his consonants while simultaneously pushing the voice more into the back of the throat. It created a muffled effect that with enough willing suspension of disbelief the audience would attribute to the dummy speaking to them while out of sight. And so Franz's performance continued:

'Comrades, I'm going to ask my volunteer a question now – wherever you are. Are you still there? I hope he hasn't walked out. That would put a damper on things. Are you still there?'

'Yes,' came a shout from the auditorium, from the spectator who had selected the card.

'Good, because I had a premonition earlier today – I had an instinct, a feeling that later on, during this evening's performance, I would meet a person just like you, and that you would mentally select a particular playing card. And to check if my premonition would turn out to be correct, I took that very playing card and turned it round in the deck so it was reversed. I'll now ask my assistant to show it to you. Before he does, can you shout out as clearly as possible the name of the card you imagined.'

'The seven of hearts.'

'The seven of hearts, I think you said. It's hard to hear in here.' More laughter from the audience, who appreciated being let in on the joke, even as the routine neared its climax. 'I'm going to ask my assistant now to spread out the pack of cards with their backs towards you.' Louis did so, maintaining his air of stoic dignity, revealing that there was indeed a single playing card reversed, facing them, and it was the seven of hearts. But Franz wasn't finished. 'Please, in case anyone thinks there is any chicanery ... To demonstrate that my prediction was actually made earlier, and that this untrustworthy fool of an assistant hasn't just done something he shouldn't have done, I actually used a card from a completely different pack. Please – show them the back.' Louis plucked the card out and reversed it, confirming what Franz had just said. The audience immediately broke into spontaneous and enthusiastic applause. And as he looked up, he saw the steely-faced woman writing in a small secretary notepad.

So now he knew that the job was not just to maintain this level of performance, but to keep building and building through the rest of the run. He'd already had an idea for how he could incorporate a routine with a floating cigarette, with Franz demonstrating his ability to move objects with the power of his (wooden) mind, thus securing Karel Kay's reputation as the ventriloquist who'd demonstrated he had magical skills too

– steering anyone from the Kolduny away from the simple idea of 'a new magician in town', should anything about that make them suspicious.

When it came to the other side of Louis' mission, his ongoing reconnoitre of antique shops and second-hand dealers had yet to yield anything concrete, but there was a flea market coming up in the east of the city, at a disused part of the Pragovka Car Factory.

Initially, walking on to the huge concrete forecourt, he felt despondent. There was a chaotic mix of stalls and stands, some no more than trestle tables strewn with what appeared to be random collections of rubbish. Some were even selling home-grown produce – cabbages and turnips mixed with jams and pickles. It wasn't exactly Petticoat Lane. The vendors were closer to amateurs than dealers with any knowledge or expertise. It was while he was at one of these counters, digging through a box of old ironwork, that he saw the old man again, the one who had greeted him in Hebrew and then Yiddish. Now Louis felt contrite about his earlier arrogance and discomfort. He'd been stupid. Here was somebody who, given his age, could well have a lifetime's knowledge to share, knowledge that might be helpful.

'Excuse me,' he said, approaching the man from behind. 'We've met before, haven't we?' This felt a little bit direct, spoken aloud, so he immediately tried to soften his approach. 'Yes, I thought so. Please. Would you let me apologise? When we met last time, I didn't understand what you were saying. I was . . . I was embarrassed. But I fear it might have come across as rudeness.'

The old man looked taken aback, frightened even. Louis' eye was drawn to two unshaven patches of short white beard under his chin and on the side of his neck. He felt guilty for even noticing them. For the briefest of moments, he recalled his grandfather, who towards the end of his life had had a similar demeanour, his importance and stature long gone, replaced by an air of lost helplessness.

'It was in an antique dealer's a few days ago. In the Malá Strana. You spoke to me in Polish, I think. I don't speak Polish, so I just walked on, which was very rude of me. I felt bad about it all day. Please allow me to apologise.'

A dim look of recollection came over the man's face, and his suspicion gave way to a smile.

'*Ikh hab gemeynt az du bist meyn bruder*,' he said in Yiddish, as much to himself as to Louis. *I thought you were my brother*. 'I thought I recognised you,' he added in Czech, providing his own translation.

'It's perfectly all right. I'm glad I've seen you. I really didn't mean to be rude. Lord knows, courtesy is in short supply in these times.' The old man smiled at this melancholy observation. 'Could I buy you a cup of coffee?' Louis had seen a little kiosk on the outer edge of the pitches. 'It's a cold day.'

'Ooh, I can't drink coffee. It gives me wind,' said the old man, laughing at the idea.

'A pastry, then.'

'I'd take a cigarette if you had one.'

Louis smiled and pulled a pack from his pocket.

'Take one for later,' he said, offering two. The old man looked at him with something approaching wonder. It appeared it had been a long time since anyone had made such a gesture.

'You're a mensch. Are you a collector? Or a dealer?'

'Oh, neither. I'm an entertainer.'

'An entertainer?' The old man pulled a face, as if this was the strangest thing he'd ever heard.

'I'm appearing at the Karlín at the moment. In the variety show.'

'A burlesque? At the Karlín?'

'Not quite a burlesque.' The word was *parodie* in Czech, but 'burlesque' was how Louis would have translated it. 'A Czech Cavalcade of Culture,' and he dared to allow a little hint of sarcasm into his voice. He doubted this old man was an enthusiastic party member.

'So what's brought you here?' said the man.

'A silly thing,' said Louis, 'a fantasy.' He could feel his cover story elaborating itself as he prepared to tell it.

'What do you mean, a fantasy?' The old man was intrigued by the word itself.

'I don't have the means to build a real collection. Or the space. But my interest is real, so I like to pretend that I do. Just to give myself permission to go looking.'

'To go looking for what?' The old man was hooked, desperate to know.

'Puppets, marionettes, automata.' In the same way his entry into Czechoslovakia had been disguised by his pairing with Elena, here he hid his true interest by combining it with two innocent elements. This technique – the use of clean items placed alongside gimmicked ones – was an endlessly useful piece of magical thinking, blurring the edges of truth and reality. It was a method that Louis and the Brains Trust fell back on again and again.

The old man looked vaguely disappointed. Maybe he was hoping for something else, something he might have been able to trade with. Louis tried to conceal any countering disappointment on his own face. It would have been too much perhaps to expect that this shabby individual was a direct passage to a dream box.

'Do you know anyone who deals in those things? Specialises?'

The old man shook his head with a regretful little laugh, as if this was a possibility so distant it was barely worth acknowledging.

'Not any more. Before the war ...' He tailed off, reluctant perhaps to even visit the memory. One of his yellowing eyes twitched involuntarily. 'But they ... they're no longer with us.' His voice faded into sadness. Louis added his own sigh.

'Like so many others.'

The old man spoke quickly, rather than leaving a silence in which the painful thought could flourish.

'I have no automata or puppets, but I do have something that may interest you. I collect cigarette boxes.'

'Cigarette boxes?'

'Yes.' The old man obviously picked up some disappointment in Louis' response, because he immediately added, 'Many of them are novelty items – for example, one is in the form of a caged bear. You pull a lever on the side and the bear sits upright holding a cigarette. Maybe you would like to see it.'

Even if this was a blind alley, the man obviously knew more than Louis did about the antiques dealers of Prague, and indeed the rest of Czechoslovakia. There was nothing to be lost by pursuing the relationship. Besides, there was something in his melancholy rheumy eyes that called out to Louis. Need, perhaps. Loneliness. Responding to that, helping another – there was sustenance to be found in that. It was reason enough to accept the invitation.

The old man withdrew a battered leather wallet from his inside coat pocket and opened it with his unsteady hands. He pulled out a creased and worn business card.

M. Gabčík
15 Přistavní
Prague

'The M stands for Marek,' he said, as if compensating for the formality of the gesture. 'Please. Call on me.' After a moment, he added, 'I would like it.'

Louis went straight to the Karlín after his encounter. It was raining hard, and it seemed preferable to wait at the theatre for a couple of hours rather than go back and forth to his rooms and submit to a double soaking.

He was surprised to find Novy waiting for him anxiously at the stage door, as if Louis was late when he was in fact more than an hour early.

'Kay, there's someone who wants to speak to you.'

'Who wants to speak to me?' said Louis, mirroring Novy's surliness straight back at him.

'Your act has . . . garnered interest.'

'From whom?'

'They're waiting in my office,' said Novy, making a point of leaving the question unanswered.

There were two men, both tall, both fair-haired, wearing match-ing green greatcoats with thick buckles and wide lapels. Both were clean-shaven, though one looked more brutal than the other, with heavy brows, and big hands clasped across his chest. He didn't speak. That was left to the more intelligent-looking of the two, whose Czech was impeccable but spoken with a Russian burr.

'Karel Kay?'

'Yes.'

'We'd like to ask you some questions.'

'OK. And you are . . .?'

'We are the people asking you some questions,' said the man drily, as his colleague pulled at his fingers, cracking his knuckles. Not a subtle gesture, but an unambiguous one.

'You've been performing here for . . .?'

'Three weeks.'

'And where were you performing before that?'

Louis looked at them. He wanted to play the part of the affronted tough-minded man who resented being questioned rather than the frightened man who had something to hide. The problem was, in that moment, he was closer to the latter than the former. He forced himself to remember his mission. This was exactly why he was here, after all, and exactly the outcome he had been working for.

'I had a pitch in front of the railway station. The central station.'

'And before that?'

There was a moment when he had to strive to remember his story. He searched for the first sentence of the monologue he'd drilled with Strath after devising his alias. As it came back to him, he was grateful for that distant officer's fierce insistence, and his perspicacity.

'Before that, I worked more haphazardly.'

'What does that mean?'

'Street performing elsewhere. Children's parties.'

'In Prague?'

'In Europe. I only came back to Czechoslovakia recently. I was living in Europe.'

'Why did you come back?'

'I'm Czech. I fled the Nazis. Once the Soviets took over, I wanted to come back.'

'Many people felt the opposite,' said his interrogator, after a moment's silence.

Louis shrugged. 'Not me. I'm a poor man. Always have been.'

'Where were you born, Kay?'

'Košice.'

'And Kay was your father's name?'

Louis gave a bitter laugh. 'Kaznelson,' he said. 'Kay is a stage name. He would have hated me doing this.'

'Why?'

'Because he thought the stage was for effeminates.'

'Are you effeminate?'

'No.'

'Karel Kaznelson, then.'

'Radoslav Kaznelson. Not as catchy on a bill.'

The officer said nothing as he wrote it down.

'Can you read minds?' he asked next, in a flat voice. The other officer, the brutal-looking one, was staring at Louis intently.

'I can make an audience think that.' This was a considered and nuanced answer, but it came to Louis straight away.

'What do you mean?'

He reached into his trouser pocket for some loose change.

'I want you to imagine you've got three coins in front of you. Say, twenty haléřů, fifty haléřů . . . and a koruna.'

The interrogator looked at him, weighing up whether to go along with this. Was it too impertinent? Louis wondered. Was he pushing things too far? But the man gave a small nod of assent, and Louis could feel that little catch of having lured someone in with the hope of a few moments of entertainment.

'Imagine them laid out in front of you, right in front of you, just there.' He nodded at the desk. 'I want you to visualise them – see them in your mind's eye. OK?'

The interrogator nodded. The brutal man's gaze remained fixed on Louis.

'Good,' said Louis. 'Now I want you to choose one of those coins. Just one. Any one you fancy. A free choice. But don't tell me what you've chosen.'

The man nodded again. Louis held up his hand, which was closed into a loose fist.

'In a moment I'm going to open my fist and reveal what's in here. But first, I want you to touch the imaginary coin you're thinking of. OK?' He nodded at the man, who reached out his finger and did so. 'Which coin is it?' Louis asked.

'You tell me.'

'I'll do better than that. Which coin?'

'The koruna.'

Immediately Louis opened his fist, revealing a single koruna in there.

'How did you know?'

'A trick,' said Louis, slipping the coin back in his pocket. 'But it creates a good effect.' It was clearly wiser to emphasise the artifice rather than pretend he had mind-reading powers. It was more direct, straightforward. No need for unnecessary layers of deception given the mission. 'But why do you want to know if I can read minds?'

'Thank you, Kay,' was all the man said. 'And how much longer are you here?'

'For the length of the run. Unless Novy sacks me.'

'He won't,' said the interrogator confidently, and both men stood up. They said nothing more as they left.

That night, the severe-looking woman was back. Louis hadn't changed his act. He and Franz were still doing his version of the Invisible Deck, enjoying the fact that he'd had an opportunity to iron out all the wrinkles. He was delighted to see that his admirer was now accompanied. On her right side sat an intense-looking man with swept-back black hair and round-framed spectacles. Louis didn't let his eyes settle on the man for any noticeable amount of time, but he wondered if that was Potash. Everything that had happened in the past few days made it feel like this was a possibility.

Nothing was said that night, but the next day Novy caught Louis on the way to his dressing room. He seemed both resentful and anxious about his own resentfulness, caught in some terrible mental bind.

'I've heard they may move you to Moscow.'

'I'm sorry?' said Louis, meaning it as a question. But he received no reply, so he had to probe further. 'Who's "they"?' But Novy just walked on, frightened perhaps that he had already said too much.

If this was the case – and Louis allowed himself a small spike of triumphant satisfaction – he had better turn his attention to the old man, to Gabčík. It was just possible that he had some information about dream boxes, and about where in Prague the unfortunate Colonel Richmond had found his.

There was no guarantee that Gabčík would be there, Louis thought as he set out to Holešovice, the industrial region of the city where the man lived. He was anticipating some small apartment or rooms in a tall, narrow boarding house not unlike his own, and was therefore taken aback when he came to the site on the corner of a nondescript road lined with squat low-roofed factories and warehouses. Number 15 Přístavní was actually a yard, with a large battered wooden gate, and were he not searching for it, Louis would barely have noticed it. Just a few planks of rotten wood, covered in fading paint.

He searched for some way of indicating his presence there, a bell push or a knocker. In the end he identified a piece of string hanging behind a crack in one of the planks that were loosely nailed together to fashion the gate. Pulling it experimentally, he heard a distant clang. He looked at his watch. It was just gone 10.30. It was possible Gabčík had left for the day, off on some time-passing perambulation of the junk shops and antiquarians of Prague, something to fill the lonely hours between now and his death. Louis immediately hated himself for having the thought.

He was about to ring the bell again when there was the sound of movement on the other side of the battered wood. Heavy things being moved, bolts being slid back. After a few moments of this, the makeshift gate creaked open a fragment and the old man's eye appeared in the gap. He looked confused at first, squinting out at Louis as if trying to remember why his face was familiar or understand what it was doing there. And then it became apparent that he was smiling as he recognised who it was. The gate creaked open wider, its bottom edge grating on the rough stone floor.

'My friend. *Mój brat!* What are you doing here?'

'I'm sorry, I didn't mean to intrude.'

'Oh, you're not intruding. It's a pleasure to receive you. To have a visit from an artiste. It's a privilege.' The old man ushered Louis through the gate. It was a proper junkyard, with piles of just about anything lined up and distributed randomly around the edges. There were old toilets and railway sleepers; lines of copper pipes seemingly emerging from the muddy ground as if they'd grown there; cloth sandbags piled against broken pianos . . . such a confusion of items that it was hard to make sense of it.

'Please, this way, this way.'

'I fear I might be leaving town soon,' Louis said.

'Oh, that's a pity, when we have just made our connection,' said the old man, who was revealing more of his Polish accent as he spoke.

'A new engagement beckons. The lot of a strolling player,' said Louis, flashing Karel Kay's more theatrical side.

'Where? Not far away, I hope.'

'I don't know exactly.'

'But you will be back?'

'I hope so, though I don't know when.'

'Well, you must come inside.'

He led Louis towards a living area, a sort of lean-to hut against the side of a larger building, an old warehouse or storage facility. Inside was a bed, neatly made, with pyjamas folded on the pillow; a small dining table with evidence of breakfast still on it; and a lone gas ring in the corner, with a stack of saucepans and pots to one side.

'You would like some coffee, no?'

'Coffee would be lovely, yes.'

Even in this living area there was more evidence of Gabčík's collection and storage: piles of newspapers and magazines, old army uniforms bundled neatly next to a line of buckets, a cardboard box full of false teeth. The man didn't seem to distinguish between what he accumulated. His collection appeared to be more a celebration of the act of categorisation itself rather than being about any possible utility or commercial value – a pastime rather than a business.

'How long have you been here?' asked Louis, wanting to make conversation. The old man did not seem to hear him.

'You have come to see my collection, haven't you? The cigarette boxes.'

'Well, actually I came to see you. But yes, I'm intrigued by them.'

'Oh, there are some very intricate items in there – some fine examples.'

Louis thought this was as good an opening as any, so he decided to seize the opportunity it gave him. 'As a collector, sir, I was going to ask: are you familiar with makers?'

'Makers?' said Gabčík, confused.

'The names of makers, I mean. Like Fabergé, the jeweller. Or Becker, the clock-maker.'

'Of course. But I cannot afford such items myself. They are beyond my means.'

'Oh, I know. Mine too. I was rather going to ask you if you knew who in Prague might deal in the products of such artisans.'

'This new appointment must be lucrative, no!' The old man wrapped a coffee-stained dishcloth around his hand and picked up a battered old kettle.

'Oh, it's a fantasy really. But also partly a prudence.'

'A prudence?'

'I've never trusted banks when it comes to life savings. A nice clock or a fine jewellery box strikes me as a more reliable pension.

If you have expert knowledge, you can buy something that will never lose its value.'

'*Yiddische kopf!*' said the old man, tapping his head. He wasn't disguising his Jewishness, and he was behaving as if he discounted Louis' denial of his own, for this phrase was Yiddish and could be translated as something like 'a canny business head' – literally 'Jewish brains'. Louis let it go. It would have been too self-conscious to have questioned the phrase. More believable to not respond at all, if he was someone who had no understanding of the man's foreign vernacular.

'So who is the maker you want to collect?' The little kettle on the gas ring started to rattle and whistle.

'Do you know Pierre Boileau?'

'Of course,' said the old man. Perhaps his affirmative response wasn't so surprising. As an average Englishman might know that Thomas Chippendale made furniture, whereas an average German might not, so an average Czechoslovakian might be conversant with his country's artisans where others would be ignorant. 'And you want to own a Boileau piece yourself?' he continued, a notable twinkle in his eye.

'As I say, it's a dream. But for dreams to be sustained, they must contain an element of possibility, don't you think?' said Louis.

'I've heard it said.' Gabčík picked up the kettle with his cloth-bound hand. 'But Boileau pieces are not just expensive. They are rare. Very rare – no?'

'Well, that's just it,' said Louis. 'There was a man I knew – well, a man I heard of, it might be more accurate to say – who put his hands on a piece fairly recently here in Prague. I'm guessing you know all the dealers in the city. I wonder if you might know who would have been likely to have sold such a piece.'

'How do you know he bought it off a dealer?' said the old man. 'Sometimes such transactions are more . . . informal.'

'That's true. But then maybe you know of other such collectors, too.'

Why did it feel like they were standing on different ground now? It was like something had shifted between them as they were talking. The boiling water trickled into the coffee-maker, sending clouds of scented steam into the air.

'A man such as me does not move in those circles,' the old man said, although there was an element of theatricality to the statement, as if he was contemptuous of anyone who might think that of him. He put the kettle down and unwrapped the dishcloth from his hand.

There was a pause in which Gabčík looked at Louis, holding him in an unwavering gaze. Then he asked:

'If you had the means – in your dream this is – would it be a small piece or a large piece that you were most interested in?' It was an oddly specific question. Perhaps sensing Louis' surprise, the old man qualified it: 'Because there are some large examples, you know. Quite remarkable.'

'It is a dream, remember,' said Louis, working to hold on to his character, to Karel Kay and the circumstances he had woven around him.

'I know. I know. But it is good to indulge our dreams from time to time.' And now the old man was smiling in a way he hadn't done before. 'I wonder ... Can I trust you?' He seemed to be speaking to himself rather than to Louis, but before Louis had decided whether he should answer, Gabčík had moved over to the entrance of the living quarters. It was obvious he expected his guest to follow.

They passed back out into the yard and then through a door that at first did not reveal that it was a door; it looked more like a collection of old planks of uneven lengths and different-coloured peeling paint, something knocked together to cover a piece of broken wall. It occurred to Louis that it had been made to deliberately misdirect.

The corridor beyond was very different from Gabčík's yard. If it reminded Louis of anything, it was the backstage area of a theatre: bare brick walls, scrubbed floorboards, and a number of doors on either side, each one closed, with matching handles. The sense of order and maintenance was in marked contrast to the shabby chaos they had just come from.

'This is all yours?' asked Louis, genuinely curious.

'After a fashion,' replied the old man, somewhat enigmatically. They rounded a corner and came to a narrow staircase leading to a lower floor. 'Mind yourself here,' he said. 'The stairs are quite steep.'

284

The staircase doubled back on itself. It led to a tighter corridor than the one above, with numerous branches that the old man navigated without pause. Again there were several doors, reminding Louis once more of a theatre, or indeed a hotel.

He was surprised when the room the old man led him into revealed itself to be spacious and ludicrously well appointed. Such was the contrast with the place they'd just come from, he was momentarily disorientated. At one end there was a roaring fire that looked like it had been recently attended. It had an art nouveau surround with bright green floral tiles. Plush purple velvet curtains hung from ceiling to floor, with generous swag. Cast-iron vents of an elaborately decorative nature ran around the top of the walls, drawing the smoke out of the room, and the furniture was equally ornate and luxurious: a pair of carved chaises longues, heavy leather armchairs, and a large mahogany desk with a spindled surround.

As he stood there taking in this unexpected luxury, Louis was already aware how far away he was from the door, from any possible escape. Not only that, even if he did get out of the room, would he be able to retrace his steps through the labyrinthine corridors before he was apprehended? He tried to calm the growing sense of panic, of being in trouble, that was beginning to freeze his belly. Why he felt like this wasn't immediately apparent, apart from the obvious revelation that Gabčík had been dissembling about his status and true identity. But it wasn't just that. It was the manner of that dissembling. It was so brilliantly done. As if Louis had been fooled by a master magician, with misdirection so strong he had been unable to see through it. The formality of the surroundings only added to the sense that he was standing in the headmaster's office waiting for the cane. He consciously began to breathe from his lower abdomen, as he might if he were on stage and a prop had jammed or a method failed. Perhaps there might yet be a benign explanation for this unexpected turn.

'This is a nice room,' he heard himself say, hoping to prompt a response that shifted things towards the good.

'Well,' said the old man, a newly sly tone evident in his voice, 'as Trotsky once said, while we struggle to change life, let us not forget the reasons for living.' He went over to the expensive-looking desk and pulled open one of the drawers. Taking out a cardboard box, he handed it to Louis. 'Have a look in here.'

Now Louis' sense of panic returned. He was fearful of what was inside. A dream box? If it was, he didn't want to be made to stare into it. He would just look away.

'Go on,' the old man said. 'See what you think.'

Louis reached for the cardboard box. Rather than being tentative, he lifted the flaps with a defiant casualness. He wasn't going to appear cowed in any way, whatever was going on. Inside, rather than the beautiful craftsmanship of the item he had seen back in Aldershot, he was faced with a cheap-looking roughly carved casket made from glued-together cedar wood. It was the kind of thing you would find on a market stall or a souvenir stand. On the front was a glossy oval with a brightly coloured picture of a riverside scene, badly printed. Something about it made him feel sick.

'Have a look. Go on, get it out,' the old man said, persisting, encouraging him.

Louis lifted the box from its cardboard container. It was lightweight, insubstantial. It had a cheap tin clasp on its front, imperfectly fitted and slightly off-centre.

'Open it, go on. You don't need to be so hesitant. Tell me what you see.'

But every instinct in Louis was to hesitate. He didn't want to see what was in that box. Was something going to spring out at him, hurt him? Was there something alive in there? He thought about shaking it, but his instinct was still to maintain the fiction that nothing had changed since they were standing in the battered old lean-to with the gas stove hissing; that this was still a slightly eccentric, lonely old man and Louis was still Karel Kay, the mordant ventriloquist, former street entertainer who'd graduated to the Karlín. With that in mind, he flicked up the catch and lifted the lid.

The box was empty. The outside was stained with varnish, but the inside was unfinished. The only adornment was a mirror fixed to the underside of the lid.

'Well, what do you see?' This line of questioning was increasingly puzzling. It was like a riddle, or onstage dialogue that didn't fit with the props he'd been given.

He frowned, trying to think what the answer to the question was.

'A cheap jewellery box ...' He stared into the grain of the unvarnished wood. 'Something mass-produced, made in bulk.' A movement caught his eye. It was in the mirror, and therefore somewhere behind him.

'You're not looking hard enough,' said the old man. His voice, close behind Louis, softer, talking only a few inches from his ear, was different now. It was the same person, recognisably the same person, but the inflection had changed, the accent was less pronounced, the pace of the speech faster, more confident, that of a younger, more powerful man.

'I can't see anything else,' said Louis, not reacting, sticking stubbornly to the reality he was invested in, out of either pride or fear, or a combination of the two.

'No? Well, shall I tell you what *I* can see?' The reflection behind him moved. Louis was bending slightly to peer into the box, and Gabčík's head appeared over his shoulder. 'I can see a fool.' The voice changed even more, the accent shifted, no longer Polish, all trace of Yiddish inflection gone. It was smooth, calm, Russian. 'I see one Louis Warlock. Well, no – that's not true – one Ludvik Weinschenk, crudely disguised, like an idiot child who foolishly thinks the cellophane bag he's pulled over his head is a mask.'

Louis turned to see Gabčík standing erect, no longer hunched, his expression and demeanour that of a man thirty years younger. He reached for a cloth from his pocket and began wiping his face. The colouring and mottling of aged skin began to vanish, smeared across his features. He wiped his hands too, removing the nicotine stains and grime. It was nothing but make-up, skilfully applied. He pushed a finger against his eyeball, separating the lids with the fingers of his other hand, and removed a large contact lens. Louis winced. Gabčík didn't. He just smiled and gestured to the open door on the other side of the room.

'Shall we?' he said casually, as if the outcome they had finally arrived at had never been in doubt. Not for a single second.

'Where are we going?' asked Louis.

'Oh, nowhere,' said Gabčík, who Louis was forced to accept wasn't Gabčík. Was this actually Potash himself? Or one of his minions? Or was there something else going on?

'I liked it in there,' said Louis. This stupid attempt at being blasé made him feel sick the moment the words were out of his mouth. His thinking was that he had yet to confirm anything that had just been said about his true identity, about him being Louis Warlock. In fact, he'd given no response at all, other than the blend of shock, surprise and cold horror that had played spontaneously on his face. Given this, he thought his only option now was to hold off from confirming anything for as long as he could, if only to gain himself some time in which to think through the best way forward. But something else lay behind that thought, something dark that was beginning to coagulate in his guts, slowly freezing him from within. There might well be no 'best way forward'. There might only be cold terror ahead, and an awful fate – and the slow freeze suddenly burst into a hot panic before he could gain control of it.

'Well,' said the man, 'we're done with all that now, I'm afraid.'

They arrived at a door larger than any of the others they'd passed, being more industrial in its appearance, and it did indeed lead into an expansive warehouse space, which had been divided up with smaller partitioned units at one end. In the centre of the concrete floor was a wheelchair, and a surgical trolley covered in a green cloth.

'Now then,' said the man, continuing in Czechoslovakian (which was something, thought Louis – maybe there was something to hang on to in that, though he couldn't think what). 'I need you to slip out of your clothes, please.'

'Sorry?'

'I need you to slip out of your clothes,' repeated calmly and firmly, in such a way as to make clear that there was no alternative. As if to reinforce the point, two black-clad figures had appeared on the opposite side of the warehouse. They stood in a military manner, and both had rifles slung over their shoulders. Whether they'd been there all along or whether they'd just entered, taking the man's instruction as a cue, Louis didn't know.

'I don't want to slip out of my clothes.'

'Take your clothes off, please.'

'No.'

Without making much of a fuss, the man lifted his arm and beckoned to one of the guards, who strode briskly across the floor, footsteps echoing off the corrugated-iron ceiling above. He was a good six inches taller than Louis, and twice his width. He stood at Louis' side, awaiting instruction.

'Please don't make me give him an order,' said the man. 'Do as you're told and take your clothes off. Now.'

Louis found that his hands were moving mechanically and he was taking off his jacket, unbuttoning his shirt. So much for resistance. Even had he been trained in the management of receiving violence, he doubted his actions now would be any different. He was in a place where he was just going to do whatever was asked of him, carried along on the rails of it. His choices were stark: immediate pain, or hold it off for as long as he could.

When he got down to his underpants, he stopped.

'No, no, no,' said the man. 'Everything, please.' Louis just stood there. 'Take them off.'

He was back at school. Mr Cooke, the music teacher, had caught him and his friends talking in the dormitory, still in their clothes when they should have been in their pyjamas. The other boys had heard him coming and jumped into their beds fully clothed. Louis, with his back to the door, hadn't sensed his approach and was caught in flagrante. He'd been shouted at, chastised and then told to strip. He'd stood there – as he was now – in his underpants until Cooke had barked at him to take those off too. He'd felt the teacher's unwavering gaze on him as he did, and his insides had curdled.

'Let's have a look at you,' said the man. He approached, touched Louis' arm, the hairs on which were raised, the skin goose-pimpling from both the cold and the fear. 'Ah,' he said, 'you're cold. I served in East Prussia during the war. My coat had rotted to nothing by the winter of '43. I got used to being chilly, while you were in your cosy school dormitory, fat on plum duff.'

'Are you police? Are you arresting me?' Louis was trying to gather himself into some sort of coordinated response: why not string them along for a bit longer? He felt a fragment of fight in him; oddly enough, not aimed at his assaulters here, but rather at Strath and the whole British establishment for throwing him into this pit with no training, no support, no preparation. He thought of those older boys at school when he first got there who were up in Spitfires and Mosquitos after a few weeks of rudi-mentary instruction and dead within days. At least there the enemy was worth fighting. This one was amorphous, dubious, but was it really any worse than the lords and masters on his side? *His side!* Had he ever had a side?

The man nodded at the guard, and Louis' back exploded into a burst of pain ballooning upwards from the base of his spine where the rifle butt had struck it. And in that moment, unex-pectedly, he thought of Eva at the Karlín, her skirt riding up over her legs, her beauty, her gift, her dignity torn from her – for what? For what?

'Please,' said the man. 'I'd like to hear from your lips, for the record, your name and rank, if they gave you any, and your mission.'

'Radoslav Kaznelson, formerly of British 313 Squadron. But shot down in—'

The man nodded, and another blast of pain came, this time in his side, winding him, doubling him up.

'I'm quite happy for this to go on all day. So carry on as long as you like. But really, you should know that it's futile.' He took a step closer to Louis as he spoke. 'Do you know why it's futile? Hmm? Because we've met before. Oh yes. Look at me. Look. At. Me.' And he nodded at the guard again, who took hold of Louis' head. He had no choice but to stare at the man, who did something very peculiar. He adjusted his posture, his demeanour, much as he'd done when he'd slipped out of the persona of Gabčík to become this well-spoken Russian tormentor. Now he seemed to become taller still. He spread his legs slightly, pushed out his chest, adjusted the angle of his neck, giving himself a more athletic bearing. Finally he removed something from an inside pocket, a pair of distinctive gold-rimmed spectacles. He slipped them on and his face became serious, grave-looking, and as soon as he spoke, in a clipped English accent, Louis knew who he was.

'Mr Warlock? Thank you for coming at such short notice, and such a late hour.' He had become Thorneycroft. Major Thorneycroft.

Until that moment, Louis had had no idea; it would never have occurred to him. It was like a fantastic magic trick. A new man appearing from nowhere. It was absurd, but the only thing he could think of was Basil Rathbone in the Sherlock Holmes films, adopting some elaborate disguise, delighting in fooling both Watson and the audience.

'Potash,' he said quietly, knowing it – which was different from suspecting it.

If there was a flicker on the man's face at the use of his real name, it was so small that Louis might well have imagined it. But that didn't alter his sense of certainty.

'So easy to fool. So easy to reel in,' said Potash, back to his native Russian accent. 'I have to confess, I gave you more credit than you deserved. I thought there was going to be some risk involved in this scheme, and it's turned out there was none at all. It's been like performing to a child.' And he contorted his face into a grotesque caricature of subservience. '"Oh yes, sir. Please let me help you, sir. I'll do anything for you, sir." Because, Weinschenk, you're just like any other Jew. You're so desperate to be accepted, to please, to ingratiate yourself with whatever authority is to hand, in search of any little scrap of acceptance, that it blinds you to anything else. Because you don't belong anywhere, do you? You're an aberration.'

Louis very much wanted to avoid displaying any emotional reaction to this tirade. He wanted to deprive Potash of that satisfaction at least, but it was impossible. The words were chosen to cut, and the cuts brought pain, which showed itself automatically on Louis' face, in his stance, in his demeanour. There was no concealing it. It was vanity to think there could be.

'Your people have been culturally redundant for more than two thousand years,' Potash continued, 'a squirming little bit of dead history, supplanted by the religion yours gave birth to, too self-absorbed to admit to that fact, so full of yourselves, so puffed up with your own story that all the little egos who are part of that story through nothing more than an accident of birth find themselves clinging to their tale of specialness and chosen-ness and elevation, even as the culture they pull around themselves like a rotten cloak repels and disgusts wherever in the world they go, whichever diseased corner of it they try and make their own. So the lightest of touches, the tiniest of pressures was all it took to get you to perform for me, like some starving seal. You only saw one of your betters – Major Thorneycroft – who you were so anxious to please, that you immediately jumped into line.'

Louis' bruises were beginning to throb: in the small of his back, his lower ribs. He hadn't noticed, but the other guard was at his side now, and he felt himself being hauled to his feet. He cursed Strath again for his ludicrous scheme, sacrificing him for nothing, making him endure a fake hanging so word would get out that he was dead. The hubris of the plastic surgery, which it had turned out had fooled nobody. None of it had made any difference whatsoever. Compared to Potash's deceptions and misdirections, Strath's operation was akin to the fumblings of a clumsy amateur. And Louis could hardly bear the dreadful irony that while his own face had been carved into with a surgeon's knife without fooling his nemesis for a second, that same nemesis only had to don a pair of spectacles and adjust his posture and Louis had been pathetically bamboozled.

'How could you tell?' he heard himself ask, in a barely audible voice.

'Hmm?' Potash cocked his head as if indulging a child.

'How could you tell? After the—'

His snorted laugh cut off the question. 'You can make all the physical changes you want. But ultimately, it seeps through your skin. Your stain. The only way to really remove it would be to drench you in acid till there's nothing left but bubbles.'

'What's it for?' Louis could hear that his tone was snivelling, just like Potash had said. 'All of this . . .'

'Well, I must admit . . .' as he spoke, Potash gestured to the guards with a casual movement of one hand, and Louis was jerked backwards towards the waiting wheelchair, 'I'm disappointed in you. I was told you might be a danger to our operation, a rival mind.' He snorted at this. 'Clearly that's not the case. So you're right in that sense: if the object of the exercise was to neutralise a potential threat, it's been a wasteful use of our resources, given that you were never any danger to my operation at all. But fortunately, there was more to the whole circus than that.'

The guards held Louis in place as Potash moved to the surgical trolley at the side of the chair.

'You're not a rival,' he said, pulling back the green cloth to reveal a large hypodermic syringe with an intimidatingly long needle. 'You're not even an irritant. You're nothing. Absolutely nothing.' And he picked up the needle, squirting out a few drops of the clear liquid within.

'The Funhouse. I know about the Funhouse . . .' Empty defiance, but it was still something – a declaration of resistance rather than surrender.

Potash laughed. 'You know nothing about the Funhouse. But you're about to find out. You're about to find out everything there is to know. Now, this is going to sting a little bit, I'm afraid,' he said, adopting the manner of a sympathetic doctor as the needle pierced the left side of Louis' abdomen. Sharp, cold pain that made him gasp, moving deeper and deeper into him. He flinched and wriggled, but the guards held him fast.

'Such a fuss,' said Potash, withdrawing the needle in one sharp movement and deftly placing a cotton pad over the injected area. 'Shh.'

'Dream boxes,' said Louis. 'I found out.' Another lie, but the need to defy continued. He was clenched, and not just from the pain, which remained even though the needle had been withdrawn.

Potash laughed lightly, a little snort, a burst of air through his nose as he wheeled Louis away from the trolley and across the room. 'Ah, the dream boxes. Yes. Let me explain, while we're waiting for that cocktail to work. The dream boxes were only ever a worm on a hook. But they were also a bell attached to the line that the hook was on. Of course, it was a particular type of worm, with a taste specifically designed to tempt you, just to speed things along. And if there were reports of anyone asking about dream boxes or Boileau – well, that was the bell ringing, letting us know that the bait had been taken, just in case we'd missed you earlier.'

'What's in the Funhouse? . . . What's in the Funhouse?' Louis found he'd repeated the question. Was it the drug beginning to work on him?

'Would you like to see?' asked Potash.

'You've gained nothing,' Louis said. He was holding on to that defiance, reaching for it like a drowning man trying to grab a rope that had been thrown to him.

'I've not quite gained it yet,' said Potash. 'But I am about to. I just have to melt away what's inside of you.'

They'd paused in front of a pair of large doors on the back wall. They looked as though they led to another space. There was graffiti written on them, painted in broad, messy strokes, a casually made joke. The same kind of joke as *Arbeit Macht Frei* over the gates of the death camp at Auschwitz. A joke that heralded the presence of evil. The graffiti here was written in the Cyrillic script of the Russian alphabet. Louis couldn't read the letters, but he guessed that they were the words Strath had spoken to him: 'Vesel'ye Zhiloy-Dom'. The House of Fun.

'Let's have a look and see what's inside.' Potash lifted the plain steel locking bar and pushed the doors open. Louis could feel the cold spreading from his side, freezing his legs, running up his spine. His vision was starting to blur and darken at its periphery. Consciousness was leaking away. It remained long enough for him to get his first glimpse of where he was going . . .

It was the strangest sensation. There was a sense of oblivion arriving – an engulfing coldness and blackness – and almost as soon as it had overtaken him, there was a slow awakening, a gradual fade-up. He was lying down, facing up. There was just whiteness. Bright whiteness. The same bright whiteness he had seen in the Funhouse, or rather the room that had been on the other side of the doors with *Funhouse* written on them. It had just been white, a large, intensely lit white space with absolutely nothing in it. It was the last thing he remembered seeing. And now he seemed to be being rolled back into it, even though he had no memory of being taken away.

Other sensations came back: a dull soreness in his side and another in his groin. He couldn't move his hands. He didn't have the strength to sit up. He drifted off again, then woke, presumably after only a few minutes, and felt himself being lifted off whatever he was lying on – a gurney of some kind – and carried for a short while, then seated on the floor. He couldn't struggle; he was still too weak. He could only look at what was being done to him. There was a cannula emerging from his wrist, and a male nurse in a white tunic and trousers was attaching it to a drip. He wanted to lie down, to fall over, but his hands were being fixed in position with straps that held him to the wall. There was more fiddling connected with the discomfort he was feeling in his side and groin; both areas were starting to throb. He tried to speak, but he didn't have the energy to open his mouth. His head lolled forward, until abruptly something started to revive him, like the burst of energy that followed the downing of a cup of espresso.

He tried to make sense of the room he was in. It was large, like a gymnasium, but there was nothing in it. The walls were white, the floor, which was hard, was lined with white linoleum. He managed to crane his neck backwards slightly to take in the ceiling, which was white too, but a brighter white that made it hard to stare at for any length of time. There was no visible light source, no bulbs or skylight or fittings, and yet it glowed as if there were. Because there was no furniture in the room and because every surface was featureless – just plain white – he found he had no sense of scale. Was it actually a normal-sized room and he'd been somehow made tiny? It was very hard to place himself in the space without any other reference to hold on to.

As if in answer to the thought, Potash appeared in front of him. Maybe he'd been there all along, standing behind him.

'Welcome to the Funhouse, Weinschenk. You're all set now.'

Louis tried to speak. He could open his mouth, but his throat was very sore. With a great effort of will, he managed to form the words:

'Set for what?'

'Your hollowing-out, ready for your repurposing.'

'What repur ... what ...?' It was harder to phrase that question.

'What will that be?' said Potash, affecting helpfulness. 'Well, there won't be much left of you, so it will be pretty simple, but you'll be serving a useful function from our point of view. Shall I explain how this is going to go, so you can understand while you're still capable of doing so?' His tone was insufferable. It was smug and triumphal and patronising and cruel all at the same time. It was like listening to an only child who couldn't bear being beaten, having just won a round of Monopoly with his friends.

'So – your brain, your mind, your sanity, your mental well-being, all of it needs stimulus, mental stimulus via the senses. You are a finely tuned machine designed to receive and process that stimulus. Well, it turns out that if we remove all stimulus, an interesting thing starts to happen: your nervous system starts to malfunction.'

Louis found unwelcome memories appearing, books he'd read about hypnotism, altered states of consciousness, darker examples of experiments in those arts that he'd dismissed at the time.

'If we create the right conditions,' Potash continued, 'your mind literally starts to consume itself. And when the process is comprehensive enough, this begins to happen after a remarkably short amount of time. Obviously, it's a highly artificial set of circumstances we have to establish. No human would encounter this in the real world. But research and development has enabled us to come up with the perfect version. The key, it turns out, like much else in life, lies in being thorough. Because the mind rebels against a vacuum, it will fill it with anything, any little scrap it can find that constitutes a stimulus of some kind, in order to offset the boredom. It needs to be able to look forward to something, anything – and it's remarkably adept at turning anything available to it into a reward. Prisoners of war know well how the promise of a scrap of bread when hungry can be as monumentally anticipated as a wedding night. Well, the principle we've devised and perfected here uses that need as a tool for scooping out the mind.

'All stimulus is removed. And I mean *all* stimulus. We create a total state of nothingness. So that means no visual stimulus – hence the room here. No sensual stimulus – it's kept at a constant thirty-seven degrees Celsius and is soundproofed and odourproof. You'll see you're connected to an intravenous drip; that provides a constant mixture of fluid and nutrients – enough to keep you alive for as long as we want, but no taste and smell or texture on your tongue, no meals to look forward to, no prisoner's banquet of a hunk of bread for you. And we've gone further. There are none of the usual bodily processes for you to enjoy either – we've circumnavigated them.'

Here Potash gestured down, and Louis saw the tube that emerged from his groin and disappeared behind him into the wall, and another, larger tube that emerged from his side.

'We've catheterised you and colostomised you; we've even stabilised your uncommonly high blood pressure. Tut tut. That's not a good sign for a man of your age. And lest you find yourself looking forward to the nightly phantasmagoria of your dream world, well, on a diurnal cycle we introduce a cocktail of barbiturates into your feed to deprive you of the stimuli of your unconscious mind. Your sleep will be blank, dreamless, contributing to your experience of endless nothing.'

He paused, patted Louis on the shoulder almost sympathetically.

'No being can stay sane under these conditions, certainly no human. Rest assured, you will be gone from yourself quite soon. In our experience, a few days, no more than two weeks. Of course, you will have no accurate experience of time, so you will quickly lose the sense of where you are in the process. When you're done, there'll be just about enough left for us to work with as we move you towards your final purpose.' A squeeze on the shoulder here. 'I hope you've enjoyed this account. They're truly the last words you'll hear as a sane human being.'

Potash smiled, released his grip and turned away. This was somehow the cruellest gesture of all, whether it was calculated to be so or not. It demonstrated what the man truly thought of him. Louis was nothing, an object, less than a farm animal, just a thing to be utilised for his own ends. Any suffering he felt was of no consequence whatsoever.

Nothing more was said. There was just the sound of the doors to the Funhouse swinging shut, being locked from the outside. And then an expansive hush settled on the room as if a giant blanket had been thrown over it. Louis coughed experimentally to see what it sounded like. The percussion of the noise was immediately swallowed up by the glutinous silence.

He sat there on the floor, tubes trailing out of him. At first, he was overwhelmed by dread. A stark, visceral horror – a physical sensation, like nausea but more profound, reaching down into the deepest part of him. There was panic in it, there was despair. There was revulsion. This continued for some indeterminate time. And then, surprisingly, abruptly, it began to subside, with unexpected speed. He guessed the body could only sustain that kind of state for so long. It wasn't quite relief – the continuing brute fact of his incarceration wouldn't allow for that – but it was enough of a shift away from the negative for it to galvanise him into taking action.

He stood up. He wanted to ascertain how much physical space he'd been afforded by the straps that held him to the wall. They were attached to his forearms with padded cuffs that ruled out any attempt at self-injury. The part of these cuffs that disappeared into the wall were on a mechanism that allowed them to slide up and down, but there was not enough slack or length in them to let him turn around. OK – so he could stand up and sit down. That was the limit of his physical freedom. But even that afforded him something, some domain within which he could act and make a choice.

A choice. A choice. He could define himself by his choices. Even here. Even in this dreadful desert, he must still be able to make choices.

Recite the Shema. There. That was a choice. *Recite the Shema in your head.* He could either do that or not do that. There was a choice he could make. Do. Don't do.

'*Shema Yisrael, adonai eloheinu, adonai echoed.*'

That was all he could remember. But he made the choice and executed it. There must be other choices he could make. Internal ones. His interior. That was his secret place. They couldn't see what was happening in there.

He had command over his secret place. He'd had command of it since he was eleven years old. And it had grown since then.

He had to keep his mind engaged. He had to utilise every fragment of discipline he had to hand. He had to use everything he had inside.

He only had to stay sane.

He only had to stay sane.

THE GOD WITHIN

It's a thing I think about often, dear
fellow magi: the memory of where it all
came from, the little spring from which the
rolling river has subsequently flowed. It's
something that's often in my head, and
always in my heart. Was it just a chance
encounter that led me to my passion? I used
to think that. I used to think it was
always in me and it would always have come
out. That it was solely mine, from my
birth. My birthright. My faculty. The
treasure I was born with. It's only
recently, as I've been pondering, thinking,
reflecting (a practice that circumstance
has allowed me to indulge of late), that it
came to me: actually, it's not so
clear-cut.

In my case, we'd have to go back to the
dark days before the war started, before
night fully fell over Germany, when the sun
was nearly down but a last few tendrils of
light remained.

It was my birthday, or at least my
birthday was imminent, and I'd been having
a hard time. I was a thinker, and a
worrier, and I was getting older,
approaching my twelfth year. I had a sense
of what the Nazis were, and what that meant

for Jewish children like me and their families. And more than that, there was the feeling in the household, which even our relative prosperity could not hold at bay.

As a consequence of all this upset, plans for my birthday had been put on hold. This information had come to me via eavesdropping. There had been a conversation about a month ahead of the date. I was in the habit of standing at the top of the banister upstairs and listening, after bedtime, whenever I heard my mother and father muttering to each other. This was partly a defensive strategy to calm my increasing anxieties. News about the political implications of some recent bit of government policy or edict was hard for me to understand, so listening to Mutti and Vati nattering was often the only way to make any sense of it. Also, I was habitually nosy, a fact that my nickname, 'bat ears', attested to. This time, though, the muttering wasn't about Herr Hitler or some new restriction, but rather about me:

'You know where he'd love to go? Zauberkönig.'

'Darling, you're not taking him eight hundred kilometres to visit a shop.'

'I want to show him something fun. Something he'll enjoy. He'll adore it. You know he will.'

I wasn't sure what Zauberkönig was. I'd heard mention of it before and knew it was some kind of novelty shop, different to a normal toy shop, but not much more than that. I loved that Vati thought it would mean something to me. Because if he said

that, then it surely would. He knew me, you
see. He knew who I was.

There was another conversation about
three weeks later. I'd been told in vague
terms that we might take a trip for my
birthday, without officially being told
where. This time the muttered chat had a
different tone, one that caused me to tense
up immediately:

'I don't want you to go,' said Mutti.
'You're tired. You're under a lot of
strain. He'll understand. We'll do
something else.'

'I know he'll understand.' This was
Vati being firm, not shouting, just being
assertive. 'But that's the problem with
Ludvik — he keeps it all in.'

'He'll be happy enough here.'

'I want to take him. We get on a train.
We get off again. We'll stay at Deitch's'
— which was a Jewish hotel — 'we'll be
welcome there. We come back. We avoid the
thugs, the SA.'

'But it's easier to—'

'I know it is. I know it is.' This was
said not in anger, but with force.

And so the day before my eleventh
birthday, we took the train north to
Berlin. The journey was long and generally
uneventful, apart from one point when two
uniformed officers, younger than my father,
got into our carriage and talked loudly.
One started telling an off-colour joke, and
I wondered whether Vati would let the
matter go rather than risk provoking
trouble. But he didn't. He coughed loudly
and firmly and nodded briskly in my
direction. He was still willing to seize

the authority in the confined space of that compartment at least.

Berlin was enormous and completely overwhelming compared to the narrow medieval streets of my home town. Red banners hung all over the place, with that black twisted spider of a swastika crouching in the centre of each one. They fell down the faces of buildings, from lines strung across the street, from flagpoles and street lights. It felt very different to home. Vati seemed unperturbed, and did not make reference to it, did not mention it at all. We were there for one reason, and one reason only. We were going to Zauberkönig.

It was south of the city centre, on a wide road called Herrfurthstrasse, in between two parks (I thought they were parks. They were actually cemeteries), and I'd never seen the like. We'd left Freiburg on the earliest train, at 6.45, so we'd arrived in Berlin just after lunchtime. Vati had promised me I would have as much of the afternoon as I wanted to browse in the shop. He'd remained deliberately vague about what I was going to find there. He just kept saying that I was going to love it.

I was in a state of considerable excitement by the time we stepped off the tram. It was probably about half past two when we arrived, but it was a gloomy afternoon and the shop front was illuminated as if it were night-time. From a distance it looked like a mosaic, or a scrambled jigsaw. There were two huge expanses of plate glass filled with a vast

confusion of items, some big, some small,
all colours, all shapes, like an explosion
in a magic-lover's imagination, scattering
its contents into every corner; a crazy mix
of chrome and coloured silk, and feathers
and painted wood and printed card. There
were practical jokes and disguises and
masks and moustaches and noses and
spectacles, but mostly there were magic
tricks, more magic tricks than I could have
possibly imagined.

It was the sheer abundance, the
infinity of impossibilities, that forever
changed my idea of what magic was. I could
have stood there for a year and not got
bored of staring, imagining what each prop
might do, how each one might work, what it
might be like to own them. It was simply
too much to take on board in one go. And we
hadn't even got inside yet.

I must have stood there open-mouthed
for quite a while. When eventually I turned
to look at Vati, he was smiling at whatever
the expression was on my face.

'Would you like to go in?' he asked
gently. I just shook my head. As we passed
through the front door, he squeezed my
hand.

Inside was just like the window but
cubed, so it filled the whole space behind.
There were display cabinets everywhere,
lined with tricks laid out in front of
their printed or typed instructions. There
were shelves full of books with coloured
dust jackets. There were puppets and props
hanging from the low ceiling. There was a
huge gravity-defying house of cards on one
side of the counter, and a series of

decorated tables with glittering chrome edges, carrying an array of painted wooden production boxes and polished brass tubes. One wall was devoted to masks, bald head wigs and rubber noses. It was fun, but it was wild, improper, maybe even dangerous in some glorious way. As with the window, it was the sheer profusion of items, the abundance, the volume that seared its way into my head. How could such a place exist?

A small man with a shiny pate and a red moustache came out from behind the counter. Vati greeted him, held out his hand to shake, and it turned out they were acquainted. I didn't really listen to their talk, as I was still drunk on the vat of pure joy I was swimming in, but I felt a kind hand on my shoulder and I was led to a tall glass display with a series of items beautifully laid out and lit.

'*Far onheyb*,' the man said, speaking Yiddish to my father. For beginners.

I looked up and down the range laid out in front of me. A set of three brown Bakelite cups with white cork balls, a nest of five colourful cardboard boxes that fitted one inside the other, three white ropes of differing lengths with coloured tape bound around their ends. Standing there imagining each one of these in turn in my possession, I tried to make a judgement as to which might yield the most pleasure. My eye was drawn to another item, two magic wands, glossily black with white tips, laid crosswise on a little wooden block. From the end of each one hung a bright red thread with a decorative tassel. I didn't know what it did, but it looked

like it had some kind of mechanism, some
kind of secret, something inside that I
could only find out about if I bought it.

And now I had another idea in mind. I
was going to choose just one thing. I was
going to choose one thing and learn how to
do it as well as anybody had ever done it.
I was going to learn everything about it. I
was going to become an expert in it. I
don't know where this thought came from. I
was surprised at myself. In theory, I
should have gone down the path of guzzling
and asked for five things, or at least
three, but it was suddenly clear to me that
I was only going to choose one. Maybe I was
making some kind of bargain. If I only
chose one thing, Vati would bring me back
here again another time.

Having made my choice, I went over to
him. He was standing at the shop counter
talking to the man with the ginger
moustache in a low, serious voice.

'You don't want to sell?'

'We've talked about it, Oskar. I'd
rather pass it to Regina. We trust her with
it until the madness ends.' The man saw me
approaching before Vati did and stopped
speaking, replacing his grave expression
with a smile. 'He's made his choice
already! That was quick, *kleyner*.'

'You know how these work?' he asked as
he unlocked the cabinet. I just shook my
head. He removed the item and began to
demonstrate how if you held the two wands
crossed together and pulled down on one
tassel, the other wand rose. Then he
switched positions, keeping the wands
connected at the bottom, and the mechanism

still worked. As I watched, he kept
adjusting their positions without
interrupting the connection. It was clever,
but it was clear the threads were joined
somehow. I couldn't wait to find out how.
But then he did something that filled me
with wonder. He separated the wands and
gave one to me before taking a step
backwards as if to demonstrate beyond all
possible doubt that any connection between
the two wands had been severed. He nodded
at me to pull at the tassel on my wand. It
was gloriously impossible, but as I did so,
the thread that dangled from the wand he
still held began to rise.

'No!'

'Oh yes,' he said, grinning
delightedly. He took the wand off me and
turned to Vati. 'Shall I wrap them?'

'You can, but he'll have torn the paper
off by the time we get to Deitch's.'

Vati tried to persuade me to choose
some other things; we'd travelled such a
long way after all. But I'd made my
bargain, whoever the bargain was with.

'We'll come again,' I said simply, and
he seemed to understand. He certainly
didn't contradict me.

When we got back to the hotel, we
suppered on bread and cheese in our room. I
was impatient to see how the trick worked,
but he was insistent that we eat first. As
we munched on Limburger and *Roggenbrot*, he
told me the history of Zauberkönig; how it
had been founded by a family called the
Kroners at the turn of the century. Arthur,
who we'd met, ran the shop with his wife,
Charlotte, who'd inherited it from her

father, Josef. Josef had lived for
conjuring and magic and his four daughters
all ran magic shops – the others being in
Munich, Cologne and Hamburg. But
Charlotte's shop was the best, the most
magical. I could hardly disagree.

I lay on my bed playing with the
beautiful props I'd discovered. The
mechanism and the method, revealed in a
neatly typed and illustrated pamphlet, was
beautiful. Across the street, visible
through the hotel window, was a red banner
with its central swastika illuminated. I
clutched my wands. I looked at my father,
who was sitting in a chair across the room,
reading by a desk lamp that he'd angled
towards him so it didn't keep me awake. I
fell asleep, perfectly happy.

I found out many years later that
Zauberkönig was still there. Shortly after
Kristallnacht, when Nazi thugs destroyed
over seven thousand Jewish businesses in
one night – a few scant weeks after Vati
and I were in Berlin – Arthur and Charlotte
had signed over the business to one of
their employees so that it was in Aryan
hands. Two of their three daughters managed
to escape Germany and made it to America.
One of them, Hilde, went on to become the
successful stage illusionist Hildeen. But
Arthur and Charlotte, and their eldest
daughter, Meta, were so in love with their
beautiful house of magic that they stayed,
hoping to get their business back one day.
In December 1942, it was expropriated from
Charlotte Kroner by a public notice in the
official gazette *Reichsanzeiger*. Meta, who
was managing the business by then, was

arrested in Alexanderplatz and taken to the police prison in Lehrter Strasse. From here she was deported to Auschwitz and murdered. Charlotte and Arthur took their own lives early in 1943, drinking poison from the same cup.

As for me, I never revisited Zauberkönig with Vati. But my love of magic, my grand passion, was confirmed and initiated by the visit. For years I thought it was Arthur and Charlotte's beautiful shop that was responsible, but it is only recently, as I have had some time gifted to me in which to reflect on such things, that I have realised the truth. Although that palace of wonders played its part, my interest, my obsession, my destiny was activated by something else.

What was the magic that freed the seed to grow? In a word, it was love. And by 'love', I don't mean mere sentiment, or warm feelings — I mean action: I mean time my father spent with me, time in which he got to know who I was, understood me enough to see what captured my imagination; and then the effort he expended even when to do so was difficult, and in this case dangerous, and to do otherwise would have been so much easier. But love is only truly love when it's demonstrated.

The consequences of my father's love survived the Nazis, who murdered him too, along with my mother. But like Zauberkönig, my passion for magic is still here, still in the world, still driving me, animating me, making me gift it on to others, and I —

26

On 12 October 1953, various foreign news services began circulating a short piece of film footage of a young British spy who had defected to the Soviet Union. It lasted about a minute and was apparently part of a larger 'confession' that was going to be released to the world's media in the next few days. At first the British newsreels and the BBC did not pick the item up, though the newspapers reported it with a modicum of scepticism. But then, quite quickly, British Movietone News broke ranks. They were motivated to because of a sensational story in the communist-sympathising *Daily Worker*. Apparently, the man in the film extract was a facially altered version of the mentally ill entertainer Louis Warlock. As far as the general public was concerned, Warlock was currently being held in a secure institution following a nervous breakdown earlier in the year. But the Soviet government source quoted by the *Daily Worker* claimed that this was a lie, and that Warlock was actually a spy working for the British government, having undergone plastic surgery in an attempt to disguise his identity.

The story was so lurid and sensational that there was no response at all from any official sources. But once Movietone had started running the footage on their newsreel, the other services immediately began to do the same. By the end of the week, British Paramount, the Universal Newsreel and British Pathé were all carrying the extract in their bulletins. There was such a sense of scandal and sensation around the item that people began visiting cinemas specifically to see it. The choice of extract – presumably made by the Soviets themselves – was designed to be as titillating and attention-grabbing as possible, hinting at more to come. The alleged spy bore the thinnest resemblance to Warlock, and certainly didn't look exactly like him. He talked in a stilted manner, giving monosyllabic answers to the questions he was asked. The newspapers said this indicated an individual who was either heavily sedated or perhaps 'brainwashed' – a term that had recently come into use in reports from the Korean War.

'Under what alias did you serve?' This from an off-camera interviewer, who spoke fluent English with a strong Russian accent.

'Karel Kay.'

'And you worked for the United Kingdom government? They sent you here?'

'Yes.' The man's voice was slurred. His eyes were cast downwards and seemed to close on occasions. Whether this was to hide his shame or a symptom of some more troubling mental difficulty it was impossible to say from this short clip alone.

'But now you have realised your error in serving the corrupt forces of international capital and imperialism?'

'Yes.'

As well as the signs of mental perturbation in his speech, there was evidence of extreme agitation elsewhere in his demeanour. His right hand rested against the side of his face, his forefinger extended across his cheek, where it drummed nervously and erratically all the time, both as he spoke and as he sat silently, his head lolling to one side.

'You're a proud citizen and comrade of the Union of Soviet Socialist Republics?'

'Yes.'

The man was surrounded by a dense bush of microphones, and every so often the film was punctuated by a burst of light, as from a clutch of offstage photographers.

'Next we will turn to the nature of your operations and what it reveals about the criminality of the degraded regime you served.'

The clip ended there, like a cliffhanger from some sensational 1930s Mascot Pictures serial.

Dinah sat in the darkened cinema on King Street in Hammersmith. The Regal was the nearest place she could find that was screening the newsreel. She'd run there as soon as she'd heard about it. Literally run there. It was Beulah who had called her:

'Darling – you need to get yourself to the pictures.' There was a gravity to her voice that belied the seemingly anodyne nature of the instruction. When she explained the situation, Dinah knew immediately that this was the confirmation she had been waiting for since the call to the Turk five months ago.

She'd had to sit through the tail end of *The Story of Gilbert and Sullivan*. She would have been bored by it under the best of circumstances, but now the slow pace was absolutely excruciating. By the time the newsreel came around, she found she was as tense with expectation as if Louis were about to be brought into the cinema in person.

Her first thought was: *is* that Louis? It was as if she'd forgotten what he looked like, as if she'd known him in childhood and was now seeing him as an adult for the first time, straining to find the person she remembered in the man on screen. It took her a minute to pin down what it was exactly that had changed. The nose was different. This one was smaller and neater. It made him (if it was him) look more . . . More what? More English? It seemed absurd. Everything about the face was neater. It looked narrower, and the eyes wider. It's not Louis, she thought. It's someone who looks a little bit like him. The monosyllabic answers gave nothing of the character of his voice, and the dead look in his eyes merely served to accentuate how far this person was from Louis as she remembered him, how he lacked Louis' perpetually animated spark. The film was black and white, of course, so there was no indication if they were Louis' dark brown irises she was looking at.

By the time all these thoughts had run through her head, the clip was over. She could have left the cinema there and then, dismissed the whole thing as sensational nonsense, Cold War propaganda, an attempt to slur and smear Louis' reputation, some kind of revenge for the scheme he'd got himself caught up in. But instead, she sat there for a moment trying to review everything that had happened. Initially she had taken Prison Officer McGarvey's testimony about Louis' hanging at face value.

The man hadn't been lying to her. She'd known that. And she'd told the other members of the Brains Trust so at the time. She'd been berated by her rational side for holding on to the hope that she hadn't lost him when all the evidence was telling her that she had. She wanted to be stoic and courageous, to invoke the spirit of all those war widows who were able to accept their bereavement with fortitude.

But when the message on the Turk had appeared, she had immediately discounted the prison officer's testimony – or at least wondered whether he himself had been fooled. Made to witness a believable hanging as part of an elaborate cover story being spun by the British intelligence services. Maybe they wished the Soviets to believe Louis dead before they deployed him, and wanted them to obtain that information through their own intelligence services. A 'secret' hanging that the Russians discovered for themselves would perhaps be more likely to convince than one trumpeted in the British press. They would congratulate themselves for having found out about it and be more motivated to believe the story from there on in.

All of this was enough to keep Dinah in her seat now, despite her doubts, waiting for the next showing of the newsreel. And there was something else calling out to her, something that nagged just on the edge of her consciousness. So convinced was she by this feeling that she stayed through the whole of the dismal second feature, as well as the insufferable Gilbert and Sullivan film. She felt herself tense up when the British Pathé fanfare began. She had to pay attention. There was something tangible she had to unearth, something she needed to work out in the scant minute or two the item took up in the programme.

Initially she felt a hollow sense of disappointment. There was no sudden rush of certainty that this was Louis accompanying the man's reappearance on the screen. But the thing still tugged at her, a maddening familiarity in what she was looking at.

And then it hit her.

She felt a sharp, jagged rush of excitement, a sudden spike of knowing what it was, as if a curtain had been pulled to one side and now she could see the thing that had been there all along, right in front of her eyes. She tried to concentrate on the screen, to confirm that what she was thinking was actually true.

Rather than staying for a third viewing of the clip, she left and made her way to Soho. She had to get hold of the others as quickly as possible. Going straight to Beulah seemed the best way to do that.

The truth was, in the months since the incident with the Turk, the Brains Trust had drifted apart, despite their vow that they wouldn't let that happen. It wasn't just a matter of Dinah clinging to a different interpretation of the Turk's message (which none of the others considered to be a message). It was rather just life taking over – the need to earn a living, to pay the rent, maintain a career. Phyllis had kept a connection, encouraged Dinah to accept the fact of Louis' hanging for her own good. But because Dinah wouldn't capitulate to that, it actually made it hard for them to get together. It was easier all round to just get on with things, as people had done during the war.

But here they were, reassembled at Maison Bertaux for the first time since their gathering round the Turk. Each member of the Brains Trust felt a different shade of discomfort, but the cause was the same. A terrible, unbearable absence. The passage of time and the human capacity to accommodate the impossible had softened the jag of it into something closer to melancholy, but now they were back in their former lair, they were all feeling something more agonising, staring at the exposed brickwork, the wall still painted black, covered in the ghosts of chalk lines from happier days. All of them except Dinah that is, who was feeling something very different, something much closer to hope.

'We've all heard the same thing,' she said, convening the assembly. 'I don't know how many of you have seen it yet, but I watched the newsreel twice. At first I thought, "It isn't. It can't be." But then, the second time around, I saw something I'd missed. I'd felt it on the first viewing without knowing what it was. Now I saw it straight away.'

'Saw what?' said Ivan, who was closest to his old self. More used to floating through life on a river of irony, maybe he was less affected by everything that had happened. A typical comedy writer, with the ultimate defence mechanism: he was always looking for the joke.

'How did Louis communicate with me, more often than not?' said Dinah.

'What do you mean?' asked Phyllis, irritated at this oblique approach. She, like the rest of them, wanted to get instantly to the core of the matter. But Dinah wasn't asking this question for dramatic effect. She was using Louis' own Socratic method, because it was the clearest and the quickest way to get them all to understand.

'How did he speak to me when we were separated from one another as far as the outside world could see? When I was upside down in a tank of water? Or if we were together but not talking to each other, or even looking at each other? How did he do it?'

'Morse code,' said Danny. They all knew that Morse was the most basic method they returned to again and again.

'The man in the film – Louis, the man who doesn't quite look like Louis – was telling me he was Louis without having to say a word,' said Dinah, gripped by excitement, disbelief, wonder. She put her hand to her cheek and started tapping her face with her index finger. 'Remember, I was having to work this out on the hoof. That clip only lasts for a minute or so. It gave me about thirty seconds once I'd realised. But I wrote it down.' She fished in her handbag for the scrap of a note she'd made on the back of an old receipt with a stub of pencil. She read from it:

'"Will go along with them for survivals sake. Have not".'

They all stared at her, not speaking, taking it in, trying to compute it.

'Are you sure?' said Ivan eventually. His doubt sparked an angry response.

'How many years were we working it, Ivan? Under the most ridiculous bloody conditions, hanging upside down in tanks barely able to breathe. Do you know how deeply I've got it in my bloody bones? I don't even have to think about it. Those dots and dashes – they're the same as spoken words to me.'

They all knew that. They all had their own version of a brain that had been rewired by their work with Louis.

'"Will go along with them for survivals sake. Have not",' said Danny, repeating what she had said. He'd already memorised it.

'So there's more in there? There's more to get?' said Phyllis.

'We need to speak to Beulah,' said Ivan, urgent and no longer detached.

'Why Beulah?' asked Dinah.

'Come on. She knows all the film people. The technicians. The lab men. She might be able to get us one of those reels so we can look at it closely.'

'How does Beulah know the people at the lab?' This was new information to Dinah.

'Darling,' said Phyllis, a little surprised at her innocence. 'How many stag reels do you think she's had shot on that stage out of hours? Don't tell me she's never asked you if you wanted to make a quick thirty quid.' Ivan coughed, indicating that perhaps Phyllis had gone too far with her revelations.

Things moved very quickly. Beulah had already seen the news-reel, having ducked into the Rialto on Piccadilly herself as soon as she'd heard. She was less sure it was Louis, but then she didn't have Dinah's knowledge of his techniques. As soon as Dinah called her, she was on the phone to her contact at Denham Studios. Within fifteen minutes, Dinah was in the back of Alan Chunz's taxi on the twenty-mile trip west.

Denham had been the home of Alexander Korda's London films before merging with Rank just before the war. Despite the fact that all the film-makers preferred it to Pinewood, it had ceased being a working studio last year. But the post-production facilities remained – the editing suites, the dubbing studios, the music stages, the film labs. Beulah's contact there – whoever they were – knew that British Pathé used it for duplication and print-ing, so it would be a straightforward matter to locate a copy of the reel. By the time Dinah arrived and was shown up to a first-floor editing suite, it was already looped up on to the Moviola, together with its accompanying soundtrack. A serious-looking middle-aged woman in a zip-up cardigan, hair coiled on her head in a tight updo, sat waiting on a bar stool.

'You from Beulah?' she said, unsmiling. Surely this wasn't the woman who cut the stag reels. Dinah took another look at her and told herself not to be so naïve.

'Can you run the piece with the spy, but slow it down?' she said.

'Sure.' The woman turned towards the bulky editing machine and made adjustments. 'You'll have to lean right over it to see.'

Dinah took out a pad and pencil and went to stand next to her. She focused on the little ground-glass screen as the editor started the motor. The sound began playing, the voice-over slurred, slowed down, low-pitched, like something broken.

'I don't need the sound, it's fine.'

The editor flicked a switch and cut the noise, which was an immediate relief. Dinah leaned as close as she could to the image, staring at the little grey line of Louis' finger tapping at his face. Don't panic, she thought. You can run it again to be sure. You can run it as many times as you like.

She began to write exactly what she saw. She felt each of the letters deep in her gut:

. . . vived Funhouse. Was in for – weeks. Am OK – I think. Will go along with them for survivals sake. Have not defected. Tell Strath SIS – Pot . . .

That was all there was. Would it be enough?

Ivan had suggested that they start with the Ministry of Defence, because of the SIS reference.

'And how do we get to the Ministry of Defence?' said Dinah, incredulous. 'Walk up to the front door?'

'Basically, that might be the best place to start.'

By now a terse denial had been issued by the British government. Their story was that this was nothing but a bizarre piece of Soviet propaganda. Mr Warlock was still being held in a secure mental institution in the UK, and it was clear from a comparison of photographs that the man in the newsreel bore very little likeness to him. The whole thing, it seemed, was an elaborate and eccentric hoax. Dinah knew enough not to take this denial at face value, but the walls of the British establishment were not easily penetrated by outsiders.

She remained absolutely determined to see her mission through regardless. She went to the ministry building in Whitehall, walking up to the reception desk, which was manned by a serving officer with a severe countenance who made her want to clam up before she'd even opened her mouth. Nevertheless, she persevered.

'Excuse me, I need to get some urgent information to an officer called Strath in the Special Intelligence Service. It's a matter of the utmost importance to national security.'

The man didn't respond to the latter part in any way; he just said, 'Strath. Do you have an extension number, please, miss?'

'I'm afraid not. I just have the information.'

He looked at her, frowning.

'What's your name, miss?' He had a pencil in his hand.

'My name's Dinah Groule. If you could tell them this is to do with Louis Warlock.' There was no reaction from the man as he wrote the name down.

'Would you bear with me, please?'

He stepped away from the desk and disappeared through an open door to one side of the reception. She thought he would be away for a while, but he returned in less than a minute.'

'They've asked if you could put your request in writing. If you just address it "General Enquiries", it'll find the right person.'

'You can put it in writing,' Phyllis said, 'but they'll just ignore it.'

'Why would they ignore it?' asked an infuriated Dinah, who was taut with frustration and anger.

'They thought you were a crank,' said Danny. 'Seen the reel at the pictures. Wanted attention.'

'We need to do something else. Or find someone who might at least take us seriously.'

But what should have been a straightforward matter turned out to be anything but. They tried going through Dinah's MP, to no avail. They tried going through the papers via Beulah's press contacts, but no one would touch it. They tried another approach via Scotland Yard through a contact Ivan had, but it got them nowhere either.

It was Dinah who worked out that they were missing the obvious. She asked for one more proper meeting of the Brains Trust back at Maison Bertaux. She told Danny to bring a new box of chalk.

'We've been going at this too straight. We haven't used our best asset.'

'What do you mean?' said Ivan, who was already helping himself to a marzipan fig.

Dinah poured out steaming cups of black coffee for all of them. Once she'd realised where she'd been going wrong, she resolved to make this a proper Brains Trust meeting in every way. That meant fresh coffee, the best cakes and pastries, the chairs spaced correctly around the table. It meant convincing each one of those brains that Louis was there amongst them, despite his physical absence. What was their greatest asset? The singular binding personality of Louis Warlock. The body around which they orbited. Not because he was better than them. Not because he was some superhuman champion. But because the machine was the totality of them. And he was the mechanism at its centre. His essence. His being. If she could get everyone in the correct frame of mind, it wouldn't matter that he wasn't physically there with them. Their combined imaginations would conjure his spirit. That, ultimately, was the essence of the Warlock effect.

'Our greatest asset is the truth of who we are,' she continued.

'All right, Bertrand Russell. Put it in plain English for the privates on parade, please,' said Ivan, brushing the crumbs from his hands.

'So far we've been going about our mission in a very ordinary and obvious way. We need to get a message to some intelligence officer called Strath. And we've worked through all the conventional ways we might do that. But that's not us, is it. That's not the Brains Trust. That's not how Louis would have gone about it. We need to think about it like he would himself. We just need to do what we always do. Crack it in the way only we can crack it.'

As she spoke, she could see that the others had immediately grasped what she was saying. Whether it was the coffee and cake, or the simple hope she'd kindled within them, the chance of getting something back that they'd thought was irretrievably lost, her approach was working. And soon the ideas were flying.

'OK, OK, this is *meshuga*, but I'm going to say it anyway, just to kick things off. What if we sent smoke signals over Whitehall. They couldn't ignore that.' This from Danny, who was keen to show his willingness to step up, as if trying to compensate for his lack of faith about the message on the Turk.

'Not smoke signals,' said Ivan, just as keen to pick up the baton, 'but skywriting over Parliament. They certainly couldn't miss that.'

'They couldn't miss it,' agreed Phyllis, who at some point had pulled a half-finished cardigan from her bag, her crochet needle now working as fast as her mind, 'but they wouldn't thank us for being so bloody obvious. That's the real challenge – we've got to somehow grab their attention without making enemies of them. There's a long way to go on this beyond just getting them the message.'

'She's right,' said Dinah.

'What about a cryptic newspaper ad? Full page,' said Ivan.

'How can you guarantee this man Strath will see it?' A fair question from Phyllis

'He doesn't need to see it. As long as it's prominent enough, we only need someone who knows him to see it. And they'll tell him.'

'That widens the net,' said Dinah, nodding encouragingly.

'Where do intelligence officers congregate?' said Phyllis.

'The Silver Cross Tavern?' suggested Ivan.

'You know what I read the other day,' Phyllis continued, ignoring him, 'A piece about serving intelligence officers being seconded to duties guarding the new Queen. Effectively being turned into royal bodyguards.'

'Well, it's easy to get to the Queen,' said Ivan facetiously. 'Just follow the royal motorcade.'

'Yeah, but we do know where the Queen's going to be in six days' time,' said Danny, a touch of excitement in his voice.

'Where?'

'The Coliseum. The Royal Variety Performance.'

'How does that help us?' said Dinah, not yet getting it.

'Come on – we could get something up on stage.'

'How?'

'Tommy,' said Ivan, as if it was the most obvious thing in the world.

'What do you mean?'

'Tommy Cooper's on the bill. He'll do us a favour if we say it's for Louis.'

Phyllis had stopped crocheting. 'He would. You know what he's like. If you tell him it's a matter of national security. He was a Desert Rat.'

'Served under Monty,' said Ivan.

'You say he'll do us a favour. But how?' asked Dinah.

'What about if we come up with some item that features our message? I don't know … Get him to produce the flags of all nations but with our message spelled out letter by letter.'

'He's not going to take a risk on his material, is he – not on a command performance. Change his act with less than a week to go?'

Ivan snorted at this. 'I wouldn't worry about that. He probably hasn't started rehearsing yet.'

'That's not fair,' said Phyllis.

'I just mean – with Tommy, he's in the moment, isn't he. He likes simple magic he can improvise around. His shtick's his shtick. I'll bet you anything he's doing Passe Bottle and Dippy Duck. You're not telling me we couldn't come up with something stronger. As long as it's funny, he'll be happy.'

'You say we need to get our message on stage,' said Dinah, 'but how does that get it to Strath? He's not going to be guarding Queen Elizabeth himself.'

'No,' said Ivan, as if it was obvious, 'but his colleagues will see it, and as long as the words 'Strath SIS' are prominent on it, you can guarantee the old bush telegraph will do the work for us.'

Dinah wanted to pick another hole in it. But she couldn't find one. Not in the moment. As always with the Brains Trust, when they were on form, their logic was impeccable.

27

'Oh thanks, Ive, thanking you. You are a gent.'

Ivan brought over a tray with two pints of pale ale and two whiskies. It was far more than he'd normally drink on a midweek night, but it was better to meet Tommy on his own turf. They were upstairs at the Green Man in Soho, the air thick with cigarette smoke and the smell of beer-soaked carpet. The choice of location was partly because it was quiet, but mainly because it was the drinking place of choice for true magicians. This was where the inaugural meeting of the Magic Circle had occurred, over forty-five years earlier.

'I need this, I can tell you,' said Tommy, his coal-black hair flopping over his eyes. 'I backed a horse this morning – twenty to one.' He wetted his lips with whisky. 'Came in at twenty past four.' And he laughed his throat-clearing laugh before downing the rest of the shot.

'I think I might have written that for you,' said Ivan, when he'd stopped laughing himself. The laughter was genuine, not a matter of politeness. You couldn't help but laugh when you were in Tommy's company.

'Stole it, I think you mean, Ive. Dan Leno did that one for George the Fifth. Which brings us to the matter at hand . . .' He put his drink down and for a moment become uncustomarily grave. 'I don't know if I can risk it, Ive. Really.'

'Tom. It's not a risk, I promise you. There's no risk. Danny's come up with something beautiful.'

'You get one shot at these shows. They don't ask you again. I don't want to end up in the Tower.'

'The only Tower you're heading for is the Tower Ballroom. The summer season. No one'll even notice. Me and Phyll have worked out some patter. It all feels one hundred per cent bona fide.'

'This business with Louis. What the hell is going on?'

'All I can tell you is we're trying to sort it out. And if you can't do it for Louis, think about doing it for Dinah.'

'Dinah?'

'She's pining for him, Tom. She needs to know she's done everything she can for him. Me, Phyll, Danny – we're all doing this for her as much as Louis.'

'But what was Louis up to?'

'I wish I knew.'

Tommy took a sip of his beer. He looked unusually thought-ful, running his hand through his thick hair, pushing it back from his eyes. 'Let me tell you a story about Louis Warlock,' he said. 'We were about five minutes from here one night. Star Café. Sat in the window. Egg and chips. Toast and tea. Me and Louis on one side, Alfred Marks on the other. We were up at the Windmill, doing our turns. Anyway, there we were, between shows, chatting away. War stories. Gossip. And you know Alfred. You can't shut him up. And I'm not quiet at the best of times.'

Ivan laughed. Even when Tommy was being serious, he couldn't resist a gag.

'Well, while we were all gassing, there's this old fella outside. Wretched. Begging. Loud with it, you know. Pleading with passers-by. Desperate. Theatregoers, city gents. Men out with their wives. Everyone hurrying past. All of them ignoring him. "Please help me. Somebody help me. Please somebody help me." This was going on all the time we were telling our stories. No one said anything. It's just London, innit. Just Soho. You turn a blind eye. You have to or you'd go mad.

'But after about – I don't know – ten or fifteen minutes of this, Louis, without making any fuss, without saying anything at all, he just quietly gets up, like he's going to the lav. Except I was facing the same way as him, so I could see through the window. He wasn't going to the lav. He steps outside. And he goes up to this old fella – who might not even have been that old. I didn't hear the conversation. I just saw Louis take his wallet out. And I swear to God, he gave him everything in it. Then he hugs him.

Holds him tight for about a minute. And then he comes back in, sits right down, picks up the chat. Didn't say a word about it. Nor did I. But I'll tell you what. I've never forgotten it.'

The evening of 2 November rolled round quickly enough. Ultimately, the thing that had swung it was that this new trick – the one they'd all worked out together and that Danny had then gone ahead and made – was constructed around a message of goodwill to the new Queen. There'd been a wobble when Danny had first demonstrated the item and the mechanism jammed, but the application of a bit of furniture polish seemed to sort it out. Tommy loved it, and had decided he was going to end with it because of its royal theme, but then on the night, just before he went on, he changed his mind.

Danny and Dinah were standing in the wings at the Coliseum, Danny there as Tommy's technical adviser, Dinah as Danny's assistant. She'd put her hair up in a headscarf and wore horn-rimmed specs, a semi-disguise. Given that her name was about to feature on stage, she didn't want to draw too much attention to her presence. Fortunately, it was so busy backstage, and there were so many bodies milling about, no one noticed her anyway. This was helped further by the fact that the act preceding Tommy was the Hastings Girls' Choir. The sheer numbers in the wings kept any heat off Dinah.

As the girls filed off, Tommy grabbed Danny. For a moment Dinah feared he was going to tell them he'd dropped the item. As it was, he just said, 'I'm opening with it, Dan.' And then he was on.

Four bars of a quick-tempo arrangement of 'That Old Black Magic' announced him, and he was straight into his routine. He sported a very smart, neatly tailored suit, pinstriped and double-breasted. He could have been a wartime spiv, if it wasn't for his red fez and the unruly black locks spilling out beneath.

'I must say, you've been a wonderful audience. And I'd like to finish now with a little song.' Roar of laughter. He had them already. 'I can always tell if an audience is going to be good or bad. Goodnight.' And he turned as if he was going to exit. More laughter, and he turned back, grinning his manic grin. One of

Tommy's secrets was the fact that, perhaps more than any other performer, he had the air of someone who genuinely enjoyed his own act as much as the audience. In lesser hands that might have been irritating. With Tommy, perhaps because of his childlike sense of mischief, it was endearing.

He pulled a white glove from his pocket. 'See that glove?' He let go of the back of it, and the other half of the pair fell down. They were sewn together at the fingers. 'Second-hand.' And his head jerked from side to side waiting for the laugh, which came immediately, of course. He threw the glove off stage and walked over to his table, picking up Danny's prop – a scarf-sized piece of material, which in its opening state was nothing but a large rectangle of black velvet.

'I was in Margate for the summer season. Friend of mine said, "You want to go to Margate. Good for rheumatism." So I went.' He paused briefly. 'And I got it.'

While the crowd were laughing, Tommy picked up the handful of loose white ribbons cut into short lengths that formed the second part of the prop. He displayed the cloth with one hand and the ribbons with the other.

'Here's a little trick I'd like to show you that I picked up. I don't know who dropped it.' He turned to the Royal Box. 'Your Majesty. Your Royal Highnesses. The magical spirits are with us tonight.' It was Ivan who'd suggested adding 'magical' – it took the trick away just enough from the occult and kept it in the realm of entertainment. 'And they'd like to convey a message for your coronation year. Thank you very much.' And he held out one hand and then the other as he said, 'Cloth. Ribbons. Ribbons. Cloth.'

Dinah's heart was thudding now, and Danny gripped her hand. How was this going to go? Was it going to play with the audience? Was Tommy risking offence? Ivan was confident he wasn't. The Duke of Edinburgh loved him. There was a lot of goodwill there. 'He's a good laugher, Tom,' Ivan had said about the royal consort. 'Everyone'll take their cue from him.'

'Ribbons. Cloth. Cloth. Ribbons.' And Tommy threw the lengths of white ribbon into the cloth, the end of which he'd flicked up so it formed a sort of bag. Immediately he let the top half go to reveal that the ribbons were now fastened to the cloth, forming a series of white letters spelling out a phrase:

STRATH S I S CONTACT DINAH GROULE

He read it aloud exactly as Ivan had written it. 'Strath SIS contact Dinah Groule.' Then he said it again, just in case any of those attending intelligence officers had missed it. 'Strath SIS contact Dinah Groule.' And he moved his head with a series of small bird-like jerks, playing his own confusion exactly as he did when any of his tricks went intentionally wrong. The audience were tittering, without fully laughing. They were searching for the joke in the odd combination of letters. Tommy helped them as much as he could. 'Who's Strath's sis? Do I know her? Sorry, Your Majesty. That's not right.' He was taking a risk here. Did it sound impertinent? Was he risking losing the audience?

'I think the magical spirits have been on the spirits.' There was a joke for them. They laughed at that. A bit of the tension eased, though not entirely. Tommy shook the cloth again, and some of the white letters fell off. Now it spelled: *RATH SI CONTA N H GROUL*. He looked at it.

'It's Scottish!' he said, and proceeded to read it out in a ridiculous broad Scots accent. '"Rath si conta N H groul." It means "cold wash only".' The Duke of Edinburgh roared with laughter and the audience followed. As the noise hit its peak, Tommy shouted, 'Spirits – don't let me down.' He turned to the audience with a drunken expression, and the laughter rose again. The audience were in the hands of a lunatic master and they loved it. This time, as the hilarity hit its zenith, Tommy held out the cloth and Danny's brilliant mechanism came into play. Dinah felt him grip her hand tighter than he had done before. The little ribbon letters darted about under their own animation, guided by a system of unseen threads and fishing weights running through little brass eyes sewn into the layers of the cloth. The audience howled in disbelief. The letters on the cloth now spelled two clear words:

HRH CONGRATULATIONS

'There you go!' said Tommy. And now the audience understood. It all suddenly made perfect sense. Another one of Tommy Cooper's tricks that went wrong, then went right.

Huge and appreciative applause followed, fuelled by patriotic sentiment. The statement that the Brains Trust had wanted to smuggle in was already forgotten by the general audience. Just a piece of random nonsense – an arbitrary anagram that had disguised the true intent of the trick. Tommy had toyed with them, made them think his routine had failed when it had all been under his control from the start. They loved it. They loved him. And he loved Danny. Of course, he threw the cloth behind him as if it was a bit of rubbish with his trademark staccato laugh. As far as Dinah was concerned, as misdirection that was even better. But had anyone got the message? Now the real wait began.

28

Dinah was in bed when the knock came. It was around 5 a.m. She pulled the curtains in her room apart to look for a clue as to who was there, but was met with only a darkness thickened by smog that made it hard to see down to the road below.

Her sister's face appeared in the crack of her bedroom door as Dinah passed, pulling on her housecoat. 'Stay there, Anne – it'll be for me.' Her heart was thudding with anticipation, excitement even. It could only mean one thing. Their plan had succeeded.

'Miss Groule?'

There were two heavy-looking men with severe haircuts at the door. One of them held out a wallet with an identity card indicating that he was a detective inspector with the Special Branch of the Metropolitan Police. 'You'll need to come with us.'

'Come with you where?'

'To Charing Cross police station, miss.'

She was allowed five minutes to get dressed.

'I'm coming with you,' said Anne, who'd been listening from her bedroom door. Dinah just shook her head.

The car was black, unmarked, and the officers said very little. But at least she was going to meet Strath. Or someone who knew Strath. Unless she wasn't. For the first time since the knock at the door, she began to feel a flicker of doubt. She remembered what had happened to Louis, how he had been sucked into this whole insane affair. Might she now be in her own version of his nightmare? What if the Brains Trust had miscalculated? What if they'd all made an incorrect assumption about how their message would be received? Was she now going to have to carry the weight of that error?

Inside the station, which smelled of sweat and stale cigarette smoke from the night shift, the desk officer informed her she was being charged with a breach of the 1939 Official Secrets Act. It had never occurred to her that she was being arrested. Her personal details were taken, along with her coat, her handbag and, for some reason, her shoes. Trying to calm herself, she asked the policeman behind the desk if she was allowed a phone call. She had never been arrested before, but she'd seen enough B pictures to know that was the routine. The man just looked at her and said briskly, 'Someone will be in to see you in due course.'

She sat there in the grim cell somewhere beneath the pavement of Agar Street, a narrow glass-blocked window above her, breathing in the smell of carbolic. Why had she allowed herself to walk into this so passively? Was this how Louis had felt when they'd come for him: desperate, frightened, helpless? And what about now, his own face stolen from him, possibly his mind too, to judge from his demeanour in the newsreel?

Pull yourself together, girl. That was her father's voice in her head, mingled with a touch of Louis. Old Louis in his pomp: confident, clever, assured.

Come on. She wasn't in the Soviet Union, and she wasn't just going to disappear. But that thought didn't tally with the memory of Louis' hanging, or the countervailing news story about his nervous breakdown. She realised with a chill that it might not be that simple. The truth was, she had no idea what she was dealing with.

Think, Dinah – come on. That was definitely Louis. Her inner Louis, telling her not to give in to panic. She wasn't alone. The rest of the Brains Trust was in on this. And Tommy Cooper. They couldn't all be made to disappear.

As if in answer to the thought, the heavy lock began to turn, rattling and clattering as oiled gears fell into place. The door swung open, revealing a smartly dressed man in his thirties with surprisingly dark skin, almost an African look to him.

'Miss Groule?' He turned and nodded to the policeman next to him. 'You can leave us, Officer, thank you. Shut the door, please. No need to lock it.'

'Sir.'

The man stepped into the cell. 'Well,' he said, taking off his gloves. 'Congratulations are in order.'

'What do you mean?' said Dinah, who didn't know whether to be relieved or scared.

'My name's Strath. And you succeeded in gaining my attention. No easy task. I can quite see why Warlock might have employed you.'

Dinah tried to catch up. This was Strath? She'd pictured some stuffy old colonel.

'Why am I being charged with a breach of the Official Secrets Act?'

'You're not,' said Strath. 'You're not going to be charged with anything. As long as you come with me now. Come on.' And from behind his back he produced her shoes, her handbag and her coat. It was clear he enjoyed the flourish.

They walked out of the police station without anyone acknowledging or being troubled by Dinah's exit from the premises. Whoever Strath was, he was clearly senior enough to have circumnavigated whatever punitive wheels had been set in motion. Dinah expected there to be a car waiting for them, but there wasn't.

'Where are we going?' she asked.

'Short walk, to Whitehall Court,' said Strath, already moving at pace. 'I can bring you up to speed as we go.'

They crossed the Strand, marching past the side of the station and down Craven Street, Strath talking all the way. 'I'm sorry we weren't able to speak sooner. And that you had to go the lengths you went to in order to make this happen. There's been some furious politicking going on. We are not of one mind in my department. And there are plenty of people who take an opposite position to me as a matter of principle.'

'What is your department?'

'Better not to use any names. Let's just say we're the department that's in charge of your fiancé's case.'

'Why did you even arrest him? He was innocent. You must know he was. He was always innocent.' She couldn't help saying it. Having this man in front of her unlocked months of contained feelings. Tears and fury had forced the words out of her.

331

'Let's focus on the matter in hand, shall we? Sufficient unto the day and all that. Time is of the essence.' He spoke quietly and seriously, as if to emphasise that fact. Somehow his manner communicated his sincerity. 'None of this is straightforward.'

They walked past the old Playhouse Theatre, which was now a BBC radio studio, and across the road, doubling back up Whitehall Place.

'Here we are,' said Strath.

'Where are we?'

'National Liberal Club. I have a private apartment here. Away from the eavesdroppers and the naysayers. You may not be surprised to hear that I don't quite fit in with the ... shall we say orthodox element of the intelligence community.'

They passed inside the grand building and Strath led Dinah across the marble-floored lobby. They took a small flight of steps up to a red-carpeted corridor and arrived at a set of lifts with polished brass doors.

'How the other half lives,' Dinah muttered to herself.

'Believe me,' Strath said drily, 'there are precious few perks to this job. One takes what one can when the opportunity arises.'

As they waited for the lift to arrive, he checked there was no one within earshot and began to talk in a lower voice.

'Now, I'd like to hear exactly *why* were you so desperate to make contact with me.'

'You don't know?' said Dinah, surprised.

'Shall we say I've got a broad idea, but I would very much like to be told about the specifics. From your point of view.'

'I was asked to get a message to you. Specifically you. You were named.'

'A message from whom?'

'From Louis. You really don't know, do you?'

Once they'd stepped into the lift and were alone, she took great delight in explaining to Strath exactly how the message had been passed via the tapped-out Morse code.

'This is extraordinary. This is phenomenal.' He was open-mouthed upon hearing it. 'Your timing couldn't be any better.'

'Why?'

'Because we've had some more film. From the same recording session as the extract that's already been issued. This one's been sent to us directly. It's the whole thing.'

'They're not making it public?'

'They will if we don't do what they want. At the moment, it's being used as a bargaining chip.'

'What *do* they want?'

'I can't go into details. But it involves the return to Soviet soil of some individuals who are currently in custody elsewhere. If we don't cooperate, what you are about to see will be made public via the same channels as before.'

The lift doors opened and Strath led her a short way along a narrow corridor to a suite of rooms. The smog had lifted outside, revealing a rather lovely view across the Thames to the south bank of the river and the new Festival Hall. He drew the heavy velvet curtains closed. There was a projector set up on a stand and a small portable screen.

'Make yourself comfortable, Miss Groule. I wasn't expecting you to have to take dictation, but it's quite possible you're going to need to do some more translation.' And Strath, who now had the air of an excitable child, started scrabbling around, looking for a pencil and paper. He handed Dinah a foolscap pad and an inky-looking biro.

The set-up on the film was exactly as in the previous reel: the off-camera interviewer, the man who could have been Louis (and it was worth noting, although she hadn't yet heralded the fact to herself, that it had now been confirmed that it *was* Louis), his head down, the absent, sickly air around him, the feeling of somebody who'd been damaged in some awful way. Dinah had a catalogue of questions she wanted to throw at Strath, but she knew he would resist, and he was using all his power and charisma to keep her focused on the task he had just set her. She guessed there wasn't much time in which to accomplish whatever it was he needed to accomplish.

'Can I watch it through first before doing the decoding? So I'm not distracted. How long is it?'

'Not long. That's a good idea.'

The off-camera figure in the film did most of the talking:

333

'Under questioning you have revealed the following: that the British military have an active biological weapons programme in contravention of the 1925 Geneva Protocol. Is that correct.'

'That is correct,' said Louis, in a slurred voice. If it wasn't for the tapping finger, Dinah would have been devastated. But the little nervous tic and what it concealed in plain sight was a life raft for her, a tiny bit of ballast that showed things were better than they appeared.

'These weapons are actively deployed, ready for use, in Korea, and soon in West Germany, despite the international obligations the imperial government of Britain proclaim to honour?'

'Yes.'

'Thus revealing the stain of their corruption and their nefariousness to the world.'

'Yes.'

'OK,' said Dinah. She didn't bother to ask any questions about the detail of what the reel apparently revealed. She just wanted to translate the code as well and as clearly as she could. She moved her chair closer to the screen and readied herself for the task in hand as the projector motor whirred in its rewind mode, and then Strath rethreaded the film for another run. She asked him if he could kill the volume. It would help her concentrate.

It turned out that Louis was repeating the message on a loop. It overlapped the entirety of both reels. Unpacked and laid out from start to finish, it ran:

Tell Strath. Message to Strath. Survived Funhouse. Was in for – weeks. Am OK – I think. Will go along with them for survivals sake. Have not defected. Tell Strath SIS – Potash there too, his alias Gabčík. Funhouse address 15 Přístavní, Prague.

There was such a look of urgency on Strath's face when he read the message that Dinah dared not even begin to ask the questions she'd told herself she would ask. Instead, she asked another simpler one.

'What will happen now?'

'You've just changed the game, Miss Groule. You and your fiancé. We were playing chess with them. Now we're playing poker. If we move fast enough, they won't know the game's been changed. And on top of that, you've given us a rather good hand.

Let's make sure it stays that way. Please keep everything you know strictly to yourself. Forgive me for dashing off. Time is very much of the essence.'

'What about Louis?'

'That's why time is of the essence. Please. Trust me. You've done your bit. More than your bit. Now let me do mine.' He was already at the apartment door, gesturing for Dinah to follow. The relief was immense, and the determined look of urgency in Strath's eyes gifted her something she hadn't truly felt in six months: hope.

Three and a half weeks later, the following report ran in *Rudé Právo*, the most widely distributed Czechoslovakian newspaper (which was also the official organ of the Czechoslovakian Communist Party):

> A large explosion that was reported in the Holešovice region of Prague last week was confirmed to be a consequence of faulty gas lines whose installation pre-dated the communist jurisdiction. The corrupt former owners of a factory facility on Přístavní had endangered workers' lives by using and installing substandard pipework with no regard to employees' safety or the lives of others. Party officials are currently working on replacing and correcting such egregious examples of the unscrupulous legacy of capital.

Naturally the paper didn't report that chemical traces of gelignite, dynamite and petroleum were found at the site of the explosion. Or that despite reports of a man being seen in the building before the incident, no body was recovered. And there was no mention of any suspicions that responsibility for this calamity lay with resistance groups operating from within the city, working in close collaboration with British Intelligence who had ordered them to detonate only when a certain individual was definitely present inside. That would never have been published in the state organ. Of course it wouldn't. Such resistance groups didn't exist.

It was not a coincidence that six minutes prior to the explosion, a prisoner swap had taken place on the Czechoslovakian/

Austrian border at Nové Hrady. Louis Warlock was passed from the Czechoslovakian side in exchange for three Soviet agents who had been arrested in Vienna trying to tunnel from the Soviet army headquarters beneath the British residence of Commandant Ernest Howard in order to intercept his private communications. The fact that the British agent, Warlock, was seen as being worth three Soviet agents was perhaps a mark of how highly he was now valued by Her Majesty's government. It was notable that the timing of the explosion in Prague was such that the detonation did not take place until he was safely in a British army transport, out of range of any bullet, stray or otherwise, that might have been fired from the Czechoslovakian side.

29

It was Strath's idea to go to Nevis.

'We have a house there – the department does, I mean. We've used it for various purposes since the war. It's a long way from anywhere, so it's very secure, and very private. No one's in it at the moment. It's in Charlestown. Right on the beach.'

Louis had been in the hospital for well over two months. It wasn't the institution in Aldershot where his journey had begun, but a smaller and seemingly better-equipped place just outside Oxford. It felt more like a hotel. He had his own room that overlooked some rather appealing gardens, and there was a sauna, steam room and heated swimming pool in the basement that he was free to use whenever he liked.

His natural sleep patterns were just starting to come back. There had been a lot of sedation in the first weeks. Not the brutal sledgehammer kind he'd been subjected to in the Funhouse. From the first day here, he could tell that this was of a gentler, more healing character. The benign intention behind it was apparent. But the restorative effects did not make themselves felt for some time. There was a lot of screaming still, in the night. But at least help and care came immediately when that happened. That did more for him than the drugs. To feel he was being held in some way.

His psychiatrist, Dr Thompson, was an ebullient figure, like a young Santa Claus. Big wiry beard, round spectacles, warm but authoritative. Precise, careful, painstaking. He also had a surgical background, having switched to the mental side of things later in his career, which meant he could keep an eye on Louis' physical recuperation too. There had been some repair required in order to reverse the effects of what they'd done to him in Czechoslovakia, when they'd prepared him for the Funhouse. It took more than one operation, but whatever the procedure was, it seemed to be holding, though he had to remain on a plain diet of porridge and stewed fruit for a number of weeks. Ordinarily that would have been a trial, but to be eating food again, any food, just to be sipping a glass of water, still felt like paradise.

The non-physical side of things was proving harder. But here Louis might have encountered a piece of luck. Dr Thompson was a world leader in the field of psychological injury, and his theories and methods were way ahead of the kind of care Louis would have received had he been recuperating elsewhere.

'There's been considerable trauma,' said Dr Thompson, 'trauma that's proved cataclysmic for others. You have to acknowledge that and accept it. You also have to be aware that you're made of pretty strong stuff. You must be, or we wouldn't be having this conversation. To be honest, given what we know . . .' and here he paused, choosing his words carefully, 'I'm not entirely sure what has led to your outcome being so different.' He was leaving it open for Louis to talk about it, without wanting to push things.

Louis remained taciturn, unwilling to communicate anything of his experience of that place. Maybe silence was the best they could hope for.

'There's every reason to expect that things will improve, if you allow time to pass and trust the process of your own healing. The nightmares, the high anxiety, the feelings of helplessness and despair, they are not going to be permanent. I want to encourage you to hold on to that thought, even when you're overwhelmed. You know about King Solomon's ring, don't you?'

Louis shook his head.

'According to legend, the great sage wore a ring that was engraved with the words "this too will pass". He would twiddle it in his fingers whenever he was faced with anything that felt overwhelmingly awful.'

Louis remembered that he had heard that story. 'He would turn it when anything wonderful happened too, wouldn't he?' he said.

'He would. But shall we just focus on one problem at a time?'

Dinah had been allowed to visit after a month. They didn't speak the first time. She just held his hand and kissed his forehead. She had been writing to him. He'd received letters most days. Of course, he hadn't been able to reply, but Dr Thompson had been keeping Dinah informed of his progress and encouraging the connection. Louis was aware that he wouldn't be there if it wasn't for her. He was also aware of something else. His faith that she would see and decode his message. He hadn't thought that at the time. At the time, he hadn't thought anything. He was simply living moment to moment. *What can I do now? What can I do now?* The idea to encode a message just came to him – an instinct. It was something else to hold on to. Another task to give himself to remind himself he had choices – to do something to affect the chances of his own survival, even if it felt like he was beyond caring. Even expressing it this way was too articulate. He wasn't thinking by the end. He was just doing. But there was something there in him that had taken over and chosen the path for him. *Just do what they say, do what they say, but inside, hold on to the truth, hold on to the truth, hold on to what you know – just hold on.*

Here he was. In a better place. Because he had been able to hold on.

Louis and Dinah were sitting in the garden together. Dr Thompson had encouraged Louis to plant some vegetables. Telling Dinah about them were the first words he actually spoke to her.

'Dr Thompson gave me some seeds that would grow in the winter. I didn't know anything could grow in the winter.'

'Of course you didn't. You were always an urban creature, Louis.'

'Did you know?'

'Yes. Father kept a kitchen garden when we were young.'

'So what grows in the winter?'

'What he's given you,' she said in a no-nonsense way, pointing to the sprouting seeds. 'Radishes, alfalfa, spinach.'

'That's right,' Louis said, full of wonder that she recognised the plants. They sat looking at the green shoots together, silent for a moment. It was a cold afternoon, but bright and sunny. Eventually he dared to express a thought: 'Will you come back and see them when they're fully grown?'

'Louis, I'm going to come back every day, if they'll allow me.'

There was a pause, then he said:

'I'm broken, Dinah. I'm a broken thing.'

'Broken things mend. You're mending.'

It was Louis who suggested that Dinah came to Nevis with him.

'It could be our honeymoon.'

'We'd have to get married first.'

'That's right. We would.' They looked at each other. Louis had spoken the words, but they didn't even feel like a choice. Just something he understood. Something they both understood.

Charlestown was quiet, ramshackle, warm like a summer's day, which was a novelty for both of them, given that they were deep into winter. There'd been a small civil ceremony that Strath had helped arrange before they left. Dinah wanted to invite the Brains Trust, but Louis asked if they could keep it just to them, with Strath as a witness.

'We can have another do. We can have a do any time.' It was a barely concealed plea. He wanted everything to be as simple as possible. Scraped right down to the bone. And Dinah wasn't going to object.

Although the service was non-religious, at the last minute Louis asked Dinah if he could place a folded handkerchief on his head in lieu of a yarmulke. She wasn't going to object to that either.

The house was an old colonial villa about a hundred yards from the beach. When you looked one way, you saw the satin blue sea; when you looked the other, you saw the gentle peak of the mountain that made the island, which was actually a volcano. It had been quite an adventure getting there, involving aeroplanes, ships and increasingly smaller boats. That was part of the therapy, said Dr Thompson.

There was a British doctor on the island who was keeping an eye on things, a gentle soul called Craddock with a soft Edinburgh burr and a leathery brown face that seemed at odds with his red hair. He'd shown them round the place, identifying the best hostelries in Charlestown. There was a gas burner on the veranda on which Dinah took to preparing eggs in various ways. There were chickens strutting around the house, so the eggs were abundant.

In the afternoons, Louis would go for long walks on the beach. At first they'd gone together, but he found himself waiting until Dinah was napping and then set off on his own. It was precisely because things were so idyllic that he was struggling. Because the idyll didn't disperse the heavy pall of doom that still settled over him regularly. The mismatch between the setting, his circumstances and the waves of black awfulness that would regularly rush over him was too much to share. So going for a walk on his own with the sea shushing in his ears seemed like the best thing to do. Dinah didn't say anything the first day, or the second. But on the third she expressed her concern.

'Louis, you can talk to Dr Craddock. You don't have to suffer.'

'I'm fine. I'm not suffering,' was all he said.

On the fourth day, he found himself walking right round the bay. He came to a deserted beach with a big semicircle of pale sand and a fringe of palm trees behind it. There was a kind of causeway that had formed naturally in the shallow water, separating a portion of the sea from itself. It might be pleasant to stride across it. It was maybe half a mile long, and he was about a quarter of a mile across it when he happened to glance out to the ocean. There was nothing. Just a vast, empty, formless blue surface and a blank blue sky above it – an infinite emptiness. He was suddenly aware that he had nothing around him to hold on to, nowhere he could get to, nothing he could reach for. He was alone in this vast bright emptiness, and an annihilating fear rushed up from inside and paralysed him. He fell to the sand and curled into a ball.

He didn't know how long he was there, but the sky was beginning to darken by the time the feeling passed enough for him to begin moving. He didn't even dare stand up. He wanted to feel as much of the ground as he could beneath him if he was going to go anywhere, so he crawled, back the way he'd come, keeping his eyes on the wet sand, not daring to look up at anything, lest the expanse brought back the mind-blasting wave of panic.

Eventually he found a tree and reached out to it, wrapping his arms around it.

Dinah found him there. He heard her calling for him before he saw her.

She led him back to the house, which was less than fifteen minutes away, where he broke down crying.

'I don't know who I am,' he kept saying. 'I don't know who I am.' He was filled with shame, with self-loathing, emasculated by his fear.

She held him gently, and then got up and went briefly into the bedroom.

'I've got something,' she said.

'What?' She handed him a handkerchief. 'A hankie?'

She laughed. How could she even express warmth in these circumstances?

'Not a hankie. A letter. Strath gave it to me before we left. Do you want me to read it to you?' She'd been wondering about when the best time to share it would be. Now seemed right.

Louis nodded, noting that his heart was racing, although he didn't know why.

'"Dear Kay".'

'That was my name out there. My alias. Kay.'

'I'd worked that out, thank you.'

'Sorry.'

Dear Kay,

I wanted to write to you though I didn't have an address. I thought if I sent a letter to the army people in Sydney who helped me when I arrived they might know how to get it to you. I don't know if it ever will. But I want to try.

I'm called Helen now. I have a new life. I am living in Canberra, which is much warmer than Czechoslovakia! I started working in a bank. My English is not so good though it is better than it was, but I have a gift for numbers. Shortly after starting there I met a young man who is older than me – also an immigrant, but from Italy. He fought in the resistance there at the end of the war. It felt like we had something in common, he said, though I would never have said that myself.

Things have moved quickly for us and we are married and we're going to have a baby.

I wanted to thank you, Kay, for doing what you could to help me get back from Czechoslovakia. For taking care. I know you would say it was nothing, or your duty. But you gifted me the rest of my life.

You never told me who you really were. What your real name was.

I wanted you to know that whoever you are, you are good. A good man. I wanted to thank you for it. If the baby is a girl we're going to call it Kay. It's a girl's name here.

Yours,

Helen (Elena) Amato

Louis sat there for a moment. And then he started crying. Sobbing in small percussive yelps.

Dinah reached for him. She held him tightly as he wept, and wept . . . and wept.

'I need you to do something. I think it will help,' he said eventually. His voice was quiet. He spoke quickly. Dinah could hear the fear, hear that he was risking something, as if he was seizing upon some inner moment that the tears had precipitated, some little opening of a container that had been hitherto tightly sealed.

'What? What do you need?'

'I need you to take dictation.'

They could only find an old typewriter and a stack of paper, covered in dust.

'I could go into town, get a pen.'

'It has to be now, I think. Otherwise I don't think I can.'

She looked at him, trying to understand. 'What is it?'

'I wrote a book.' The statement hung there for a moment. Dinah tried to contextualise it. Louis continued. 'I . . . composed a book. When I was . . . imprisoned. I committed it to memory. Word by word. I didn't move on until I had each page fixed in my mind. That's where I went. It kept me together.'

He paused while she took that in.

'I want to get it out of me. So I can forget. I didn't ever think I could speak about it. I can only do it once. I think it has to be now.'

They found a typewriter ribbon in a little yellow tin box. The machine itself was a Remington. There was just a bare steel peg where the letter 'P' key should have been, with an uncomfortably sharp-looking point, but otherwise it was in good working order.

'It'll hurt. When you're typing.'

'It doesn't matter.'

'Not when you start, maybe. But it will by page twenty.'

'I don't care, Louis,' she said, rolling the first sheet of paper into the machine. 'Just begin. Just start dictating.'

She sat down at the machine, her fingers poised over the letters.

'The first page – you've got to centre the text.' He told her how to type it. He had it exactly in his imagination. She'd torn a bit of loose leather from the strap of her handbag and wrapped it around the tip of the third finger of her right hand, which would be taking the brunt of the 'P's.

THE READER'S SECRECY COVENANT

I, ...
as an admirer and appreciator of magic,
understand that within this book

'That's it. Are you all right?' he asked.
'It's fine. Keep going.'

THE READER'S SECRECY COVENANT

I, ...
as an admirer and appreciator of magic,
understand that within this book I will learn
many of the secrets behind the numerous
effects with which the author has built his
reputation. In signing this covenant I give my
word to never share the revelations described
herein. I do so out of respect for the noble
art of magic and in acknowledgement that these
are the wishes of the late Louis Warlock.

        Signed _____

        Date ___ / _____ / _____

NB After the initial print run has sold,
the printing plates of this book will be
destroyed.

344

THE WARLOCK EFFECT

by
LOUIS WARLOCK

LINE DRAWINGS
by
DINAH GROULE

'I imagined you were doing the line drawings,' said Louis. 'I hope you don't mind.'

'I can add them in when you're done. Just tell me where to leave a space.'

'OK.'

'Go on.'

'This is the book proper now. Starting.'

'Yes. Louis . . . start.'

Hello my friend.

Forgive me for thinking of you as my
friend, but first and foremost I think
that's what you are to me. A kindred
spirit. Some kind of magic has happened if
you're reading this. The mere act of me
imagining that you might one day read this
book has brought it about in actuality.
That is a miracle.

Dinah stopped typing. She looked at Louis, whose face carried a
broken expression.

'I was thinking of you,' he said. 'I was writing to you.'

She nodded, continued to type, despite her tears.

It's an act of faith, composing these
words. What's made it happen? What's helped
bring this miracle into being? It's the
fact that we share something, you and I,
dear friend, dear reader, something
profound.

I'm not used to thinking in this way,
but I'm allowing myself to do so now. As I
close my eyes and bring you to mind and odd
though it may sound, I've already spent
many hours doing that, this is what I know
about you. You're endlessly inquisitive.
You have a genuine sense of fun, which is

an underrated quality. I think it may be the secret to a happy life. Most importantly, in fact essentially, you still feel connected to the person you were as a child. And that is why magic appeals to you. It's a direct line to the wonder we all see at the start of our journey. Magic's biggest trick is that it keeps us excited and ready to make humdrum moments sparkle, for ourselves and for others.

As I begin thinking about committing these secrets to the page - revealing the real modus operandi that lies behind the headline-grabbing stunts and effects with which I've made my name - time and again I find myself reaching the same conclusion. It's all about simplicity. Everything begins with blankness, with empty space. Empty spaces can be terrifying. The temptation is to fill them with all kinds of nonsense.

But if you open yourself to empty spaces, you can fill them with truth. And the truth is never wrong.

Here's the truth.

I love you, fellow magician.

What I have to offer to you, these secrets, take them as a gift. I want them to fill you with joy every day.

You are my friend.

I love magic . . .

And I love you . . .

ACKNOWLEDGEMENTS

Firstly we'd like to thank our editor Myfanwy Moore for lighting the fuse and then for skilfully shepherding the book to its final form. Her notes, questions and suggestions were invaluable, and we remain indebted to her skill and insight and grateful for her faith, encouragement and enthusiasm. Thanks too to Lily Cooper and her team for all their care and attention in readying the book for publication.

We'd like to thank Emily Senior for reading an early draft and providing immensely useful feedback. And we are grateful to our agent Simon Trewin for his continuing support and expertise. Many thanks to Nicky Clarke-Dyson for her wonderful and period-accurate magical illustrations. We are also indebted to Jane Selley for her sharp eyes and attention to detail. Thanks too, to the Estate of Tommy Cooper for their generosity in allowing us to include some of Tommy's wonderful jokes. And we are grateful to David Britland, Mike Slosberg, Louise Abbott and Macy Nyman for their help with final corrections.

Several books were invaluable as sources of information when we were composing the story. Peter Hennessy's *The Secret State: Whitehall and the Cold War* (2002) and Gordon Corera's *The Art of Betrayal: Life and Death in the British Secret Service* (2011) were excellent guides to the post-war machinations of the intelligence services. Zuzana Palovic and Gabriella Bereghazyova's *Czechoslovakia: Behind the Iron Curtain* (2020) gave us visceral insight into the realities of post-war life in the Soviet satellite state.

Louis Warlock himself takes inspiration from the example of many 20th Century magicians who remain heroes to this day.

Dinah and Louis' close relationship and hit radio show is inspired by Sydney Piddington and Lesley Pope (who would go on to be Sydney's wife). Their BBC radio broadcasts as The Piddingtons were hugely popular after the war and their methods were closely guarded. Martin T Hart's *Piddington's Secrets* (2015) details some of them. The idea for a secrecy contract with the reader comes from this book.

Robert Harbin was a magical genius whose inventions and methods still fool today. Much of Louis' thinking – including his commitment to solving every problem – is inspired by Harbin who revealed some of his secrets in *The Magic of Robert Harbin* (1970) – which, as Louis' book does – insisted that its own printing plates must be destroyed after the initial print run.

Al Koran was a hugely popular mentalist in the 1950s. Martin Breese's *Magic of Al Koran* (1983) details some of his methods which are as agile and creative as Louis'.

David Berglas is another truly inspirational and extraordinary magician. Like Louis, David was a childhood refugee, though his interest in magic didn't develop until early adulthood, and his schooldays were mercifully happier than Louis'. Also like Louis he was challenged (albeit in a more friendly way) to find an object hidden anywhere in London by *Picture Post* Magazine and succeeded under impossible circumstances, as detailed in David Britland's wonderful *The Magic of David Berglas* (2002) which reveals some of David's incredible thinking.

Another Jewish magician who was subject to a challenge after claiming he could read minds on a BBC radio show – was Maurice Fogel. Journalist Arthur Helliwell was determined to expose him as a fraud and wrote an article doing just that. It didn't affect Fogel's standing with the public. Much of his wonderful thinking is detailed in Chris Woodward and Richard Mark's excellent *Maurice Fogel – In Search of the Sensational* (2007).

Louis' technique for simulating the memorisation of a pack of cards is actually one of the oldest published card tricks in existence – dating back to a book from 1794 entitled Breslaw's Last Legacy.

The Card to Matchbox trick Louis refers to was first published in Will Goldston's T*he Young Conjurer – Part 1* in 1910, though the actual inventor may have been Goldston's shop manager Stanley Collins. As early as 1911 it was commonly available for a few pence from magic shops and other magicians started publishing more advanced handlings for the box.

Louis' 'Fibbing Archie' trick was inspired by an item from Vol 14, No.5 of *The Magigram* magazine from January 1982 called 'A Head for Figures' by Len Saunders.

Many of the names in the book are those of real magicians, they are all there as a nod to their collective brilliance and their advancement of that wonderful artform.

The history of the Zauberkönig magic shop in Berlin is true and is memorialised in artist Gunter Demnig's Solpersteine project. (https://www.stolpersteine-berlin.de/en/biografie/355). The shop itself is still open and trading in 2022.

JEREMY DYSON AND ANDY NYMAN

Jeremy & Andy have been best friends since the age of 15 – their shared love of magic, movies and horror is as alive today as it was then. As a team they co-wrote and co-directed the smash hit play *Ghost Stories*, which has had three highly successful West End runs as well as numerous productions across the globe. They then co-wrote and co-directed the acclaimed film version that won the Fangoria Chainsaw Award for best first feature in 2019.

They have recently written an episode of Amazon's *Good Omens 2* entitled 'Nazi Zombie Flesh Eaters'. They are currently working on their next play and film.

In their individual careers, Jeremy is best known as one quarter of the multi-award winning comedy team The League of Gentlemen. Beyond the League he co-created and co-wrote the BAFTA nominated comedy drama series *Funland* and the Rose d'or-winning, all-female comedy series *Psychobitches*, as well as writing for and script-editing numerous TV series including *Killing Eve*. Jeremy's first novel *What Happens Now* was published in 2006. He has written three collections of short stories including Edge Hill Award winner *The Cranes that Build the Cranes*.

Andy is a multi-award-winning actor, writer and director. As an actor he is best known for playing Churchill in *Peaky Blinders*, Dan in the Oscar winning film *Judy* and Tevye in Trevor Nunn's 2019 west end revival of *Fiddler on the Roof*. His two 'Golden Rules of Acting' books are best sellers within the acting world. As a magician and creator, Andy has been Derren Brown's main collaborator for over twenty years. Together they devised and wrote many of Derren's startling TV specials including *Russian*

Roulette and *How to Win the Lottery*. Andy has co-written and co-directed eight of Derren's stage shows as well as inventing tricks in his own right that are performed by magicians the world over. In 2018 Andy was awarded the Magic Circle's prestigious Maskelyne Award for 'Services to British Magic'.